THE
CLOUD

RAY HAMMOND

Ray Hammond is a novelist, dramatist and non-fiction author. He is also a futurologist who lectures on future social and business trends for universities, corporations and governments. He lives in London and can be found on the web at www.rayhammond.com.

Also by Ray Hammond

EMERGENCE
EXTINCTION

unknown deep space. The discs had included 115 images of Earth, recordings of human languages, diagrams of the human form, local star maps and, because it was the 1970s, even samples of whale songs.

But the international group of scientists, linguists, mathematicians, philosophers and anthropologists charged with composing the new radio communication felt a far heavier weight on their shoulders than had the NASA team responsible for composing the Voyager message. Now Earth's communication was to be beamed towards a specific intelligent life form, and one living not too far away.

The arguments about what to include in the greeting, and how to say it, were intense. It was agreed that although this was Earth's first contact with an extra-terrestrial civilization, it would almost certainly not be the Isonians' first contact with other alien intelligences. Earth's technological civilization was very young indeed and statistically it was extremely likely that the more advanced Isonians would have made contact with many other cultures before. It was possible, indeed likely, that there was a galactic protocol established for this kind of communication and information interchange. But those on Earth would have no chance of knowing the correct way to respond and introduce themselves; they would just have to say 'hello' politely, and hope that as newcomers to the galactic community they didn't cause any offence.

In the end it was agreed that a first initial message lasting about twenty minutes should be broadcast, to be followed by a series of regular daily transmissions which would explain and amplify further details of Earth's civilization. The first programme of signals to be beamed to the Isonians would take almost two years.

Basdeo Panday, the United Nations Secretary-General,

THE
CLOUD

RAY
HAMMOND

PAN BOOKS

First published 2006 by Pan Books
an imprint of Pan Macmillan Ltd
Pan Macmillan, 20 New Wharf Road, London N1 9RR
Basingstoke and Oxford
Associated companies throughout the world
www.panmacmillan.com

ISBN-13: 978-0-330-44187-2
ISBN-10: 0-330-44187-6

Copyright © Ray Hammond 2006

The right of Ray Hammond to be identified as the
author of this work has been asserted by him in accordance
with the Copyright, Designs and Patents Act 1988.

All rights reserved. No part of this publication may be
reproduced, stored in or introduced into a retrieval system, or
transmitted, in any form, or by any means (electronic, mechanical,
photocopying, recording or otherwise) without the prior written
permission of the publisher. Any person who does any unauthorized
act in relation to this publication may be liable to criminal
prosecution and civil claims for damages.

1 3 5 7 9 8 6 4 2

A CIP catalogue record for this book is available from
the British Library.

Typeset by IntypeLibra
Printed and bound in Great Britain by
Mackays of Chatham plc, Chatham, Kent

This book is sold subject to the condition that it shall not,
by way of trade or otherwise, be lent, re-sold, hired out,
or otherwise circulated without the publisher's prior consent
in any form of binding or cover other than that in which
it is published and without a similar condition including this
condition being imposed on the subsequent purchaser.

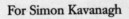
For Simon Kavanagh

ACKNOWLEDGEMENTS

Copy editors are usually the last people to amend a novel's text before it goes to the printer, but for this book Nick Austin was kind enough to help with ideas, suggestions and research tips when I was just beginning to plan the story – well over a year before he received the final manuscript. I'm grateful to him both for his initial creative input and for his usual meticulous copy-editing skills.

Simon Kavanagh, my agent at the Mic Cheetham Literary Agency, proved himself to be far more than just an enthusiastic and skilled literary representative. Throughout the development of this narrative he challenged, encouraged, berated, cajoled and threatened me to develop my story, to strike sections that didn't work well enough and to build up aspects he was sure would improve the book. He was nearly always right and I owe him a great debt, both creatively and commercially.

At Pan Macmillan my editor, Peter Lavery, has supported, encouraged and guided me over the past five years. His powerful commercial instincts and his continuing, infectious enthusiasm for story-telling makes me proud and grateful to be a member of his illustrious stable of writers. I'm also thankful to his colleagues Rebecca Saunders, Stef Bierwerth and Kate Eshelby at Pan Macmillan for all their help and support over the years.

For guidance on space affairs, astronomy and other technical matters I am indebted, not for the first time, to the writer and journalist Simon Eccles and to the distinguished astronomer and broadcaster Dr Bruno Stanek of Astrosoftware, Switzerland. For advice on computer science and the hypothetical alien mathematics used as a central device in this narrative, my thanks go to Professor David F. Brailsford of the School of Computer Science and Information Technology, University of Nottingham, and to the feasibility expert Peter Stewart. Although all of my technical advisers helped me greatly, any errors or mistakes in such detail remain my responsibility entirely.

On a personal level, I am grateful for the loving encouragement that my partner Maria Fairchild provided when she read the initial draft of this novel, and for her understanding when my writing kept me so often in solitary confinement. I'm also grateful to Alan Phillips, who had to listen to me trying out some of the early ideas for this story during many evenings at The Ladbroke Arms, and to Elaine Cooper, who has provided me with speedy, reliable and valuable criticism of all my novels.

I would also like to thank the management and staff of Orpheus Island Resort in Australia's Great Barrier Reef for making my stay so memorable that it led to me purloining their magical atoll for my own purposes. Despite what you may read in these pages, Orpheus Island remains one of the most beautiful and welcoming resorts in the world. Thanks must also go to Dagmar O'Toole and Alex Krywald of Celebrity Speakers Associates whose development and management of my public-speaking career has allowed me to visit Orpheus Island and many of the other locations that I have used in this book.

Finally, as always, I owe a huge debt to Liz Hammond for her patient, diligent and intelligent reading of my many drafts.

THE BEGINNING

April 2033

When it finally came, the alien contact was so weak, so minuscule among the noises of the great universe, that it was almost overlooked. Had it not been for the success of SETI's ten-year fund-raising campaign to build a listening post on the far side of the moon, humankind might never have learned that other forms of intelligence exist in the cosmos.

The director, council members and regional representatives of the SETI Institute (the loose grouping of maverick scientists and astronomers who made up the organization known as the Search for Extra-Terrestrial Intelligence) had raised almost $7 billion for the massive lunar construction project, mostly from public donations. Even then they were forced to beg passenger rides and cargo space from NASA, the European Space Agency, the Chinese and a few of the many private aerospace corporations who were now busily building habitats, launch sites, maintenance facilities, fuel dumps and even tourist accommodation on the Earth-facing side of the moon.

But it was the *far* side of the lunar surface that attracted SETI – the side which always faces away from Earth, the side which is shielded from the mother planet's massive out-pouring of radio and television signals, laser beams, electro-mechanical transmissions and all of the other electronic 'noise' that is produced by a young but rapidly advancing technological society and which spills out heedlessly into surrounding space.

Uniquely among the 138 major moons that circle the sun's planets, Earth's satellite is the only one to have a permanently shielded surface. In radio terms, it is the quietest place in the entire solar system, and it was the perfect location for the manned research outpost that had become known as 'Setiville'.

'Come on, come on!' shouted Desmond Yates impatiently as he stared up at the main communications screen, willing it to flicker into life. 'What are they doing? What's taking so long?'

Joan Ryder, a more mature and more seasoned SETI warrior, laid a calming hand on the young astrophysicist's shoulder.

'What do you think they're doing, Des?' she reasoned, as she too stared up at the blank screen. 'They're checking and double checking, just as we would. This is far too big for them to risk making a mistake.'

Yates nodded, ran his fingers impatiently through his thick dark hair and gently pushed himself up out of his low-gravity chair. As a twenty-five-year-old researcher, only one year out of his doctorate course at Stanford and a member of the SETI lunar team for less than three months, he would normally have been merely assisting his two more experienced colleagues. But it was he who had discovered the strange signal – a transmission that he now firmly believed to be both electronically generated and of genuine alien origin.

Strictly speaking, it was SETI's powerful analysing computers that had identified the unusual signal amongst all the myriad noises produced by the galaxies. But it was Des Yates who had chosen to target that particular patch of sky, Yates who had selected which range of frequencies to scan and Yates who had opted to pursue, amplify and home in on the 'possible contact' that the computer systems themselves ranked as being only of 'ETI Category 22 (minor interest)'. This 'contact' – now hastily reclassified as 'ETI Category 1 (most promising)' – was all Des's, and his two SETI colleagues agonized for him as they all waited to hear back from the Parkes radio telescope in Australia and England's Jodrell Bank Observatory.

Soon after its first informal establishment in 1960, SETI laid down strict checking and verification procedures to be followed whenever a signal was detected that might possibly be of alien origin. The organization's founders had been far-sighted. Over the seventy years during which the search had been conducted there had been no fewer than 635 'strong' false alarms, seventeen of them so convincing that SETI had been on the verge of announcing 'contact' to the world before the mundane truth of each of these signal's man-made origin was finally discovered.

Recently the Institute's 'ETI signal verification procedure' as laid down in the SETI operating manual had been strengthened, as if the organization's elders had anticipated that their new lunar research centre might produce a rash of supposedly positive contacts. Now, once the three Setiville duty scientists in the lunar observatory had all agreed that a contact was a 'strong possible', a copy of the signals received along with all of the relevant computer records and astronomical location information were to be sent for verification to two SETI-affiliated but independent observatories in opposing hemispheres of the Earth.

Yates and the SETI computers had first identified the

strange transmission ten days earlier. He had been alone, working a 'night shift' – the habitat's lighting and internal environment were set up to mimic the Earth's own circadian rhythms – when he saw the frequency graph spike at the same point on three repeated sweeps of the microspectrum he had chosen to explore.

For the rest of his life Desmond Yates would be unable to tell questioners what it was that prompted him to investigate this particular minor spike – especially when there were so many other larger peaks on the graph that seemed more worthy of exploration – but that is one key difference between humans and machines: Yates was working on a hunch.

For no reason other than fulfilling his romantic notions of the hunt for extra-terrestrial intelligence, the youthful researcher had then switched on the audio circuits so that he could hear the faint narrow-band signal on which he was instructing the computers and the sixty-four-metre dish outside to focus. He had watched too many science fiction movies.

The small control room – in which almost every wall surface was covered by high-definition 3-D screens – was suddenly filled with a jumbled cacophony. Yates could hear a low roar, like the sea, and higher notes that seemed to pulse with irregular and complex rhythms, but it was hard to pick out any detail.

He reached forward and set the parameters of a mathematical analysis he wanted the systems to run on the mysterious signals. Then, as his hunch suddenly grew, he asked the system to run a directional trace on the origin of the transmission and display the result in the small holo-theatre that occupied the centre of the control-room floor.

Seven minutes later Yates was on his feet circling a laser-projected hologram which shimmered as it hung in space in the centre of the holo-display area. From all around came the low roaring, interspersed with the shrill higher notes.

What the holo-image displayed was a computer-gener-ated rendition of H-712256X, an 'Earth-like planet' (known to astronomers as an ELP), that was 14.8 light years away in the constellation of Aquarius.

Yates had never before known a signal trace to point so clearly to a particular planet. But he quickly reminded him-self that he was less than a year into his career as a SETI researcher and a total new boy to lunar-based observations. Perhaps such apparently interesting traces had occurred many times before.

Suddenly an alarm sounded and Yates spun on his heel to scan the display behind him.

<u>SIGNAL IS NARROW-BAND – SIGNAL IS MODU-LATED</u> read the screen, the red underlined capitals flashing as they were supposed to do when such an unusual trans-mission was identified.

'Narrow-band' and 'modulated' were the key words when it came to any radio signal that might possibly be of extra-terrestrial origin. 'Narrow-band' meant that the signal was produced by some form of electronics or machine. 'Modulated' meant that the radio signals had a coherent pat-tern to them, a pattern that could not occur in nature, but could only have been created artificially by an intelligence for the purposes of meaningful communication.

'Holy shit!' Yates said out loud, and he moon-bounded out of the control room and along the short corridor to the residential quarters where his two colleagues were sleeping. A few minutes later, they too were staring open-mouthed at the computer announcement and the shimmering hologram of a planet that looked something like Earth, but was almost fifteen light years away – or about 142 trillion kilometres.

Their first task had been to eliminate all possible radio signals and electromagnetic interference that could be of man-made origin. Although 'modulated' was the most exciting alert they could be given by their analysing computers, it was also the most worrying. Usually it meant that the supposed narrow-band ETI signal was very much man-made; perhaps a transmission from a passing spacecraft, signals being beamed back home by a probe launched decades before or even stray signals from one of the deep-space telescopes that were now parked in locations well beyond the Earth-moon solar orbits.

But the SETI computers were able to dismiss such suspicions quickly. Their database had files on every commercial spacecraft launched by all of the world's nations in the last eighty years and, by a combination of careful observation and tip-offs from sympathetic scientists around the world, it also contained details on almost every 'covert' space craft, satellite and weapons systems any of the world's nations had launched. Within thirty-six hours of first receiving the alien signals the three members of the SETI lunar staff were all convinced that they were receiving genuine alien signals which were both 'ultramundane' (originating from beyond the solar system) and clearly of mechanical origin.

What really convinced Kim Mukerjee that young Des had made a genuine ETI contact was the fact that whilst the SETI computers could identify regular frequency shifts and amplitude variations that clearly indicated modulation in the radio signal, there were in no way able to decipher any of its content. At forty-eight years old, Mukerjee was the senior member of the Setiville lunar team and he had been employed by the SETI Institute for over twenty years. He had also been present in various Earth-based observatories when three previous 'positive contacts' had been made, all of which had finally turned out to be of man-made origin. He understood that the quantum encryption techniques used by the world's governments for their military satellites and weapons systems were totally impenetrable, but SETI's computers were always able to detect that quantum encryption was in use, even though they were unable to make any sense out of the constantly altering states of the signal itself.

But this signal was completely different. The computers did not identify the oscillating natural randomness that is the signature of quantum-encrypted transmissions, but neither could they suggest any form or shape for the content that was being transmitted. What was clear, however, was that the signals were both artificial and deliberately transmitted.

Now, ten days after the signal had first been identified and continuous recording begun, Des Yates and his two co-workers were all on edge as they waited for a response and the verdicts from the Parkes Observatory and from Jodrell Bank in the UK.

The protocol was clear. The Parkes and Jodrell Bank astronomers were checking copies of Setiville's signals, running their own analyses of them and attempting to pick up the signals for themselves (despite the appalling radio pollution in Earth's dense atmosphere). But neither group would say anything publicly about the contact, negative or positive, until and if SETI itself decided to make an announcement.

Contact with an alien intelligence was what every astronomer, astrophysicist, cosmologist and imaginative person in the street dreamed off, whether the professionals wanted to admit it or not. Proof that there was another form of technologically capable intelligence in the universe was what an increasingly irreligious world fantasized about. For many, the concept was a replacement for God.

'Setiville, this is Gus Wilson at Parkes,' boomed a voice from a wall speaker.

All three members of the lunar team spun round as the main communication screen came to life and revealed the features of a middle-aged man with a bald head and a red, weather-beaten face. They all knew the image and formidable reputation of Professor Gus Wilson, Director of the Parkes Observatory.

At a nod from Mukerjee, Des Yates responded, hardly able to get his greeting out of his mouth.

'We confirm your signal ST86901XT as positive, repeat positive, Dr Yates,' said Wilson, an excited, intense look on his rugged face. 'We've been able to pick up the signal ourselves, although it was worse than minus 600 – so faint we'd never have noticed it down here on Earth. We've also eliminated every possible known man-made source and we've enquired about that particular frequency range with all government, academic and commercial regulatory bodies – nobody is using the 17.655 gigahertz frequency band. We too confirm that the signal is modulated, and that your presumed point of origin, ELP H-712256X, is correct as proved by the Doppler drift – although why the hell it should have come from somewhere so relatively close, somewhere that we've all looked at many times before, beats us.'

The Australian scientist paused for a deep breath, then delivered his organization's formal pronouncement.

'Our unanimous vote is that this signal is a positive contact with an unknown but demonstrably intelligent alien source. Written confirmation of our decision should be with you by now. Congratulations – and we all hope you get a second confirmation.'

'Yes! YES!!' yelled Yates, punching the air as the comms screen faded to black.

'Hold on, Des, hold on,' said Mukerjee. 'You know we've got to–'

'Setiville, this is Jodrell Bank,' said another voice as the screen flashed back to life.

The three SETI scientists turned again and saw the severe, pinched features of Sir Kevin Kelly, the director of Jodrell Bank and Britain's Astronomer Royal. Mukerjee nodded at Yates once more.

'Good day, Sir Kevin,' stammered Yates, hardly able to contain his excitement. Dread filled him suddenly; was this internationally famous astronomer about to reveal him as a stupid geek, an over-obsessed enthusiast who had confused alien-chasing with the pursuit of real, scientifically based research?

The Astronomer Royal straightened his tie and cleared his throat, as though he were preparing to make a public announcement.

'We are able to confirm that your signal meets the three internationally agreed criteria and should be treated as a confirmed reception of a modulated signal generated by an intelligent extra-terrestrial source,' he said carefully.

'First, we have been able to pick up the signal ourselves, here at Jodrell Bank, albeit very weakly. Second, we confirm that it is modulated by electromechanical or other artificial means. Third, we agree with your identification of the planet H-712256X as the most likely point of origin and, finally, we have been able to eliminate all known forms of human-originated radio transmissions.'

'YES!' yelled Des once more, punching the air and

leaping from the ground so hard that he was catapulted upwards and hit his head on the habitat's soft roof lining.

Sir Kevin's severe expression creased into a smile at this display.

'I understand that you've already received a confirmation from Gus Wilson at Parkes – he and I have been speaking about this for some days. We think this is the real thing, Dr Yates. Congratulations to you – and to the rest of the team at Setiville. I look forward to your announcement.'

'Thank you, thank you very much, Sir Kevin,' Des managed to blurt as the screen image faded.

Now even Mukerjee was excited. He grabbed both Yates and Joan Ryder and hugged them to his slight frame, the three of them moon-bouncing around the control room, making footmarks on the polished floor of the holo-theatre and fending themselves off from the soft walls and ceiling as their low-gravity dance produced numerous collisions.

'Quick, get the champagne,' Mukerjee told Joan, as he finally released his dancing partners. But she was already heading for the refrigerated cabinet which held the sole bottle of alcohol that was officially allowed to be kept on the far side of the moon.

Yates grabbed three plastic cups and as Mukerjee popped the cork the fountain of champagne shot right up to the ceiling. The senior team member quickly directed the remaining wine into the plastic containers and, as their celebratory drinks were poured, the small group suddenly became subdued and solemn.

The trio of scientists stood in a little semicircle, still flushed and breathing heavily from their dancing, but now sobered by the realization that others had confirmed their momentous discovery. It had suddenly become real. They glanced at each other, unsure what to drink to, and Des's colleagues both nodded to him to make the toast.

The first human being to make confirmed contact with alien intelligence raised his paper cup to head height. 'To ET,' he said.

'To ET,' echoed Mukerjee and Joan Ryder, lifting their cups in turn.

As soon as they had drunk what little of the wine they had managed to salvage, their serious mood returned once again. They all had the feeling that they were present at a momentous event, something they would later have to describe over and over again for the benefit of strangers.

'Well, we know what the manual says we must do now,' said Mukerjee, breaking the silence. 'I think you should be the one to make the call, Des – it's about eleven a.m. in California.'

Des Yates nodded once, drained the dregs from his plastic cup, allowed it to float down into a waste basket, and then, with a deep breath, he seated himself in the main comms chair.

'Thank you for calling the SETI Institute,' said a female voice and image as the screen lit up. 'How may I direct your call?'

'Please connect me personally with Professor Jackson,' said Yates.

'I'm sorry, the director is in a trustees meeting all morning, Dr Yates,' said the operator. 'May I take a message?'

'Please interrupt him immediately,' said Yates as Kim Mukerjee leaned over his shoulder to point out the relevant paragraph in the manual. 'Please tell him that this is a Code 42 call. I repeat, a Code 42 call. I'll hold the line.'

Headline from the *New York Times* website, 26 July 2033

WE ARE
NOT ALONE

SETI astronomers pick up confirmed alien transmissions.

To Des Yates's growing fury, the main board directors of the SETI Institute had delayed announcing the discovery of confirmed alien signals for nearly three months.

At first Director Jackson told the lunar team that he wanted to personally check out the signals for himself, as did several other SETI board members. He reminded the excited Setiville researchers that irreparable damage could be done to the Institute – and its hopes for future fund-raising – if a premature announcement were made and the signals turned out to be non-alien after all.

'We only get one shot at such an important announce-ment,' Jackson told the lunar team forty-eight hours after they had first reported their success to the SETI Institute. 'We're going to advance the Setiville duty rota and relieve you early. We want you down here with us next week while we discuss how best to proceed.'

'But he has seen the independent confirmations!' fumed Yates to his colleagues when the connection to the direc-tor's office was closed. 'What else does he want, pictures of little green men?'

Mukerjee calmed his younger colleague, patiently explaining the sort of political wrangling that was probably taking place at the highest levels of the Institute's adminis-tration. He warned the discoverer of the alien signals that things were no longer going to be so straightforward for him.

While they were waiting for their replacement duty team to be ferried up from Earth, Mukerjee and Joan Ryder urged Yates to occupy himself by thinking up a name for the Earth-like planet from which the signals originated. They couldn't use 'H-712256X', the planet's astronomical desig-nation, in a press release; people would want a simple name that they could understand and latch on to.

Yates spent his free time scouring on-line dictionaries and reference works, his study filled with the low roar of the alien signals that he kept patched through to his personal quarters from the control room. He wanted to be sure that the transmissions were still being received.

The astrophysicist finally decided upon the name 'Iso' – from the Greek word meaning 'equal' – as the planet H-712256X was about the same size as the Earth and had a biological 'signature' that was also very similar. From the composition of its atmosphere, it seemed likely that Iso also supported abundant biological life and Yates found himself fantasizing – even doodling – about the sort of creatures who might inhabit the planet and who might be sending such complex radio signals out into space.

Back on Earth and visiting the SETI Institute building in Mountain View, Northern California, Dr Yates was treated to a crash course in senior management politics. The first row was over when to make the momentous announcement.

Professor Jackson wanted to wait until the content of the alien signals had been decoded. Three independent cryptanalysis laboratories had been hired. Without being told that the signals on which they were working might be of alien origin, they were given copies of the transmission and charged with extracting its meaning. Two weeks into their work, all three were reporting that the encryption appeared to be of an unknown type, but they were sure they would soon be able to make progress in at least identifying the type of security used.

Other members of the SETI board argued that an announcement about the signals should be made as soon as SETI had completed its own internal investigation. This should not take very long, Desmond Yates and the other members of his lunar roster were assured. SETI's own in-house specialists had already reconfirmed what had been vouched for by the Parkes and Jodrell Bank facilities, but the Institute team was now devoting a huge effort to ensuring that there wasn't even the slightest chance that the signals could have some obscure man-made origin.

'What about the national security implications?' asked one board member, during an emergency meeting to which Yates and his colleagues had been invited. 'Won't the Pentagon want to slap a National Secrecy Order on us and impound the recordings for themselves?'

'They might very well try to classify it,' admitted Director Jackson, 'which is why I would really prefer to have the message decrypted and the content available to all. Then it would be too late for the government to try to keep it for themselves.'

'Our major announcement protocol has been clearly laid down for over fifty years,' broke in Dr Denise Logan, the Institute's Director of Publicity and Corporate Affairs. 'SETI was established to bring the benefits of communication with an alien intelligence to all humankind, not for the benefit of just one nation, let alone one government. I insist that we must make the announcement by the procedures we have established and that it must be made simultaneously around the world.'

Eventually SETI's hand was forced. The pressure within the scientific community for an announcement to be made became acute, with both the Parkes and Jodrell Bank directors doubting how much longer they could rely on their own teams to keep silent about such an important and exciting discovery. Then it became clear that the three decryption labs were not going to make fast progress in cracking the alien code. All were reporting a security system of previously unknown design and all were asking for more time to work on the problem.

Finally the SETI board agreed that the formal announcement of first contact with an alien intelligence would be made at press conferences on Saturday, 26 July 2033 at twelve noon Pacific Time – nine p.m. GMT – and that the announcement would be made simultaneously in Washington, London and Sydney. Des Yates would speak at the Washington afternoon press conference, Dr Mukerjee would appear in London in the evening and Dr Ryder would make the breakfast-time announcement in Sydney.

Copies of the press release would be flashed simultaneously to all international news agencies along with video, photographs and biographies of the discoverers, sound recordings of the alien signals, copies of the independent confirmations, and computer-generated 'best-guess' images of what the planet Iso looked like. Interviews would then be immediately set up for Des Yates and his colleagues while the directors of Jodrell Bank and the Parkes Observatory would add their own contributions to keep their local press happy.

The media went wild. The headline **WE ARE NOT ALONE** occupied almost all of the front page of a special edition of the *New York Times* which was posted both on the web and rushed onto the streets as a souvenir print publication.

ALIEN SPACE SIGNAL DETECTED trumpeted the London *Times* and images of Des Yates, and to a lesser extent those of his co-discoverers, appeared on every news bulletin around the world. Talk shows were filled with instant experts who pontificated about the likely nature of the aliens, what the planet Iso might be like, how quickly Earth could get a message back to the Isonians, and what technology could be used to allow humans to travel through space on a mission to visit Iso. The fact that such a journey would in reality take hundreds of years only added to the romance of the story. Suddenly space exploration made sense to everybody.

The story of alien contact was treated as the ultimate good-news story all over the world. In America, the White House announced that President Don Randall would make a presidential address to the nation.

In Britain, seventy-year-old Sir Charles Hodgeson, the internationally famous best-selling science fiction author and futurology guru, told the British media that the discovery of the alien signals 'is an historic first encounter with the cosmic community, just as I predicted in my very first book, *Signature of Life*'.

In Italy the Pope called on all Christians to pray for peaceful and fruitful dialogue with the aliens.

'This is God's voice sending us clear instructions,' said Archbishop Tyrone Underfield as he addressed a specially convened meeting of the Alabama Chapter of the Rasta-mendolian Church of the True God.

All over the world, special services were held in churches, mosques and temples, and prayers were offered giving thanks and welcoming contact with the new intelligent beings.

Des Yates almost lost his voice. In the first three weeks after the official announcement, he flew 100,000 miles and made almost ninety network television broadcasts around the world. On the flights and during transfers in between TV appearances he was accompanied constantly by television crews and print reporters. Even though he could do little except simply repeat how he came across the signal and how it felt when it was first confirmed to be of alien origin, his questioners never seemed to tire of hearing the same stuff over and over again.

On some TV shows animation artists produced renderings of possible aliens for him to comment on; on others he was asked to speculate about what it was that the aliens might be trying to communicate to the inhabitants of Earth. Even his mother and father were rooted out of their suburban home in Denver to provide accounts of how the young Des had first fallen in love with the stars by gazing up at the heavens through the clear air of his high-altitude home city.

It was during an evening talk show in Chicago that the words 'Nobel Prize' were first uttered in Yates's presence. 'There are rumours that you are to be nominated for a Nobel Prize,' said the anchorman. 'How do you feel about that, Dr Yates?'

Eight months after the public announcement, Desmond Yates's life had changed beyond all recognition. He had been given his own office at SETI's Mountain View headquarters along with a full-time assistant. Her job was to deal with the huge volume of requests for media interviews, enquiries from fellow scientists and invitations for her boss to give lectures, attend meetings and make celebrity appearances.

Yates's new office window looked out onto a building site where a large extension to the main SETI building was now under construction. The news of positive contact with aliens had led to a flood of new money pouring into the Institute.

US Congress members keen to display their forward thinking, their proactive engagement with space technology and their awareness of the benefits that knowledge of alien technologies might bring to the nation, voted to provide

SETI with annual research funds so large that even NASA was made jealous. This ongoing grant was enthusiastically endorsed by a public that had suddenly become space-mad. Every teenage boy – and many girls – now wanted to be astronomers, cosmologists, astronauts or 'alien hunters', as the media had dubbed the SETI researchers.

Overseas governments – keen to buy into any knowledge that could be gleaned from alien communications – also donated significant funds and thousands of rich individuals made gifts, planned legacies or set up trusts to further SETI's endeavours to put humankind into useful contact with alien civilizations.

Director Jackson found that his working life had also been changed completely by the announcement. He now spent most of his time closeted with the fund managers who looked after the Institute's new wealth or with rich potential donors who wanted personal tours of the Institute – and a handshake with Desmond Yates himself – before finally parting with their money.

A new director of research had been hired and SETI was already using its increased resources to expand its lunar listening base on the far side of the moon. As well as adding two new ultra-large radio dishes to the Setiville complex they were also building a ten-metre optical telescope to take advantage of the superb lunar viewing conditions. None of the new money was being spent on building or developing Earth-based observatory facilities.

Immediately after SETI made the public announcement that alien signals had been received from the planet Iso, every radio-telescope observatory in the world had started to scour its own records to see why it had failed to spot the extra-terrestrial radio transmissions. No fewer than nine observatories subsequently announced that they too had been receiving the Isonian signals all along, but the transmissions had been so faint that their computers had categorized them as merely being part of the universe's background noise. Within the astronomical scientific community it was agreed that the alien transmissions would never have been noticed by any radio-dish observatory on Earth. From that moment on, all new money and development plans were switched to lunar and space-based observatories.

Des Yates was made a Fellow of the SETI Institute and, despite his youth, was given the singular honour of being invested as the 'Howard Regis Professor of Extra-Terrestrial Communication'. He wasn't expected to teach, or to conduct new research; his job was to oversee the decryption of the Isonian signals and to direct the Setiville teams who were continuing to monitor and record every bit of information being received from Iso.

Now thirty-six different decryption laboratories had been given copies of the alien transmissions to work on. A dozen of these were commercial forensic computing establishments, a further ten were labs located in the world's leading universities and the remainder were secret government computer-science establishments dotted around the world.

But the newly promoted Professor Yates had one private worry that he couldn't shake off: he kept wondering whether a government-owned computer laboratory would be honourable enough to disclose any success it might have in deciphering the alien transmissions. He knew that governments possessed the most powerful and advanced computer networks in the world, some so powerful that there was already an international protest movement calling for limits and treaties to control computer development and proliferation – much like those that were in place to limit the development of nuclear weapons – and he knew that any government offered the opportunity to read the alien signals would face a tremendous temptation to keep such potentially advantageous knowledge to itself. Statistically, the Isonian community was almost certain to be thousands or even millions of years ahead of Earth's civilization and would be very likely to possess technologies that would be of immense military, commercial or economic benefit. Who could resist?

The US government had already made its own position clear. The administration had been completely wrong-footed by SETI's simultaneous international announcement and by its liberal distribution of digital copies of the alien transmissions.

In a private phone call to Director Jackson, the US Secretary of State had told the SETI chief that many in the White House and the Pentagon were furious that the Institute had not been sufficiently patriotic to provide its mother nation with a private preview of such an important discovery. Jackson had politely reminded the Secretary that SETI was an international organization, with affiliations to the United Nations rather than to any single country. The call had ended on a decidedly chilly note.

Yates had ensured that each laboratory entrusted with the complete alien data stream had signed an undertaking that any knowledge extracted from the signals belonged in the public domain. But he still had the nagging suspicion that perhaps one of the government labs had already made sense of the transmissions and had secretly passed the knowledge on to its military or political masters.

But all of the lab directors he spoke to were telling him the same thing: their cryptologists had established that there was a clear but unfamiliar mathematical base to the signals and there appeared to be 'boundary lines' which might possibly indicate that some form of software was embedded in the data. But without knowledge of the alien radio technology, languages, software codes or its computer architecture it was going to take more time to make any sense out of the signals.

If governments were peeved that they had no exclusive rights to the alien transmissions and the potential treasures they might contain, their electorates made it abundantly clear that they were very happy that at least one other form of technologically capable intelligence existed in what had seemed up until then to be a vast, hostile and empty universe. Suddenly humankind belonged to a family, even though it had yet to meet the relatives.

There was a fundamental change in the world *Zeitgeist*; science fiction, space fiction, futurology, astronomy and cosmology, previously uneasy bedfellows and the preserve of geeks, now became part of mainstream popular culture. Sir Charles Hodgeson, already the doyen of great science-fiction storytellers, became the unofficial figurehead of this quasi-religious movement, appearing on TV shows, internet forums and magazine covers in almost every country in the world. He had been confidently predicting such contact for decades.

To celebrate the momentous discovery, Hodgeson had completed a new novella called *The Isonian Window* which his publishers rushed onto the web and into print, and which now topped the best-seller book charts in most English-speaking countries. Translation editions were being produced as quickly as possible and a film adaptation was already in production.

Then, on an American combined TV network show and internet broadcast, Sir Charles called on his millions of fellow alien-life enthusiasts to take future communications with the planet Iso into their own hands.

'I want everybody who owns a radio transmitter, no matter how low-powered, to transmit greetings of welcome and peace to the planet Iso over the coming week,' he told the viewers. 'The Earth is currently in a favourable position for radio communication with the constellation of Aquarius and if people broadcast UHF signals just two degrees south of Pegasus, we can be sure that the Isonians will receive our friendly messages in less than fifteen years' time.'

Hodgeson hit a public nerve. Amateur radio enthusiasts throughout the world trained their directional and even non-directional antennae approximately on the dim constellation and broadcast whatever messages they felt like sending to the alien civilization. Many people who had never owned radio equipment before went out and bought UHF transmitters and rigged up transmitting aerials, few of them worrying about licences or controlled radio spectrums, and broadcast wildly across all frequencies, as if they were bellowing into the night sky.

From an ancient Winnebago in an Arizona trailer park, a group of alien-life enthusiasts created a network of 287 separate radio transmitters around the state and then started to beam such powerful UHF signals out into the night sky that all flights had to be diverted away from the central-southern states of America until police could be dispatched to forcibly shut down the endlessly repeating transmissions.

'Hello people of Iso,' their message ran. 'We send greetings of peace from the planet Earth. Please come and visit with us.'

*

'On behalf of the people of the United States, I am proud to present you with the Presidential Medal of Freedom,' said President Don Randall as he shook Des Yates's hand.

About eighty people were present to witness the ceremony being conducted in The East Room at the White House; SETI board members and scientists mingled with NASA officials, administration personnel and favoured politicians. Yates's parents stood proudly at the front of the group as the official photographer asked the President and the latest recipient of the nation's highest civilian honour to shake hands once again for the benefit of the cameras.

When the formal part of the ceremony was concluded, President Randall greeted Yates's parents, complimented them on their son's achievement and then, to the surprise of his aides, quietly asked the young SETI celebrity if he could spare a further few minutes of his valuable time to join him in the Oval Office for a private discussion.

Almost a year had passed since the moment when Des Yates had first selected the weak Isonian signals for further investigation, but no further progress had been made in deciphering their content. Now some of the cryptanalysts were even questioning whether the alien signals were encrypted at all. 'It might just be that their own spoken language and electronic designs are so different from ours that we don't know where to start,' the director of the Rand Laboratory in Berkeley told Yates. 'We've thrown petabytes of networked power at the task, but we're not making any progress.'

'Well, young man, what should we do now about these alien signals of yours?' asked President Randall, once he, Yates and a handful of advisers were ensconced in the Oval Office's comfortable couches.

'Well, sir, I think we should respond officially,' replied

Yates, still somewhat overawed by his surroundings and the august company he was keeping these days.

'At least the decision about whether or not to respond to the signal has been taken out of our hands,' interjected one of the senior NASA officials to whom Yates had been introduced earlier. 'Thousands of crazy dingbats all over the world are already pumping out their own greetings.'

The President nodded thoughtfully, then turned back to Yates. 'So what should I say?' he asked.

The newly honoured, recently promoted, international celebrity scientist swallowed as he steeled himself to make the only reply that he knew was correct.

'With respect, sir,' he began, 'it isn't for the United States to respond officially. This has to be an international diplomatic response, one that is made on behalf of all the world's people.'

'Oh God, not the UN,' groaned Randall as he glanced across at his Chief of Staff.

For all of the public's excitement about the world's first confirmed contact with aliens, it took the United Nations organization a further ten months to agree on and to compose Earth's first official response to the signals that were still being received from the planet Iso. Much discussion and preparation had taken place before the historic meeting of the General Assembly during which the greeting would be formally transmitted.

Back in 1977, in the very earliest days of space exploration, NASA had optimistically prepared for contact with forms of extra-terrestrial intelligence by attaching twelve-inch gold audio discs to the sides of the twin space probes Voyagers 1 and 2, a pair of spacecraft that were due to explore the local solar system and then head out into wholly

stood at the large lectern facing the General Assembly and the world's TV cameras. Beside him was a clear plastic column surmounted by a large red button.

'Samples of every major language used on Earth, along with their grammatical rules, are included in our message of peace and greeting,' the Secretary General told the UN Assembly representatives and the worldwide viewing public. 'We have also provided examples of our mathematics. In addition we are sending video streams which show the beauties of our own home planet – as viewed from the surface and from space – and we have included detailed star maps and locators which will pinpoint our precise position in the galaxy, relative to Iso's own location in the Aquarian constellation. We have also included a variety of intelligent software tools to help the Isonians read our message. I only wish they had done the same for us.'

There was widespread laughter in the Assembly Chamber. Almost two years after the continuous stream of alien signals had first been detected, Earth's most distinguished cryptanalysts were still unable to decipher what it was that the Isonians were trying to communicate.

'Later transmissions to Iso will include a full set of encyclopaedias, geographical and historical information about our planet, details of our own solar system and samples of non-proprietorial technology designs.'

Panday paused, partly for effect and partly because as the time approached he too felt the immensity of the moment. He moved across from the lectern to stand at the elevated push-button.

The Secretary-General cleared his throat, and then announced clearly, 'On behalf of all the world's peoples, we send this message in a spirit of peace and with the hope of mutual and beneficial cooperation between our worlds in the years to come.'

His hand fell onto the large red mushroom-shaped button and simultaneously eighteen international radio observatories and 187 military radio-transmitting stations on Earth and in space began to transmit the laser-pulsed message at maximum power. It was the most powerful synchronized radio signal ever transmitted from Earth and travelling at the speed of light it would take fourteen years and eight months to reach its intended destination.

ONE

April 2063 – thirty years later

'Look at the size of it!' remarked Walker Donahue, a reporter from *Time* magazine, as the balloon-tyred moonbus crested a ridge and the lunar complex came into sight. 'I had no idea it was so big.'

'Setiville now covers three thousand acres of the moon's surface,' announced Melody Barron, SETI's media relations executive, as she stood in the aisle of the pressurized bus, trying to keep the carefully selected and highly privileged group of fifty journalists, reporters and camera operators informed and happy. She knew that her charges had been less than pleased to leave all their personal networking and communications equipment behind at SETI's main guest hotel but, as she had explained to them over and over again, no radio communication whatsoever was allowed on the far side of the moon. Nothing could be transmitted that might pollute the precious radio-free environment.

'There are sixteen arrays of radio telescopes which are each made up of over four hundred separate dishes,' she told the group. 'The individual dishes are more than two hundred metres in diameter.'

As the media party drove down the gentle incline towards the vast scientific complex, they could see row after row of ultra-large radio telescopes angled towards the brilliant night sky. 'Welcome to Setiville' read a large, softly illuminated sign at the entrance to the settlement, a township that appeared to boast scores of separate buildings, all interlinked by hermetically sealed walkways. Some of the buildings were two or three storeys high and the scientific establishment seemed almost as large as the main Lunar City on the Earth-facing side of the moon.

The journalists had been invited to visit Setiville as part of the anniversary celebrations that SETI was holding to mark the thirty years since the radio signals from the planet Iso had first been detected. Those signals were still being constantly received, and Setiville had become the natural home for the ongoing search for other alien signals.

Over the three decades since the discovery SETI's wealth had become legendary. Each year more and more donations and bequests rolled in to the organization and, as the visiting journalists were told, most of it was being spent on carefully exploring the many parts of the universe that were still unsurveyed and unmonitored by radio listening equipment.

The media visitors were shown around a permanent exhibition that was housed inside a huge pressurized plasti-glass dome. The enclosure was sufficiently large to cover the original sixty-four-metre dish which had first captured the Isonians' radio signals, and other exhibits included a holographic re-enactment of the moment when the young Desmond Yates had first picked up the alien signal and had realized that the primitive computers of the time had identified it as being 'Modulated'. A copy of his Nobel Prize citation was displayed proudly in a wall case.

'Of course, Professor Yates is now the Emeritus Chairman of the SETI Institute,' explained Melody to her large group. 'And he's also the senior Space Affairs Adviser to the White House.'

The party then moved on to look at another holographic exhibit which showed a computer-generated model of the planet Iso and its own local star, Giliese 76.

'We're unable to observe Iso optically – it's too far away,' explained Melody. 'But spectrum analysis has allowed us to make very educated guesses about the likely amount of water and even the size of the land masses that the Isonians have on their home planet.'

At the back of the group, Walker Donahue yawned. He wasn't even bothering to take notes or make any recordings. The alien signals were no longer exciting news - they had been considered old hat for years - but the thirtieth anniversary celebrations had provided just enough of a news hook for him to be able to justify leaving his New York office to join this expensive luxury junket. He'd never been to the moon before, but he was already coming to the conclusion that he wouldn't return quickly. Moon-bouncing was fun, but there was nothing special to see on the lunar surface. The luxury space-station hotels which orbited the Earth offered even better views of the home planet as well as wonderfully sybaritic weightless accommodation.

Donahue desultorily followed the party into Setiville's main lecture theatre, took a seat at the back and stifled another yawn as a fit-looking middle-aged man bounced onto the stage.

Dr Lee Kaku, Setiville's resident director of research, welcomed the reporters and quickly moved on to the main topic of the day; he understood that the media needed a constant stream of new information to keep them interested.

'Ladies and gentlemen, you have been invited here

today to hear an important announcement. We are going to visit the planet Iso. In partnership with NASA, SETI will launch an unmanned spacecraft to the Aquarian constellation this coming August.' As Kaku spoke, a 3-D holographic image of the spacecraft appeared, floating above the visitors' heads.

The Setiville director stepped forward to the edge of the stage and pointed a laser highlighter up towards the large image. 'We are calling our spacecraft *Friendship*. It will take four hundred and twenty-five years to reach Iso and it will carry three of our most advanced computer personalities on board. With the special permission of the United Nations Directorate of Computer Control, these personalities will be given fully humanoid form.'

Now there was a buzz of excitement among the members of the press. A mission to Iso in four months' time, and a temporary lifting of the worldwide ban on computer intelligences occupying adult humanoid form; this was real news.

Director Kaku provided more details about the craft and the journey it was going to undertake. The reporters learned that despite its crew of androids and its hybrid-nuclear power source, the mission was a relatively low-cost project and that over half of the money had come from SETI's own reserve funds.

'We realize that none of us will live long enough to see the benefits or the results of this investment,' explained the director. 'But we owe it to future generations to go and see what is on Iso for ourselves. This is the modern-day equivalent of fifteenth-century European galleons setting out for the New World.'

'You've cracked the code, haven't you?' shouted a woman reporter at the front of the theatre. There were other shouts as more journalists picked up the cry. Over the years there had been recurring press speculation that the continuous stream of signals being received from Iso had long since been decoded by either SETI itself or by one of the world's major governments and that the contents of the transmissions were being kept secret from the people.

'Are you in current communication with the people of Iso?' shouted another voice.

The director raised his palms. 'Absolutely not,' he said firmly. 'If anyone had managed to crack the Isonians' languages or data packets, SETI would have told the world immediately. It is a fundamental part of our charter that all our work should be conducted in the public domain, for the benefit of all society.'

'So why are you launching this spacecraft now?' shouted a voice in the darkness.

'To celebrate the thirtieth anniversary of our first alien contact,' said the director, 'and because if the Isonians did receive the first responses that were sent them thirty years ago, we should be receiving their reply – assuming that they chose to make one – any day now.'

The I-95 interstate highway runs all the way between Maine in the north and Florida in the south and, where it passes through Massachusetts, it becomes a high-tech corridor. This trend began in the late 1960s as technology firms began to be spun out of the Massachusetts Institute of Technology, the University of Boston, Cambridge University, Harvard and the other colleges that make up America's North-East Coast cluster of academic excellence. These firms chose locations near to the highway for ease of access and for the obvious distribution advantages.

The owners of the themed retail outlet known as 'The

Adoption Center' chose Deer Park Valley on the I-95, fifteen miles south of Boston, for the same reasons – and because of the opportunity it gave them to capture passing trade. Large billboards placed beside the highway – ten miles, five miles and one mile before the north and south turn-offs – told passing motorists that the Center had a wide range of infants available for adoption, from newborn to twenty-four months, and of all ethnic groups.

Inside the adoption nursery, forty infants were sitting, crawling, playing or standing according to their age and level of physical development. A dozen of the youngest babies were in playpens, watched closely by three of the dozen white-uniformed nurses who had the care of this boisterous group. In other parts of the floor area children were playing with toys, doing drawings, exercising in activity centres or being fed by the smiling, friendly staff.

Baby Luke, just eight months old, was seated in the middle of a large rubber mat and he was clearly unhappy. His wails filled the room, as wails filled these particular premises so often; clearly, he needed either feeding or changing, perhaps both.

Nurse Anne Loman turned away from a small two-year-old girl with golden curls and started to cross towards Luke, her arms outstretched.

Suddenly the double entrance doors leading from the main customer parking lot were forced open violently – doors that for security reasons were always kept locked from the inside.

Three youthful figures, all dressed in black and wearing black ski masks, burst into the nursery, each holding a large sinister-looking weapon with a complex metal contraption at its muzzle.

'PUT THE BABIES DOWN – NOW!' shouted the man at the front of the group.

The infants all wailed at this violent and unexpected invasion of their playtime but none of the nurses moved. They were all frozen with fear.

'MOVE AWAY NOW!' shouted the group's leader, directing his weapon threateningly at the nurse nearest to him. All around the room, security cameras silently recorded the proceedings. 'MOVE AWAY NOW, NURSES – YOU WILL NOT BE HURT,' yelled the leader.

The intruders advanced menacingly into the nursery, threatening the adults with their weapons, until each nurse had risen and had gone to stand at the side wall of the nursery, as directed by the attackers' gun muzzles. The children stared up at these interlopers with wide, frightened eyes. There was now complete silence in the nursery, as if the infants had realized that something so serious was happening that it was beyond crying. As they had risen, several of the female nurses had instinctively gathered up individual babies in their arms.

When the nurses were clear of the main group of frightened children, the leader nodded curtly to his companions and the three attackers fired their high-voltage laser-channelled electrical pulse weapons directly into the crowd of infants.

The babies, some no more than a few weeks old, burst into flame, their skin frying as if it were plastic, their hair catching light immediately as they were struck by 50,000-volt charges.

The attackers continued to fire pulse after pulse of high-voltage power into the group of children and suddenly blood burst from the victims' bodies as they began to explode under the sustained onslaught. The attackers and the nurses were sprayed with gore as veins and arteries burst and a vast dark pool began to spread slowly outwards from beneath the group of bodies.

One of the three black-clad attackers suddenly started to scream – a female cry of anguish – and ripped off her mask to reveal pretty features that belonged to a face no more than twenty years old.

'LOOK AT THE BLOOD, KURT!' she screamed at the group's leader as she lowered her heavy weapon. 'LOOK AT THE BLOOD!'

'It's just their latest feature,' the leader shouted back, still engaged in firing powerful bolts of electricity, his weapon whining repeatedly as its booster charger prepared each burst. 'Come on, the warehouse is through there.'

He ran around the pile of burning children, his co-attackers following, and burst through a white door at the back of the nursery.

The trio suddenly arrived in a large, cold warehouse in which wooden pallets were stacked thirty feet high. On each pallet were piled between twenty and thirty rectangular plastic boxes.

The woman who had ripped her ski mask from her face ran to the nearest stack of pallets and prised a box from the pile. She glanced at the packaging and then smiled, holding up the weighty pack for her fellow attackers to read.

MY BABY BOY, TEN MONTHS OLD, read the large letters on the front of a transparent window from beneath which a naked infant boy appeared to be staring out at the world. 'NOW, WITH LIFELIKE BLOOD' proclaimed words on a yellow flash that had been applied to the packaging. **Another fine product from Someone To Talk To, Inc.,** read a smaller line of text.

The leader nodded with grim satisfaction, then signalled for his grinning accomplice to stand aside.

Standing shoulder to shoulder, the three attackers raised their weapons again and fired high-voltage bursts of electricity into the vast piles of cartons. Immediately the boxes and the pallets burst into flame and the attackers directed their fire at other shelving units in the warehouse. From somewhere nearby a loud alarm started to wail, then water sprinklers came on all around the building. But the attackers showed no sign of a desire to flee.

A loud crack suddenly cut through the noise of the flames and a bullet whined off a nearby concrete pillar.

The third attacker, a male, turned quickly and saw an elderly security guard puffing his way towards them through a spray of water, raising his pistol for a second shot.

'Don't–,' shouted the leader, reaching out a restraining hand. But even as he spoke his partner lifted his stun-weapon and on reflex fired back at the old man carrying the raised pistol.

The security guard was knocked backwards off his feet by the high-energy pulse. Unlike the plastic computer-based toy dolls at which the group had been previously firing, though, he did not burst into flames.

Followed by his two accomplices, the leader sprinted towards the fallen man. As he arrived beside the prone form, the leader ripped his own mask from his face, not caring about the many security cameras dotted around the warehouse, and threw his stun-gun aside.

Dropping to his knees on the wet floor, he felt for a pulse in the right side of the fallen man's neck. The guard's face was paper pale and smoke was still rising from his thin grey hair.

'He's still alive,' shouted the group's leader over the

noise of the crackling inferno all around them. 'Help me get
him out of here, Mitch. Zoë, you call an ambulance.'

Mitch, the gang member who had fired at the security
guard, now discarded his own mask and weapon. The two
men took an arm each and dragged the old man out through
the billowing smoke towards the daylight that they could
see at the far end of the warehouse. Zoë was shouting to
the emergency services on her communicator as she ran
alongside.

Once outside, the group's leader immediately started
full CPR on the felled security guard. He opened his shirt
collar, checked the air passageway, felt again for a pulse and
then began to massage the old man's chest forcefully. As he
worked his co-conspirators stood helplessly by, all their
weapons and masks now discarded.

'He's dying on me,' shouted the leader furiously as he
pummelled the old man's chest. He bent and put his mouth
onto the wet, cold lips, blowing hard to inflate the security
guard's lungs.

'But my gun was only on stun!' protested the attacker
who had felled the guard.

The group's leader ignored him, continuing his frantic
resuscitation attempts as the minutes raced by, pausing only
occasionally to catch his own breath.

Loud siren wails suddenly filled the air and the tall
metal gates to the loading dock at the rear of the warehouse
burst open as an armoured SWAT vehicle raced into the lot,
followed by a string of police cars, sirens wailing, emergency
lights strobing. Then the smoke-filled air was compressed
with a deep and repetitive thudding as a police helicopter
descended to hover low overhead.

'Throw away your weapons and lie face down on the

ground,' ordered an amplified voice, so loud that it seemed to rattle the attackers' chest bones.

The gang leader leaped to his feet.

'This man needs a doctor,' he shouted at the top of his voice, over the thwacking of the helicopter blades, the wailing of the sirens and the roaring of the inferno in the warehouse behind them.

'THROW AWAY YOUR WEAPONS AND LIE FACE DOWN!' repeated the police voice, now with even more amplification.

The leader glanced at his two friends, shrugged as if to apologize, and then raised his arms high, got down on one knee and, with an awkward half-roll, lowered his body onto the hard, gritty tarmac. As his two followers did the same, heavily armed SWAT team members poured out of the back of their armoured transport and, with automatic weapons raised and pointed at the prone gang members, began to inch their way forward to make their arrests.

'And now, I'm pleased to introduce a very special surprise guest,' Director Kaku told the lunar visitors. 'He's making a rare visit to Settiville, so please join me in welcoming SETI's chairman emeritus and the man who first discovered the Isonian signals, Professor Desmond Yates himself.'

The group of journalists clapped politely as a tall, distinguished-looking man with a full head of wavy dark hair strode into the spotlight. The years had been kind to the famous astrophysicist and his movements were so energetic that he seemed like a much younger man.

'I'm not going to say much,' Yates told the now attentive group, 'But I want to underline how pleased I am that we are finally going to send a mission to Iso – it's long overdue.'

The SETI chairman then went on to describe several key design features of the mission that he had personally overseen. He explained that a nuclear-powered Orion drive would be used initially to boost *Friendship* to a very high velocity, after which an ion drive would continue to provide gentle acceleration for most of the long journey towards the Aquarian constellation. Then, on its final approach, large solar sails would be deployed to slow the spacecraft down, capturing the solar wind from Iso's own star to create a braking effect. He explained that the crew of computer personalities would carry out all maintenance and repairs to the spacecraft during the mission and, after telling the journalists that he was going to be available after the briefing if they had any questions, he came to the conclusion of his short presentation.

'Finally, I would like to remind you of what the Isonian signals actually sound like in real time,' Yates told the audience, looking at his watch and turning to where Director Kaku was sitting at the side of the small stage. 'If my timing is right, we should be receiving a handover of the signals from the Parkes Radio Observatory in Australia any moment now.'

The Setiville director nodded, then rose from his seat and signalled into the wings.

The audience shifted in their seats as Professor Yates waited expectantly at the lectern. At the edge of the stage they could see that Director Kaku was now engaged in some urgent exchange with an unseen person. Then the director nodded before walking back to the centre of the stage to stand close beside SETI's chairman. He whispered in Yates's ear, then turned to face the audience.

'Ladies and gentlemen,' the Setiville director announced, 'I am afraid that due to a technical hitch you will not be able to listen to a live stream of signals being received from the planet Iso on this particular visit. But recordings of the original signals can be found in your press kits, and Professor Yates has kindly consented to make himself available for interview immediately after this event. If you would like to follow Miss Barron, she will lead you back to the main reception centre, where cocktails will be served.'

From the *New York Times* website, 20 April 2063

ET HANGS UP

Alien Radio Transmission Ceases Abruptly After 30 Years

Thirty years after they were first detected, radio transmissions from planet Iso have ceased abruptly. No signals have been received from the source since April 16th.

Professor Desmond Yates, the original discoverer of the alien transmissions, said, 'It's probable that the interruption is only temporary – a solar flare in the Aquarian solar system, or an occlusion by another planet. Or they could have switched their range of frequencies for some reason. I'm sure we will re-establish contact soon.'

'Not a Coincidence'

Other ETI experts were less confident. 'They switched off their transmission just when we were expecting an answer from them,' said Dr Jim Burns, NASA's Director of Extra-terrestrial Communication. 'It's difficult to consider it a coincidence.'

To the casual gaze of the people thronging the corridors of the Boston County Court, Bill Duncan looked more like a musician waiting to go on stage than a witness being called to give evidence. His thick brown hair was worn collar length and a small silver earring in his left ear accentuated rather than softened a long, aquiline face. His white T-shirt, denim jacket, jeans and black cowboy boots all added to the impression that he could have been a lead guitarist from a successful rock band of the late twentieth century.

Despite functioning in what was now a very high-tech networked society, criminal justice remained a wholly human process. The proceedings in most civil cases were now conducted virtually with the plaintiffs, defendants, lawyers, juries and judges meeting only within the networks to plead, argue and receive judgements. But legislators still believed that for the most serious criminal offences the law should be administered in the old-fashioned way. Many modernizers argued that this expensive anachronism was merely maintained at the behest of lawyers who wished to maintain their exorbitant fees and monopoly over trial proceedings. But for hearings such as the one now proceeding beyond the closed oak doors across the corridor from where Bill Duncan waited, there could be no method of justice other than that conducted in real time, in person and face to face. The three young defendants in the hearing were each facing a murder charge, and in the state of Massachusetts a conviction would lead to a life sentence without parole.

The courtroom door opened and a petite, smartly dressed woman peered round it. She saw Bill and then crossed quickly to sit beside him on the bench where witnesses were required to wait before being called to give evidence.

'The prosecution has agreed to drop the murder charges,' she told him in a low voice. 'But all three defendants now face aggravated manslaughter charges, which could still carry a life sentence when it comes to the main hearing next year.'

The witness shook his head and ran his fingers through his hair.

'They're just kids doing what they thought was right,' he said, with a shake of his head. 'All they wanted to do was protest this grotesque trade in imitation babies. They had no intention of hurting anyone.'

'Well, that's exactly what we want you to say, and with luck you'll help them to get bail. You'll be called in a few minutes, once Mr Cohen has finished laying out our defence. Is there anything you need?'

Just over an hour later, Bill Duncan stepped up into the witness box of Boston District Court Number 9, refused the Holy Bible and read out loud the words of affirmation printed on the card.

The crowded courtroom was large, airy and panelled in a light maplewood. The public seating and press benches were crammed as this case had already attracted considerable media attention. Behind the long defence table Bill could see his three former students, all now severely and smartly dressed, their faces pale and drawn. The defence counsel had tentatively suggested that Professor Duncan too might like to remove his earring and wear a dark suit for the occasion, but the look his proposal had drawn from the witness had quickly prompted the lawyer to move on to other topics.

As soon as the swearing-in was complete, Counsellor Paul Cohen rose from behind his table, crossed to the centre of the floor and faced his witness squarely.

'Please tell the court your full name, age, address and occupation,' he said.

'I'm William Andrew Duncan, I'm forty-four years old, I live on a ship called the *Cape Sentinel* which is moored at Pier Sixty-Seven in Boston harbour and I teach and conduct research at the Massachusetts Institute of Technology,' Bill told the attorney and the court in a clear strong voice.

'In fact, you hold the Juliet M. Hargreaves Chair in Computer Personality Psychology and you are the Director of the Cognitive Computer Psychology Lab at MIT, aren't you, Professor Duncan?'

'That's correct,' agreed the witness.

'And isn't it also correct that you are a MacArthur Award-winner for science and a member of the National Academy of Sciences?'

'This is only a pre-trial hearing, Counsellor,' broke in the judge. 'I just want to get a flavour of the testimony, not the witness's entire life story.'

'Of course, your honour,' agreed Cohen. 'I merely wanted to establish Professor Duncan's pre-eminence in the field that is under discussion today.'

The attorney turned his attention back to his witness.

'To put it plainly, Professor Duncan, you are the world's leading authority on the development, psychology and pathology of artificial intelligent life, commonly called computer personalities, aren't you?'

'Well, I suppose I'm probably one of them,' agreed Bill.

'And would you tell us something about your three students here, and what might have been their motive for staging such a theatrical incursion into a retail outlet selling computer-personality toys?'

The lawyer had coached his witness for two hours on what he was expected to say. Bill drew a deep breath before summarizing what had prompted the protest, a stunt that had been organized for the sake of publicity but a stunt that had gone terribly and fatally wrong.

'I know the three defendants well, and I know them to be upright, decent people who would never deliberately hurt anyone. I also know that they were protesting against the obscene trade in lifelike baby androids that are now being sold to childless couples, to children and to lonely old people without any consideration for the psychological damage that can be caused to vulnerable humans who strike up relationships with these machines. This is a trade that must be banned – just as the manufacture of adult humanoid computer personalities has been outlawed.'

'Your honour, what has this got to do with this brutal killing?' asked the prosecuting counsel, rising from behind his table.

'I was about to ask the same thing, Mr Cohen,' said the judge.

At the back of the courtroom a smart but soberly dressed woman in her mid-thirties watched the MIT professor's face carefully as he gave evidence. Federal Agent Sarah Burton had guessed that given the chance Bill Duncan would use the witness box to denounce both the American computer industry and the US government for its lax attitude to computer regulation. She'd been secretly investigating the radical professor and his circle of friends for six weeks now and she was getting to know how the man's mind worked. Not for the first time she wondered why the prestigious Massachusetts Institute of Technology was prepared to condone such anti-establishment expressions by a senior staff member, and an attitude that was so opposed to the interests of the computer industry itself. It seemed as if Duncan was a cuckoo in MIT's hallowed computer-science nest.

'What it's got to do with this sad but accidental death is that millions of children all over the world are becoming more attached to these machines than they are to their own parents,' broke in the witness, ignoring Cohen's frantic hand signals for him to shut up. 'I know of children as young as eight who have self-harmed or committed suicide when they have been forced to give up their relationship with a computer personality.'

'Professor Duncan–' began the judge firmly.

'People have no idea of the emotional damage these computer personalities are causing and the social harm that is being stored up for our societies – not just in this country, but all over the world,' continued the MIT luminary, ignoring the judge's interjection.

'That's enough, Professor,' ordered the judge.

'These machines are turning children into psychopaths,' shouted Bill, eyes blazing, his gaze shifting from the judge to Attorney Cohen, to the defendants and to the main courtroom. 'And they also encourage old people to commit suicide. That's why I'm here, isn't it? I'm a psychologist as well as a computer scientist, and I know the damage that is being caused by this heedless, greedy exploitation–'

Three loud bangs resounded around the courtroom as the judge pounded his gavel.

'That's more than enough, Professor,' he shouted at Bill Duncan. Then he turned his stern gaze on the defence attorney. 'If your witness has nothing of relevance to tell the court, I suggest you excuse him and move on.'

TWO

'It is quite true that *Friendship* will take four hundred and fifty years to reach Iso,' agreed Professor Desmond Yates, responding to a question, 'But all the time the spacecraft is travelling it will act as a mobile observatory and interstellar probe, continuously reporting its images and valuable data back to Earth. It will provide the most fantastic opportunity for astronomy, long before it arrives at its destination.'

The SETI Institute's chairman was making a crucial presentation, one that would help to decide whether the *Friendship* mission was now to be cancelled or whether it should proceed as planned, despite the continuing loss of the signals from Iso. His small but illustrious audience included President Maxwell T. Jarvis himself, the White House Chief of Staff, the Secretary of State, the Director of NASA and various Treasury officials who already seemed keen to abandon the whole project. They were meeting in one of the small White House Cabinet rooms adjacent to the Oval Office and Yates had spent fifteen minutes briefing them on the project's progress, describing *Friendship*'s hybrid power source, the three humanoid computer personalities who were going to crew the ship and the procedures they would adopt as they approached the source of the alien radio transmissions. Now, having answered the question, he returned to his prepared presentation.

'Throughout the voyage *Friendship* will transmit powerful radio signals ahead of itself informing the Isonians of its approach. Once there it will go into orbit, radioing down for permission to dock with any space stations present or to land on the planet's surface. The three computer personalities are, of course, entirely autonomous and will have full control of the mission themselves. They are able to learn an infinite range of new languages and they will broadcast repeated reassurances that they set out in a completely sterile condition and that they bring no foreign bacteria from Earth.'

'How are they going to communicate with the aliens when we still haven't been able to translate any of the signals from Iso?' asked one of the Treasury officials. 'Isn't it all pointless if we can't understand them and they can't understand us?'

'But we'll get visual images back,' protested Yates, 'And we'll be able to see what it is we are dealing with.'

'But not *us*, Professor,' broke in a second man from the Treasury. 'It will be our far-distant descendants seeing the pictures, won't it?'

Yates was used to this objection. He'd been handling it for seven years, ever since the *Friendship* project was first mooted.

'You're right, of course,' he agreed. 'But if we don't set out to visit Iso now, humankind will never learn anything about our near neighbours in the cosmos. It is our duty to provide future generations with this vital research tool.'

'And anyway, most of the budget's already been spent, right?' It was President Jarvis, speaking for the first time since Yates had begun his presentation.

'That's right, sir,' agreed the SETI chief. 'The project was designed to be low cost in the first place and we've already spent over eighty-five per cent of the budget on building the spacecraft, the computer personalities and the various on-board systems.'

'But the signals from Iso have now dried up,' protested the first Treasury official. 'There's another eight hundred million dollars of public money that still has to be spent just to send a robot spacecraft to a planet that's gone silent on us. The voters won't like it, Mister President.'

'Well, I'm sure the interruption in the Isonian signals is only temporary,' countered Yates quickly. 'It's probably caused by a local solar flare in the constellation of Aquarius, or from occlusion by another star – or it could be that the Isonians have merely switched frequencies for some reason. After all, we now know that we've been receiving their signals on Earth ever since radio astronomy began – it's just that they were too faint to be detected by dishes based on the Earth's surface.'

'Yes, but–'

'And an opinion poll taken yesterday,' continued Yates, cutting off the Treasury man before he could frame his next objection, 'shows that sixty-two per cent of the American public are in favour of launching *Friendship* to visit Iso, provided the majority of the cost comes from private funds. As you know, the SETI Institute has provided almost three quarters of the money spent so far.'

'Look, NASA's already been allocated its share of the budget for the launch – am I correct?' interjected President Jarvis, his patience now visibly running out.

Everyone in the Cabinet room nodded, but both Treasury men leaned forward as if they had still more to say on the subject.

'Then let's do it,' ordered Maxwell, standing up abruptly. 'We're going to Iso but I don't want to hear that there has been a single dollar overrun on this project – is that clear?'

'Yes, sir,' said Desmond Yates.

At an altitude of 15,212 feet, the Carl Sagan Ultra-Large Optical Telescope was both the highest and most powerful astronomical viewing instrument in the world. It perched on the summit of a mountain called Cerro Samanal in the Atacama Desert in northern Chile and the observatory complex was usually staffed by a team of six astronomers. These resident professionals individually rotated their duties between capturing fresh optical data during the night and analysing the results during the day shifts.

In the early-morning hours of Tuesday, 13 August 2063, Brian Nunney, an Australian-born astrophysicist and a world authority on the behaviour of information in the proximity of black holes, was projecting a live optical image from 'Big Carl' straight into the observatory's main holographic display area.

'Come and take a look at this,' he called over his shoulder to Suzi Price, a Californian intern who was also simultaneously studying for her PhD in alien planetary biology.

'The computers have flagged up a strange area of density in deep space – in the direction of the Antila constellation,' he explained as Suzi arrived at his side. 'It's causing some of the stars in the region to oscillate. What do you make of it?'

A large patch of scintillant night sky was displayed in the holo-theatre in front of them – simulating a small part of the brilliant constellations on show overhead. Magnified by the telescope's giant lenses, mirrors and high-resolution electronics it appeared 20,000 times larger than could be seen with the naked eye.

'Hey, that really is weird!' agreed Suzi, tapping her screen stylus against her gleaming white teeth. 'It looks as if something's obstructing our view, but we've got completely clear skies tonight.'

'The closest star in Antila is eleven m.p.c. away – that's about thirty-five million light years,' Nunney explained to the intern. 'Look, I've sampled a few frames from that region of sky which were captured in the last year. I'll run them at fifty times speed.'

The establishment's senior astronomer and the popular young PhD student watched with puzzlement as the computers showed the same patch of the constellation photographed at different times and from different angles over a period of twelve months.

'It's as if some of the stars are being turned on and off,' said Suzi. 'How come nobody's noticed this before?'

'Antila's not particularly popular with optical astronomers,' explained Nunney. 'There's nothing much going on in that direction – well, until now, at least.' The astrophysicist looked at the data read-outs as the simulation arrived at its conclusion, then turned to his companion. 'Add some density interpolation to the area, will you, Suzi?'

The student punched in the necessary instructions and a thin red mist appeared across the centre of the constellation.

'Well, whatever it is has got some form of mass,' observed Nunney as he keyed in instructions for the computers to measure the distance and density of the patch that had appeared in front of the distant stars.

'Look at that,' he said. 'The distance can't be measured optically. It must be some form of matter that doesn't emit visible light.'

'This could be an important find, couldn't it, Brisie?' exclaimed Suzi excitedly. 'What are we going to do now?'

'*We're* not going to do anything,' said Nunney thoughtfully. 'I've got a couple of old mates who I want to take a look at this. One's at the Parkes Radio Telescope in Oz. The other is at Setiville, on the far side of the moon. Let's see what they make of it in the radio wavelengths.'

The US government's Department of Computer and Network Security, popularly known as the CNS, had been formed in 2022 by the amalgamation of the CIA's cyber-surveillance division, the FBI's computer-fraud unit and the National Security Agency's anti-cyber-terrorism facility. It had become clear that the computer networks were the natural habitat of criminals, terrorists, cranks and sociopaths and some real specialization within government forces was needed. In less than a decade, the CNS's reach had become global as well as national and its annual budget exceeded that of the CIA.

CNS agent Sarah Burton had been with the agency for seven years and she enjoyed her demanding work. Most of her time was spent investigating, catching and prosecuting computer hackers and cyber criminals and, with a doctorate from Berkeley in forensic computing and communications, her speciality was catching the 'ultra clever' fraudsters, 'techno-terrorists' and those criminal hackers who considered themselves far too brilliant ever to be brought to justice.

But her current assignment seemed more like small beer, she thought idly as she sat in her car gazing out at the MIT professor's houseboat where it lay beside an old jetty in Boston harbour. She'd watched Bill Duncan deliver his outburst in court, and she and her two field assistants had now been gathering information on the radical academic and his bizarre group of computer wizards for almost two months.

She didn't underestimate the technical capabilities of either Duncan or his strange circle of high-tech followers; from speaking discreetly to the authorities at MIT she had established that it was only the professor's brilliance as a computer psychologist that persuaded the Chancellor to put up with his eccentricities. Normally a department as prestigious as MIT's Cognitive Computer Psychology Lab would require a rather more suave academic to be its director, an urbane figurehead who could charm the corporate sponsors to part with even more money for research. But Duncan's reputation in computer science was internationally established and well deserved, even if his political views made him suspect to some.

It was the activities of the group of hackers and crackers who surrounded the maverick professor that had caught CNS's attention and had led to this investigation. The team jokily called itself HAL, an acronym derived from 'Hackers At Large', and many members of the group were ex-students of Duncan's who had completed postgraduate studies at MIT. But instead of applying their gifts and expensive educations for the benefit of corporations or government departments, they had been infected by their professor's radicalism and were now engaging in cyber war against some of the most powerful governments and most successful IT corporations in the world.

Agent Burton sighed and switched off the reading panel of her communicator. She would pay her first visit to *Cape Sentinel*, to see what her gut instincts made of Bill Duncan. Despite spending almost all of her working life policing in virtual precincts, she believed firmly in the value of a 'meat meet', an old-fashioned face-to-face encounter.

Stepping from her black government-issue sedan, Sarah Burton straightened the dark jacket of her trouser suit and strolled along the jetty towards the old lighthouse ship – a vessel that she knew to be over a century old. It was a bright sunlit morning in late August.

Her suspect was up on deck, using a squeegee mop attached to a long pole to clean the windows of the old ship's wheelhouse. He was wearing an old white T-shirt and cut-off denim shorts over his athletic frame and the agent noticed that he'd acquired a deep suntan since she had last seen him in court.

'Good morning. May I have permission to come aboard?' called the smartly suited woman who had appeared at the bottom of the gangplank.

Bill laid the mop aside and jumped down onto the deck to steady the walkway for his visitor. She was below middle height, maybe five-four or -five, and her shoulder-length dark hair framed a face with an Irish cream-skinned complexion in which were set a pair of vivid blue eyes.

'Careful,' he said as the woman grasped the thick rope handrail. 'It can sway when the boat moves. Who are you looking for?'

Instinctively Bill held out his hand to steady the new arrival as she stepped down onto the metal decking.

'Thank you. I'm looking for Professor William Duncan,' said Agent Burton, knowing full well to whom she was speaking.

'That's me – and who might you be?' asked Bill with a smile, as he gazed down at the attractive but soberly dressed woman standing on his deck.

The federal agent slipped her communicator from her pocket and showed him her badge and its digital verification.

'CNS, Professor Duncan. I'm Agent Burton. I would like a few words with you.'

Bill froze, then took a step backwards. He had a poor regard for the CNS. As he and his circle often complained, they were a bunch of biased and incompetent government enforcers who were completely failing to uphold laws and regulations on computer intelligence – safeguards that he considered vital for the safety of society.

'I'm very busy,' he said coldly.

'I saw you give evidence on behalf of your three students,' said the agent, snapping the communicator shut and putting it back in her pocket. 'I heard what you had to say about the computer toy industry and I wondered if you, or your friends, had ever decided to take any other form of direct action yourselves.'

'I'm sorry, I don't have any time for your agency,' Bill said, with a curt shake of his head. 'I think you should leave.'

'This is a friendly visit,' said Agent Burton, now sounding far from friendly herself. 'Just to let you know that we have been aware for some time of the activities you and some of your former MIT students get up to here on this boat.'

The CNS woman took a few steps forward until she stood in the centre of the deck and gazed down through the open double doors to the main living area below. On either side of the large cabin were long benches on which was perched an array of the very latest high-tech gadgetry. The walls were covered in large 3-D screens and in the centre of the cabin she could see a small holo-display area. She already knew that enough radio and cable bandwidth was connected to this ship to provide data services to an entire town.

'Looks like some pretty heavyweight stuff you've got

down there,' she said with a wave towards the cabin. 'Is all of it legal?'

'Take a look around, if you think you'll understand what you're looking at,' retorted Bill, as condescendingly as possible.

'What will you do with yourself now that you've been suspended from your university post?' countered the federal agent, turning back to face the subject of her investigation.

Bill looked at the agent as if he were considering throwing her over the side. But for some reason he decided to humour his unwelcome visitor a while longer.

'I'm only suspended while they carry out an investigation into the accident at the retail outlet,' he told her. 'I wasn't involved in that, so I'll be back at work soon.'

'But it seems very odd for an MIT professor of computer science to be campaigning *against* the development of advanced computer intelligence?' suggested the agent.

'It wouldn't do, if you had bothered to read my book on the subject.' *The Rise and Rise of Techno Sapiens*, Bill's first academic publication, had found unexpected success in the popular-science book charts ten years earlier. His powerful polemic had then gone on to fuel many public debates on the wisdom of developing ever more capable computers.

Following his surprise publishing success, Bill had campaigned for years about regulatory insouciance on the subject. He had publicly berated governments and public corporations for their unheeding and reckless development and exploitation of computer personalities – forms of machine intelligence which frequently exceeded all regulatory limits.

'What exactly are your political affiliations?' asked the agent, ignoring the jibe about his book.

'You will have already checked me out,' said Bill, now

growing angry. 'You know I don't belong to any party, nor do I have what you call any "political affiliations".'

'Don't you believe in American progress, Professor Duncan?' asked his visitor, deliberately provocative.

'How dare you?' snarled Bill. 'I love my country, but that doesn't mean that I have to love our computer industry, or our government. And so long as this is a free country, get the fuck off my boat.'

'Thanks for your time,' said Agent Burton as she stepped back unassisted onto the wobbly gangplank.

'Well, it seems to be a large interstellar cloud of gas,' announced Lee Kaku to the rest of the Setiville duty team. 'And it's heading towards our own solar system at quite high speed – at about a thousand kilometres per second.'

Three days earlier the sophisticated SETI observatory on the far side of the moon had received a request from the team at the Carl Sagan Telescope in Chile. The Setiville team was asked to track and measure a patch of peculiar space matter that had been identified at a location in the direction of the Antila constellation.

Although almost all efforts at Setiville were now concentrated on trying to relocate the missing Isonian radio signals, Director Kaku had granted permission for the lunar base's second-largest dish array to be temporarily focused towards Antila.

Now he and Stephanie Duval, the French member of the team who had been given the task of tracking and analysing the strange area of misty density, were explaining their findings to a dozen or so off-duty members of the Setiville team.

'The cloud is between fifty and sixty billion kilometres away from the outer edge of our solar system at present, and it appears to be made mostly of hydrogen gas, which is why nobody's spotted it before,' added Stephanie, in the cute French accent that many of the male Setiville astronomers adored. 'As you know, natural hydrogen does not emit visible light. But the mass emits the characteristic twenty-one-centimetre radio wavelength of hydrogen, which I think is fairly conclusive.'

Stephanie turned to the computer-enhanced radio image of the space cloud displayed on a wall screen. 'In terms of size, it's about one hundred and forty million kilometres across – that's about one AU, the same distance as between the Earth and the sun.'

'And it also seems to contain some helium,' interrupted Kaku. 'And some dust, ice particles and enough unidentified gases that we are likely to be able to see it soon with optical telescopes. Of course, such high-velocity clouds are quite common around the edges of the Milky Way, but it's very unusual to see an HVC so close. We are getting very good radio images.'

'If this thing is coming our way, shouldn't we alert the Asteroid Defense Network?' asked Pieter Gustafson, an extra-terrestrial biologist who was on short-term secondment to Setiville from Munich University.

'No, I don't think that's necessary,' said Kaku. 'As their density is so light, space clouds are affected strongly by a whole variety of gravitational forces. It will probably change its heading, or even disperse, long before it gets anywhere near our solar system.'

The director turned back to the French astrophysicist. 'E-mail our affiliate observatories, Steph. See if they can pick it up with their optics and ask them to keep an eye on it. Oh, and ask them to keep this news confidential for the moment.'

*

From the outside the 156-year-old former lighthouse vessel *Cape Sentinel* did not look like anyone's idea of a high-tech network centre. The converted sixty-five-foot ship was painted black with a thick red stripe along her iron hull, but rust had appeared in several places since her last paint job and another coat would soon be needed. Several panes of glass in the squat lighthouse tower also needed replacing.

But from four p.m. onwards on most weekdays, the innards of the old boat were lit up with such sophisticated computer and network analysis equipment that even CNS itself would have been envious. The technology had been partly installed by MIT guru Bill Duncan during the three years he had lived on the vessel following his divorce, but most of it had been donated by a small group of well-connected – and well-heeled – alumni from his Cognitive Computer Psychology Lab.

Many of those who had studied with Bill at MIT had been lured away to highly paid jobs in software and network development, either in the Boston high-tech corridor or in Silicon Valley, But many had returned to linger in Bill's orbit, enthused by his radicalism and his certainty that human society had to place more stringent limits on the development and production of artificial intelligence.

As a computer scientist – indeed, as a specialist in the psychological disorders of computer personalities – Bill did not object to computer technologies *per se*; he objected only to their irresponsible exploitation for military, government and commercial purposes.

Many of his students – among them some of the most able minds of their generation – had come to share his point of view. A hard core of about twenty of his former researchers had formed HAL – Hackers At Large. Five times a week a dozen or so of this group, of which Bill

Duncan was the unelected and unofficial figurehead, turned up at the *Cape Sentinel* to light up the networks in what was, in fact, a vigilante search-and-destroy action against the use of computer power that exceeded internationally agreed limits.

'Got another one to test,' announced Christine Cocoran loudly from the lower cabin. 'It's in Beijing and it's speaking Mandarin.'

Christine took off her headphones, turned away from her screen and swung round in her swivel chair. 'One for you, Levine-san,' she called up the companionway.

'OK, let's have it, Chris,' shouted back Paul Levine, a self-employed artificial memory designer who was seated at a screen in the main upper cabin.

Christine transferred the details of the network location up to Levine's monitor and then rose, stretching her lean body after a long shift spent monitoring the world's vast web of networks.

'Coming up to watch, Chris?' asked Bill poking his head down the companionway.

'In a moment,' replied Christine, shooting him a warm smile. Then she relit a joint she had allowed to go out in her ashtray.

Upstairs, Bill and five of the other volunteers gathered behind Levine to watch him test the capacity of the network entity in Beijing. Their game plan was simple: if their tests revealed that a network or processor cluster exceeded statutory power limits they didn't bother reporting its existence to either the national or the international authorities. They simply sat back down at their terminals and, acting in concert, deployed an array of their own specially developed and highly proprietary virus-based attack technologies to disable the illegal computer entity and to drive it from the networks. They were good at what they did – the best in the world, they believed – and without knowing precisely who to blame, many operators of illegally high-powered computer systems had found themselves victims of Duncan's vigilantes.

'It's definitely another illegal,' declared Levine after only four or five minutes. 'Over fifteen terraflops – the Chinese just won't give it up.'

'Let's close it down, guys,' said Bill quietly as Christine arrived at his side. 'But be careful to leave no trace – we don't want CNS poking around again.'

'Darling, a reporter from the *New York Times* wants to talk to you,' called a voice from the doorway.

Desmond Yates sighed and removed his arm from around the shoulders of Alethea, his ten-year-old daughter. It was a Sunday, and Yates was enjoying a quiet family afternoon at his home in the Washington suburb of Belvedere.

'He says it's something about a space cloud heading towards the Earth,' added Gail, his second wife.

Yates frowned, then stood up. 'I'll take it in the den,' he told her.

'This is Randall Tate of the *New York Times*,' announced the caller unnecessarily – his ident was already clearly displayed. 'What's your take on this large space cloud that's heading towards our solar system?'

'No comment, I'm afraid, Mr Tate,' said Yates firmly.

'Does this mean that you don't know about the cloud?' asked Tate.

'It means no comment,' repeated Yates.

'I even have a picture of the cloud,' persisted the reporter, and an image with which Yates was already wholly familiar appeared on a data panel on the wall of his den.

'And I have details of its location, heading and speed,' added Tate, transferring the coordinates to Yates's screen. 'Doesn't the President's senior Space Affairs Adviser have any comment on this phenomenon, or haven't you been told about it yet?'

Yates sighed inwardly. All those to whom he had talked about the cloud had agreed that its existence should be kept confidential until more was known about its composition. But he told himself that he ought to have guessed that there would be a leak somewhere along the line.

'Well, such high-velocity space clouds are common around the Milky Way, Mr Tate,' said Yates after a few moments' consideration. 'And some are bound to pass through the galaxy occasionally, But they're harmless.'

'No danger to Earth, then, Professor?' pressed Tate.

'No danger at all,' said Yates firmly.

From the *New York Times* website, 12 September 2063

HUGE GAS CLOUD HEADING FOR SOLAR SYSTEM

By RANDALL TATE, science correspondent

Could Pass Near to Earth

Scientists at the Carl Sagan Ultra-Large Telescope in Chile have identified a large cloud of interstellar gas that is heading towards Earth's solar system. The cloud, almost 140 million kilometers across and many million times the size of Earth, is of variable density and is believed to be made up of hydrogen gas and space dust.

'Clouds of high-velocity interstellar gas are quite common in and around the Milky Way,' commented Professor Desmond Yates, senior Space Affairs Adviser to the White House. 'It is unusual for a cloud to pass so close to our small solar system but it poses no threat to the Earth. It is still about fifty billion kilometers from the outer edge of our solar system, but we will observe its progress with interest.'

Cloud 'Could Contain Deadly Bacteria'

Astrobiologist Dr Sam Golding of the Jet Propulsion Laboratory, Pasadena, said yesterday, 'It's possible that this cloud could contain forms of bacteria unknown to humans. If any were to filter through our atmosphere and fall on Earth, the effect could be devastating. I urge everybody to ensure they stock up with sufficient protection masks for all their family members.'

Since the founding of the Massachusetts Institute of Technology in 1861, the Court of the Governing Council had met formally to discipline a member of the faculty on only three occasions. Each time it had been to consider revoking a professorial tenure, a difficult procedure and one that carried considerable legal implications.

Bill Duncan had been shocked to learn that he was to be called before such a disciplinary hearing. He knew that his radicalism and outspoken beliefs about the development of artificial life and computer personalities were unpopular with many other faculty members, but he was sure that he had done nothing personally to warrant a summons to appear before such a serious tribunal.

The hearing was being held in the oak-panelled Grand Hall of the Killan Court building, the white-domed and pillared edifice which looked something like Washington's Capitol and which was always shown by the media when they were covering stories about MIT.

Behind a long oak table sat the university's President, Chancellor and Provost along with a dozen other men and women who Duncan knew to be lawyers and human-resources staff.

The recalcitrant professor himself was seated in the centre of the hall behind a smaller oak table, beside the lawyer whom he had hired hastily for the occasion.

The hearing had lasted most of the day. MIT President Cornelius Swakely led the attack, arguing that although the results of the internal investigation had cleared Professor Duncan of personal involvement with either the planning or the execution of the violent protest that had led to the death of a security guard, it had become clear that Duncan's radical 'anti-establishment' views had been a clear and serious incitement to such action.

Chancellor Cassandra Quinn had then added her voice to the case for the prosecution.

'From what we have heard, your highly political tutorials have been nothing but repeated calls to radical action,' she said accusingly. 'And this has been going on for years. You urge your students to take direct action against those companies and government departments of which you personally disapprove. Professor Duncan, I find it hard not to see you as an accessory to murder.'

At this point, Counsellor Paul Cohen laid a restraining hand on his client's tense forearm. Bill had hired Cohen to represent him in this hearing simply because the attorney was also representing the three students who were now in jail awaiting trial. Both men knew full well that the murder charges had been dropped and that the Chancellor's comments were outrageous.

Provost Walter M. Williams then contributed to the proceedings by summing up the university's position and repeating the complaints about the professor's radicalism and his anti-government and anti-computer industry stance.

'The entire faculty recognizes that you were one of the most gifted of our young cryptanalysts when you first arrived here as a postgraduate student,' said the Provost at the conclusion of his summation. 'But your more recent specialization in machine-life psychology seems to have led you astray. On behalf of the Governing Council, I must now ask if you can offer any reason why you should not be deprived of tenure and dismissed from your position at this university?'

Bill was appalled. He shot a look of disbelief at his attorney, then began to heave himself to his feet.

'Permission to confer with my client?' asked Paul Cohen

quickly, placing a strong hand on Bill's shoulder to force him back down into his chair.

The two men had agreed that all of the talking during the hearing should be done by Cohen, and the attorney had even managed to persuade his client to wear a black linen suit and white shirt for the occasion. But now Bill seemed determined to speak.

'I strongly advise against it – you'll just antagonize them more,' the attorney hissed into Bill's ear.

But Bill ignored his lawyer. Standing upright, he walked round to stand in front of the table.

'Members of the Governing Council,' he began in what sounded like a steady and controlled voice. 'It is true that my views about the development of computer intelligence may seem strange to some members of this faculty who care more about technology than people, but I have never advocated anything other than peaceful protests against those who flout the regulations.

'I should also like to remind the Council that there is a long and honourable tradition here at MIT of senior faculty members dissenting from the mainstream views on their disciplines. One hundred years ago Professor Joseph Weizenbaum, one of the very first incumbents to hold my illustrious chair, wrote a seminal book called *Computer Power and Human Reason* in which he called for the responsible development of computer intelligence. I ask merely for similar rights to express my opinions.'

Bill paused and turned to glance at his attorney. Cohen nodded cautious approval; his client was managing to remain calm.

'Computers are now many times more powerful than the human brain,' continued Bill, 'and we cannot allow their development to continue unchecked. A century ago

Professor Weizenbaum identified the issue that confronts us all: it is nothing less than who will become the dominant species on this planet, humanity or intelligent machines?'

There was absolute silence in the Grand Hall as the maverick professor delivered his own defence speech. All present were familiar with Bill Duncan's extreme views.

'I condemn the actions that led to the *accidental* death of the security guard,' continued the accused academic, 'but I condone the motives that lay behind them. We at MIT should be more than just cheerleaders for the inexorable march of technological progress. We also have a duty to guide and advise society on its use. I hope that, as my colleagues, you will respect my position and allow me to continue in what I consider to be vitally important work.'

Bill finished with a brief nod and then returned to sit beside his lawyer.

'Very good,' whispered Cohen. 'Couldn't have done better myself.'

At the main table, the council members were conferring. Both Bill and his attorney expected that there would be a recess, but the President suddenly cleared his throat and all faces swivelled in his direction.

'Professor Duncan, whilst we understand your feelings on these matters, we are unanimously of the opinion that you have gone too far and that you have brought disrepute on your own reputation and on this Institute's. Many commercial sponsors of the Cognitive Computer Psychology Laboratory have raised questions with me and with other council members about their continuing support while you remain in charge. We have also been distressed to learn that you are now the subject of a federal investigation by the

Department of Computer and Network Security. Having taken all this into consideration, we are left with no alternative but to ask you to resign your chair and leave this university forthwith.'

THREE

'I'm going to miss you, Des,' said Melissa softly. 'We've always got along very well and it may not be so easy once there's a longer time delay.'

'I'm going to miss you, too,' agreed Desmond Yates sincerely. 'I've grown very fond of you as well over these last three years.'

There was a silence as the two friends pondered their imminent separation. Both were in Yates's den at his home. It was late on the eve of *Friendship*'s departure on its long journey to the planet Iso. Yates, the chief designer and driving force behind the mission, was seated on an old, comfortable couch. Melissa, the captain of the *Friendship*, was present in holographic form, shown sitting in a black armchair in the centre of Yates's home holo-theatre. She had long blonde hair, beautiful features and an outstanding figure. Her physical presence, her actual 'body', was a human-size android female made of synthetic skin, tissue, bone and blood, that was now orbiting Earth awaiting the launch. A complex chain of communications satellites and base stations bounced Melissa's synthetic voice and image down to the Yates household almost in real time.

'May I ask you something, Des?' queried the image of the android astronaut.

Yates nodded, knowing that full visual telemetry was being returned to *Friendship*.

'What do you really think we'll find when we get to Iso?'

Yates couldn't suppress a snort, which then turned into a laugh. He'd been asked the same question thousands of times by journalists and TV people.

'OK, forget it!' snapped Melissa suddenly. 'I only wanted to–'

'I'm sorry, Missy,' said Yates, holding up a placating hand. 'It's just that, well, I thought you'd have heard me answer that one many times before.'

'I wanted you to tell *me*,' said Missy, almost petulantly. 'I want to know your *real* thoughts.'

Yates sat back in his couch, ran a hand over his late-night beard stubble and considered.

'Everything about their planet looks like the Earth,' he began. 'That means the life forms that exist there are likely to have a similar chemosynthesis and biology to our own. Therefore the laws of physics and evolution suggest that whatever the Isonians look like, they'll swim, walk or fly – just like the creatures on this planet.'

'You mean they'll be flesh and blood,' cut in Melissa.

'Probably,' agreed Yates. 'At least, that's why we've given you, Charlie and Pierre full humanoid form – so that you represent us as accurately as possible. The laws of gravity suggest they won't be much bigger or smaller than us, otherwise they wouldn't have evolved successfully. But as to what they'll actually *look* like, I've got no idea.'

'I've made an anamorphic image of what I think they might be like,' said Melissa. 'Would you like to see it?'

'Certainly,' said Yates, thrilled by the idea of seeing what a machine mind imagined an alien life form might be like.

A figure appeared beside Melissa's chair, standing in the

dim light of the holo-theatre. It was a foot or so shorter than an average adult human, but it was far more bulbous, with short legs, stubby arms and what appeared to be a recessed head. It was pale-skinned and naked, but apart from what appeared to be a pocket or flap at the bottom of the body, Yates could make out nothing equivalent to genitals.

'Fascinating,' breathed Yates as he sat forward.

'I compared Zilhinlanski's research to the work by Dr Gumingharber,' explained Melissa. 'You know that neither of them are convinced that the long-bodied humanoid form is the ideal evolutionary adaptation. Then I reassessed the likely gravitational forces acting on Iso's surface, bearing in mind that we now think the planet has three moons. Local gravity, biology, geology and climate are the four governing factors behind my model.'

'What about predator adaptation?' asked Yates, glancing at the long row of data and calculations that Melissa was now scrolling beside the representation of an alien figure. 'After all, predator-avoidance shaped all species on Earth.'

'An unknowable variable,' said Melissa quickly. 'But I–'

'Des!' complained a voice from the hallway. 'It's almost three a.m! You've got to be at NASA by seven.' Then Gail Yates entered the room and saw the virtual visitor seated in the holo-theatre.

'Oh, hi, Missy,' called Des's wife. 'I didn't know you two were talking. But it *is* very late, Des.'

Yates nodded. 'I'll be up directly,' he said.

As Gail left the room, he turned back to the image of the senior *Friendship* crew member. 'I'll be talking to you again from mission control in the morning,' he told her. 'But I wanted to just have a few more words in private.'

The humanoid super-computer dissolved the anamorphic image of the imagined Isonian, then turned to face her creator. Although her networks, processors and humanoid shell had been built and constructed by the Zynteel Corporation of San Francisco, and despite the fact that her compressed high-speed education had been provided by a dozen of the most distinguished virtual schools and universities in the world, it was Des Yates who had been her mentor, the man who had patiently tried to answer the many questions she had had that were not covered by her formal education. As her IQ and mental processing capacity were several times that of even the brightest human, Yates had frequently found himself floundering. But, if such a thing were possible between a man and a machine, the two had become friends. Working with Melissa had helped Desmond Yates understand fully why there were international treaties limiting the development of super-capable computers and why there was a worldwide ban on incorporating them into adult humanoid form. He had frequently felt as if he were dealing with a superior species.

'Are all of your approach procedures and contact protocols clear?' asked Yates for the ten thousandth time.

'Yes, Des, and all the alternatives,' said Melissa with a soft smile. 'We all know how much trust you are placing in us. We won't blow it.'

Yates laughed out loud at her use of such a youthful retro expression. For a moment he had a wild fantasy image of Earth's ambassadors arriving at Iso and behaving like delinquent teenagers.

Suddenly Melissa's mood changed. 'I won't be able to have any more real-time chats with you after tomorrow, will I, Des?'

Yates sighed. He too dreaded the parting. Over the last three years Gail had frequently chided her husband for spending more time with the beautiful captain of the

Friendship than with her. But in the end his younger wife had understood. Coaching humanity's first ambassador to meet an intelligent life form on another world *was* an important and worthy task.

'No . . . Missy,' said Yates, hesitating because he had almost used an endearment to her, the sort of word he might have used to his wife. 'But I want to hear about everything you see. We'll talk every day, even if there is a time delay.'

'Forgive me, Des, but that's not going to be for very long, is it?'

For a split second Yates wondered what she was talking about. Then he understood.

'No, Missy. By your standards that won't be very long. But I promise that as long as I am alive, we'll talk every day.'

From the *New York Times* website, 23 November 2063

ROBOT MISSION LEAVES FOR ISO

By RANDALL TATE, science correspondent

Journey Will Take 450 Years

Friendship, an $11 billion spacecraft built jointly by SETI and NASA, successfully blasted out of Earth's orbit this morning at the start of its 450-year mission to visit the planet Iso.

Crewed by three advanced computer personalities installed in humanoid bodies, the spacecraft will continuously radio back astronomical data during its journey.

Critics have claimed that the mission is a waste of money since the alien radio signals from Iso dried up last April.

<u>Live link to *Friendship's* on-board cameras</u>

'Goodnight, Paul, 'night, Steve,' called Bill Duncan as he let
the last but one of his band of volunteers out into the warm
night air. He closed the large wheelhouse door and slid on
his hands down the polished mahogany rails of the companionway stairs and back into the *Cape Sentinel*'s main
cabin.

A month had passed since his summary dismissal from
MIT and Bill was now wondering whether network
activism was going to be all that was left to him. Although
his lawyer was assuring him of a very generous pay-off from
the university, it seemed unlikely that he would now be able
to find any academic post to rival the one he had just lost.
Perhaps he would have to write another book.

'Shall I switch everything to standby?' asked Christine
Cocoran. She was the only one of the volunteers left on
board and it had been a long monitoring shift. It seemed
that no matter how successful the team was at driving illegals from the networks, another company or government
launched a new one almost immediately. Bill understood
why, of course. Computer processors no longer had any
value when they were forced to function in stand-alone
fashion. Only when they were connected to the world's vast
networks – and the web now stretched far out into space,
around the moon and even to the pioneer colonies on Mars
– could a system's real capacity and potential be tested. It
was then that their presence became visible on the net, and
then that Bill's volunteers could take them down. But sometimes it seemed as if they were merely sticking their fingers
in a dyke. Despite the annual re-ratification of the treaties
on maximum limits for processors and system power, governments and corporations were still seeking ways to bend
the rules – sometimes to flout them openly – all for national,
militaristic or commercial advantage.

Christine shut down the top-level functions of the many powerful systems installed on the old ship and then handed Bill a cup of camomile tea. It had become customary for Christine to hang around after the others had gone and Bill was beginning to take the hint. But he wondered whether he was ready for a romance again after the lingering pain of what had been a very hostile divorce.

'I've got something for you,' Christine said shyly as she sipped her herb tea. 'You know they've given Skinner the directorship of your lab . . .?'

Bill nodded. He guessed that the Governing Council had already lined up Joe Skinner to take over his department even before they had carried out his public sacking. Skinner was a systems specialist, an expert in quantum processing, but Bill was appalled that a man with such a practical background in hardware 'plumbing' should be put in charge of a laboratory concerned with the psychological development of machine intelligence.

'Well, he must have some very powerful friends in the computer industry,' she went on. 'The hardware that's been arriving in the lab in simply amazing. I've brought this for you.'

Christine slid her hand into her large shoulder bag and produced a shiny metal case, about the size of a laptop computer. Following her boss's dismissal, Christine had talked about resigning her own research post in the Cognitive Computer Psychology Lab, but Bill had quickly talked her out of making such a useless emotional gesture.

'I thought you might be able to make use of this,' she said, opening the slim case.

In a transparent neoprene enclosure sat a gold and white object that glowed dully at its centre. It was about the size of a hand and it looked like a cross between an internal human organ and a spider. Stamped on both the lid of the case and the neoprene safety moulding were the words:

<u>**US DEPARTMENT OF DEFENSE**</u>
CLASSIFIED COMPUTER COMPONENT
UNAUTHORIZED POSSESSION IS A
FEDERAL OFFENSE

'This is a prototype of a new-generation organic-molecular processor,' said Christine excitedly. 'The Rand-Fairchild Corporation has given our lab ten units to test on some of our largest personality simulations. It's weapons-grade, the most advanced atto-scale quantum processor ever built. It produces pure random bits and it employs quantum entanglement and superpositions to do billions of calculations at once. It's rated at eighteen yottaflops!'

'Jesus!' exclaimed Bill, running his hands worriedly through his thick hair. 'What have you done, Chris? That thing's classified! There are whole treaties against processors that powerful!'

'Don't worry,' said Chris with a nervous smile. 'I called Rand-Fairchild and told them that one of their units was defective. They're going to replace it, but not for another six weeks. That means you can have it for that time to see what it can do. I've signed it out of the Lab.'

'For fuck's sake, Chris!' exploded Bill. 'You know that I've had the network cops poking around. What if they raid us and find this? We'll end up in jail.'

'But we're not doing anything illegal,' protested his longest-serving and most loyal volunteer. 'We're only fighting those who are breaking the law – and we can't do that without knowing the sort of technology that we're up against. Half the stuff in here we've brought home from the lab!'

'But that was when *I* was the boss,' Bill told her, only slightly more calm. 'Then it was my responsibility, now *you're* breaking the law!'

Christine's face fell. 'Well, I'm sorry. It's just that . . .' She tailed off and closed the lid of the small high-security case containing the prototype processor.

'I couldn't even take the risk of connecting it to the networks, Chris,' Bill went on in a softer tone. 'I'm sure that CNS is monitoring all our traffic – that's why we're having to run all of our operations from remote servers. If I connected this much power to our bandwidth we'd light up on the networks like a Roman candle.'

'OK, Bill, OK. You've made your point,' snapped Christine huffily. 'I'll see if I can sneak it back into the lab. But are you sure there isn't anything useful you could do with it?'

Everybody who was not already standing in the packed Situation Room rose to his or her feet as President Maxwell T. Jarvis entered. He was accompanied by his Chief of Staff, a personal secretary and two aides.

'OK, OK, let's get on with it,' said Jarvis irritably as he took his own seat at the head of the table. 'What was so important that it couldn't wait until after this afternoon's Cabinet meeting?'

Desmond Yates stepped forward.

'Mister President, I have disturbing news,' he said gravely. 'News that I knew you would want to share with your Cabinet.'

The room was now attentively quiet. A few of the most senior NASA and Defense Department officials knew what was to follow, but nothing had leaked beforehand. Others present presumed that almost a month after its successful launch there was now bad news about the *Friendship* mission or perhaps about the Iso signals themselves – although neither of those topics would normally warrant this sort of emergency briefing.

Yates raised his arm towards the large holo-theatre and, as the lights in the Situation Room dimmed, a portion of the night sky appeared in a 3-D image. In the centre of the display area, and obscuring a large part of the constellations, was what appeared to be a long, thin line of red and grey mist.

'As you know, a large gas cloud was identified six months ago travelling in outer space, at about sixty billion kilometres' distance from our own solar system.'

Yates paused to see if he needed to remind his audience of the details. No one stirred.

'We've been tracking the cloud's trajectory very carefully and it is now forty billion kilometres closer. I'm sorry to have to tell you that if it continues on its present heading it will almost certainly collide directly with the Earth in eight months' time.'

There was another silence, this time followed by a low hubbub as people whispered remarks or questions to each other. Eventually, the President spoke.

'I presume this thing is very serious, Professor Yates? I mean, if it were to hit us, would the effects be severe?'

The White House senior Space Affairs Adviser drew a deep breath and then nodded.

'I'm afraid so, sir. According to the latest measurements we have been able to take from the cloud, it is sufficiently dense and is travelling at such a high speed that it will strip the atmosphere from the Earth's surface as it passes over this planet. In a period of between fifty and eighty days, all elements of our atmosphere will be sucked away into space.'

A massive stunned silence now filled the room. The president glanced from NASA's Director to his Secretary of Defense. Both men gave little nods of confirmation; their organizations had been helping Yates to prepare this briefing.

'We concur with Professor Yates's projections,' said Roy Wilcox, NASA's director. 'We've built our own models and they too predict that the cloud's most likely transit through our solar system will intersect with the Earth's position in eight months – give or take a few days.'

Now the hubbub in the room returned again, only much louder this time.

Desmond Yates coughed loudly to regain their attention. 'As it traverses our solar system, the cloud will probably be travelling much more slowly than at present – as it encounters the force of the solar winds and the magnetosphere,' he continued. 'We estimate its velocity will then be about two hundred and twenty thousand kilometres per hour, but that will still be sufficient to rob us of our atmosphere.'

Now they were quiet again.

'I'm afraid that's not all,' added the space-affairs adviser. 'Our models suggest that as it approaches the Earth the cloud will first radiate reflected heat from the sun back towards our planet, then it will begin progressively to blot the sun out. In the first few days of the cloud's final approach, temperatures around the world will start to rise rapidly, perhaps by as much as thirty or forty degrees centigrade. As a result of this heating, there will be torrential rainfall everywhere. Then, as the sun's light is progressively occluded, the rain will turn first to sleet and then to snow.

After about ten days, temperatures will go racing down still further. At the end of the first two weeks we will have twenty degrees of frost. Rivers will freeze and mobility will be severely restricted. Communications may be affected. Within six weeks it will be about one hundred and twenty degrees centigrade below freezing. All the oceans will freeze over and mobility will be impossible. Radio and land-line communications may still work, but everything with moving parts that is exposed to the elements will become inoperable.'

Yates paused to draw breath and to gather his thoughts. The Situation Room, the location from where so many disasters, wars and terrorist battles had been managed, was filled with an appalled silence. Now nobody exchanged remarks with their neighbours. All were struggling with the awful scenarios that the Nobel Prize-winning scientist was laying out before them.

'There's still more,' said Yates in a low voice. 'It is possible that we may not even live long enough to see the world freeze over. NASA's gas dynamicists tell us that the cloud is largely made up of hydrogen with some helium which is mixed with a lot of dust – mostly minute ice particles, no more than a millionth of an inch in size. But the problem is this: when the cloud comes into contact with our atmosphere, the hydrogen and oxygen will mix – and when they're thrust together they are violently unstable chemicals. The whole of our atmosphere could blow sky-high, like one enormous thermonuclear blast.'

The silence that now pervaded the Situation Room seemed thick as a fog.

'And assuming there is no explosion,' continued Yates, 'my geophysicist colleagues tell me that the approach of such an enormous mass so close to our planet would cause wild internal gyrations in the Earth's core and mantle. This in turn would lead to huge earthquakes, tsunamis and global-scale volcanic eruptions.'

Yates paused and looked directly at President Jarvis. The world's most powerful man had closed his eyes and was pinching the top of his nose between his thumb and forefinger. He stayed like this for so long that some standing members of the packed audience started to shift uneasily from foot to foot.

Eventually the President looked up. 'Is there any more you have to tell us, Professor Yates?' he asked in a small voice.

'I've prepared a number of simulations, sir,' said the White House adviser. The image in the holo-theatre now changed to show an image of Earth's own solar system.

'These simulations have been prepared to illustrate the sequence of events I have described, sir – other than the possibility of a sudden hydrogen-oxygen explosion.'

Yates stepped back as the simulation began. As the huge space cloud began to approach Earth, the image switched to show computer renditions of the climate heating up, then freezing as the massive cloud slowly engulfed the planet. At the end of the sequence Earth was revealed again as the space cloud moved away, but now it was a lifeless sphere, stripped of its atmosphere and turning slowly, wholly unprotected from the glare and the lethal rays of the harsh sun.

'Surely there must be some error?' asked President Jarvis, glancing from face to face around the room.

Nobody spoke.

'Well, there must be *something* we can do?' he protested.

'We plan to dispatch some high-speed probes to carry out more measurements in the cloud,' Yates told him.

'There's a chance that we could be wrong about its trajectory – or the cloud's internal density could shift and change its course. The gravitational forces acting on a large cloud of such variable mass are very hard to predict. But it will be some time before we get further results. Of course, we're going to keep the cloud under close observation throughout.'

'Very well,' said Jarvis, shifting in his chair. 'I'd like to study this information for myself.'

One of Yates's assistants stepped forward with a Digipad and a file of hard-copy print-outs that had been prepared for the President.

'Sir?' It was Nick Connors, the President's National Security Adviser.

Jarvis nodded for him to speak.

'Above all, this must be kept quiet,' urged Connors. 'Imagine the public panic if this were to leak.'

Jarvis nodded again and then rose from his chair.

'People, Mr Connors is right. There must be an absolute information blackout on this,' said the President, now seeming as if he had regained his full composure. 'We must use the eight months we've got to prepare for a worst-case situation. There's nothing we can do if the atmosphere does explode, but I want the Federal Emergency Management Agency briefed immediately and placed on full alert.'

He glanced around to make sure that his aides were taking notes. 'Tell FEMA that I want an immediate stockpiling of oxygen supplies and I want production of oxygen and oxygen-making equipment scaled up as far as possible, to wartime levels, without alerting the public or causing alarm. I want all of our underground command centres made ready and reprovisioned for a very long stay by the executive – we're also going to have to build a lot of new bunkers, as many as we can in the time. If we become unable to use solar power, we're going to need supplies of gas and oil again. And if there's even an outside chance that we're going to have to live on a planet without an atmosphere, we should start manufacturing hermetic habitats, like the pre-fabs they use on the moon and on Mars.'

The President turned back to Yates. 'Will our atmosphere re-form naturally, Professor? How long will it take?'

Yates shrugged. He'd spent two weeks frantically trying to find a flaw in the calculations that predicted a collision with the cloud, then a hectic few days preparing for this crucial briefing. He had had no time to even think about what might happen after the cloud struck Earth.

'I'm sorry, sir. I've no idea,' he admitted.

'Find out,' ordered Jarvis brusquely. Then he turned and swept his stern gaze around the whole room. 'And above all, everyone start working on ways to head off that cloud.'

FOUR

By the seventh decade of the twenty-first century, it was no longer uncommon for humans to live to be 100 years old. Medical science was now prolonging life so effectively that several people had already celebrated their 150th birthday and tens of thousands were living to be more than 120 years old. It was now being said that the body was no longer the final barrier to extreme longevity; rather, it was the mind. It appeared that humans might be psychologically unprepared to live for extremely long periods. In the end, people simply got bored.

Not Sir Charles Hodgeson, thought Randall Tate of the *New York Times* as the small seaplane banked and began its final approach to land on the smooth surface of the bay. The young reporter had been reading up on great centenarians in preparation for his forthcoming exclusive interview with the world-famous British science-fiction writer, futurist guru and sometime poet and it was clear that Hodgeson was still as active as ever.

With a far harder bump than Tate had anticipated, the four-seater seaplane touched down on the surface of the Pacific. After a rapid deceleration, it turned in a spray of foam and began to taxi towards a white platform that floated in the water 500 yards from the island's main beach. A small motor boat waited to ferry the reporter ashore.

Tate was visiting Sir Charles at his Orpheus Island home, a private atoll in the Great Barrier Reef, thirty miles out from Australia's Gold Coast. The interview was to mark the great man's one hundredth birthday and the publication of his latest novel, *Destiny*.

'Sir Charles is in the observatory,' said the fresh-faced young man in a blue T-shirt and shorts who met the reporter at the jetty. He pointed to a building on the crest of the island's central ridge. 'It's a bit of a climb.'

Forty minutes later a heavily perspiring Randall Tate was shown into the gloom of the central observation chamber. A large reflector telescope on massive hydraulic mounts occupied the centre of the viewing area and all around the curving walls were electronic screens that displayed various sections of the night sky.

'Mr Tate!' called a vibrant voice. 'Come on in.'

As the reporter's eyes adjusted to the interior gloom after the bright glare outside, Tate saw a small, wizened figure in a white singlet and baggy shorts crossing the room, gnarled hand outstretched.

'Welcome to Orpheus Island,' crowed Sir Charles Hodgeson, shaking the American's hand enthusiastically. 'Journey OK? Good, good. Well, come along, I'm going to show you the island.'

After an hour's walking under the strong Pacific sun, Tate was forced to asked if they could rest for a moment. The vigorous centenarian had marched the reporter around his luxurious hilltop mansion, a dormitory building where several hundred of what Hodgeson called 'his students' resided, the main canteen, the medical clinic and the staff accommodation. Now the old man was proposing that they should hike back up to the observatory.

'How do you stay so fit, Sir Charles?' asked the younger

man, as he sat on a rock and mopped his brow. 'Do you use gene therapy?'

'It's all in here,' said Hodgeson with a chuckle, as he tapped his temple with a bony forefinger. 'It's an attitude of mind.'

'Right,' said Tate, still wanting at least another ten minutes' rest. 'So what do you make of the space cloud that's heading towards us?' he queried in an attempt to buy time before his host began the next section of their route march.

'Don't you think it odd that it has appeared at exactly the same time that we lost contact with the signals from Iso?' asked Hodgeson with his head on one side, birdlike. 'And at just the time we were expecting to receive a reply to the messages that my loyal supporters and I sent to the aliens thirty years ago?'

'Now, I'm not sure what you are going to feel, but I'm about to connect up,' said Bill Duncan. 'Are you ready, Nadia?'

'I'm ready, Bill,' agreed Nadia, the computer companion that Duncan had been coaching, developing and 'bringing up' for almost fifteen years.

'Then here we go,' said the former MIT professor, as he switched on the final ultraband radio connection to the smart processor-bus he had built to house the classified Rand-Fairchild processor.

After sleeping on the problem, Bill had decided to hold on to the molecular processor that his loyal volunteer had purloined for him, at least for a couple of weeks. At eighteen yottaflops – a processor capable of computing eighteen septillion mathematical calculations per second – it was by far the fastest stand-alone processor that he had ever personally handled. It was also capable of producing genuinely random information from within its quantum design and that gave it the potential to do things way beyond anything conventional computers could achieve. He also knew that he was unlikely now to get personal access to such advanced hardware – at least until, or if, he found another senior post at a university. But which other university enjoyed the sort of high-level access that MIT could provide?

He was alone on *Cape Sentinel* at noon on a Saturday, and he'd been working for several days to configure a system that would allow Nadia to act in 'stand-alone' mode with the new, ultra-powerful processor.

'You understand that I will have to disconnect you from all the networks,' Bill had explained to faithful Nadia as he worked. 'We can't risk a processor of this power being noticed on the web. We'll have to find some task you can use it for on your own.'

'I've still got some of the old Iso signals, Bill,' Nadia told him. 'Shall we have another crack at those?'

Bill chuckled and shook his head at her cheeky suggestion. Like so many other young computer scientists, he had spent his student years dreaming of becoming the first person to decipher the alien messages. Because he had a natural gift for numbers and pattern recognition, he had chosen to specialize in computer-based encryption theory during his seven years of study at Stanford, and for almost a decade he had tried everything he could think of to make sense of the weird signals that had, until very recently, been received continuously from the distant planet.

Years after he had abandoned cryptology in favour of studying human and computer-personality psychology, Bill had still occasionally pulled out sections of the old Iso recordings and tried yet another new approach that had occurred to him. Now, at least ten years since he had last made an attempt, Nadia was suggesting that they should dust off some recordings of the old transmissions and try again.

'OK, why the heck not?' Bill had told her with a smile. Perhaps the pure strings of randomness this quantum processor could create might begin to highlight any patterns or macro-structures that existed in the alien signals.

'How does that feel?' he asked now as the data read-out indicated that the super processor had come on line to augment Nadia's already considerable processing power.

'I don't know yet,' said Nadia. 'It feels strange – but rather good.'

Bill nodded. *So it should*, he thought to himself. Nadia's processing power had now been multiplied to the power of six – she was suddenly a million times more powerful than before. His personal computer was now technically in breach of all national and international regulations governing computer power.

'Want to make a start?' he asked, as he pulled old recordings of the Isonian signals from the database. Over the years he had developed and written hundreds of different software algorithms in his attempts to crack the Isonians' code, and now he reloaded them all and told Nadia to start over from the top. He knew that some of his routines were so processor-hungry they had never been fully tested, but now he too was keen to see if this ultra-powerful system could make any headway.

'I'll leave you to it,' Bill told his faithful and uncomplaining companion. 'I'm going fishing.'

From the *Sydney Morning Herald*, 3 March 2064

GIANT SPACE CLOUD TO HIT EARTH

'EARTH'S ATMOSPHERE WILL BE STRIPPED AWAY'

By Gino Bardini,
Space Reporter

Collision in 8 months
Scientists in NASA and the European Space Agency have secretly come to the conclusion that the giant gas cloud now heading towards Earth will collide with the planet and will strip away all of its atmosphere. The cloud is expected to hit the Earth in October this year.

In an exclusive interview with the *Sydney Morning Herald*, Italian astrophysicist Dr Francisco Martelli, a director of the European Space Agency, said, 'It is wrong to keep the world population in ignorance. On present estimates the cloud will pass across the Earth at high speed and strip away all our atmosphere.'

Continued page 3

Despite its best efforts, the Washington administration had failed to persuade all the other members of the international space community to remain silent about the menace of the onrushing space cloud.

Soon after Desmond Yates and NASA had realized the seriousness of the situation, astronomers in Europe, South America and Australasia had come to similar conclusions about the dangers presented by the cloud – as had many of the international space scientists who were staffing the large orbiting telescopes and space stations. Not all of them agreed with the American government's decision to keep the information from the general public.

The news was finally broken to the media by an Italian member of the European Space Agency who believed profoundly that the public had a right to know as soon as possible about such a dangerous situation. The only real surprise was that he had chosen to make his initial announcement to an Australian national newspaper rather than to one of the global news channels. But then it turned out that the reporter who broke the story was the scientist's brother-in-law, an Italian migrant who had settled in Sydney.

Within minutes of its publication the news was top of every bulletin in every country. At first reporters and anchor people reacted sceptically, describing Dr Francisco Martelli as a 'maverick' and a 'lone voice' in the space-science community, but as the story developed it became clear that there was far more to the report than simple scaremongering.

Now that the news was out in the public domain, internationally respected scientists were keen to confirm their own knowledge of the dangerous situation and to provide their own predictions for a likely outcome.

In the United States, Professor Desmond Yates accepted

an invitation to appear live on the nationally networked *Tonight Show*. During the lengthy interview he acknowledged that present estimates suggested that the cloud might indeed collide with the Earth and, yes, one calculation suggested that the force of the collision could strip away the planet's atmosphere. But, he was quick to add, there were many factors that were likely to affect the cloud's trajectory over the coming months and nothing was yet certain.

All over the world excitable factions of the public reacted as if Armageddon had been officially announced. Following Yates's broadcast, crowds began to gather outside the White House, many of them protesters who carried placards demanding government protection for *all* American citizens. Within twenty-four hours police estimated that the crowd in the Washington Mall numbered over one million people. President Jarvis drafted the National Guard into the city to help the police control the demonstrators and he ordered the military to mount guards at all government bunkers, command posts and underground facilities around the United States.

In London, alarmed crowds filled Parliament Square and in Paris a mob tried to storm the presidential palace. In all of the world's major cities, protesters took to the streets certain that their governments could be forced to do something that would provide them with protection from the cloud.

Other citizens adopted a more practical approach to securing their own personal safety. Huge lines formed at camping and survivalist stores as people stocked up on oxygen cylinders, water and canned food. Fights broke out as supplies began to run low and individuals used their fists or weapons to grab as much as their vehicles would carry. There was a run on building materials as the practically minded started to excavate gardens and yards to build shelters, wholly uncaring about zoning laws or planning permission.

But the most powerful force of all was rumour, usually unfounded and wildly inaccurate. Scare stories and crazy ideas were transmitted between mobs like mosquitoes hopping between cattle. *The government is going to leave the planet to take up exile on a space station. Mountainous regions are the safest places as air pockets will be trapped in the valleys. The cloud is poisonous, so there's nothing we can do.*

In an attempt to calm the panic, the White House announced that the President would make an address to the American people.

Meanwhile, news of the approaching space cloud, and of the worldwide panic that was ensuing, had completely failed to penetrate the consciousness of the three people who were shut away on board the *Cape Sentinel* in Boston harbour.

For almost four days Bill Duncan, along with his close friends Christine Cocoran and Paul Levine, had been working non-stop. All normal activities had been suspended, and the hacker volunteers who normally showed up whenever they felt like it were told that network monitoring was being temporarily suspended for a few days.

The trio was working feverishly, unearthing new copies of old Isonian signals from the world's databases and feeding them to the now supercharged 'Nadia' computer personality. Every single storage device housed on the old ship had been disconnected from the external networks and was now linked together to create a vast private network of electronic memory. The work they were doing was *very* processor- and memory-intensive.

Only twelve hours or so after disconnecting Nadia from the public networks and augmenting her capabilities with the ultra-powerful prototype processor, Bill Duncan had been shocked and thrilled to discover that his computer companion was making significant headway in extracting recognizable patterns from the Isonian signals.

'I got to thinking that there must be some redundancy in the signal, perhaps the FM duplicated in the AM, so I wrote an algorithm for Nadia to split out the FM and AM content,' Bill told Christine later that evening when he called to invite her over. 'Then I slowed down one minute's worth of the transmissions by just over two hundred million times – something that needed a whole lot of horse-power. And guess what? Out popped a minute section of state-switched pulses!'

Christine Corcoran and Paul Levine had arrived shortly after receiving Bill's excited calls and for ninety-six hours they had worked almost constantly, their thoughts running together as tightly as schooling fish. They had snatched sleep when they could, heedless of the outside world and wholly unaware that a large proportion of the world's population was reacting in panic to the news of the approaching space cloud.

The emergence of 'state-switched pulses' from within the massive data stream suggested for the first time that there was binary or digital content buried within the alien transmissions. That was what first got the three MIT-trained scientists really excited. Thinking that the AM/FM redundancy might be mirrored by the use of multiple base duplication, they agreed to write and then insert another extraction routine into the signal to search for binary, trinary, octal and hexadecimal content. Less than an hour later Nadia had presented them with more segments of binary code, along with what seemed to be fragmentary maths on a base-sixteen model and masses of infill data which they guessed contained the complex higher-base layering.

'This small section's perfect!' gloated Bill as he stared at the digital representation of the signal displayed on Nadia's screen. 'Its analog byte and word lengths are far longer than I've ever seen, but this segment is *pure* binary code.'

Then had come the task of trying to make sense out of the binary representers. Numbers were easy to extract and after a few hours strings of integers, primes and other recognizable values had emerged. But the streams of what were surely graphic characters – many of them rich with what looked like vector arrays and unknown weightings – were not so easy to interpret.

Earth-developed languages share common patterns: humans are hard-wired for language, and no matter what the dialect, common rules for grammar and construction apply to most forms of spoken and written communications.

But it quickly became clear that the Isonians did not share any of humanity's instinctive language rules. Even with her immensely increased processing power, the symbols that Nadia produced from the short unspecified binary strings were wholly unrecognizable characters and hieroglyphs.

'It's definitely some form of mathematics,' said Duncan to his two excited companions. 'Look, these things seem to be operators and that's clearly some form of set disjunction. And those are definitely factorial coefficients in an infinite series. Wait a moment! This bit looks like a rewriting of the Riemann zeta function in a weird way!'

Christine and Levine hit a high five behind Bill's back and he spun round quickly to join them.

'We've begun to crack it,' shouted Christine, excitement blazing in her hazel eyes.

'Hold on, hold on,' said Bill, raising his hand. 'Do you realize the immense size of the task ahead of us? If we want to understand what the Isonians have been transmitting, we have thirty years' worth of their data to search through, data that was transmitted at a speed two hundred million times faster than this small sample that I've slowed down.'

Paul Levine, whose first degree was in pure maths, completed the calculation.

'That means that at a speed we can understand, there is just over six billion years' worth of data to decrypt and read. Then we've got to strip away all the redundancy, all the error-correction data and learn the language they're using.'

This daunting information sobered the little group for a few moments.

'That's incredible,' said Bill quietly. 'Just think about what it means. In the thirty years since we've been listening to them, the Isonians have generated as much information as our society could have done if we had started on the day when the Earth was first formed.'

'They must be thousands of years ahead of us in terms of their technology,' observed Levine. 'Perhaps tens of thousands of years.'

The friends glanced at each other, now awestruck as the civilization on which they were eavesdropping was suddenly made to seem both more real and even more alien.

'But still, just the fact that we're cracking it will be the biggest news story ever,' said Christine, wholly unaware of the media storm and public panic raging outside. 'Who should we tell?'

Bill and Paul Levine exchanged grins.

'Oh no, not the gov-ern-ment,' they sang together in a

ragged unison, picking up one of the group's most popular impromptu refrains.

'Who do we tell, then?' demanded Christine, smiling indulgently at her happily clowning companions.

'Well, normally I would say no one, at least not until we had finished,' said Bill, 'But we're going to need the most enormous amount of processing power, networks and networks of it. I think we need to get the media involved as soon as possible – to attract some serious funding, and to prevent the government trying to step in to take it off us.'

Paul and Christine quickly nodded their agreement.

'But there's one major problem,' Bill reminded them. 'We've done this with a highly classified molecular processor that we're not supposed to have.'

'How about Mr Randall Tate?' asked a voice from the wall.

Bill swivelled to face Nadia. Even though she had no physical embodiment, he still spoke to her main screen as if she were physically present.

'That's it, Naj!' he exclaimed. Then he turned back to the others. 'Randall Tate is a science reporter for the *New York Times*. I met him at an AI-psych conference last year. Perhaps I could trust him with the story.'

'My fellow Americans,' said President Maxwell T. Jarvis, gazing straight into the camera lens. 'It is my duty and pleasure to address you this evening because I want to calm your mistaken but understandable fears about this so-called space cloud.

'It is true that a large interstellar cloud of gas and dust is now approaching our solar system, but it is still a very long way away and we cannot yet say for certain whether it will have any effect on the Earth or, indeed, on our solar system at all. What you have been seeing on television and reading in the press are nothing but worst-case scare stories which have little bearing on the true situation.'

If the three hundred million Americans who tuned in to the broadcast could have seen their President two hours earlier, they would not have been at all convinced by his soothing words and unruffled demeanour.

Then, President Jarvis had been personally chairing a meeting of the hastily established Cloud EXCOM, an Executive Committee of government-agency principals that had been formed to consider how best to prepare for the most dire eventuality. Members included the President's National Security Adviser, who also served as the chair of the National Security Council, the Director of the Central Intelligence Agency, the Chair of PSAC – the President's Scientific Advisory Committee – the Director of the Federal Emergency Management Agency, the Chairman of the Joint Chiefs of Staff, the Directors of NASA and the Defense Department, the Director of the National Economic Council, the Director of the National Military Command Center and the Director of the National Asteroid Defense Network.

Drafted in as permanent advisers to the Cloud EXCOM were Professor Desmond Yates and the Director of the White House Communications Agency. Two large support committees consisting of departmental deputies and agency assistant directors were formed to mirror the format of Cloud EXCOM. Their job was to meet at other locations to refine and pass on information and issues for consideration by the main committee.

Even as the principals of Cloud EXCOM were assembling, a crowd estimated variously at between a quarter-million and half a million strong was still protesting on the green slopes beyond the White House railings.

'I want to accelerate our construction of prefabricated habitats and underground shelters,' Jarvis had instructed the meeting. 'I want maximum effort in the manufacture of chemical-based oxygen manufacturing systems, water recycling units, food production and all other items necessary for extended survival underground. And I want our plans for dealing with a major federal emergency updated.'

Since the news of the impending collision with the cloud had first broken, Jarvis had put all other business aside and had personally studied every file and every document available on the pool of gas, its present trajectory and its projected course. He was no astrophysicist, but he was a fast learner, and with the help of Professor Yates, advisers from NASA and other consultants drafted in from various universities and government departments, he had come to the unavoidable conclusion that the dire warnings he was being given were wholly justified.

The first thing he asked the experts for were casualty estimates if the cloud did indeed collide with the Earth as projected.

'One hundred per cent, sir,' a planetary biologist from Harvard predicted confidently. 'Except for those in hermetically sealed underground shelters. And they would be able to last only as long as their air, food, water and fuel held out.'

Accordingly, the first responsibility of the Cloud EXCOM was to decide who, in addition to the Washington executive and those legislative figures required for constitutional reasons, should get places in the many airtight shelters that were now being hastily manufactured and installed all around the country.

As one presidential aide put it to a colleague: 'They're drawing up a list of people to be saved.'

The committee quickly agreed that civil security must

be the first concern. Chosen military units, the National Guard and elite police forces would be needed to keep public order as the moment of impact approached and, if they were to be relied upon, these personnel would have need to be guaranteed space for themselves and their families in regional shelters.

Then it was agreed that some elements of local government administrations would also need to survive. There was considerable discussion about which categories of American citizens would be important to the society that continued to survive after the cloud had passed. It was decided that those on the preferred list must include doctors, scientists, lawyers, teachers, religious leaders and other important social contributors.

Finally, the meeting had agreed unanimously to set up a secret lottery system. It would use randomly drawn Social Security numbers to select which citizens within these groups would be discreetly offered family places in the shelters.

Now coming to the end of his broadcast, the President squared his shoulders and produced one of his famous, vote-winning smiles for his large TV audience. 'The truth is that this space cloud is so vast and its composition so variable that it is impossible to predict its course precisely. We can't tell how the gravitational pull of the larger planets in the outer solar system will affect it and it is by no means certain that it will even pass near to the Earth.'

The TV director ordered the main camera to close in on the President's face.

'Probes have been launched to take further measurements of the cloud and I have instructed both NASA and the Director of the National Asteroid Defense Network to develop contingency plans for all situations. In addition, I am going to request that the United Nations convene a special meeting of the Security Council to discuss the situation at an international level.'

There had been much argument between the President's political advisers and the White House speech-writers over this last paragraph. Many felt strongly that the President should only calm public fears and make no mention of space probes or of the UN Security Council – it was as if he was saying, 'I'm telling you there's nothing to worry about, but I don't believe it myself.' But wiser political heads had prevailed.

'If he doesn't spell out what steps he is taking to deal with it, it will just be a gift to the opposition,' insisted his Chief of Staff.

But there was general agreement that he should sweeten the pill at the end.

'Most of these scare stories are pure speculation,' concluded President Jarvis with a twinkle in his eye. 'For all of us here in the White House it is business as usual and my wife and I are looking forward to the state visit by the Emperor and Empress of Japan next week. Good evening to you all.'

'I need you to sign this document before we go any further,' Bill Duncan told Randall Tate of the *New York Times*. The two men were standing in the arrivals hall of Terminal 7 at John F. Kennedy Airport, New York. Bill had just flown down from Boston and he handed a two-page legal agreement to the reporter.

'This gives me the right to vet anything you decide to print or broadcast,' Bill explained as Tate ran his eyes over the text. 'And it says that the copyright and intellectual property of the decoded signals belongs solely to me.'

Once he had decided to tell the media about his break-through in decoding the Isonian signals, Bill had asked for Counsellor Paul Cohen's advice on the best way to go about it. The lawyer had then drafted the agreement that the journalist now held in his hand and had even contacted Tate on his client's behalf to sound him out.

'You do realize that everybody in the media is obsessed with this cloud story,' Cohen had warned Bill before making the preliminary call. 'Maybe they won't be very interested.'

But Tate had responded enthusiastically and the lawyer had fixed up a conference call between his client and the *New York Times* correspondent.

'You mean you can *really* read the signals from Iso?' Tate asked disbelievingly over the encrypted phone connection that the lawyer had insisted upon.

'Well, yes, small parts of them,' Bill confirmed. 'We're getting some clear binary code and graphics, but we don't yet know what they mean. We need you to help us get others involved in the task.'

'Who else have you told?' Tate had demanded. 'Have you spoken to any other reporters?'

Bill had assured the journalist that he was offering him an exclusive story.

Now, as they stood together in the JFK arrivals hall, Tate signed the legal agreement with a flourish and handed it back to Bill.

'Come on,' said the *New York Times* writer, already hastening towards the exit. 'My car's in the parking lot.'

Ten minutes later Bill Duncan found himself in the reporter's powerful sports car, being driven away from JFK airport at high speed.

'I've got you a safe house to stay in,' Tate told Bill as they raced along the Brooklyn-Queens Expressway. The excited journalist switched off the computerized highway auto-control and changed lanes abruptly, pulling out in front of a truck.

Unheeding of his car's computer warning him of the spot fine he had incurred, and of the furiously blaring horn behind, he continued, 'Anyway, the public's getting fed up with this goddamn cloud story. They want something new. My editor will clear the front page for this.'

Tate swerved to the right and accelerated, narrowly squeezing between a school bus and a white van as he threaded his way through the late-afternoon traffic.

'A TV crew is arriving at the house in an hour,' the journalist continued. 'We'll record the first interview for a broadcast which will go out tonight to tie in with our nine p.m. edition. Then we'll run the full details in the paper tomorrow.'

'Right,' agreed Bill hesitantly. He had his right arm braced against the car's dashboard as the reporter jumped lanes again before exiting on the Atlantic Avenue ramp at the very last minute.

'Listen, Professor, I know it's a lot to ask,' said Tate as he pulled down hard on his steering wheel and swung into a scruffy tree-lined *cul-de-sac*. 'But I'd like to write the official book about your discovery. What do you think?'

The reporter slammed on the brakes and pulled into the driveway of a faded-looking clapperboard house at the end of the street. He switched the engine off.

'Well?' asked Tate, swinging round excitedly in his seat. 'We could do a great book together, Prof.'

FIVE

When the United Nations complex in New York had been finally rebuilt in 2050, the redevelopment had taken place amid much grumbling about the huge sums of money involved and many questions about the continuing relevance of a global institution with decidedly limited powers.

Many Americans felt that the United Nations was an ongoing threat to the US's rightful leadership of the world. Many Chinese felt that the organization was too heavily influenced by its host nation to be of any real value to the rest of the international community. And the Europeans were so smug about the spectacular growth and financial muscle of their own new federation that they too found the United Nations to be almost an irrelevance.

'The UN will only find its true purpose when the Earth has to fight a battle with aliens,' ran an old saw.

As forty-eight distinguished international scientists gathered at the UN headquarters to discuss what could be done to neutralize the menace of the approaching space cloud, it felt for the first time as if the UN had both a clear purpose and a mandate to represent all the planet's people in what was a truly global threat.

Professor Desmond Yates had opened the meeting by repeating the presentation he had made for the US President and his staff. But on this occasion he was able to include considerably more scientific detail and introduce many more subtle caveats to his prognostications. He knew that this group of astrophysicists, astronomers, astrobiologists, planetary geophysicists and those from related disciplines represented the cream of the world's scientific elite. There were sixteen other Nobel Prize-winners in the audience.

After Yates had made his initial presentation – a briefing which included the very latest data about the cloud and its continuing trajectory towards the Earth – he invited Dr Okuno Pigiyama, the chief designer of the American-European-Russian-Chinese anti-asteroid shield, to bring the meeting up to date about the defensive assets available in distant orbits.

The Japanese-born thermodynamicist rapidly reminded the attendees that the Asteroid Defense Network consisted of 214 nuclear-warhead-tipped missiles that were parked at strategic points in a large defensive sphere around the Earth and at key locations in deep space.

'We are wholly confident that we can now stop even large meteorites and asteroids hitting the Earth,' said Pigiyama. 'But how can we stop a cloud?'

The meeting then broke up for two hours as the scientists huddled in informal groups, exchanging ideas and querying all the available data.

As the gathering's informal leader, Desmond Yates went from huddle to huddle, listening in on the ideas that were being generated. Sometimes he stopped to join a group and to contribute suggestions himself. Sometimes he merely paused to observe, then passed on by.

At the end of the afternoon he called the meeting back together. It was planned that a two-hour break would now follow before the scientists met again for a working dinner which would also be held within the secure confines of the UN complex. Then the debate would begin again on the following morning.

'This afternoon's discussions have thrown up one idea I thought should be shared,' Yates told the meeting. 'I want to hand over to Dr Demetrios Esposito from CalTech.'

A squat, swarthy man with a severe weight problem stepped up and took over the stage from Des Yates. He patched some graphics up onto the large presentation screens and turned to face his audience.

'I've been working on this for the last few days,' he explained, his brow glistening under the lights. 'I think we should carry out a series of closely timed nuclear explosions within the heart of the cloud. This will start a chain reaction that will cause all the oxygen and hydrogen molecules in the cloud to ignite spontaneously.'

There was absolute silence as the CalTech theoretical physicist went on to provide his calculations and demonstrations of how the chain reaction could be started and the likely force of the resultant explosion within the cloud.

Suddenly, a thin cadaverous man rose to his feet at the back of the room. He was shaking with anger.

'Good grief, man,' he shouted in a broad Scottish accent. 'You must have taken leave of your senses. Such a huge blast could disrupt every planetary orbit in the solar system!'

All heads turned to stare at Sir Hamish McLeod, the well-known geophysicist from Edinburgh University. Some other heads in the audience nodded their own concerns.

'I don't think so,' ventured Esposito. 'Not given the volumes of space available for shock-wave dispersal.'

The argument in the meeting then raged for almost an

hour, before Des Yates was forced to step back to the lectern to bring the afternoon's proceedings to a halt.

'We're going to have a further chance to discuss this over our evening meal,' he said. 'In the meantime, I propose we set up a working party to model the explosion that would be produced if we did succeed in detonating the gases within the cloud.'

There were many nods of agreement from within the audience.

'One thing more,' said Yates. 'I know that I don't need to remind you, but everything we are discussing here must be kept completely confidential. You can imagine how the media would react if they discovered that we were even considering a nuclear attack on the cloud – let alone if they found out we thought that there might be some risk that it could cause a misalignment of planetary orbits.'

A few audience members nodded their understanding but most sat stony-faced, unused to being formally reminded of their professional responsibilities.

'See you at dinner, then,' said Yates.

Bill Duncan was obsessed with his decoding work. In the hour in which he had been left alone in the safe house in Brooklyn, he had covered the walls of the living room with scraps of paper on which he had scrawled fragments of the formulae and mathematical operators that he had managed to extract from the Isonian signals. He was reverting to the way he used to work as a young cryptographer: he was looking for patterns, for clues that were non-obvious.

Bill had Nadia with him in his communicator. Although her system now lacked the ultra-fast computing power available on board *Cape Sentinel*, he had stored as much of the decoded Isonian signals as her memory systems could contain.

After ensuring that the safe house was indeed secure, the excitable Randall Tate had warned his exclusive interviewee not to open the front door to anybody but himself. He had then left to make the final arrangements for the interview and TV broadcast that were to follow later the same evening.

Bill felt an urgent need to translate parts of the Isonian transmission into coherent content for the public. He knew that other mathematicians would recognize the operators and mathematical components that had emerged from within the signals, but he desperately wanted to be the first to translate some of the information into plain language, into something that the person in the street could understand.

Despite his overwhelming obsession with the fragmentary alien maths, on his journey down from Boston even Bill had been finally forced to acknowledge that another major story was dominating the public consciousness. There was an air almost of panic hanging over Boston's Logan Airport, with passengers exchanging gallows-humour jokes about aircraft safety and how it might be better to die quickly in a plane crash rather than to wait for the space cloud to strip away all the Earth's oxygen.

While he had waited for his flight, he had caught up with what the newspapers and the TV channels were saying about the mysterious interstellar cloud. It was definitely a threatening situation, he realized, but, as a scientist, he knew that many unknowable variables would come into play during the eight months between now and the point at which the cloud was due to cross the Earth's orbit. Like many other people, he had pushed the problem aside.

There might even be something in these signals that could be of use in tackling the space cloud, Bill thought now as he gazed at the many sheets of paper he had Blu-Tacked to the living room walls.

He walked slowly around the room, allowing his gaze to settle on each scrap of formula for a few seconds before moving on to the next. He was constantly trying to make patterns, trying to see how the apparently unrelated mathematical arguments linked together.

Despite his absorption, Bill suddenly found his concentration disturbed by the loud wail of police sirens. He pulled himself away from the mass of hieroglyphics on the walls and saw bright blue strobe lights flashing against the net curtains. Then car doors began slamming.

Even as the doorbell chimed, Bill heard a loud thudding as someone started to break the door down. Leaping across the room he started tearing his notes from the wall, gathering sheet after sheet in his hands, folding them quickly and stuffing them back into his briefcase.

'POLICE, POLICE, POLICE,' came the cry from the hallway as the front door was smashed in.

Bill was trying to grab the last of his papers just as three armed cops in full body armour burst into the room. They immediately pointed their automatic weapons in Bill's direction and he raised his arms in a bewildered reflex. Then other cops ran past to secure the rest of the house.

Into the room stepped CNS Agent Sarah Burton. Dressed in a black trouser suit and crisp white shirt, her businesslike elegance was in sharp contrast to the ungainly body armour and helmets worn by the police.

The federal agent pulled her badge from her pocket and showed it to Bill as if they had never met before. 'Agent Burton, CNS,' she announced. Then she turned to her police escort. 'Thank you, gentlemen,' she told them. 'You can stand easy. The Professor isn't going to cause us any trouble.'

The cops lowered their weapons but remained in the room, keeping a watchful eye on their suspect. Agent Burton glanced around the room and then turned to the wall and to the half-dozen snippets of mathematical formulae that Bill had been unable to remove.

'What are these?' she asked after studying the symbols for a few moments.

'You tell me,' said Bill Duncan.

'The damn thing has shrunk,' said Brian Nunney disbelievingly as he stared at the computer displays. 'It's gone from being over one hundred and forty million kilometres across to just under one hundred and twenty. And that's in just two days! It's incredible!'

'Well, I've double-checked all the computer measurements,' Suzi Price assured him. 'I'm certain we haven't made an error.'

They both stared at the large, red-and-grey-coloured mass that filled the 3-D screens of the Cerro Samanal mountain observatory. Since the space cloud had drawn close enough to the solar system to be visible in the optical wavelengths, all normal astronomy had been suspended. Every night the massive domed building housing the Carl Sagan Ultra-Large Optical Telescope opened up to the night sky with the sole aim of monitoring the space cloud as it rushed headlong towards the Earth.

'But what could have suddenly happened to nineteen billion cubic kilometres of space gas?' asked the Australian astronomer. 'It can't just disappear.'

Suzi knew that she wasn't really required to come up

with an answer. She was just being used as a sounding board by her senior colleague.

'Has the density of the main cloud altered?' she asked.

'We can't tell from this distance,' admitted Nunney. 'That's why NASA has sent out the probes. As they get closer they'll be able to bounce laser beams off the gas to measure just how dense it is.'

'If it can change that much in two days, it could change completely in a few months,' suggested Suzi. 'I think people will be very glad to get your new measurements.'

'You're right,' said Nunney as he sat down at a keyboard. 'I'd better inform NASA immediately – and Des Yates. I think he's in a top-level meeting at the UN. They're trying to figure out what can be done to head the cloud off.'

'How can they stop a cloud?' asked Suzi.

Bill Duncan glanced up as Federal Agent Sarah Burton re-entered the interview room. They were in a police precinct house in Lower Manhattan and Bill knew that Randall Tate was also being held in another room in the station. The reporter had arrived back at the safe house just as Bill was being loaded into a police car and although Tate had executed a rapid U-turn and sped away, a cruiser stationed at the open end of the street had flagged him down and brought him in.

'William Andrew Duncan, I am arresting you for the illegal possession of a classified computer component,' Agent Burton had told him coldly as they stood in the living room of the safe house. 'You will also be charged with attempting to sell or give information about the said classified processor to the media.'

While the agent read Bill his statutory rights one of the

cops handcuffed him. Three more CNS agents then entered and began a thorough search of the house.

'The processor you're talking about isn't here,' Bill told the woman who had arrested him. 'It's still on my boat in Boston. And I'm *not* here to sell secrets about any goddam processor.'

'You can tell me what you were doing when we get to the station,' the federal agent had told him sharply.

'So how long have you had me under surveillance?' asked Bill now as Sarah Burton sat down again at the interview table.

The federal agent didn't answer, but she glanced down at a Digipad on the table in front of her and made some notes. Eventually she looked up.

'You have admitted to the illegal possession of a classified computer component, Professor Duncan,' said the agent icily. 'That is an offence under federal law. If we go to court on this you are likely to be sentenced to between five and eight years in jail.'

Bill Duncan stared back at the CNS officer, appalled by what she was saying. Over the last two hours he had waived his right to have an attorney present. He was certain of his innocence of anything other than a technical offence and he had explained as patiently as he could that as an academic he had no interest in the proprietary design of the Rand-Fairchild processor – other than in its use in decoding the alien transmissions. He had also explained that his meeting with Randall Tate had not been set up to discuss the existence or design of the classified processor, but had been arranged solely to bring the story of his decoding breakthrough to the general public in the hope of attracting funds for more research.

Now Agent Burton sat back in her chair and regarded

her suspect quizzically. When she finally spoke, Bill noticed a change in her tone.

'It is possible that we may not proceed with charges if you are prepared to return the processor immediately,' she told him.

'Well, of course I will,' agreed Bill. 'But I was hoping to continue my work on the signal decoding. I think you'll agree that it is something of national importance.'

'And you can only do it on this particular processor?' asked the agent.

'Well, even the Rand-Fairchild prototype processor isn't really powerful enough on its own,' Bill explained. 'One of the reasons I wanted to break the story in the press was that I was hoping to get some research funding – to buy access to more powerful networks.'

Sarah Burton ran the tip of her forefinger around the edge of the electronic notepad that lay on the table.

'If we drop the charges, would you be prepared to withhold the news about your breakthrough from the media for a short while, Professor?' she asked. 'I want to introduce you to somebody – somebody who might be able to help you with decoding the signals.'

'Sorry, but it's too late to stop the story,' Bill told her. 'I've already given some of the information to Randall Tate.'

'Yes, I've just spoken with Mr Tate,' said Agent Burton with a sharp nod of her head. 'He's prepared to cooperate and sit on the story. But he has one condition.'

'A condition? What condition?'

'He insists that the *New York Times* must get an exclusive when the story does break.'

Bill shrugged. 'So who is it you want me to meet?'

The agent sat back in her chair. 'Someone I was introduced to at a seminar in Washington last year – Professor Desmond Yates. He was the one who–'

'I know who Des Yates is,' broke in Bill irritably. 'But he's a White House adviser these days. I particularly don't want the government involved in this. That's why I was talking to the media first.'

Agent Burton sat forward in her chair. 'I know what you think of our government, Professor,' she said. 'But I think you'll agree that things are more than a little sensitive at the moment. The public has been really panicked by the news of this space cloud.'

'Damn it!' shouted Bill, banging his fist on the table. 'I am NOT taking my work to Washington!'

'There's no need for you to go to Washington,' the federal agent told him. 'Professor Yates is in New York for a meeting at the United Nations.'

SIX

'Agent Burton, a pleasure to meet you again,' said the tall, distinguished-looking man who strode into the ante-room. 'Forgive me for keeping you waiting.'

It was almost eleven p.m. and Sarah Burton and Bill Duncan had been waiting for over an hour to meet Desmond Yates. While he waited Bill had found himself in the grip of powerful mixed feelings. On one hand he was furious with the CNS agent for blackmailing him into sharing his breakthrough with a representative of the White House. But on the other he was genuinely excited by the prospect of meeting the man who had first discovered the Isonian signals, the man who had been his scientific idol since boyhood.

Agent Burton rose and shook Yates's hand, then turned to introduce Bill Duncan.

'Ah yes, Professor, your reputation precedes you,' said Yates genially. 'I was sorry to read about that business at MIT.'

Bill returned the older man's smile, but said nothing. The contrast between the elegantly suited Nobel Prize-winning celebrity scientist and the denim-clad, long-haired radical computer psychologist seemed very marked.

'So,' continued Yates, glancing from Bill to Agent Burton. 'I suppose this must be about something important?'

There were to be no further preliminaries. Both visitors knew that Yates had just come out of a very high-level seminar with the world's top scientists – a meeting in which they were deciding what could be done about the threat posed by the space cloud. Only by insisting that she needed to communicate with Professor Yates on a matter of the highest national security had the federal agent been able to persuade Yates's secretary to interrupt her boss and arrange this hurried ten-minute interview.

Sarah Burton turned to the man she had arrested and nodded brusquely.

'I've decoded small sections of the signals from Iso,' Bill said, feeling so coerced and cornered that he found the words difficult to get out of his mouth, words that he had been expecting to say with pride one day. 'It contains digital information, pure binary code. I've extracted some sections of math, some graphics operators whose function I've yet to determine and some hieroglyphs of unknown meaning. I have about forty petabytes of the analog digitized so far and I need expert help in working out what it means – as well as a lot more processing power and network capacity.'

Yates started in shock as he heard the news. He took a small step backwards and his mouth opened. Then he shook his head.

'Jesus, after all this time! And it's digital! How did you do it? What have you got? Can you show me?' The questions tumbled from his mouth.

Bill hesitated. 'I'm sorry, Professor Yates,' he began, 'but I have to tell you that I'm very reluctant to share this information with you as a government representative. I am only doing so under duress and I wish to make it clear that I intend to retain my rights to all proprietary information regarding my methods of signal conversion and analysis.'

Yates glanced from the computer psychologist to the CNS agent and back again.

'Duress?' he asked. 'What duress?'

'Hardly duress,' broke in Sarah Burton mollifyingly. 'Professor Duncan has been helping us in our inquiries about the misuse of a classified processor. I merely suggested that he should inform you of what he has been doing with it.'

Bill glowered at the federal agent and Yates cleared his throat.

'Look, if it's of any help, we can agree to keep this unofficial,' he offered. 'I give you my word, Professor Duncan, that I will keep what you are going to tell me confidential until you agree otherwise. Fair enough?'

Bill considered for a moment, gave a short nod, then took out his communicator from the pocket of his denim jacket. He flipped open its lid and selected the projector function.

An hour later, Desmond Yates and Bill Duncan were still standing at the room's white-painted wall on which the projection was slowly scrolling past. Both men were in shirt-sleeves, both had electronic marker pens in their hands. They had been writing their thoughts and their attempts to complete the partial alien formulae on the room's electronic whiteboard.

The former MIT scientist had explained that the key to beginning to unlock the analog alien transmissions had been to slow them down by two hundred million times, and then look for redundancy in both the FM/AM signal components. Then, when it was clear they that contained digital elements, to look for more redundancy within the bases that had emerged.

Yates had grunted with excitement as recognizable values and mathematical operators appeared on the wall. Then the two men began to piece together what were almost certainly sections of equations. Initially Sarah Burton had tried to keep up. Her own maths was rusty, though still serviceable, but she found herself lost as the two men started to speculate about the possibility that the fragments of calculations appeared to be illegal mixtures of quantum theory, base-sixteen digital code and Einsteinian-style traditional astrophysics.

'How much more have you converted and digitized?' asked Yates when they had exhausted the files carried in the small personal technology assistant.

'I've got about eighteen minutes' worth of binary altogether,' explained Bill. 'But there's so much more analog data – six billion years' worth on even the fastest stand-alone system.'

'That's no problem,' said Yates enthusiastically, as he lifted his own communicator and began a series of rapid calculations. 'If we distribute small segments of the task over the networks – like we did years ago with the old "SETI" at Home program – we can ask the public for help and use the power of the world's thirty billion processors. We can have the conversion done in a few months.'

'With respect, Professor,' interjected Sarah Burton, speaking for the first time in half an hour. 'That would only be OK if you don't mind what it is the public finds out. At present, only Professor Duncan knows how to translate the Isonian signals. Don't you think we should consider carefully before we give it all to the world – especially at such a sensitive time as this?'

Both men looked at the government security agent as if she were a massive killjoy. Then Yates put down his communicator, re-fastened his collar and tightened his tie.

'You're right, of course, Agent Burton,' agreed Yates as he plucked his suit jacket from a chair back. 'We don't know what it is we're going to find, nor whether it could be any use to us with the space cloud.'

The older scientist eased on his jacket and, formal again, turned to face Bill Duncan.

'Would you be prepared to bring everything you've got to Washington, to show my colleagues at NASA and the White House?'

Bill glanced from Yates to Agent Burton. Every instinct he possessed made him want to yell 'NO' and tell them to go to hell. He could tell them both to jump in the lake and take whatever sort of rap was coming to him. It hardly mattered, now that he no longer had an academic career or a family to worry about.

But on the other hand, the approach of the space cloud and the awful, terrifying threat that it brought had changed everything. It now seemed as if all normal considerations had to be suspended until the threat was averted.

'OK, just so long as you understand that I will remain free to talk to the press when the time is right,' said Bill, snapping his communicator shut and pulling on his own jacket. 'I will just have to go back to Boston to pick up my things.'

'We'll have that done for you,' said Agent Burton quickly. 'I can arrange a hotel here for you tonight. Let's meet up again in the morning.'

From the *New York Times* website, 20 April 2064

NUCLEAR ATTACK PLANNED ON CLOUD

By SONIA MAXWELL, special correspondent

'Risk that Solar System Could Break up'

Scientists meeting at the United Nations to discuss potential methods of diverting the space cloud away from Earth are considering detonating nuclear weapons at its center. The aim is to create a chain reaction explosion that will incinerate the entire cloud. Their proposal will be put before the UN Security Council in the next two days.

'The idea is lunacy,' Sir Hamish McLeod, professor of geophysics at Edinburgh University, Scotland, said yesterday. 'If the cloud were to explode, the blast would be so great that it could wreck the delicate equilibrium of the whole solar system. Disrupting the Earth's orbit could destroy our entire civilization, even before we are sure that the cloud will collide with our planet and before we can be sure of what the consequences of such a collision might be.'

Nobel Prize-winner Professor Desmond Yates dismissed concerns about the proposed nuclear attack. 'Before the very first atomic weapon was exploded, some scientists believed that such an explosion would set fire to the Earth's atmosphere,' he told the *New York Times*. 'We are building computer models of the proposed strike to ensure that if any nuclear action against the cloud were to take place, it would not harm Earth or any other part of the solar system.'

'What do they hope to achieve?' groaned President Maxwell T. Jarvis as he watched TV images of a huge crowd surrounding the United Nations headquarters building in New York. The television sound was down and the dozen or so other people gathered in the Oval Office wondered if his question was rhetorical or whether they were expected to come up with an answer.

Since news of the plan to detonate nuclear warheads inside the cloud had been deliberately leaked to the press, the whole of the east side of mid-Manhattan had ground to a standstill. Hundreds of thousands of protesters carrying banners and placards proclaiming 'NO TO NUKES', 'SAVE OUR SOLAR SYSTEM' and 'MILITARY OUT OF SPACE' had blocked the roads and made all normal business impossible.

Because of the protests, the scientists attending the supposedly secret meeting at the UN had been unable to reconvene and the seminar had been abandoned. Instead they had agreed to continue their urgent discussions in the privacy of the networks.

'I'm not at all sure the protesters know what it is they want to achieve themselves, sir,' Desmond Yates told the President. 'But their actions do seem to be having an effect on political opinion. The Security Council members are now deadlocked over whether a nuclear strike should be made against the cloud or not.'

'So what should *we* do?' asked the President, turning to the room in general.

'We must act unilaterally, sir,' said the Chairman of the Joint Chiefs of Staff firmly. 'We should mount an all-out nuclear strike in the very near future, while the cloud is still well outside our own solar system. If Professor Yates says there's minimal risk, that's good enough for me.'

Jarvis glanced at Yates for his confirmation.

'Well, the majority view among our group of scientists was that it is the right thing to do, sir,' agreed Yates. 'The computer models we've built suggest that the risk is minimal.'

'But what if they're wrong?' groaned the President with a shake of his head. 'Think of the responsibility!'

The Cabinet members, aides and advisers stared at the President as he wrestled with the concept of the United States launching a unilateral nuclear attack on the cloud.

'If the UN can't agree, perhaps I can at least get agreement from the other major powers,' Jarvis said at last, turning to his senior foreign affairs adviser. 'Henry, set up calls for me to speak with the leaders of Europe, Russia and China – in that order.'

SEVEN

'So, Agent Burton, I presume you've been told to keep a very close eye on me while I'm in DC?' Bill Duncan said with a resigned sigh. The pair were belted into neighbouring seats in the business section of a plane waiting to take off for Washington.

'That's understandable, given your feelings about our government, isn't it, Professor Duncan?' replied Sarah Burton. 'I'm afraid you're stuck with me for the duration.'

Bill nodded and wondered again whether he was right to be taking his discovery to the Washington administration. He'd already had one major row about it with Christine Cocoran, his most loyal volunteer. He'd called her to arrange for Boston-based CNS agents to visit the *Cape Sentinel* to collect the Rand-Fairchild processor, his personal memory-storage systems and some clothes. During the call he had been forced to admit that he was about to share their precious breakthrough with NASA and the White House.

'How could you?' Christine cried. 'After everything you've said about them. You know our government is completely irresponsible about the development of AI personalities and machine life. Think what they could do with *this* material.'

The phone call had ended on a sour note, but Bill now knew that his personal effects had been collected promptly and were already on their way to DC. Christine had begrudgingly agreed to remain on board the *Cape Sentinel* to boat-sit for him while he was away. 'I want you to carry on the good work,' Bill had urged her, trying to make it clear that he hadn't completely sold out. 'Keep knocking those illegals off the networks.'

'So, Professor,' said the federal agent as she flipped open an in-flight magazine. 'How well do you know Washington?'

Bill glanced sideways at his travelling companion. As usual she was wearing her uniform of a dark trouser suit and a bright white shirt, but her medium-length brown hair now seemed fuller, and done in a less severe style than before.

'Only too well,' said Bill. 'But I can't say I know the city.'

The jet engines suddenly increased their power and the plane began to accelerate quickly towards take-off.

Thirty minutes later Bill was beginning to regard his fellow passenger in a rather different light. He had learned a little about her own studies in forensic computing at Berkeley and he had been surprised to discover how much she knew about artificial life and the principles of cognitive therapy for computer personalities. He had also learned that her role in Washington was not solely to keep an eye on him – she had also been seconded to provide him with practical assistance.

'I think that CNS hopes to share in whatever comes out of your work,' she admitted. 'Who knows what we're going to find? Stuff that could be of real use to the Department, maybe.'

'That's what worries me most,' said Bill.

'Thank you for waiting, people,' said President Jarvis as he entered the Situation Room. Motioning for the members of the Cloud EXCOM to sit, he took his chair at the head of the table.

'I've just got off the line with President Olsen,' Jarvis told the meeting. 'He's formally agreed that Europe will join us in the strike against the cloud. He had a lot of arguing to do with his Cabinet colleagues, but the majority view was that we should go ahead.'

There were nods of approval from the committee members and the other advisers and aides who had been called together to learn the outcome of the negotiations.

'But neither the Russians nor the Chinese will take part,' added Jarvis. 'Lee Jian seems unable to make up his mind and President Orotov said an outright "No". That means it's us and the Europeans going it alone.'

There was a short silence while the others in the meeting waited to see if the President had anything to add. Then Desmond Yates stood up.

'Sir, I've got an update on the cloud's position – and on its behaviour,' he told the meeting as the holo-theatre at the end of the Situation Room lit up. All present saw a graphic of the solar system with a dotted line passing through the orbital ovals of the outer planets before intersecting with Earth's own orbit, closer to the sun.

'We've been monitoring the cloud continuously for the last nine weeks,' explained Yates, 'And it's still clearly on a heading that will lead to a direct collision with Earth – in fact, we'll be plumb in the centre of the cloud as it passes by.'

A few EXCOM members seated at the large table shook their heads anxiously, while others made jottings on their digital notepads.

'But something odd has occurred,' continued Yates as the image in the holo-theatre changed. Now those in the meeting saw an image of the vapour mass itself, thick and red with extensive grey bands. 'The cloud seems to be shrinking, or perhaps I should say condensing. Over the last few days its volume seems to have become seven per cent smaller.'

'How might that be possible, Professor?' asked Lillian Bayley, the director the National Asteroid Defense Network.

'We just don't know,' admitted Yates. 'The cloud's still well outside our solar system so it can't be because of any gravitational effects from the sun or from the outer planets. The only theory that makes any sense is that there's some sort of chemical reaction occurring within the cloud itself, something that's making it shrink from the inside.'

'You mean it's not *passive*?' asked President Jarvis. 'The briefing material I've read describes the cloud as being made up of *passive* gases.'

'Well, all of our spectrometry and other forms of measurement suggest that it is made up of nothing but passive gases, sir,' agreed Yates. 'But we can't account for the change in the cloud's length and volume.'

There was a short silence in the room. Then the President asked, 'And is the cloud travelling at the same speed?'

'It's slowing quite a bit, sir,' Yates told him. 'It's now travelling at approximately three hundred thousand kilometres per hour. We now calculate that it will begin to strike the Earth's atmosphere five months from now – at eleven twenty-one a.m. GMT on October twenty-fourth.'

Each person in the meeting digested this news in silence. The President drummed his thick fingers on the writing pad in front of him.

'So do we go ahead with a nuclear strike?' he asked the

Cloud EXCOM. 'Europe will join us, but no other nation in the world is prepared to take part. Can we take the risk?'

'I think we should,' said Yates. 'It is more risky to do nothing.'

Turning to the head of the Joint Chiefs of Staff, the President asked, 'How many warheads can fly if we just use our own part of the Asteroid Defense Network and the sector that is controlled by the European Union?'

'Twenty-four, Mr President,' said General Thomas Nicholls promptly. 'Approximately three hundred and fifty megatons of nuclear power in total.'

'Is that enough?' asked Jarvis.

'More than enough to start off the chain reaction,' Nicholls assured his commander-in-chief. 'My people have double-checked with Professor Esposito at CalTech. He's the scientist who worked all this out.'

'How soon can we launch?' said Jarvis.

'Well, we're currently on the other side of the sun from our main deep-space missiles, so we'll have to use the Martian colony as our strike command,' Nicholls explained. 'Mars is also on the other side of the sun to us at present so it's three hundred and fifty million kilometres nearer to the cloud than we are. It has good line-of-sight communications with the missiles and there will be a much shorter time delay in their command communications. We can be ready in just under ten days.'

'And the cloud will still be a safe distance away from us?' Jarvis asked, turning to Desmond Yates.

'About half a billion kilometres outside our solar system,' said Yates. 'But we don't want to delay too long. It's travelling at very high speed.'

President Jarvis nodded, then sat with his eyes closed for a few moments.

'Well, should we go it alone with the Europeans?' he asked, suddenly looking up. 'Formal votes, please.'

The President glanced around the members of the executive committee.

'I agree – let's do it, sir,' said Coleville Jackson, the Secretary of State.

'Yes, let's do it,' said General Nicholls firmly.

'I say yes,' said the White House Chief of Staff with a quick nod.

One by one all present were polled. Although some were slower than others to agree, all finally gave their assent.

'Very well,' said President Maxwell T. Jarvis. 'Let's do it.'

Dr Bridget Mulberry, an astro-mineralogist and the serving mayor of the American Martian settlement, glanced round at the eleven other members of the Township Council and announced, 'Twenty seconds to go.'

The council meeting had been convened in the settlement's main assembly hall following notice that an emergency broadcast of the gravest importance was to be transmitted from Earth. The President of the United States was going to address the councillors of the American Martian colony.

There were two sizeable habitat-settlements on the surface of Mars. The oldest, and largest, was the American habitat – now more like a small town – which had first been established as a scientific base in 2038 and which had since been enlarged several times over. Now the settlement consisted of seventeen separate domed buildings which were connected by hermetically sealed walkways.

Over eighty volunteers lived in the American outpost, most of them scientists, and the personnel rotated every three years as the planet's low gravity took its toll on the human skeleton, forcing the temporary settlers to return to Earth for a lengthy recuperation.

The other major settlement, located over 200 kilometres further south on the Martian surface, was the more recently built Russian-Chinese township which now boasted almost forty colonists. Once a month, the residents of the two colonial outposts got together in one or the other habitat for socializing and information exchange. The next party was due to take place on the following day in the Russian-Chinese settlement. It was an event to which all of the colonists had been looking forward.

'I hope this message won't spoil our party,' grouched Foster Robinson, the settlement's writer-in-residence. Robinson doubled as the township's only journalist and Dr Mulberry had invited him to the meeting so that he could report on proceedings for the benefit of the rest of the settlers.

The large screen flickered to life as Washington's encrypted transmission reached Mars after its twenty-one-minute outward journey. Then they saw the grave features of President Maxwell T. Jarvis.

The broadcast lasted only seven minutes. When it ended there was complete silence in the habitat meeting hall.

'Want to see it again?' asked Dr Mulberry. There were many nods, and she quickly punched up a replay.

At the end of the second showing she turned to Major Marshall Peters, the senior military officer resident in the American settlement.

'I guess I must officially hand over to you, Marshall,' she told him. 'Now that we've become a military base.'

The US President had updated the Martian colonists with the latest information about the cloud and had then outlined the plan for the nuclear attack on which the US and the European Union had agreed.

'As Earth is currently on the other side of the sun to the missiles that are nearest the cloud, we want you to launch and coordinate the attack,' President Jarvis had told them. 'I therefore place the United States Martian settlement under US military law and I order Major Marshall Peters, as the senior officer on the base, to take control of the settlement and to form the team that will execute NASA's instructions to launch components of the Asteroid Defense Network into the cloud.'

The broadcast had ended with a rendition of the American national anthem played over a long shot of the Capitol, in Washington DC.

From the *New York Times* website, 1 May 2064

U.S.– EUROPE TO DETONATE 24 NUCLEAR WARHEADS INSIDE SPACE CLOUD

by RANDALL TATE, science correspondent

In a bilateral action taken without the agreement of other major world powers, the United States government and the European Union executive have agreed to launch a massive nuclear strike against the giant gas cloud that is currently heading towards Earths solar system. The attack will be mounted and co-ordinated by the American military command on Mars.

'The plan is to set the cloud on fire and to disperse it with the blast,' said Professor Desmond Yates, Space Affairs Adviser to the White House. 'We cannot take the risk of the cloud entering our solar system. It could carry unknown forms of bacteria and many astrophysicists conclude that it could endanger our planet's atmosphere.'

DISGRACEFUL AND RECKLESS ACTION' – SIR CHARLES HODGESON

British science-fiction author and centenarian space guru, Sir Charles Hodgeson,

yesterday described the bilateral US–European plan to launch nuclear warheads at the space cloud as 'disgraceful and undemocratic.'

Speaking from his island home in the Western Pacific, Hodgeson went on to accuse the governments of 'reckless and irresponsible behaviour. 'This is our first chance to study a large space cloud at close hand. Destroying it before we fully understand its nature is a barbaric response.'

'Good morning, welcome to the Pentagon,' said Desmond Yates cheerily as he walked across the marble floor, hand outstretched.

Bill Duncan and Sarah Burton both shook hands with the White House adviser and then stepped through a metal and weapons detector.

'Settling in to DC OK?' asked Yates as they received the all-clear. He handed a digital security pass to Bill; the CNS agent had already flipped her Federal badge and digital ID to the outside of her jacket pocket.

The government – Bill was unsure which department exactly – had provided him with a two-bedroomed duplex apartment only fifteen minutes' walk from the main Pentagon building. When he had arrived in the flat he had found his clothes, personal effects and Nadia's main processor array waiting for him. But the classified Rand-Fairchild processor had not been among his things.

'We've found a private room for you two to use in the Advanced Computing Lab,' explained Yates after they had descended two levels and completed a long walk along a windowless corridor. He punched a code into a combination lock, pushed open a door and ushered the visitors into a cool, dimly lit room.

The walls were covered in a variety of screens – 3-D, laser panel, HD-2D and holo – and a small holo-theatre occupied one corner of the computer laboratory. Along a bench against one wall Bill saw half a dozen linked processor units and, at the end, the housing unit he had constructed to hold the Rand-Fairchild component that Christine Cocoran had purloined for him from the MIT lab.

'We've managed to smooth things over with the Rand-Fairchild corporation,' said Yates, 'And they've been kind enough to lend us a further six of their prototype processors. Do you think they'll help in the conversion process, Bill?'

'Well, they'll make a great start,' agreed the former MIT professor as he examined the array of advanced equipment.

'One thing I must ask is that you don't remove anything from this room at the end of your working shifts,' said Yates. 'This is a secure area and your work is regarded as classified, so I don't want–'

'Hey, hold on a minute,' objected Bill. 'I haven't agreed to my work being classified. The deal is that I publish what I want, when I want.'

The older space scientist regarded the computer expert quizzically. 'I understand,' he said after a few moments. 'But these processors are classified units, so they can't leave this room. Is that OK?'

'That's OK,' agreed Bill as he slipped his slim communicator unit from his pocket. 'But this unit and Nadia, my PA, go with me everywhere, along with whatever I'm working on. You understand?'

'OK, that's fine,' agreed Yates reluctantly. After a pause he added, 'The President has been informed of your achievement, Bill. He asked me to congratulate you, and he's very keen that you should get all the assistance you want.'

'Well, that's helpful,' agreed Bill. 'But I'm not sure quite what I'm going to need yet.'

'There's a list of the departments within the Advanced Computer Lab on the wall,' said Yates, pointing. 'If you need technical support, hardware, or any other sort of help, they've been told to give you top priority. Agent Burton knows where the Pentagon canteens and all of the other facilities are.'

'Great,' said Bill, still feeling very unsure about whether he was doing the right thing.

'Copies of all the Isonian signals that have been received are in those memory packs,' said Yates, nodding towards the bench. 'How long will it be before you've got real-time digital conversion up and running again? We need to demonstrate what we're doing for SETI, NASA and a couple of the other agencies.'

Bill glanced at his federal minder. The agent was already slipping her jacket off, ready for work. 'Well, with the help of my new assistant, I should have something in a few days,' he told Des Yates.

From the moment that martial law had been imposed, the pace of life at the US settlement on Mars had accelerated dramatically. Like many colonial outposts of previous centuries, life in the Martian habitat had previously been rather sleepy. Things got done, but at a pace that suited the remote community, rather than at a speed to suit those back home on Earth.

Now everything had changed. The eighteen military personnel at the base had commandeered all the scientists' surface transporters and had been busy erecting an array of six high-power radio antennae to augment the already powerful transmitters that the settlement used for its regular communications with Earth, and with various space stations. Now the military command on Mars needed to be in constant, close-to-real-time radio communication with twenty-four nuclear-tipped spacecraft as they flew into the high-velocity space cloud and detonated in a carefully timed sequence.

The software to control the fleet of spacecraft, and to time the precision explosions, had been up-linked to the

Martian colony from the Asteroid Defense Network headquarters in Pasadena, California. Once it had been received, Major Marshall H. Peters, the officer in charge, had checked and double-checked with his technology specialists that the software was working properly and that communications with the two dozen nuclear-weapon delivery vehicles were in good order.

'We have A-One telemetry with each and every bird,' confirmed Chief Communications Sergeant Morrison Laburke. 'We've carried out six rehearsal launches – everything's working fine, sir.'

'What precisely will we see when the warheads explode in the cloud, Major?' asked Foster Robinson as he gazed into his video viewfinder. Since the announcement of military rule and the critical mission given to the base, the resident reporter had been galvanized into a flurry of activity, sending report after report back to the news organizations on Earth.

'There will be a huge explosion low down on Mars's southern horizon,' said Major Peters, looking straight into the camera lens, as Robinson had instructed. 'For a while it will seem as if a night sun is burning. Then, after about an hour or so, the light will die out as the hydrogen and helium are consumed. That will be the end of the cloud.'

EIGHT

'I don't like the look of this at all,' Brian Nunney said worriedly to Suzi Price. They were waiting impatiently for Desmond Yates to return an urgent call that the Australian scientist had placed earlier. 'I think this news is definitely going to spook them in Washington.'

Over the last three days all duty astronomers at the Carl Sagan Ultra-Large Telescope in Chile had been checking and cross-checking some very strange optical data: it looked as if the giant space cloud had abruptly changed course.

The huge pool of interstellar gas had now reached the outer limits of the solar system and although the powerful gravitational effects of Neptune, Pluto and Uranus had been carefully modelled and the calculations fed into the cloud's anticipated trajectory, nothing could account for what looked like a sudden course change eighteen degrees to the solar south and thirty-two degrees to the east.

'But it's no longer going to hit the Earth, is it?' pointed out Suzi for the tenth time. 'It's the best news we've had in months.'

Nunney's communicator beeped and he glanced down at the screen. Professor Yates was finally calling back.

Taking a deep breath, Nunney returned Yates's greeting and then delivered the message that he had been mentally rehearsing for hours.

'We think the cloud has changed its heading, Professor Yates,' he said carefully. 'We've been tracking it constantly and there is a discrepancy between the trajectory our computers predict and the cloud's actual position. The longitude discrepancy is plus twenty-nine seconds and the declination is out by minus seventeen seconds.'

Nunney listened intently as Yates fired a series of questions at him.

'Yes, we're quite sure,' Nunney assured the world-famous astrophysicist. 'I've already e-mailed our data to you on a secure link.'

The Australian nodded down the phone as Yates asked for yet more details.

'Yes, we've modelled the new trajectory,' Nunney said. 'If the cloud stays on its new heading it will miss the Earth completely, by about two hundred million kilometres.'

Brian Nunney glanced anxiously at Suzi as he listened to Yates express his relief at the other end of the line.

'But there's something else you should know, Professor,' Nunney broke in. 'On its new course, the cloud is now heading directly for Mars.'

Two days later Randall Tate received an early-evening call at his desk in the *New York Times* building. Glancing at his handset he saw that it was originating from a small island in the Great Barrier Reef.

'Hello, Mr Tate. How nice of you to take my call.'

As always, Tate wondered whether the over-elaborate manners of the British were sincere or whether they were subtly sending up everyone with whom they had contact.

'Always a pleasure, Sir Charles,' said the reporter, responding in kind. 'What can I do for you?'

'Have you talked to any of your astronomer friends

about how the space cloud is behaving?' asked Sir Charles Hodgeson. 'I mean, in the last couple of days?'

Tate frowned into his communicator. They hadn't selected visual.

'What's on your mind?' asked the reporter, irritated by the Englishman's obtuseness.

'Call me back when you have,' said Hodgeson, closing the connection.

A little over 9,000 miles away, the centenarian science-fiction guru stared at his now blank communications screen, then glanced up at a wall clock. It was five a.m. on Orpheus Island – seven p.m. in New York – and Hodgeson had spent the night in the island's observatory, taking careful observations and measurements of the space cloud.

'How long before he calls back, do you reckon?' Hodgeson asked Amrik Chandra, one of his most devoted students.

The young man who had worked through the night with the great visionary shrugged. 'Depends on how good his contacts are. And how much they're prepared to tell him.'

A little over fifteen minutes later Randall Tate called back.

Hodgeson greeted the reporter again and listened to what he had discovered.

'Well done, Mr Tate' said Hodgeson, more than a little condescendingly. 'So the cloud is now heading straight for Mars, for the control centre that is planning to attack it. What does this suggest to you?'

'Nobody's prepared to offer any theories on the record,' Tate admitted. 'My contacts merely confirm that the cloud has changed direction and is now heading for Mars. They say they don't know why it has happened.'

'Well, *I'm* prepared to tell you something on the record,' said Hodgeson assertively. 'It is quite clear from its behaviour that this so-called cloud is a form of alien life – and intelligent life, at that! It is obviously responding to the preparations now being made to attack it. This means that any attack we make against the cloud would be an act of unprovoked aggression against another form of life. What sort of barbarians are we?'

'So you believe we should do nothing?' asked Tate.

'Remember, this cloud has caused us no problems so far,' insisted the space guru. 'This insane pre-emptive strike must be called off before something terrible happens. We should be transmitting peace messages, not launching nuclear weapons.'

'So what exactly should we be saying to the cloud, Sir Charles?' asked Tate sceptically.

'We should be welcoming it. I am personally calling on like-minded peace-loving people to transmit radio signals of welcome to this alien being. I myself am already doing so. This is something I have waited my entire life to see. The idea of attacking a form of alien intelligence before it has revealed its own intentions shows how barbaric the human race remains. It is probably merely curious and is coming to visit us.'

'Just what the hell are we dealing with here?' demanded President Jarvis, glaring up from behind his desk. 'At first you tell me that this cloud is just a harmless pool of gas that is moving vaguely in the direction of our solar system, then you tell me it's going to hit the Earth and strip away all our atmosphere. On your recommendation I ordered our forces on Mars to prepare to make a pre-emptive nuclear strike and now you say this goddam thing has changed course all on its own and is now heading directly for the people who are planning to attack it. I repeat, what *is* this thing?'

Desmond Yates stood in front of the President's desk in the Oval Office along with the director of NASA and the head of the Joint Chiefs of Staff. There was no informality about this meeting and, for the first time since he was a teenager, Yates had the overwhelming feeling that he was being carpeted – which was patently unfair.

'Sir, we have no idea,' he admitted. 'We have examined the cloud optically, by radio-telescopic analysis and by interferometry, and all we can detect in its interior are giant pools of gases – hydrogen, helium and other gaseous elements – that are of varying density. We've bounced radio waves from one side of the cloud to the other, and from the top to the bottom. There are no heavy elements in the cloud, no structures, no nucleus that we can detect. It appears to be just a large pool of gas and dust.'

'But a pool of gas that can change direction when it wants?' snapped the President.

Yates glanced sideways at NASA director Roy Wilcox.

'Professor Yates is correct, sir,' confirmed Wilcox. 'We've applied our most sophisticated techniques to look inside this cloud, right inside, and it's just gas – all the way through.'

The President flicked the end of a silver letter-opener on his large blotting pad and then nodded once, sharply.

'OK, sit down, gentlemen,' he said, waving at a row of empty chairs which stood in front of his desk.

He swung round in his own high-backed swivel chair and glanced briefly out at the Rose Garden. Then, when his advisers had taken their seats, he swung back round and stared at Yates and Wilcox in turn.

'I realize that you two are scientists and that you're not used to making wild speculation,' he said. 'But in the privacy of this room, and off the record, I must ask whether you believe this cloud might have some form of intelligence and, if so, whether we should be trying to deal with it in a different way?'

Neither of the men held by the President's gaze volunteered an answer, until finally Jarvis raised one eyebrow and glared directly at Desmond Yates.

The White House space-affairs adviser drew a deep breath. 'I personally do not believe that we have seen any signs from within the cloud, or any behaviour by it, that could be described as exhibiting evidence of intelligent behaviour,' he began carefully. 'I agree that it seems bizarre that this pool of gas should suddenly change its heading, apparently in response to an attack that is being prepared, but it would be even more bizarre to ascribe intelligence to a simple pool of gas without more proof. Once we have had sufficient time to analyse the cloud properly – and we are still only beginning to build computer models of what is, after all, over forty billion cubic miles of rapidly shifting gas – and once we have calculated all of the thousands of variables affecting its course, such as gravity, solar wind, internal chemical reactions and so on, I think we may find an answer to why this change of heading has occurred.'

The President listened patiently as Yates made his considered response, Then he turned to the NASA Director. 'And what's your take on this, Roy?' he asked.

'I believe in the principle of Occam's Razor, sir,' said Wilcox.

He saw the President frown.

'Occam was a fourteenth-century Scottish philosopher,' he explained. 'He said that when something looks very complicated, and when there are many different possible explanations, the most obvious solution is likely to be the correct one. I've learned the wisdom of that approach and I too see no reason why we should leap to any wild speculation about possible intelligence inside this cloud.'

'And what about the fact that it appeared at the same time the signals from the planet Iso dried up?' asked Jarvis. 'And at about the time when we were hoping that we might hear back from the Isonians?'

'I admit that it does seem strange, sir,' agreed Yates. 'But these things are most likely to be coincidences, nothing more.'

'But what if they're not, Des?' asked Jarvis, sitting forward anxiously. 'Shouldn't we be trying to contact this cloud – just in case we could communicate with it?'

'Thousands of people are already doing that for us,' broke in Wilcox. 'That crazy science-fiction author in Australia is getting all of his fans to radio this pool of space gas. They're pumping out messages of welcome every hour of the day. If there was anything inside this cloud that was going to respond, we've have heard from it by now.'

Bill Duncan and Agent Burton had been waiting impatiently in their Pentagon laboratory for over two hours. Professor Yates's personal assistant had assured them that her boss would be with them by three p.m., but it was now almost five-thirty and they had heard not a word of explanation or apology. In an age when communication was constantly available everywhere, his lateness and lack of contact felt like a gross discourtesy.

Working closely together, Bill and his official CNS minder had re-established the redundancy-stripping and conversion processes for the Isonian signals. To his considerable surprise and pleasure the specialist in machine psychology had discovered that the CNS agent seconded to help him was herself a highly capable network specialist and was also a much warmer and friendlier woman than he had imagined. She had asked him to call her 'Sally' – 'No one calls me Sarah, it's so severe' – and Bill found that he needed to explain very little to his new assistant as they set up their cluster of super-capable processors and designed new software that would distribute the analog-to-digital conversion tasks across the additional computing power.

Nadia, Bill's personal computer companion, was now coordinating the efforts of the seven classified Rand-Fairchild prototype processors that they had been given to carry out the work. Along with Nadia's own limited power, the new processors made up a private network that Bill Duncan reckoned must be one of the most powerful stand-alone circuits in the world. And they were making some progress, progress they were keen to share with their contact in the Washington bureaucracy.

'I'm sorry, so sorry,' said Des Yates when he finally walked through the door. 'The boss kept me in a long meeting and I couldn't break out.'

Bill and Sally exchanged glances. They understood which 'boss' their visitor was referring to and they both noted that the Presidential adviser looked very tired, almost exhausted.

'So, how are you two getting on?' asked Yates.

'We're up and running,' reported Bill with a smile. 'And we've extracted further snippets of coherent binary strings – along with a lot of what appears to be redundant garbage.'

The ex-MIT man nodded to Sally, who punched data up onto the main wall screen.

'As you can see, like the first section I decoded, these short segments also seem to be made up of binary, quantum and base-sixteen mathematical sets.'

Yates moved closer to the screen and stared up at the display.

'Anything that works, or that we can understand?' he asked.

'Not yet,' Bill admitted. 'But there's so much compressed analog data that we can't even make a dent on it – even with this set-up.'

'Yes, I understand,' said the White House man, an absent look on his face.

'In fact, even with this network we haven't got nearly enough power,' continued Bill, gesturing at the chain of superfast organic nano-scale processors. 'I think we're going to have to revert to your original idea and throw the task open to the public networks. If we get every hobbyist with an interest in alien communications to download a tiny part of the data to work on, we might be able to make some progress. After all, even at our fastest computing speeds we've got over six billion years' worth of signals to convert.'

'Quite, quite,' murmured Yates, his glazed eyes fixed in the middle distance.

Bill glanced again at Sally, who shrugged her shoulders. Their visitor was behaving very oddly.

'Either that,' said Bill, 'Or you've got to get me another million of these new processors.'

'I'll see what I can do,' said Yates distantly.

'I thought they were prototypes!' objected Sally sharply, annoyed by their visitor's vagueness. 'I thought they weren't even in mass fabrication yet?'

Her abrupt tone summoned Des Yates's mind back to the topic under discussion, and to the pair of computer specialists standing expectantly in front of him.

'I'm sorry,' he said, with a shake of his head. 'There's a

lot going on at the moment. I'll put in a request for you to get some more processing power.'

'A *lot* more processing power,' stressed Bill.

'Yes, a lot more,' agreed Yates distantly. A worried look crossed the astrophysicist's face again, Then he looked directly at Bill, then at Sally.

'Sorry, but I might as well tell you what's on my mind,' he said. 'You're going to be reading about it tomorrow, anyway.'

Yates took a deep breath and shook his head. 'The trajectory of the space cloud has changed. It's now heading directly for Mars. That's why I was so late getting over here.'

Bill and Sally looked blank. Very little news about the cloud and its progress had permeated through to the confines of the Pentagon's Advanced Computing Laboratory. Over the last week or so Bill and Sally had been totally absorbed in setting up their private network system.

'It means that people are starting to question whether this is just a simple gas cloud,' explained Yates, seeing their incomprehension. 'And it means that I'm going to have trouble getting anyone to focus on the work you're doing here – at least in the short term.'

CLOUD CHANGES COURSE FOR MARS

By RANDALL TATE, science correspondent

Risk to Earth Averted – but No Time to Evacuate Colonists

Astonished NASA astronomers confirmed last night that the giant space cloud approaching the solar system has now changed its heading by over 40 degrees and is on a new trajectory which will cause it to pass over Mars beginning July 22. NASA confirmed that with Mars in its furthest position away from Earth, there will be no time to evacuate the Martian colony before the cloud arrives. Space scientists also say that on its new heading the cloud will no longer come into contact with Earth.

Scientific opinion is divided about what might have caused such a dramatic change of direction. Many experts have concluded that the cloud has been diverted as it has encountered steadily increasing solar winds. Others suggest that distant galactic gravitational forces may be responsible.

'Cloud Will Cause Little Damage on Mars' – Yates

Presidential Space Affairs Adviser Professor Desmond Yates told the *New York Times*, 'I suspect the cloud is merely responding to the strong gravitational forces that surround our solar system. If it does pass over the surface of Mars, there is little atmosphere for the cloud to remove and all Martian colonists are protected inside secure habitats that have been robustly constructed to withstand the fierce Martian storms.'

'DIRECTION CHANGE NO COINCIDENCE'

By Randall Tate, science correspondent

Author Calls on Public to Radio Peace Greetings to Cloud

'A change in direction of this magnitude can be neither accidental nor a simple co-incidence,' said Sir Charles Hodgeson, speaking from his Orpheus Island home last night.

'This cloud is clearly intelligent, or is the product of intelligence,' he claimed. 'In some way it has sensed that we intend to attack it from our base on Mars. I call on the United Nations to act swiftly to stop America and Europe from carrying out their primitive and barbaric attack.'

Hodgeson went on to say, 'I have already begun transmitting welcome messages towards the cloud from my own transmitter and I urge all supporters of peace and tolerance to do the same. The ordinary people of the world must distance themselves from the actions of their warlike and irresponsible governments.'

'Above all, it is our duty to communicate with this cloud. Under no circumstances must we harm it.'

By special invitation of the Secretary-General, the American President Maxwell T. Jarvis was addressing an emergency meeting of the General Assembly at the United Nations headquarters.

The large meeting was being televised and broadcast to the world and, as Jarvis's political advisers had realized, it allowed him to make an appeal both to the world's population and to his own domestic electorate at the same time. Plus it placed the Chief in a setting that demonstrated who was really the power behind the UN throne. It was now time for the US to assert strong global leadership, the President's aides insisted.

Jarvis was trying to reassure the meeting, and the billions of TV viewers, that there was no reason to panic because of the space cloud's strange behaviour. He knew that his words were also being transmitted to the colonists who were trapped on Mars as the cloud approached.

'One change of course is insufficient to suggest that the space cloud is anything other than a simple pool of gas,' he assured the meeting. 'Although I am told that it is unlikely to do much physical damage if it were to pass over the Martian surface, it *is* possible that it could contaminate the planet with hostile, long-lived bacteria.'

He paused to sip from a small glass of water.

'With the cooperation of the Russian and Chinese space agencies we expect to be able to return the one hundred and eighty-two Martian colonists safely to Earth once the cloud has passed – and once we have applied stringent decontamination procedures – but it has to be faced that if the cloud does contain dangerous bacteria we may no longer be able to return to the planet.

'In addition, there is also the remote possibility that the cloud could change direction once again, whether caused by gravitational attraction or some other force, and resume its collision course with Earth. This time, the direction change might occur when it would be too late for us safely to do anything about it.'

Jarvis paused as he came to the main section of his important speech.

'For these reasons, the United States, with our European Union allies, intends to proceed with the precautionary nuclear detonation within the cloud in an attempt to disperse it or to modify its course while it is still in the outer reaches of the solar system.

'I call upon all delegate nations to join us in our attempt to divert what could still turn out to be a significant threat to our planet.'

'Put it over there, over there,' shouted Sir Charles Hodgeson irritably to his building foreman.

With a nod and a tip of his finger to the peak of his blue hard-hat, the foreman turned and shouted directions to the driver of the large yellow dump truck.

Over a one-month period Orpheus Island had been transformed into a vast building site, as if a movie company had suddenly descended on the peaceful Pacific atoll and turned it into a giant film set.

But there was nothing temporary or cosmetic about the construction that was now going on all over the island. Half of the main hill ridge had been scooped out by two huge yellow earth-movers and prefabricated steel roof beams and wall supports – flown to the island by giant Sikorsky Load-Mover helicopters – were now stacked against the hillside, awaiting their positioning.

There was no deep-water port at Orpheus Island, but a fleet of flat-bottomed barges was busy ferrying ashore sand, cement, cables, pipes and all of the other items necessary for a major building project from ships that were anchored far out to sea.

Cranes, cement mixers and building blocks had also been flown in by the powerful Sikorskys, as had the large-bore ventilation system, air-conditioning units and oxygen-manufacturing equipment. Already four tall radio transmission antennae had been erected on the hilltop, suddenly giving the skyline of the beautiful island the sinister appearance of a military base.

Hodgeson himself was the site's project manager and he was also its chief architect. Technically Orpheus Island was part of Australian sovereign territory, but its centenarian owner had not bothered about niceties such as planning permission or zoning laws before he started erecting his new radio transmission towers and begun carving into the hillside of his island home. Lacking all faith in the world's governments to respond peaceably towards the gaseous extra-terrestrial visitor, Hodgeson had decided to take extreme precautions and had applied his huge personal wealth and his boundless energy to get the project moving.

The science-fiction guru had made his initial fortune almost by accident. Over sixty years earlier *The Wars of Galetea*, one of his first space fantasy adventures, had been made into a movie which went on to achieve worldwide cult status. That success had made the author financially independent, but had not provided him with truly great riches. But then an American software house had purchased the rights to create an interactive internet game-domain based on the book. They then poured so much time and effort into recreating Hodgeson's fantasy world in cyberspace that the company had bankrupted itself before it had earned a single cent from a paying customer.

Charles Hodgeson – then still two decades away from his knighthood – had bought the American company from the receivers for a song and within six months *The Wars of Galetea* had become the most successful immersive multi-sensory gaming environment on the web. Subscriptions boomed and for almost two years Hodgeson wrote nothing but new virtual-reality scenarios for the space-battle game, keeping his millions of addicted fans happy and the sub-scriptions pouring in. At the peak of its popularity over two million people were playing against each other and the game's virtual characters in every twenty-four-hour period. The game's success made Hodgeson seriously rich. Then he had begun buying whole blocks of residential property in London, New York and Beijing, back in the 2020s, when smart city addresses were still reasonably affordable.

'Start pumping the concrete,' Hodgeson ordered into his walkie-talkie. His radio crackled a confirmation and he shielded his eyes to watch as the first load of aggregate and cement began to flow, forming the foundations of what would become the vast underground bunker he had been designing for the last three months. The steel-reinforced, air-tight and lead-shielded building would house a new observatory control room and accommodation units for Hodgeson himself and his staff, and for the 130 young stu-dents and followers who made a pilgrimage to Orpheus Island. New recruits came annually to study with the great man – an author who was now regarded as a world-famous guru, philosopher and quasi-religious leader. Hodgeson never referred to a god in his talks, but each year thousands of young people applied to his website for the privilege of coming to work for no pay on Orpheus Island, just to be near their hero and to attend the visionary workshop dis-cussions he led three times a week.

'Sir Charles?'

It was the foreman climbing back up the side of the small rise on which Hodgeson stood as he surveyed his emergency building programme.

'The first desalination unit is arriving,' announced the building supervisor, pointing into the sky.

Hodgeson glanced up and saw a giant twin-rotor helicopter approaching the bay at low altitude. Beneath it was slung a large stainless-steel device about the size of one of the many Portakabins that had been erected on the island to house the Australian construction crew. All of the workers were earning quadruple rates for this round-the-clock project, plus a completion bonus so large that it had outshone all of the many other offers the rich were making to such workers. In addition, Hodgeson had made the contractors one additional offer they could not refuse: he offered them space for themselves and their families in the Orpheus Island bunker, if they chose to take it up.

'Lower it straight into its housing,' ordered Hodgeson, raising his voice as the beating helicopter blades began to drown out all the other noises being made around the vast site. 'I want it up and working by tomorrow.'

From the *New York Times* website, 18 June 2064

COMBINED NUCLEAR STRIKE CONFIRMED

By RANDALL TATE, science correspondent

Explosions Will Be Visible from Mars 2.20 p.m. Eastern Standard Time, June 30

By an overwhelming majority, the United Nations General Assembly last night voted to authorize the U.S.–European nuclear strike against the gas cloud currently heading towards Mars. China and Russia have now offered use of their components of the Anti-Asteroid Shield to be used in the attack. Over 700 megatons of nuclear weapons will now be deployed.

'Sensors aboard NASA's intercept probes have confirmed that the cloud is indeed composed of hydrogen, helium and other passive gases,' said Desmond Yates, the White House's senior Space Affairs adviser. 'I anticipate a complete destruction of the cloud whilst it is still in the outer reaches of our solar system.'

The 48 nuclear explosions and resultant conflagration will be visible from Mars and images of the strike will arrive at the Earth 21 minutes later.

Thousands of Alien-Life Pacifists Transmit Greetings to the Cloud

U.S. military and civil authorities are monitoring a sharp rise in high-power radio transmissions sent by disciples of British-born space guru, Sir Charles Hodgeson.

'So many signals are being directed towards the cloud that we are experiencing interference with our normal satellite communications,' said a spokesman for the Federal Communications Commission.

Hodgeson Builds 'Illegal Radio Station' – Installs 'Mercenaries' as Security Guards

Queensland authorities have declared 'illegal' a number of high-power radio masts and a large underground construction that billionaire science-fiction guru Sir Charles Hodgeson is building on Orpheus Island, his private territory on the eastern flank of the Great Barrier Reef, Australia.

Authorities in Cairns are to apply to a Queensland county court for permission to land on Orpheus Island and remove the transmitters.

Speaking from his home, Hodgeson said, 'I have no faith in any of the world's governments to do the right thing. If this foolhardy attack on the cloud proceeds we may all need the very deepest shelters we can build.'

Asked whether he will contest action by the authorities to enforce local zoning laws, Sir Charles said, 'I will resist any attempt to prevent me from using my own private territory as I wish – especially at this time of global emergency. I have employed a highly trained body of military troops to protect this island against all comers.'

'I don't think I have ever seen anything more beautiful,' an excited Foster Robinson told his interplanetary audience. 'These pictures you are seeing now are being transmitted from the nuclear missiles as they are actually flying inside the cloud.'

The images that the Mars-based journalist was receiving and forwarding to his viewers on Earth were truly breathtaking. Towering multicoloured columns of what looked like smoke rose through the centre of the cloud, stretching upwards for millions of kilometres, like pillars in a staggeringly vast cathedral.

'I can see a background of deep red gas,' Robinson said over the pictures, 'and there are blue, green and white funnels, or cyclones, rising up inside the cloud.'

A total of forty-eight missiles, each armed with a nuclear warhead, had been launched from dispersed locations in deep space to arrive in the centre of the cloud in a carefully timed sequence. Each missile also carried an array of cameras that were now feeding back images to those overseeing the countdown on Mars, and to the anxious billions back on Earth who were receiving the pictures twenty-one minutes later.

Foster Robinson was seated at the small TV editing suite he used to put together his normally prosaic weekly news reports from the red planet. When the first Martian colony had been founded thirty-nine years earlier, Robinson's predecessors had found that their video reports were eagerly received by Earth's broadcast media. But the public had quickly become bored with pictures of Mars's rugged, monotone landscape and the distant community's mundane doings.

But now the whole of the home planet's population was hanging on the words and pictures flowing back from Mars.

On the other side of the main habitat floor-space Major Peters and his team of eighteen military personnel were overseeing the computers that controlled the mission. At Foster Robinson's request, strike command had even patched through to him a digital read-out of the countdown timer so that the viewers could count off the minutes and seconds as the moment for the synchronized detonations approached.

Robinson switched from the video images streaming in from one of the missile nose cones to a long-distance picture of the cloud taken by the Asimov Deep-Space Telescope, an instrument that was parked in a solar-stationary orbit between Jupiter and Saturn, over 300 million kilometres away from the pool of gas. Normally this powerful optic was used for surveying the giant outer planets, major solar events or constellations outside the solar system, but now the twin-mirrored, six-metre telescope was focused on the vast mass of the space cloud that was rushing headlong towards Mars.

'Detonation is due in two minutes,' Robinson reported as he mixed an overlay of the digital counter into his live picture stream. For the hundredth time during this long broadcast he wished he had a video editor at his side so that he could concentrate solely on providing the best possible commentary. *But here comes my Emmy*, he thought to himself as he tightened the framing on the cloud.

The telescope's image showed the gas pool clearly, as a grey-red mass against the black background of space. The countdown display indicated that there was just over one minute to go.

'The theory is that these forty-eight carefully timed explosions will start a chain reaction which will cause the cloud to burn up completely,' Robinson told his viewers.

'The cloud is still two hundred million kilometres away from Mars and over six hundred million kilometres distant from Earth. I am assured that as the cloud is still so far away its incineration will not cause any harm to Mars, or to any other planets in our solar system.'

The counter flicked down to thirty seconds.

'What we'll see in a moment will be a series of flashes from inside the cloud as the seven hundred megatons of warheads start to explode,' said Robinson quickly. 'Then the whole thing will suddenly go up in a single gigantic ball of fire.'

Robinson glanced down at his video feeds, wondering which of them to supply to his billions of viewers on Earth as the moment approached. All were being recorded so he decided to leave the distant view of the cloud from the Asimov Telescope as the main live feed.

'Five seconds,' announced Robinson. 'Four, three, two, one . . .'

On the monitor he saw a tiny pinpoint of light shine from within the centre of the distant cloud. Then another. Then another, followed by a rapid sequence of small flares, like starbursts from a far-off rocket display. Then there was nothing but the image of the cloud as it had been before.

STRIKE FAILS TO HALT CLOUD

By RANDALL TATE, science correspondent

Will Engulf Mars in Three Weeks

The White House confirmed last night that the multilateral nuclear strike made in an attempt to disperse the space cloud had failed. It is now crossing through the asteroid belt and is expected to pass over Mars and its colonies beginning July 12. It is estimated that the planet will be hidden from sight by the cloud for 45 days.

'Perhaps the interior of the cloud is less dense than we thought,' said Desmond Yates, the White House's senior Space Affairs Adviser last night. 'If so, it is a good sign for the Mars colonists. A less dense cloud will do very little damage to the Martian structures.'

MARTIAN COLONISTS TOLD TO PREPARE FOR CLOUD'S IMPACT

The U.S., Russian and Chinese governments have told their colonists on Mars to prepare for the arrival of the space cloud. The colonists have plentiful supplies of water, food and oxygen and, in recent weeks, the communities have been reinforcing their permanent habitats.

'Well, we tore a great hole in the cloud, but it's still heading directly for Mars,' reported Desmond Yates gloomily. 'The hole we created is over one million kilometres wide but, as we all know, there was no subsequent chain reaction. All we've achieved is to make the cloud more radioactive than it was before.'

The White House adviser was in the Situation Room addressing President Jarvis, other members of the Cloud EXCOM and various guests and other advisers.

'So do we assume that the helium, hydrogen and oxygen atoms were too dispersed, or just too inert to sustain a chain reaction?' asked a disgruntled Dr Demetrios Esposito, the man who had devised the attack plan. 'Seems very strange to me. Everybody knows that hydrogen is far from inert. It should have gone up in a flash.'

'You're right, Doctor,' said Yates in a conciliatory tone. 'And that's not all. Our laser instruments suggest that the hole we created is already beginning to fill in once more.'

'That's incredible,' exclaimed Esposito. 'I'm no gas dynamicist, but that seems darn strange behaviour for a cloud of passive gas.'

Yates nodded and glanced around the rest of his audience. Most of them, especially the President, seemed confused by this strange turn of events.

'And there's something else,' added Yates. 'From our spectrographic analysis of the parts of the cloud that were burnt during the strike we now know that the gas pool contains particles of many rare and exotic elements. These include cerium, promethium, samarium and ytterbium as well as many elements that we have so far been unable to identify.'

There was a silence as the group struggled to digest

this information. Yates waited a few moments before he continued.

'More importantly, however, we have discovered that the cloud contains large amounts of the isotopes helium-3 and helium-4. These are known to be by-products of nuclear fusion.'

'You said "fusion", not "fission", Professor?' queried Dr Esposito quickly. 'You're saying these isotopes didn't come from our own warheads?'

'That's correct,' agreed Yates. 'And, what's more, when we blew a hole in the cloud, our optical instruments could momentarily see right into its centre. They identified patches of hot plasma, all at varying densities, which are swirling around in their own internal magnetic fields.'

'Jesus!' exclaimed Esposito, half rising out of his chair in surprise.

'Do you mind helping us out here, gentlemen?' asked the President. 'Please explain – we're not all rocket scientists.'

Yates glanced at the CalTech theoretical physicist and nodded for him to provide the elucidation.

'Well, sir,' began Esposito, 'from the information that Professor Yates has just given us, a nuclear physicist would be likely to conclude that the cloud is producing its own internal form of energy by a process of self-contained nuclear fusion.'

'Energy?' echoed the President, looking from Esposito to Yates. 'Energy for what?'

Neither man answered immediately. Then Yates cleared his throat.

'For propulsion, sir,' he said.

There was a short silence. Then the President asked,

'Do I take it that you have now changed your mind about the true nature of this space cloud, Professor Yates?'

The White House space-affairs adviser gave a small nod. 'It seems that the normal laws of physics are being violated within the internal structure of the cloud and it also appears to have its own energy source. For these reasons I am afraid we must conclude that there is some form of basic organization within the structure – a form wholly unknown to us.'

'You mean it's intelligent?' pressed Jarvis.

'We simply don't know, sir,' said Yates. 'Intelligence is a difficult concept to define. So far all we've observed is a series of events which are apparently coincidental. There's been nothing to suggest any form of higher intelligence as we would understand it.'

'I'll ask you again, Professor Duncan. Are you prepared to sign a Level One National Secrecy Agreement?' asked the chairman of the combined security panel. 'With all that such an undertaking implies?'

Bill Duncan glanced sideways at Sally Burton. Both were seated on the other side of a table from the five men who were conducting the interview. The Pentagon meeting room was windowless and well below ground. The air-conditioning was humming powerfully and the atmosphere had turned decidedly chilly.

This long-overdue meeting had been set up by Desmond Yates, but at the last moment he had cancelled his own participation, claiming that urgent matters connected with the space cloud prevented him from attending.

After a lengthy delay, Professor William Duncan was finally being interviewed, or interrogated, by a joint security vetting panel consisting of representatives drawn from the

National Security Agency, the Pentagon, the CIA, CNS and the White House. The meeting had been set up to discuss Bill's request for the additional computing power he needed to work on converting the Isonian transmissions.

'You see, even at the speed of the fastest processor we possess, there are over six billion years' worth of analog data to slow down and convert,' Bill had told the meeting in his opening presentation. 'What I need is permission to distribute the task over the public networks. I want to get the media involved and to get the millions of space and sci-fi fans all over the world to do some of the conversion work using the idle time of their own computer processors.'

'I'm afraid your work on converting and decoding the Isonian signals has just been classified by direct order of the Secretary of State,' said the man from the NSA firmly. It had been at that point that the meeting had started to go rapidly downhill.

'CLASSIFIED!' shouted Bill. 'I came to Washington only on the clear understanding that I was free to publish at any time.'

'Professor Duncan,' broke in the man from the White House administration, the official who was standing in for Desmond Yates. 'You must understand that these are not normal times. The National Guard has been called out in some parts of the country to control looting and violent crime has increased by five hundred per cent in the last three months. The government is gearing up for a massive civil emergency. Martial law may be declared any day.'

Bill sat back in his seat and shook his head. During the last few weeks he and Sally had been so absorbed in their conversion work that they'd paid hardly any attention to the news. Bill knew that a nuclear strike against the approaching space cloud had failed and that it was now due to pass over the surface of Mars, but he knew nothing beyond the main headlines. He was unaware that civil unrest had become so serious.

'Your work on the alien transmissions has been classified under the highest military category,' continued the NSA representative. 'You must not discuss your work with anyone who does not have Level One clearance and under no circumstances may you distribute copies of the signals or of your conversion software to any third person.'

Bill let go a large sigh of frustration. All of his suspicions and mistrust of the government were being rapidly confirmed but, he was forced to admit, these *were* highly unusual times.

'Then how do you suggest I make any progress with my binary extraction?' he asked quietly.

The NSA panel member twisted in his seat. 'Over to you, Dr Kramer,' he said, looking at the scientific representative from the Pentagon, a man who wore the uniform of an Army colonel.

'Professor Duncan, I've been an admirer of yours for many years,' said Colonel Kramer. 'I used to be at Harvard and your paper on adaptation psychosis in artificial-life personalities has been widely read there, and in my current department.'

'Which department is that?' asked Bill.

'I may have a solution to your problem,' continued Kramer, ignoring the question. 'It is possible that we could grant you privileged access to a top-secret military computer network with far more processing power than you have now. In fact, a network with more processing power than you've ever dreamed of.'

Bill frowned, struggling to imagine what sort of network the man could be referring to.

'But there's a condition,' said the NSA representative who was chairing the meeting. It was then that he had stated his request that Bill should sign a National Secrecy Agreement.

Now Sally Burton responded to Bill's glare with a small shrug, a gesture half offering apology, half urging pragmatism.

'I'll ask you again, Professor Yates. Are you prepared to sign a Level One National Secrecy Agreement?' demanded the panel's chairman. 'I should also add that if you choose to do so you will become a full-time Pentagon employee with a salary equivalent to what you were earning at MIT. You will be granted every facility possible to continue with your important work.'

Bill struggled with conflicting feelings. He knew that he was making slow progress with the signals, and he knew that, above all else, he needed much more computing power. But he hated being cornered like this.

The panel chairman touched a button on the table top and a wall screen flickered to life.

'Just so that we understand each other,' the chairman continued, 'We have the file on you that CNS Agent Burton prepared, so we are fully aware of your activist campaigns to limit the development of computer intelligence.'

On the wall screen Bill saw images of himself going aboard *Cape Sentinel* and pictures of Christine Cocoran, Paul Levine and the other HAL volunteers arriving at his house-boat. Then he saw a network usage analysis chart and what looked like screen grabs from some of his own monitors. One of them displayed a HAL screensaver that Christine had designed in an idle few minutes. The chairman shut the projection down before Bill could make out any more of what the surveillance operation had captured.

Bill felt a rush of fresh anger rise in his throat. In recent months he'd been getting on very well with the CNS agent who sat beside him, but now he felt betrayed all over again.

'So you will understand why we need you to sign a National Secrecy Agreement,' continued the NSA man. 'We need to know that your loyalty to your country, and your commitment to our nation's need to learn anything of use that the alien signals may hold, will supersede all your previous political sympathies. We will require you to sever immediately all connections with your organization of network activists, and with all similar groups, now and in the future. If you agree, you will be provided with a level of security clearance which, if breached, makes the offender liable to immediate imprisonment. It's your choice whether to proceed or not, but your choice will be final.'

Sally Burton now stared straight ahead, not wanting to make eye contact.

At least she has the grace to be embarrassed, thought Bill.

'I need to few days to think about this,' he said. 'In fact I need a few days off. Time to clear my head.'

'Very well,' agreed the chairman, glancing at the other panel members to see if there was any dissent. 'We'll expect your decision in one week. In the meantime please be aware that you can't discuss these proceedings or these options with anyone outside this room – other than Professor Yates.'

NINE

'The cloud is now visible from Mars with the naked eye,' said Foster Robinson into his helmet microphone. 'For the last ten days my fellow colonists have been taking short breaks from their frantic work schedules simply to come outside and stare up at the incredible beauty of this scene.'

The resident reporter was fully spacesuited and was standing on the Martian surface about two hundred metres away from the American settlement's central habitat. Beside him, a remotely controlled TV camera mounted on a balloon-tyred transporter was panning slowly from horizon to horizon.

'As you can see, the entire sky is now dominated by enormous columns of what looks like smoke,' explained Robinson. 'But the columns themselves are the most beautiful shades of magenta, green, blue, purple and black.'

He allowed the camera to dwell on the awful magnificence of the onrushing cloud for a few moments, then used his hand-held remote joystick to pan the camera back round so that it focused on the main group of habitat buildings. Everywhere there was the scurry of intense activity as spacesuited colonists attached additional steel guy-ropes to the main buildings and piled bags of Martian sand around the airlocks.

In the distance two of the three mini-bulldozers on the

red planet were scooping up surface soil and rock and piling it high against the walls of the domed habitats. The third earth-mover was in use at the smaller Russian-Chinese habitat where it would be busy carrying out similar tasks.

Robinson panned thirty degrees to the right and zoomed in on two suited figures working beside a glinting steel tripod.

'In consultation with colleagues on Earth, our Chief Science Officer has devised a series of experiments that will be conducted as the gas cloud passes over this planet,' the journalist explained. 'These should give us a lot more information about the cloud's density, its composition and its likely future behaviour. The American community on Mars is proud to be able to provide this information as a service to all those on Earth.'

Then Robinson panned a few more degrees to the right until the camera settled on a huge concrete bowl that had been hastily constructed inside a depression on the surface of the Martian desert.

'That large saucer is the reinforced concrete communications dish that the American military unit has constructed to allow contact with Earth to continue after the cloud has arrived,' he explained. 'At present, all pictures from here are being sent to Earth by relay satellites that are in orbit around Mars, but it is expected that as the cloud strikes these will be blown out of position, or out of orbit altogether. Then we will need to transmit to you directly from the surface of this planet using that big dish.'

The reporter swung the camera around until it focused on his own suited figure.

'The cloud is due to begin passing over this planet in forty-eight hours' time,' he said, looking straight into the camera lens. 'Everything that was loose has been tightly secured and every building structure has been reinforced. When it arrives the cloud will be travelling at a velocity of two hundred thousand kilometres per hour but it has such low density that its effects are predicted to be no worse than those of one of the many violent dust storms we suffer regularly on Mars.'

Robinson took a breath and zoomed the camera in tighter on his helmeted face. When he got back to the video suite he would edit all this recorded material together to form two-, three-, four- and five-minute packages for distribution to the news channels back on Earth. After decades of showing little interest, they all now wanted to carry regular reports from Mars.

'When the cloud strikes, every colonist will be safely inside the habitat buildings,' he continued. 'They will be wearing their own personal spacesuits for safety and, as a precaution, they will be instructed to lie down on the floor. All members of the American community, and our friends in the Russian-Chinese settlement, have been given individual supplies of oxygen, water and food which will be topped up at regular intervals. In this way, we will wait out the forty-five days that it will take for the cloud to complete its journey across this planet. This is Foster Robinson reporting from Mars.'

'Well, here it comes – less then one minute to impact,' said Desmond Yates, even though he knew that the images that were about to arrive from Mars were of incidents that had actually occurred over twenty minutes earlier.

The President, his Chief of Staff, NASA's Director, two army generals, a clutch of White House aides and all of the other members of EXCOM were all gathered in the Situation Room to watch events unfold as the cloud engulfed

Mars. The images from space and from the Martian surface were projected within the large holo-theatre at one end of the room.

'We've got multiple feeds from cameras orbiting the planet and from those on the ground,' explained Yates. 'Let's stay with the orbital shots,' he said, addressing the technicians in the AV booth.

Yates stepped back to his seat to observe with the others.

'Five seconds,' he said quietly.

Suddenly the image in the holo-theatre turned into a wash of grey, then the signal disappeared.

'The relay satellite has gone,' a technician said over the talkback system

'Switch to one of the surface cams,' ordered Yates.

The holo-theatre lit up again and the White House party saw a dim image of the American settlement. Even though it was daytime there was now very little light on the Martian surface. As they watched the light seemed to grow even dimmer and then, abruptly, the signal disappeared.

'Go to one of the other surface cams,' Yates told the AV people.

'Sorry, sir, we've lost all surface signals from Mars,' said a voice from the gallery.

'OK, go to the Asimov,' said Yates grimly.

The holo-theatre came back on and those present saw an image that was being transmitted from the deep-space telescope over 300 million kilometres away from the red planet.

'Where the hell is Mars?' asked President Jarvis.

Desmond Yates looked at the image of the huge green, grey and red cloud that was being sent back by the telescope.

He knew that the lenses had been trained directly on the planet.

'It's now inside the cloud, sir,' he explained.

'This is Foster Robinson reporting,' said a faint voice over a loud background roar. 'I don't know if you can hear me, or see anything, but I'm going to keep transmitting for as long as possible.'

Mars had now been engulfed by the cloud for two days. When the signals from the orbiting satellites and from the video cameras on the planet's surface had disappeared, NASA's technicians had initially reported that all contact with the planet had been lost.

A few moments after receiving this news Maxwell Jarvis had stood and abruptly ended the meeting. But forty-eight hours later NASA had reported that a signal from Mars was being received once again and the President had hastily reconvened the meeting in the Situation Room.

The image now displayed in the holo-theatre showed the interior of the main American habitat on Mars.

'The incoming signal is very weak, and there's a lot of background noise,' apologized an AV technician over the talkback. 'But we're boosting it as much as possible.'

'Just don't lose it,' snapped Yates.

'This is Foster Robinson on Mars,' the reporter said again, his voice sounding feeble.

The twenty-one-minute time delay in receiving the signal made any two-way conversation impossible. Yates and the others were forced to watch in mute anxiety as Robinson turned the hand-held camera away from himself and panned it around the habitat. Bodies were lying across the floor like a human carpet. All were spacesuited, but from a movement here and there it was clear that the colonists, or at least some of them, were still alive.

'We lost our landline connection to the ground dish,' said Robinson, turning the camera back onto himself. 'The force of the cloud is much stronger than predicted and it ripped away everything that was outside, even stuff that was buried. Major Peters and two of his men went out to repair the link. They didn't come back.'

Those in the Situation Room could hear a background roar like continuous thunder as the cloud's internal winds tore at the habitat's exterior.

Robinson tilted his head back in his space helmet, and puffed quickly, like someone trying to increase their oxygen levels. After a minute he sat up and stared into the camera lens again.

'I hope you are receiving this,' he said. 'I have spent the last forty-eight hours hooking up all of the habitat's local-area transmitters. I just hope their combined signal power is strong enough to reach you on Earth.'

'Well done, Mr Robinson,' said President Jarvis quietly, echoing the feelings of all in the room.

'The habitat has been standing up fairly well so far,' added the reporter, just as the signal flickered and recovered. 'But the winds now seem to be getting much stronger. And it looks as if storms are developing within the cloud. I am now going to hold the camera up to one of the habitat windows.'

Robinson's small but exclusive audience on Earth watched in awestruck horror as the camera relayed images and sounds of the huge electrical storm that was raging outside the habitat. Flashes of almost continuous lightning revealed that a howling dust storm was in progress. Even as they watched there was another blinding flash of lightning and a huge crack shot down the habitat's triple-glazed window.

Suddenly the image in the holo-theatre turned head over heels. Then there was blackness.

'Have we lost the signal?' demanded Yates after a few moments.

Before the AV engineers could provide an answer the signal returned. The camera now lay on its side, about two metres from where the dimly lit figure of Foster Robinson lay prone. All present in the Situation Room leaned their heads to one side to try to make out what they were viewing. They could no longer see the interior lights of the habitat, nor its domed walls. A loud howling sound accompanied the visual signal.

'This is Foster Robinson,' called a faint voice over mounting sounds of destruction. 'The habitat is being destroyed. One wall has gone and–'

The holo-theatre went dark and the sound of static replaced the last words to be heard from Mars.

From the *New York Times* website, 22 July 2064

MARS COLONY DESTROYED
182 FEARED DEAD

Two days into its progress across the Martian surface, the space cloud finally destroyed both human habitats, almost certainly killing all 182 colonists. The community included 83 Americans, 21 Britons, 26 Russians, 23 Chinese nationals, 16 French citizens, 12 Germans and one Swedish national. President Jarvis is today sending messages of condolence to the families of all Americans who lost their lives.

'Cloud Acted in Self-Defense' – Hodgeson
Sir Charles Hodgeson last night claimed that in destroying the Martian colony, the 'cloud was merely acting in self-defense'.

'After all, the colonists on Mars had attacked it with 700 megatons of nuclear weapons,' he said. 'This is the result of Mankind's aggression. We must redouble our efforts to make contact with the cloud to assure it of our peaceful intentions in the future.'

TEN

On a beautiful Sunday morning at the end of what had been a glorious month of July – a period of sustained fine weather that for Bill Duncan had gone almost entirely unnoticed – the former MIT computer psychologist left his government-supplied apartment near the Pentagon and crossed the Potomac River via the 14th Street Bridge. For the first time since he had arrived in the capital, he had decided to see the sights.

He walked around the man-made lake known as the Tidal Basin and skirted the shining white Jefferson Memorial. His intention was to stroll on towards the tall white obelisk of the Washington Monument and then head across the lawns to see the White House itself. But, even before he arrived at the Mall, he was stopped by yellow police barriers.

The cop was unimpressed by his Pentagon pass. 'If you want to join the protesters, use the south-east gate down by the Smithsonian on Independence Avenue. If you don't want to protest, stay away from the Mall.'

In the distance Bill could see a massive crowd of people gathered around the Washington needle, spilling over onto the surrounding lawns. Mounted police circled the group and helicopters hovered overhead.

With a shrug he gave up the idea of sightseeing around

the capital and turned back towards the East Potomac Park.
He sauntered on through the trees for fifteen minutes, the
sun hot on his face, and then came to the end of the narrow
strip of land that separated the main Potomac River from
the Washington Channel.

Despite the brilliance of the day, the leafy park seemed
almost deserted and Bill found an empty bench at Haines
Point, at the very tip of the isthmus.

Just across the broad Potomac was Washington's
National Airport. Planes were constantly taking off and
landing, but instead of finding this noisy activity a distur-
bance Bill found the regular movements reassuring, a
symbol of normality in what seemed to be an increasingly
unreal world.

He was due to provide his answer to the Pentagon's vetting panel on the following day. He was either going to
accept their terms and sign a top-level National Security
agreement to gain access to what he'd been promised would
be enormous computing power, or he was going to walk
away from all involvement with the government. He had
still not decided which course of action to take.

In the week's break he had taken from his decoding
work, Bill had returned home to the *Cape Sentinel* in Boston
and, to some extent, had patched things up with Christine
Cocoran and his other hacker volunteers. He was unable to
tell them precisely what the Pentagon was offering him, nor
the terms they were attempting to extract, but he was able
to make them understand that the looming threat of the
space cloud had pushed all normal considerations to one
side. His point had been heavily underlined for him; during
his week's vacation the cloud had engulfed Mars and had
killed all the pioneer colonists on the planet.

Despite Bill's many concerns, the beauty of the day

pressed in upon him. The sun and gentle wind created rippling rows of flashes on the surface of the river, like flotillas of miniature warships frantically signalling the shore. A mallard swam past with ducklings bobbing along behind her as if they were a garland of flowers. The air was swollen with grass and pollen and the river bank was alive with bees picnicking on buttercups the colour of condensed sun. It was the sort of day that mocks the single.

'Mind if I join you?'

Bill spun round on the bench to see Sally Burton standing behind him. She was no longer dressed like a federal agent, but was now wearing a white sports top and a pair of scarlet running shorts. She looked sensational.

Bill felt a leap of joy at the sight of her, a feeling that surprised him. Then he felt annoyed.

'How the hell did you know I'd be here?' he demanded. Since starting his week's leave he hadn't seen the CNS agent once.

'May I?' asked Sally as she sat down on the bench. Bill noticed that despite her running gear and trainers she did not look as if she had been jogging. He turned around on the bench and scanned the park behind him. He saw her black sedan parked fifty yards away.

'What answer are you going to give them tomorrow?' asked Sally, staring out over the scintillant water.

Bill shrugged. 'I still haven't decided. On one hand it seems obvious that if there's anything in the signals that might be of use in tackling the cloud, I have no choice but to agree to their terms. But what if I discover that the military has developed something really insane, some computer technology that's a real threat? Am I just supposed to keep quiet about it?'

Just as Sally opened her mouth to reply, Bill's communicator rang.

'It's Des,' he explained as he lifted it to his ear.

Bill greeted the White House adviser and then listened for a few moments. 'Hold on,' he said. 'I'm with Sally now. There's no one else around. Mind if I put you on speakerphone?'

He laid the communicator on the bench between them.

'Hi, Sally,' said Yates's disembodied voice. 'I was just explaining to Bill that we received some strange data from the instruments that were set up on the surface of Mars. They only managed to broadcast for a short while before they were destroyed, but they picked up some radio signals that we think may have been produced by the cloud itself. The signals appear to be modulated – to be artificial.'

'That's incredible, Des,' said Sally. 'Doesn't that suggest that–'

'We can't be sure of anything yet,' broke in Yates. 'But I know that Bill is due to meet the Pentagon people again tomorrow and I wanted you two to have this information. It's now even more imperative that you get that extra computing power, Bill. We need you to see if you can make any sense of these new signals that we've picked up from inside the cloud. We desperately need to know what it is we're dealing with.'

After closing the connection Bill and Sally stared out across the slow-moving river together, both lost in thought.

'If the space cloud is generating its *own* radio signals . . .' said Bill after a while, not even bothering to finish his sentence.

'Terrifying, really scary,' agreed Sally. Then she turned to face her companion. 'Please say you'll do it?' she asked, earnestness filling her blue eyes. 'I think the appropriate phrase is "Your country needs you."'

'You may be right,' agreed Bill. 'But I'm going to need a lot of help from you.'

Sally swung round to gaze out over the river once more.

'I've been ordered back to New York, Bill,' she told him after a pause. 'My boss thinks that after the Mars catastrophe all the cranks are going to come out of the woodwork. He's predicting a sharp rise in network fraud and cyber-terrorism and he wants me back to run the Manhattan operation.'

They both stared at the water and Bill suddenly felt a profound sense of disappointment welling up from deep within him.

Three weeks after the space cloud began its passage across Mars, President Jarvis reconvened the Cloud EXCOM for a formal meeting in the Situation Room.

'For some unknown reason, the gas cloud seems to have picked up speed,' Desmond Yates told the group. 'The last vestiges of vapour have now cleared the planet's surface. Although we are no longer receiving any radio broadcasts directly from the planet, long-distance spectrographic analysis suggests that what little atmosphere Mars did have has been completely sucked away into space.'

'Where's the cloud heading for now?' demanded Jarvis.

'Straight for the centre of our solar system, sir,' said Yates, taking a step backwards so that the image in the holo-theatre would not be obstructed. 'At present we calculate that its trajectory will take it across the orbital paths of both Venus and Mercury but it won't collide with either of those planets. Then it will head straight on inwards, towards the sun itself.'

'And what will happen then, precisely?' asked the President testily.

'We're not sure,' admitted the Space-Affairs Adviser. 'If it behaved like a normal pool of gas I would say that it would get trapped by the sun's gravity and would burn up. But we now know that we can't make such assumptions.'

'How long before we can be certain about what's going to happen?' asked the President's Chief of Staff.

'We should know better in a week, perhaps two,' Yates told him.

'Well, since we can't rely on the cloud burning up in the sun, I'm going to double our programme of shelter building and habitat production,' announced the President. Then he turned to Freddy Truelson, director of the Federal Emergency Management Agency.

'Are FEMA's plans for government evacuation ready?' he demanded.

'They are, sir,' replied Truelson. 'We've been working on them for three months. We're ready to go.'

'Very well,' said the President. Then he turned back to face the full committee.

'I also want the necessary documents prepared in case I have to declare a full-scale national emergency – including the imposition of martial law.'

From the *New York Times* website, 14 August 2064

TV BROADCASTS JAMMED BY HODGESON'S CLOUD ENTHUSIASTS

By RANDALL TATE, science correspondent

Commercial television transmissions all over the world are suffering intermittent interference and jamming because hundreds of thousands of licensed and unlicensed followers of science-fiction guru Sir Charles Hodgeson are radioing messages of peace and appeasement to the space cloud using all available wavelengths. Over two hundred megawatts of continuous radio transmissions emanating from transmitters on Hodgeson's Orpheus Island home have severely disrupted commercial television services in northeastern Australia.

'We must attempt to communicate with this cloud,' Hodgeson said from his heavily guarded island retreat. 'We must make our peaceful intentions clear.'

A spokesperson for Australia's Department of Communications said, 'We are considering how best to deal with the situation on Orpheus Island. We understand that Sir Charles has now imported a number of armed security aguards to protect his property and we are in consultations with other government departments about how best to tackle this problem.'

As he stepped into the cavernous underground facility, Bill Duncan's first impression was that he had entered an endless shopping mall. The brightly lit space was so large that it seemed to stretch away towards infinity in both directions. On either side of a broad central aisle were rows of glass-fronted units like retail outlets, only there were no window displays and there was nothing for sale. In each of the nearest ante-rooms, Bill could see groups of people working in front of terminals, data boards, wall screens, laser panels and small holo-displays.

The air-conditioning system in the subterranean nerve centre was powerful and the temperature cool, but Bill detected a faint smell of ozone in the air, the unmistakable signature of hot electronics. He was standing just inside the main entrance area of the Pentagon's Virtual Warfare Center – known internally as the VWC – which was located somewhere deep under the Earth's surface, a twenty-minute subway ride away from the main Pentagon headquarters building.

After much agonizing thought, Bill had accepted the government's conditions and signed the Level One National Secrecy agreement. He realized that it was the only way he was going to gain access to significantly greater computing power.

Before being granted the clearance, he had been required to undergo lengthy personality profiling and psychological modelling tests -- tests which, as a psychologist himself, he would have found ludicrously easy to cheat. He had then sworn a new oath of allegiance, specifically agreeing to henceforth keep everything he was shown and told by the virtual-warfare team secret for the rest of his natural life. Following that, it had taken almost two weeks to set up this first introduction to the people who were going to provide him with the additional processing power he needed to work on the old Isonian signals and the cloud's newly discovered internal radio emissions.

Earlier in the morning Bill had reported to the Pentagon reception desk where, as arranged, he was met by a VWC duty officer and handed the new digital and biometric pass which would provide access to the top-secret military establishment. It had been the preparation of this pass – an ID which contained samples of Bill's DNA, his iris scans, fingerprints and voice print – that had taken so long and had driven the ex-MIT professor to call Desmond Yates on three different occasions in an attempt to hurry up the Pentagon's grindingly slow bureaucratic process.

Once through the Pentagon's main security gateway, the duty officer had led him to an elevator at which an armed Marine stood guard. Their passes were checked again, then they had seemed to descend for ever until the doors opened onto a station platform. Two more Marines were waiting beside a small unmanned rail shuttle. Their IDs were checked once more and then they began a journey deep underground which had lasted for almost twenty minutes.

Now Bill heard a quiet beeping from behind him and he turned to see a low electric vehicle gliding silently towards him along the central passageway.

'Professor Duncan, welcome to the VWC,' called the man at the wheel of the buggy. It was Colonel Dr Otto Kramer, one of the men who had sat on the Pentagon security vetting panel. The Harvard-trained computer scientist was now dressed informally in a white short-sleeved shirt and dark trousers and was grinning from ear to ear.

Kramer leaped out of the vehicle and shook Bill's hand vigorously.

'I meant what I said about admiring your work, Professor,' said the colonel. 'It's good to have you as part of the VWC team.'

'Hey, hold on just one minute,' objected Bill. 'I'm only here to work on one particular project, as you know.'

The Pentagon scientist nodded, then put his head on one side. 'I'm sure you will take an interest once you see what we've been doing,' he said. 'Jump in, I'll take you to your new lab.'

Kramer did a U-turn in the centre of the 'mall' and drove swiftly along the broad aisle between the many glass-fronted units.

'These teams are mostly monitoring the world's radio and cable networks,' said Kramer, with a casual wave of his arm. 'Something you know a bit about yourself.'

Bill said nothing, but he noted the huge number of people who seemed to be employed in the task.

The vehicle arrived at what seemed to be a central point in the vast facility and the colonel turned left along a shorter corridor.

'How many people are employed here?' asked Bill as they passed a much larger glassed-in area in which at least twenty people were working at laser screens and monitors.

'Depends on the state of alert,' said Kramer. 'When it's quiet, about twenty-five hundred. Double that in a crisis.'

The colonel arrived at a space between units and pulled up beside double white doors.

'You've been given exclusive use of this lab and holo-theatre,' said Kramer, nodding towards the entrance. Stepping out of the vehicle, he touched his pass to a wall plate and held open one of the doors.

Inside, the room was gloomy but as his eyes adjusted

Bill saw a small holo-ring surrounded by banked seating for forty or fifty people.

'I want you to meet somebody who's going to help you with your work,' said Kramer. He pulled a slim remote control from his shirt pocket and the holo-ring suddenly lit up. Then Bill saw the image of a young, fresh-faced man with fair hair, perhaps eighteen or twenty years of age, standing at the edge of the circle with his arms crossed. The figure wore an open-necked shirt, tan slacks and a pair of brown suede loafers. He looked like an affluent college student – East Coast rather than Californian.

'This is Jerome,' said Kramer. 'He's our new VTW – that's a virtual-theatre weapon.'

'Hey, I'm not here to use any weapon,' objected Bill quickly. 'I was simply promised a lot more processing power.'

'There are no processors more capable than Jerome,' said the Pentagon scientist smoothly. 'He is a *virtual* processor – a processor without any hardware components – and he is entirely location-independent once he's deployed. He is able to expand his own intelligence and processing power infinitely and he can become as capable as you want. He acquires multiple processors of all designs to add to his own architecture at very high speed – that's his overriding goal. In an extreme case, such as all-out global war, he can acquire almost every processor on the planet and add them to his own architecture. He then becomes the sum of every computer in the world.'

'How exactly does he do that?' enquired Bill, unable to keep the disgust and scepticism out of his voice. Kramer's commentary seemed wholly incongruous with the image of the smiling, good-looking young man who was standing before them, a slight grin on his face. Bill knew that anthropomorphic interfaces had become almost mandatory on advanced computing systems but he was on record as having spoken out many times against giving complex computer programs the look and feel of a human personality. He felt certain that such simulations would only tempt program designers to add more and more human-type features to their creations, a trend that could one day result in disaster for humanity.

'Of course, Jerome has many appearances, and many identities,' Kramer said, ignoring Bill's question. 'The best way to think about him is as a super-virus to which no processor is immune – or perhaps as an aggressive virtual cancer – because he takes over entirely any host with which he comes into contact. He is so powerful that only the President and the Chairman of the Joint Chiefs can authorize Jerome to be used in full weapons mode.'

'This is *exactly* what I feared!' Bill exclaimed, his voice rising in anger. He spun round to face the smug Pentagon scientist. 'I've always suspected that you lunatics in the military couldn't be trusted. You can't just go building weapon entities like that! Don't you realize that this thing is almost certainly in clear breach of every international computer treaty that exists?'

'Please don't be alarmed, Professor,' said Kramer, laying a reassuring hand on Bill's shoulder. 'We've taken extreme safety measures. Until he's deployed, Jerome remains totally location-dependent – his locus can't function outside of physical components we've embedded in this room. We've also denied him all physical form and mobility. He's quite safe, but he's very, very powerful.'

Kramer abruptly turned back to the figure of the young man. 'Local acquisition mode, please, Jerome,' he said.

The Pentagon scientist then shot Bill a penetrating look.

'Tell me Professor Duncan, for someone with a world reputation for training and educating computer personalities, what type of software assistant do you choose to organize your own life?'

'Just an ordinary commercially available and *legal* software personality called Nadia,' said Bill, pulling his communicator from his pocket. 'I've been training her for fifteen–'

The computer psychologist broke off in mid-sentence. As he opened his communicator he saw an image on the screen that should not have been there.

'Hello, Professor Duncan,' said Jerome, speaking from within Bill's communicator. 'I can feel how close you and Nadia have become, but perhaps you and I can also be friends.'

'Jesus!' spat Bill, glaring up at Kramer. 'How the hell did you do that?' He shot a look at the holo-ring, but the figure of Jerome had now disappeared.

'I have *absolute* firewall security on my system,' insisted Bill, as he punched up a system-restore routine on his communicator's keyboard. Then he realized that all the keys were locked. He hit the master hardware-reset button, but that too was unresponsive. Then he tried to turn the unit completely off, but the power switch itself seemed to have been disabled.

'You'd have to destroy the entire unit to get rid of Jerome,' said Kramer quietly. 'And even then he'd manage to migrate and survive.'

'But how the hell did he get in?' demanded Bill again.

'Like I said, Jerome is an ultra-aggressive processor – and network-acquisition personality,' explained Kramer. 'When so instructed, his job is to assume control of all processors in a given area or of a given profile, whether connected by radio, laser, optical, landline, cable or molecular networks. We've provided him – well, at the risk of being immodest, *I've* provided him – with all the means necessary to work out for himself how best to overcome physical barriers, hardware defences, and software defences – even the total loss of electrical power. He can come up with invasive procedures and techniques that no human could think of. Allow me to demonstrate further.'

Kramer glanced at the image on Bill's screen, then said, 'Jerome, please restore Professor Duncan's companion personality unchanged and resume home location.'

The figure of Jerome reappeared in the holo-ring with a smirk on his face.

'What happened, Bill?' asked a female voice from his communicator. 'I was crashed, but I don't know how.'

'Nor do I,' Bill told his restored computer personality. 'But I'll find out and let you know later.'

He snapped the communicator shut and turned back to his host.

'Where is all of this leading, Dr Kramer?' he demanded.

The army scientist turned back to the virtual figure standing in front of him.

'Jerome, please acquire the network approved for use by Professor Duncan,' he said.

The college student nodded and then joined his hands together in front of his body and, ludicrously, started twiddling his virtual thumbs. After a few moments he looked up directly at Kramer.

'Network acquired, ninety-nine point three per cent active and available,' he reported.

'Jerome, please tell us the number of individual processors you have acquired and the total processing power that is now available,' said Kramer.

'Six hundred and eighty-two million, three hundred and twenty-one varied processors of quantum, neural and molecular design,' announced Jerome. 'Total processing network power available is three-point-two-seven trillion petabits. I've put a network map up on Screen Two.'

Both men turned and saw that a large wall screen had now lit and was displaying a dense red 3-D network matrix.

'Is that enough power to be of use, Professor?' asked Kramer.

Despite his earlier anger, Bill could not suppress his astonishment. 'That's amazing. How the hell did he assemble such a network so fast – and whose processors are they, exactly?'

'Your decoding work has been given top priority,' said Kramer. 'Jerome has been given authorization to acquire the processors used by all branches of the US military, all offices of government and all US public-service organizations. That gives you your hundreds of millions of processors to use. But he is only acquiring them partially for your project, he's just using the ninety-per-cent-idle cycles that almost all processors have available. If he were deployed in full weapons mode, he would be acquiring processors totally, taking over complete control of their function, even down to the level of the chips in light switches, locks, home utilities and vehicles. One of this model's major roles in war is the acquisition of all enemy processors, whether on Earth or in space, with the aim of denying service to the enemy and putting them to use on our side. What he's going to be doing for you is well below his maximum capabilities.'

Bill shook his head, partly in wonder and partly in disgust with himself. After years spent protesting against the unrestrained development of computer power he was now about to make use of a computer system that was itself far more powerful -- and far more dangerous – than anything he had previously imagined.

'I'm looking forward to working with you,' said Jerome. 'I too am an admirer of your work, Professor Duncan.'

ELEVEN

'Sir, the cloud has now reappeared from behind the sun,' said Desmond Yates. 'And it is once again on a direct heading towards Earth.'

There was a silence in the Situation Room as the President and the members of the Cloud EXCOM digested this news.

'Then this has become very serious,' said the President gravely. 'We must now suspect the worst about this thing, whatever it is.'

Des Yates nodded. Along with the rest of the world's scientific community he had spent the last five weeks observing anxiously as the cloud approached the far side of the sun and was then lost to direct view. Throughout the period he had had live feeds from both the SETI lunar optical telescope and the Carl Sagan 'scope in Chile patched to his office in the White House, to his home and even to his personal communicator. Like so many other astronomers around the world, he had found himself checking on the cloud's progress every hour.

Dozens of large computer models had been built by governments, universities and scientific establishments, all of them simulating the likely behaviour of the giant pool of gas as it approached the all-consuming sun. The immense gravity of the star prompted every one of the models to predict that the cloud would contract as it approached, then accelerate rapidly before being burned up while still millions of kilometres away from the solar surface.

But the brightness of the solar radiation meant that even a deep-space telescope such as the Asimov had been unable to provide clear views of what was happening on the far side of the sun and the star's powerful radio emissions meant that all radio astronomy in the solar region was also impossible. The many anxious observers just had to wait.

Then, against the predictions of even the world's most sophisticated computer models, the cloud had reappeared from behind the sun, as if it had merely sidestepped the immense gravitational force.

'The cloud is now more dense and it is travelling much more slowly,' explained Yates, pointing at the model in the holo-theatre. 'It's still millions of times larger than the Earth, of course, but it is now travelling at around five million kilometres a day. If it continues at this velocity and remains on its present trajectory it will strike the Earth in one month.'

'And is it still likely to damage our atmosphere?' asked Jarvis.

'It is,' confirmed Yates. 'Even at this relatively slower speed, it will still strip most if not all of our atmosphere away within six weeks.'

The President closed his eyes and shook his head. Nobody else in the room spoke.

'I think we have only one option open to us,' continued Yates, after a pause. 'When we fired nuclear missiles from Mars into the cloud, we managed to tear a huge hole in it, a hole that lasted for some days before it was completely filled in.'

The President opened his eyes and looked up.

'There will be just one opportunity to launch another,

much larger, attack on the cloud,' said Yates. 'We could try to disperse part of the gas cloud immediately before it hits the Earth. If we leave it until the last possible minute and position the explosions correctly, perhaps our planet will be able to pass safely through the hole we create.'

President Jarvis shook his head again, then sat back wearily in his chair.

'That sounds like a very long shot,' he groaned. Then he leaned forward once more and scanned all the faces present. 'Are we sure there's no other option?'

Heads shook around the table and members of the Cloud EXCOM glanced at each other and shrugged.

'Nuclear force is all we have to deal with something of this scale,' said General Thomas Nicholls, Chair of the Joint Chiefs of the US military.

'Very well,' said Jarvis. 'Let's get the plans drawn up.'

The general nodded and the President swivelled back to address the entire meeting.

'In the meantime, does anybody here think that we should be trying to talk to the cloud – trying to radio it officially in some way, trying to make peace?'

Everyone around the table exchanged glances. Some EXCOM members smiled, but none of the scientists seemed ready to offer a view.

'I suppose it couldn't do any harm, sir,' offered the White House Chief of Staff. 'Perhaps we should broadcast a welcome and say that we want peace . . .'

He tailed off lamely as he saw the expressions on the other faces around the table.

'You're right, it couldn't do any harm – could it?' asked the President.

'We just don't know, sir,' Yates told him. 'And what would you say and in what language would you say it?'

'I'll leave that to you,' retorted Jarvis. 'But it has to be worth trying and in the meantime we'll make preparations for as big a last-minute strike as possible. Now, can we keep the news of the cloud's approach out of the media for a while?'

'Impossible, sir,' said Yates. 'The cloud will be visible to the naked eye by next week.'

The President gave a short nod. 'Very well,' he said. 'This administration will evacuate to the Cancut Mountain facility in Arizona in six days' time. I want the emergency bill enacted that will allow me to declare martial law at the same time. We are going to need national dusk-to-dawn curfews to prevent looting. Things are going to get very bad out there, people.'

There was assent all round the table as those present – each knowing that they themselves and their families were eligible for long-term bunker shelter – imagined how the general public would begin to react as the cloud became visible in the sky.

'Will the military be able to cope?' Jarvis asked the Chairman of the Joint Chiefs.

The general shifted uneasily in his seat.

'For a while, sir,' said Nicholls. 'But we have only been able to allocate bunker places to eighty thousand troops. We'll have to disarm the remainder immediately and place our chosen forces around strategic targets and locations – airports, seaports, underground government facilities and so on. There will be some regions of the country, some quite large regions, that we won't be able to police. I'm afraid they'll have to be militarily abandoned.'

'Make a start on it, General,' ordered the President.

'The future of humankind lies in your hands,' Sir Charles Hodgeson said earnestly into the camera lens. 'We now know that the alien space cloud is once again heading directly for Earth. It is up to us, we who are best prepared for alien contact, to make sure that this incredible and beautiful entity understands that we mean it no harm.'

The science-fiction guru was seated in his newly built TV and network studio inside his private bunker on Orpheus Island. He was making a live network broadcast, an appearance that his huge fan base had been chattering about excitedly for days.

'Our governments have already demonstrated their instinctive warlike response to the unknown,' continued Hodgeson. 'It is as if they are still cavemen acting on unrestrained evolutionary impulses to kill before running the risk of being killed. This only emphasizes humankind's lack of development. It will be seen in very sad contrast to more developed life forms in the universe.'

Seated on the other side of the small studio, one of Hodgeson's acolytes mixed in an image of the space cloud so that it appeared as a background to the great man's head.

'We have a duty to make it clear that not all humans are so poorly evolved,' continued Sir Charles. 'I want all of you with radio transmitters to broadcast continuous messages of welcome and of peace towards the cloud. Stand by for our visitor's new coordinates and for our suggested range of radio frequencies on which to broadcast.

'This is Charles Hodgeson from Orpheus Island wishing you all peace. Please extend your greetings and welcome to our honoured visitor.'

From the *New York Times* website, 20 September 2064

CLOUD HEADING FOR EARTH AGAIN

By RANDALL TATE, science correspondent

Will Arrive in 4 Weeks – 2nd Massive Nuclear Strike Planned

The giant space cloud which destroyed the Martian colony has now orbited the sun and has emerged on a new heading which, if maintained, will cause it to collide with the Earth in 28 days.

The White House has announced it is leading an international effort to assemble a large force of nuclear weapons in Earth orbit prior to an all-out attack on the cloud. If a large hole can be blasted in the centre of the cloud, the Earth may be able to pass through unscathed.

Part of Night Sky Now Obscured

Astronomers at the Carl Sagan Ultra-Large Telescope in Chile have reported that the cloud is already obscuring part of the night sky.

Although the cloud is heading towards Earth from the direction of the sun, and is therefore lost to sight in the sun's glare during the day, Dr Brian Nunney of the Carl Sagan Observatory reports that it is possible to observe the cloud indirectly just before dawn.

'Shortly before sunrise the area of the sky which normally contains Pegasus is now obscured,' said Dr Nunney. 'We can expect this area of occlusion to grow rapidly in the next few days.'

Well done, Jerome!' said Bill Duncan enthusiastically. 'I'm not even going to ask how you did that.'

The virtual computer personality stood at a virtual white board just inside the holo-theatre's display area. Jerome had just finished writing a series of calculations on the electronic board, figures and formulae that were also appearing on a large 3-D screen on all of the theatre's wall screens and on Bill's own communicator display.

'It was an easy calculation, Bill,' admitted Jerome. 'Very straightforward. I just kept trying different multipliers against different harmonics in the signal. Bingo! Fifty-seven octaves below exactly.'

The computer psychologist sighed with amazement. He knew theoretically how much processing capacity Jerome had at his command – the total network availability was continuously updated and displayed on a second wall screen just outside the holo-theatre – but he had never before felt the full force of so much brute number-crunching power. Jerome was in command of over 680 million powerful processors that belonged to different branches of the US military, government and public service agencies and he was harnessing and managing all of them to run in parallel, to allow him to carry out the most fantastic computations.

Bill and Jerome were now working to try to extract some sense or, at least, some coherence, out of the mass of modulated radio signals which had apparently emanated from within the cloud itself. They had been working on the problem for several weeks, operating with the sort of comfortable rapport that can only exist between two intelligences wholly incomprehensible to each other. They were trying to isolate anything recognizable to man or machine from within the vast amount of electrical noise.

Finally, at Bill's suggestion, they had decided to assign musical values to each discrete modulated frequency and then go hunting for correlators – things that would make patterns. That was when Jerome had made his breakthrough.

'Get me Des Yates, please, Naj,' Bill told his assistant, Nadia. He waited for a few moments and then the White House adviser came on the line.

'We've made some progress with interpreting the cloud's internal signals,' Bill explained. 'Jerome's figured out that the transmissions are a partial sine wave, with a median tone about fifty-seven octaves below middle C.'

'That's very good news,' said Yates. 'And we certainly need some good news right now. So the cloud is producing a sort of music, is it?'

As Desmond Yates spoke, Bill glanced over to where Jerome was standing with his arms crossed and an amused smile on his face. He had been forced to admit that Otto Kramer and his team had done a wonderful job with their anthropomorphization features for the personality. He looked as human as could be.

'Well, it *is* a sort of music – or, at least, a sound,' confirmed Bill. 'But it's not something that we ourselves could hear. Jerome tells me that fifty-seven octaves below middle C is a trillion times lower than the lowest limit of the human hearing range.'

'This just gets weirder and weirder,' said Yates. 'I presume you're going to speed it up so we can hear what it sounds like.'

Bill grunted. 'Do the math, Des. How much computing power will I need to hold the analog signals in storage, speed them up a trillion times and then start analysing their structure?'

There was a silence at the other end of the line. The

numbers were vast – way outside of even the capabilities of the giant military computing network that Jerome had commandeered.

'We still need a lot more power, Des,' said Bill. 'I never thought I'd hear myself saying this, but I'm going to have to ask the Pentagon to authorize Jerome to acquire even more processors.'

'I'll have a word with the President,' said Des Yates. 'Apart from trying to fry the cloud with more nukes, the work you're doing is our only hope – however slim. We've been radioing to the cloud in an attempt to communicate with it, but it would be much better if we could do so in its own form of music, if it is a music. I'm sure I will be able to get you more processing power from somewhere.'

There was chaos on the floor of the *New York Times*. Over 200 broadcasters, journalists, editors and technicians were engaged in trying to keep up with the torrents of news that were pouring in from all over the world. Science correspondent Randall Tate was particularly busy as he tried to sample information coming in over the news wires, via cable feeds and from official sources. Later in the day he was due to host a live debate about the approach of the cloud on the *NYT* television network and he needed to gather as much up-to-date information as possible.

'**CLOUD NOW TWENTY-SIX DAYS AWAY**' was the headline announcement on NASA's home page.

'**VAST NUCLEAR FORCE ASSEMBLED IN SPACE**' read a wire from Associated Press.

'ARMIES ON STREETS OF MOST CAPITAL CITIES'
reported Reuters.

'WHITE HOUSE ADMINISTRATION MOVES UNDERGROUND' the *NYT* Washington bureau reported.

'CAPITAL'S ELITE EVACUATED'

Then there was the international media to digest.

As Tate scrolled through the headlines and sampled snippets of TV news bulletins he realized that the stories seemed to be similar all over the world. Everywhere there was panic buying of oxygen and oxygen-manufacturing systems, water, tinned food, fuel and the other goods and equipment necessary for extended survival. Over the previous few months manufacturers had ramped up production as news of the cloud's approach had spread into the public domain, but there were still insufficient stocks to meet demand and people were now killing each other for essential supplies. Armies and police were fighting to keep control, but they were frequently failing.

In all parts of the globe human beings were making efforts to build themselves shelters, some using machinery, some digging by hand. In many cases individuals were scooping out simple earth burrows in the hope that they would provide adequate protection from whatever evils the space cloud would bring.

In some cities communities were banding together in an attempt to try to convert subway rail systems into makeshift shelters and, in a few countries, governments were making financial aid available for these efforts. But there were four common shortages: oxygen-making equipment, water-recycling systems, fuel supplies and non-perishable food. Despite governments making heroic efforts to increase production of these essential items, most domestic and public shelters would only be able to offer the hope of survival for a month or two at most after the cloud had passed – if, as threatened, it did strip away all of the Earth's precious atmosphere.

As Randall Tate read these reports and fast-forwarded through TV pictures of the frenetic survival preparations that were in hand, he thanked his good fortune that he and his co-workers around him had been allocated space in New York Times Inc.'s corporate shelter, should it be needed. In the developed world there were two premium types of bunker space on offer: official government refuge and the shelters provided by large corporations for their key employees.

Like many other major businesses in Manhattan, the *New York Times* had been busy converting part of its own office building to serve as a shelter for its executives and senior employees. The lower eight floors of the forty-six-storey high-rise had been bricked up and completely sealed to create air-tight, self-sufficient and self-sustaining accommodation for over 600 staff and their immediate family members. Oxygen-making systems had been installed, along with air filters, generators, fuel, water-recycling systems, food stores and all the other paraphernalia necessary to sustain life for a long period.

A small force of armed security guards, who had also been offered bunker space, now protected the prepared facility around the clock for when it was needed. The company's management was not saying publicly for how long the corporate shelter could sustain its inhabitants in the sealed-floor areas, but the office rumour was that they should be able to hold out for at least five years.

'ELECTRICAL SHOCKS COULD FRY PLANET'
Tate read in a British newspaper.

'OCEAN CURRENTS WILL CEASE AS ICE AGE GRIPS' proclaimed the translation from a German news service.

A Toronto-based news agency was explaining that 'the atmosphere will be peeled off in layers, over the course of six to eight weeks'.

'Earthquakes, tsunamis and volcanic eruptions expected all over the globe,' reported the Auckland *National* in New Zealand.

Tate sighed and flicked back to his TV feeds. With such headlines being published it was no wonder that mass looting had broken out in many cities. Outside, army patrols were on the Manhattan streets and the *Times* science correspondent switched from one scene of rioting to another. People were not only shooting each other for survival supplies: armed mobs were gathering around key government buildings demanding that the shelters be opened up to admit them, and were engaging the undermanned protection forces in long-running gun battles.

Then Tate noticed one human-interest side effect of the public panic. News outlets were reporting a massive upsurge in religious activity, with crowds streaming into churches, cathedrals, mosques and synagogues. The reporter dipped into an interview being broadcast from Pennsylvania.

'Our representatives are being welcomed on every doorstep,' said a gleeful spokeswoman for the Jehovah's

Witnesses. 'We are making full use of this opportunity to bring Jehovah's message to the people.'

Three hours later Randall Tate took his cue from the floor manager, smiled into the camera lens and read the autocue introduction to his live TV debate.

Every television and radio channel was suffering from a serious shortage of experts who were willing to be interviewed about the crisis. Every TV news programme wanted to invite those who had specialist knowledge to discuss the likely effects of the cloud's approach, but many such scientists were fully occupied trying to create a safe sanctuary for themselves and their families. Only those experts who were already guaranteed places in government, university or corporate shelters had time to make themselves available – and there were too few of them to go around.

But the prestigious *New York Times* TV network still had plenty of influence. The producers had managed to persuade three eminent scientists, all of whom had already been offered government-run shelter space, to take part in this debate.

Tate finished reading his introduction and turned to Professor Nils Harmon, a senior climatologist from Columbia University.

'Professor, perhaps you could tell us what we'll notice first as the cloud approaches?' the science correspondent asked.

'Well, at first it's going to get very hot,' said the lanky climatologist with slow deliberation. 'This is because as the cloud approaches our planet it will begin reflecting a lot of the sun's light and heat back towards the Earth. We could see temperatures in New York go up to as high as sixty or seventy degrees Celsius – that's up to one hundred and fifty Fahrenheit. It will feel very unpleasant out of doors.'

Tate nodded, urging his rather pedantic guest to continue.

'Then it will suddenly start to become colder again as the cloud comes between Earth and the sun and starts to block out some of the sun's rays,' Harmon went on. 'As a result we should expect torrential precipitation as the atmosphere suddenly cools down and the water vapour that was trapped in the warm air is released.'

Once again Tate was forced to nod vigorously, encouraging his ponderous academic guest to get on with delivering his bizarre weather forecast.

'The torrential rain will turn first to sleet, then to snow,' explained the Columbia University professor, unwilling to be hurried. 'And there may be some very dangerous hailstorms. There will also be very high winds, perhaps as high as two hundred miles per hour in places – winds unlike any that have existed on Earth for billions of years – and these will whip the hail and snow into driving blizzards.'

The bony climatologist shifted in his seat, folded his hands together between his long thighs and sat forward earnestly in his chair.

'Widespread destruction will be caused both in the cities and in rural communities,' he continued, his voice lowering in register. 'And within two weeks people who venture outside will start to notice a decrease in the oxygen level in the air. Temperatures will continue to fall and, as more of the sun is obscured, it will get down to as low as minus fifty degrees Celsius. At that point all of the oceans will freeze over.'

The weather scientist recited his awful predictions calmly, almost prosaically. But Tate felt a sudden chill creep over his body as, despite the bright lights of the studio and the adrenalin rush of hosting a live TV debate, the import of the professor's words sank in.

'Thank you, Professor Harmon,' he said gravely. Then he turned to the image of a portly middle-aged woman which was displayed on a screen beside him. 'Marjory Beer, you're Professor of Human Biology at the University of Texas. What impact would these predicted conditions have on humans and on other life forms on this planet?'

Even as he asked this prepared question, Tate was aware of a feeling of total unreality. How could he and these experts be sitting around calmly discussing such events, as though they were about to happen to other people who lived on another world?

'Well, *if* Professor Harmon's predictions are correct,' began the biologist, 'the only humans likely to survive will be those who shelter in hermetically sealed and heated chambers with plenty of air supplies, water, fossil or solar fuels and the ability to regenerate oxygen chemically – or the means to produce it from sea water by electrolysis.'

'I see,' said Tate, suddenly imagining the effect this broadcast would be having on its viewers. But this was his job, wasn't it? The public deserved to know the truth, no matter what. 'And what about other life forms on the planet?'

'Well, most plants, reptiles, birds and all large mammals will become extinct within five to six weeks,' said Marjory Beer. 'A few species that can burrow and hibernate might stay alive for a few more months. Some deep-water fish may also be able to survive and there may be some pockets of warmth trapped in the oceans which will allow other ocean dwellers to hang on for a few more weeks or even months.

Of course, some seeds and some simple cellular organisms would remain viable for many years.'

'Jesus, try to get something positive going,' said the producer's voice in Tate's left ear. 'Ask them how quickly things will return to normal.'

The reporter turned to his second studio guest, a rotund planetary geophysicist from Yale.

'Assuming that the worst happens, Professor Roger Guttman, how long will the Earth's atmosphere take to reform?' he asked.

The geophysicist shifted uneasily in his chair. 'I'm not sure that it ever would. If all the plants have been killed, what's going to create an atmosphere?'

'Well, the moment the cloud leaves this planet the sun is going to heat the oceans up again,' broke in Professor Nils Harmon. 'And as soon as that happens you have water vapour, then rain, then plant growth. That's the beginning of an atmosphere.'

'No, I don't think so,' countered Guttman, jabbing the air with his finger. 'If there's no atmosphere to protect the Earth, the sun's rays will be so powerful that they will not only melt the frozen oceans, they will cause them to boil away completely in a matter of a few years, if not in a few months.'

'Which causes water vapour, which creates an atmosphere,' insisted Harmon.

'Professor Beer, do you have a view on this?' asked Tate turning to the screen image of the biologist.

'Well, I'm not an expert in atmosphere regeneration,' she began. 'But I would have thought that even if the boiling oceans did produce water vapour it would be many thousands of years before anything that could be called an atmosphere could be produced. For that you would need a breathing ecosystem with abundant plant life.'

'Do you agree with that, Professor Harmon?' asked Tate turning back to his studio guest.

'Yes, of course,' said the climatologist, nodding vigorously. 'Although I am sure that an atmosphere will re-form around this planet eventually, the process will indeed take many thousands of years.'

Bill Duncan had come home early from his Pentagon lab, eaten a solitary carry-out Chinese meal in his government flat and was now flicking through the channels to see what information the TV networks were transmitting. His mind badly needed a rest from months of almost continuous intense intellectual labour.

He switched to a news channel and suddenly recognized the image of Randall Tate. He put the remote control aside to listen in to the debate that was being chaired by his former contact at the *New York Times*.

It was fearful and depressing stuff. Within two minutes Bill was sitting forward on the couch, his head in his hands, wondering if he should rally his tired body and mind once again and go back over to the lab for yet another all-night shift. He had no idea whether he would be able to extract any information from the alien signals, or from the cloud's own radio emissions that would be of help but he felt that a breakthrough was tantalizingly close. If only he had more computing power!

Then, out of nowhere, Sally Burton's face swam into his mind, as it seemed to do whenever he took a little down time.

He flipped open his communicator. 'Get me Sally, please, Naj,' he told his personal-technology assistant. A decade earlier one of his best-received pieces of research had been on the value of good manners when addressing artificial personalities. Although it seemed illogical that humans should worry about their manners when talking to machines, he had proven through systematic research that even the most basic types of machine intelligence performed better when good manners were employed during communication. The phenomenon was something to do with the way humans interacted with their machines when they themselves chose to be polite.

'I was just about to call you,' said Sally, the communicator's small screen lighting up with her smile. Bill smiled involuntarily in return and touched two icons, one that would return his own image to Sally, the other to patch the image of her face onto the large wall screen, to overlay the depressing picture of the TV debate.

During the next ten minutes Bill brought Sally up to date on his work with Jerome, explaining that he had been working up to 130 hours a week, by way of apologizing for not having called before. Then he listened to the federal agent talk about the vast increase in cyber crime that her department was trying to cope with.

'It's as if this cloud thing is giving every pervert and every fruitcake a licence to rush onto the net and do whatever they want,' she explained. 'They figure that all of the law-enforcement agencies will be too busy to do anything about it. And they're largely right!'

Then they talked a little about the cloud. Sally had been watching part of the same *New York Times* debate as Bill. She asked him what Des Yates was now saying about the emergency.

'I haven't seen Des in weeks,' Bill told her. 'His assistant says he's closeted almost continuously with the President, but I don't know whether he's at the White House or whether they've already gone underground.'

There was a silence. Then Sally cleared her throat. 'Would you like to come up to New York and see me this weekend, Bill?' she asked. 'It sounds like we could both use a break.'

The computer psychologist gazed steadily into the image of Sally's blue eyes.

'I'd like that very much,' he said. 'But I don't think there's a hope in hell's chance of me getting a seat on a plane out of here. I saw something on the TV earlier that said every flight in the country is overbooked with people trying to get home to be with their families.'

'I've got a new one in Hamburg, and two more in the Paris area,' shouted Paul Levine over the din in the houseboat cabin. 'And they're massive!'

'Just log them carefully,' shouted back Christine Coco-ran from where she was sitting at another terminal. 'Make sure you've got a good profile and then move on. We haven't got time to deal with them individually.'

Eleven volunteer members of Hackers At Large were working busily on board *Cape Sentinel*, using their own pro-prietary technology and the network-access systems that Bill Duncan had procured to monitor the world's data net-works. Huge numbers of 'illegals' – computers that exceeded national and international regulations on process-ing power – had now started to appear on the networks in many parts of the world and the vigilantes did not intend to pass up this outstanding opportunity to map as many of them as they could.

'Governments must be wheeling out all their top-secret computer stuff to try to process information about the cloud,' Paul Levine had suggested. It seemed as if he was right.

At first the hackers had whooped with joy at having so many worthy adversaries and had set to work deploying their own advanced technology in an attempt to drive the illegals off the networks. But then Christine had struck a cautionary note.

'Maybe we should just let them do whatever it is they have to do,' she advised. 'After all, the cloud is only a few weeks away.'

The members of the small team glanced at each other. In recent weeks they had all been busy making their own sophisticated arrangements to take shelter during the period when the cloud would be passing over the planet. But they knew that there was one widely touted theory which predicted that there would be no atmosphere at all remaining after the cloud had passed.

'I agree,' said Paul Levine. 'We have to let them do everything they can, but this is our chance to log every one of the bastards. When this thing's over we'll have enough evidence to name and shame the lot of them.'

TWELVE

Public order first began to break down seriously when the cloud was still three weeks away from the Earth. As soon as the people could see it in the sky for themselves the threat suddenly seemed real. Even those who had paid scant attention to the news and to the experts' many dire warnings now began to panic.

During the day the sky took on a strange pearly luminescence as the cloud began to reflect more of the sun's gigantic energy output back towards the Earth. By night a major part of the night sky was totally obscured. As predicted, temperatures began to rise dramatically and the air became as thick and hot as soup.

Even in the world's most advanced societies – in America, Europe and parts of Asia and Australasia – mobs began roaming the streets. Governments were forced to put their carefully drafted emergency plans into operation.

Those police and military units who had been selected for 'social continuity assignment' (the euphemism used in the USA for those who had been allocated shelter spaces) were withdrawn from general duties and immediately redeployed to protect key government installations, communications facilities, airports and other sites considered vital to the continuance of national administrations. But there were large areas that went wholly unpoliced and unprotected from those who were intent on looting, robbing, fighting, raping and burning in mad, perverted or opportunistic responses to their own impotent fear.

The rich barricaded themselves away in their newly built shelters, protected by their heavily armed and highly paid guards. The middle classes made whatever small provision they could. Most households now had shelters, either within bricked-up and tightly sealed areas in their own buildings, or constructed in gardens, yards and even in the open countryside.

During the months in which the cloud's approach had been monitored, sufficient quantities of oxygen, food and water had been produced to theoretically provide most citizens of the developed world with supplies for a month or two, but these were very unevenly distributed. Widespread instances of robbery, bribery and armed force meant that many people were left with supplies for only a week or two.

Some governments managed to set up public shelters. In Sweden there were places for almost two million citizens who were admitted on a points system based on sex, age and skill sets. Women under thirty with medical or public-service qualifications found themselves at the top of the admission list. Men of retirement age or over were at the bottom.

In London the extensive underground rail network was readied for public occupation. Train services were halted, Tube station entrances were partially bricked up and planking was hurriedly laid across rails as the 253 miles of tunnels were adapted and converted to house up to six million people. It was announced that when this enormous shelter opened places would be allocated on a first come, first served basis. Many citizens began to camp outside the entrances, forming queues which stretched for miles. All who arrived seeking admission were expected to bring their own water and food for at least six weeks. Similar schemes were under way in Paris and Berlin, while Manhattan's subway system was also undergoing high-speed conversion to become a public shelter.

In the less-developed nations there was general chaos as the ruling elites grabbed as many supplies as possible for themselves and withdrew to their own hastily built bunkers. Among their abandoned populations there was a rising mortality toll as temperatures in equatorial regions of the globe soared to over forty degrees Celsius. Those strong enough to survive the cauldron of daytime then had to endure the panic-stricken mass violence that was unleashed in their communities at night.

The 6,000 occupants on board space stations and orbiting tourist hotels weighed up carefully whether they should remain in space for the period of the cloud's passing or whether they should return to Earth. As part of their normal security and survival measures most of the larger space stations and hotels had sufficient stocks of water, oxygen, fuel, food and other supplies to last for months. However, most visitors and residents feared that the space stations themselves might be blown out of orbit and they elected to return to Earth to be with their close family members and friends.

There was a similar response on the moon. In Luna City only a volunteer skeleton staff chose to remain behind to keep key systems running. At the Setiville complex all but two SETI researchers chose to return to Earth.

It was a time to be with family – if you had a family.

From the *New York Times* website, 26 September 2064

TEMPERATURE HITS 150F IN NEW YORK CITY

By RANDALL TATE, science correspondent

Many Districts Evacuated Tens of thousands of people have fled Manhattan and its suburbs over the last three weeks as temperatures have reached as high as 150 F (65°C). Many parts of downtown areas are virtually empty as residents and business owners have fled the city seeking relief from soaring temperatures.

'Over the next few days we can expect conditions to become even hotter,' said Spiro Larmar, a spokesman for the U.S. Meteorological Office. 'The space cloud is reflecting so much extra sun back towards the Earth that record temperatures are being recorded in all regions.'

'Strange to think we have that cold fish Otto Kramer to thank for this,' said Sally Burton, propping herself up on one elbow. She bent her head and gave Bill a small kiss on the side of his mouth.

Bill smiled and pulled her head back down for a longer embrace. 'How he managed to get me a seat out on that plane, I'll never know,' he said between kisses. 'But I'm sure glad I'm here.'

Sally and Bill were in bed, in Sally's government-supplied apartment in the Federal Plaza complex in Lower Manhattan. Dr Otto Kramer, technically Bill's senior officer in the Pentagon scientific hierarchy, had not only author-ized his request for a weekend's R&R, he had also found him a return seat on a military transport plane that was busy ferrying troops and equipment between Washington and New York.

'Take a long weekend off, Bill,' Kramer had insisted. 'Working too hard is counter-productive. You'll feel fresher after a break.'

How right he was, thought Bill as Sally lay contentedly in his arms. *I feel like a whole new person.*

There had been chaos at JFK Airport when Sally had met him and the federal agent had driven back into the city with her badge and gun prominently displayed on the dash-board. During the journey Sally had pointed out the shopfronts that had already been looted and they drove through whole districts that now seemed to be totally aban-doned. Hundreds of wrecked and burned-out vehicles lined the sides of the streets, heaped into grim piles by army bull-dozers.

Then they were halted by an army checkpoint that had been set up across the whole width of Broadway.

'Certain parts of the city are now no-go areas without a

government pass,' Sally explained as she waited for the soldiers to process her electronic ID. 'It's the only way of keeping some areas of the city intact.'

As soon as the CNS agent let Bill into her apartment, she warned him that they would be sensible to stay indoors for the duration of his visit.

'You'll just have to suffer my lousy cooking,' she said with a grin. 'There aren't many restaurants open – they can't keep their staff and they're almost certain to be robbed.'

Bill nodded as he lowered his shoulder bag onto a chair and for the first time wondered why on earth he had come to Manhattan to see this woman – a woman he hardly knew. Why hadn't he used his precious few days off to go back up to Boston to see Christine and his other friends?

'We're already getting our food supplies from government stores,' explained his host as she prepared pasta. 'I wouldn't really like to go outside to do food shopping now.'

Sally's apartment was fully air-conditioned, but even with the cooling dial turned up to maximum the temperature inside the three-room flat was still close to eighty degrees Fahrenheit. Outside the temperature was almost 130°.

They swapped cloud stories as they ate – snippets of information picked up from the TV, from Sally's colleagues, from Pentagon sources – and Bill talked about his growing certainty that he was close to finally extracting some meaning from the alien signals, and from the cloud's own interior transmissions.

Almost two bottles of wine had been drunk with the meal and Bill and Sally had unconsciously moved their chairs closer so that they could gently exchange small touches as they talked. Almost imperceptibly the touches became more frequent until they were finally almost holding hands. Then their senses started to take over from verbal exchanges until the moment came when Sally's face hovered tantalizingly close to Bill's. He leaned his head forward and kissed her. She kissed him back, and then they were entwined in each other's arms.

For several minutes they kissed, taking only short intervals for breath. Then Bill pulled his head back from Sally's and, with his arms still looped around her neck, stared deeply into her sparkling dark blue eyes.

'I want you, Agent Burton,' he told her.

'Do you indeed, Professor Duncan?' she asked with a single raised eyebrow. Then she kissed the tip of his nose.

'Very much,' said Bill, holding her gaze steadily.

'Well, on the strict understanding that our senses are over-stimulated because we are all in imminent danger from this space cloud,' she said, putting her palm on her chin, her index finger on her cheek, her elbow in her other hand, mocking the posture of thought. 'And in the wartime spirit of all couples facing separation and adversity . . .'

As she made her teasing speech Bill felt himself grinning back at her, hugely, stupidly.

'Yes . . . what?' he prompted.

'Well, do you want to come to bed?' she asked at last.

They had made love, slept, made love again, and had wakened to a bright, but unnaturally hot, Sunday morning in late September. They had made love one more time, taking their pleasure as if an executioner was waiting behind the door, and then Sally had gone to the kitchen and made them both coffee. Now the couple were luxuriating in the pleasurable afterglow of their lovemaking – and in a warm muggy heat that the air-conditioning couldn't fully control.

Suddenly the wall screen flickered to life.

'Sorry,' said Sally, reaching for the remote. 'I've programmed it to come on automatically for anything important.'

Then President's Jarvis's face filled the screen. He appeared to be in the Oval Office. Sally put the remote control down again and sat more upright in bed.

'My fellow Americans,' began the President gravely. 'The space cloud is now only twenty days away from colliding with the Earth. However, there may still be time to prevent the worst of its consequences. The day after tomorrow I will be visiting the United Nations to call on other nations to join the United States in launching a very large-scale nuclear attack against the cloud. It is our plan that the strike should involve the detonation of at least 20,000 nuclear warheads.'

Despite the heat in the small bedroom, Sally pulled the sheet up under her chin and shivered as she listened. Bill put his arm around her naked shoulders and drew her to him.

'The cloud is still eighteen million miles away from the Earth,' continued President Jarvis, 'And I am assured that there is no risk of nuclear contamination to our planet. If the strike is successful, however, it is likely to blast a hole in the cloud large enough for the Earth to pass through relatively unscathed.'

The camera now closed in on the President's face.

'While this strike is being organized, it is my grave but necessary duty to place this nation under martial law, starting at noon, today, Eastern Time. All authority will now be vested in national and local military forces, under my command. All state, regional and local administrations are suspended and, from now on, there will be a dusk-to-dawn curfew in all major cities. All civil aviation and all public road, rail and sea transportation will also be suspended from noon. All non-essential government buildings will be closed and I have also issued orders for all non-essential commercial premises to be closed.'

He paused and the camera zoomed in still further.

'I will speak with you again once the strike against the cloud has been carried out. Stay indoors, keep media access open and follow all advice that is broadcast by our civil defence units. God bless you all.'

The image on the screen faded and then switched to an anchor woman in a busy TV newsroom. Sally quickly muted the sound.

'I don't know how I should be feeling,' she said helplessly. 'A moment ago everything felt so wonderful, but now . . . Well, it feels so odd to think that there's a chance that everyone's going to die in a few weeks – including us.'

Bill nodded. Then he took a deep breath, and said something he had been preparing to say ever since he'd woken up that morning.

'Sally, they've offered me a place in a government shelter,' he told her in a rush. 'They think that my work on analysing the signals from inside the cloud is so important that they are relocating me with Jerome and all my equipment. I'm going to somewhere called Cancut Mountain in Arizona as soon as I return to DC – that's why Otto Kramer told me I could take this weekend break. It's so that they can pack up all my systems and fly them down to the bunker. It's where the President and his administration are evacuating to.'

Sally seemed about to interrupt, but Bill laid a gentle, hushing finger on her lips.

'I've been offered a non-parental family place in the shelter, Sal,' he continued. 'And that allows me to take one other person in with me – if that person is my partner. Will you come with me?'

Sally caught his hand in hers and kissed his fingertips.

'Thank you, Bill,' she said. Then she leaned across and kissed him gently on the lips. 'That is a wonderful, wonderful offer. But my job is here, and I'm really needed. The crazies are having a field day in the networks because there's so little law enforcement – there's no one but us.'

'Sally, it's the main US government shelter that I'm going to,' insisted Bill. 'It must be the best and safest facility in the world – the ultimate hot ticket. Surely you–'

'No, Bill,' she said firmly. 'As a federal agent I've already been allocated a place in the New York government shelter, the one beneath Central Park – and I'm really needed here.'

She saw the look of exasperation on his face.

'Look,' she explained. 'Just as it's your job to work on the analysis of the signals, so it's my job to prevent terrorists, freaks and those with a grudge against the state from exploiting the situation and making the networks unusable at a time of crisis. I've been ordered to stay at my desk and I intend to do just that.'

Ambassadors and delegates to the United Nations had been meeting in almost continuous session for three weeks. Scientists had been summoned from scores of nations to advise the national representatives on all matters to do with the approaching space cloud. Advice was plentiful but, in truth, nobody could know for certain how the vast pool of gas would affect the Earth as it came closer. The United States and some other governments had been trying to address the cloud directly by radioing continuous peace messages towards it and inviting it to make contact. But there had been no response – or no response that was recognizable as such to those on Earth.

Inside the UN facility daytime temperatures had

reached over 100 °F despite additional portable air-conditioning units being installed in all the chambers, meeting rooms and public areas. Delegates gathered in their shirt-sleeves, mopping their brows as they wrestled with all the possible options.

When the UN complex had been rebuilt in 2050 a large, bomb-proof bunker had been constructed below ground as a precaution against major terrorist incidents occurring in Manhattan. Now that same bunker had been extended and converted to provide semi-permanent accommodation for key members of the UN executive.

On the first Tuesday morning in October, representatives of 247 of the world's nations and over 2,000 of their assistants and advisers reconvened in the General Assembly chamber to hear an important speaker. President Maxwell T. Jarvis had arrived by helicopter and was about to make what many expected to be a vital address – a speech that would outline what the mighty United States military-industrial machine intended to do about the rapidly approaching cloud.

As he strode on stage, even President Jarvis was in shirt-sleeves.

'You all know why I am here,' he began. 'The cloud is only eighteen days away and we must act now.'

United Nations proceedings had rarely been popular TV viewing, but now millions of people, some of them already hunkered down inside their sealed home shelters, were watching. What was the miracle that the American president was going to propose? Many of the viewers had a touching, almost naive faith that the American government would have some wondrous master plan to announce.

President Jarvis nodded to an aide in the wings and suddenly the large screens behind the central dais lit to show a breathtakingly beautiful picture of the cloud. The image had been taken by a space probe from relatively close range and the audience in the chamber, and the TV viewers at home, saw massive columns of what looked like swirling smoke – funnels that were red, brown, green, blue and bright yellow.

'Now that the cloud is so much closer, we have been able to get much better data on its composition,' said the President. 'It's made up of a lot of different gases and other elements, some of which we are familiar with, others that we don't know, but we are now sure that it contains no harmful bacteria. And we also know that the cloud won't ignite or explode even if it were to collide with our atmosphere.'

As the President paused there was no sound from anywhere in the hall. Many delegates were sitting forward in their seats, anxious to hear what he was about to propose.

'I call on every nation which possesses nuclear warheads to join the United States in mounting one last, all-out attack on the cloud,' he told them. 'It is our intention to blow a hole in it large enough for this planet to be able to pass safely through.

'I want every national government to donate whatever functioning nuclear warheads it has – even the secret and classified weapons that have not been admitted to publicly – and, with the help of our friends from the European, Russian and Chinese space agencies, we will ferry each and every one of them into space, using every cargo transport and shuttle available. Even as I speak, a crash construction effort is proceeding under conditions of wartime emergency to build the delivery systems necessary for propelling the warheads into the centre of the cloud.'

Jarvis paused again and allowed his gaze to sweep around the assembly room.

'I repeat, I want you to volunteer every nuclear warhead above one megaton that you possess, *every single warhead* – this is no time for holding back. When we launch our strike, we will have just the one chance to create a gap in the cloud through which this planet may pass safely.'

From the *New York Times* website, 14 October 2064

CLOUD WILL OBSCURE SUN TOMORROW

By RANDALL TATE, science correspondent

Heavy Rainful Expected as Temperatures Plummet

Beginning at 2p.m. EST tomorrow, the space cloud now approaching the Earth is expected to begin what scientists predict will become an almost total eclipse of the sun.

Meteorologists forecast that as the sun's light is occluded, the recent high temperatures will start to fall rapidly, leading to rapid cloud formation followed by widespread heavy precipitation across the globe.

The yellow sands of Arizona had turned to mud. The normally wide-open blue sky above the desert was now filled with menacing dark clouds and torrential rainfall drenched the airfield, sweeping across it like enormous sheets of chain mail. The space cloud had now begun to obscure the sun and although it was still only mid-afternoon at Cancut Mountain, all was in a deep gloom.

'Straight down the stairs to bus Number 3, sir,' shouted a young Infantry Reservist with a clipboard. Professor Bill Duncan stepped out of the front fuselage door of a large army transport plane and into what felt like a wall of intense, wet heat. Global temperatures had now begun to fall once again, but it was still almost 130° Fahrenheit in the Arizona desert.

Bill pulled his black baseball cap firmly down over his eyes, but hot rain lashed under its peak as his gaze took in the scene of energetic activity going on all around. The large military airfield was located beside a mountain range with one central dominant peak which, Bill presumed, had to be Cancut Mountain itself.

Two broad parallel runways, at least two miles long, stretched away into the distance and both the airfield apron and the surrounding skies were filled with noisy aircraft. Despite the poor visibility a dozen large helicopters were either taking off or landing and more were hovering around the perimeter of the airport, waiting their turn to set down. Many of the twin-rotor choppers had large cargo payloads strung in huge container nets beneath their bellies.

Bill turned his face into the driving rain and, shielding his eyes, he saw that two more huge military transport planes had now descended from the dark, lowering clouds and were on final approach, their powerful wing-mounted landing lights brilliant in the rainswept gloom. Presumably they were carrying more people and cargo destined for this underground facility.

As Bill walked carefully down the wet and slippery aircraft steps he saw that beyond the airfield's wire-fence perimeter lay a highway. Both lanes were filled by a long one-way convoy of trucks, cars and buses that was slowly inching towards a large semicircular cavity in the mountain itself, an opening that looked like the entrance to an alpine road tunnel.

An armed National Guardsman in full wet-weather gear was waiting at the door of the bus. He checked Bill's personal ident and his newly issued electronic pass to enter the Cancut Mountain facility – the third such check that Bill had been subjected to since he had started his journey at Andrews Air Force base in Washington – and then nodded for him to board. Behind him followed a gaggle of people, mostly government employees Bill guessed, many of them with families and children. He seemed to be one of only a few travellers who were making the trip into the mountain alone.

The traffic waiting to enter the underground facility was so backed up that it took over an hour for the bus to make its one-mile journey through the mid-afternoon gloom. The vehicle was air-conditioned, but temperatures inside were still so hot that, like all the other passengers, Bill was thankful that water bottles had been provided on every seat.

While they waited in the long queue he had the chance to examine the adjacent vehicles in the convoy. There were other buses transporting more evacuees, but there were also trucks hauling containers whose markings and stickers indicated an extraordinarily wide range of goods and products – food, rubber, candles, bedding, office furniture, books, soap, computers, medical supplies, Bibles. Also waiting patiently in the twin slow-moving lanes to enter the mountain were dozens of military and commercial tankers, although whether they were carrying water, oil or some other liquid or gas Bill couldn't tell.

The torrential rain never ceased throughout the journey but the bright white glow from inside the mountain became steadily brighter. As the bus finally inched into the light, Bill saw that just inside the tunnel the mountain suddenly opened out into a giant cathedral-like cavern that had been carved inside the rock. Its builders had created a vast, brilliantly lit space with a dual-carriage central highway. On either side of the road were large diagonal parking bays for scores of buses, trucks, tankers and smaller vehicles. The main highway continued on through the middle of this gigantic cavern and then, in the far distance, split into two before re-entering tunnels bored into the rock.

Overhead were high steel walkways and gantries from which soldiers with walkie-talkies directed the traffic and oversaw operations on the ground below. As Bill's bus passed by the many occupied and busy parking bays, he saw that huge conveyor belts had been constructed to rapidly offload the contents of the containers and transport them directly into the interior of the mountain. Everywhere there were scenes of frantic activity as military personnel used fork-lift trucks and small mobile cranes to unload the vehicles and ferry the contents to the conveyor belts. Some bays with low concrete walls around them were fitted with large pipe fittings to which tanker drivers had attached hoses and which were busily pumping the vehicles' contents into some distant holding tanks.

Eventually, the coach carrying Bill and his fellow evacuees turned out of the slowly moving column and pulled into a vacant parking bay, alongside three other buses which were now disgorging their own contingents of arrivals.

'Welcome to Cancut Mountain,' said the army driver over the bus's PA system. 'Please report to the table outside that bears the initial of your family name. You will then be provided with transport which will take you to the residential sector of the facility.'

The first thing Bill noticed as he stepped off the bus was that it was cool inside the mountain. Instinctively he looked up to see if he could spot the giant fans or cooling ducts that were working this miracle, but his gaze was blinded by the hundreds of brilliant halogen lamps suspended from high above.

Bill saw that a row of reception booths had been set up – like delegate registration desks at a conference or convention – and above each one was a sign indicating which section of the alphabet they served. Bill hitched his backpack higher on his shoulder and joined the end of a long line waiting in front of the A-D registration desk.

In the middle distance, beyond the reception tables, he saw that there were two rail or tram tracks let into the floor of the cavern. As he watched, a low-slung, open-sided train – like those used for theme-park rides – glided silently up to a raised platform. Twenty or thirty arrivals who had already been through the reception process quickly boarded and the train pulled away to enter yet another tunnel which appeared to head on into the interior of the mountain.

'Professor Duncan?' A young, very attractive woman with a distinctive Southern accent had appeared at Bill's side.

'I'm Sue Snook, Professor Yates's personal assistant,' she announced. 'He sent me to collect you – to spare you all this.' She waved at the long parallel lines queuing in front of the reception desks.

'I'm very grateful,' Bill said as he turned out of the line and followed the smartly dressed PA. He realized that the White House dress code had not been altered just because the administration had relocated to the inside of a mountain.

Des Yates's assistant walked Bill around to the back of the registration table, had a quick word with one of the army men processing those arriving, and then led her charge towards the low platform used for boarding the shuttle trains.

'How long have you been here, inside this mountain?' asked Bill as they waited.

'I came down with Des – with Professor Yates – three days ago,' the PA told him. 'He's hoping to meet with you later this evening.'

More newly processed evacuees joined them on the wooden platform and then a shuttle glided silently alongside.

'This is quite some facility,' Bill said to the young woman as they began their journey into the mountainside.

The PA nodded. 'I think they first started building it almost a century ago – when the government of the time thought that a nuclear war might make the whole country uninhabitable. Every so often various administrations have extended it, added extra accommodation and so on. And, of course, over the last year there's been frantic development work going on here. Navy Seabees are still finishing some of the sectors.'

'How many people can this place house?' asked Bill as they entered a brightly lit tunnel.

'That was the first question I asked,' the assistant told

him with a smile. 'But I didn't get an answer – I think the information may be classified for some reason. But it must be quite a few thousand.'

'And how long can such a population be sustained?' asked Bill.

The PA laughed. 'That was also *my* second question. I was told that there's an underground spring in this mountain which produces 100,000 gallons of fresh hot water a day, which is why they built the bunker here in the first place. They make oxygen from that and they also recycle everything they can. The rumour is that there are sufficient non-reusable supplies to last us for at least twenty years.'

Bill saw a bright light ahead, and then the tunnel exited into another, much smaller, well-lit cavern, which was fitted out like a modern metro station. At the end of the platform a pair of stainless-steel escalators moved silently up and down, connecting to a higher level.

'I'll take you to your domestic quarters,' said Des Yates's PA as they stepped off the shuttle. 'After that I'll show you where they are setting up your new lab.'

THIRTEEN

It was as if a veil was being drawn over the sun. Hour by hour the amount of light and heat reaching the Earth was steadily reduced as the giant cloud of interstellar gas drew closer and came between the planet and its star, its source of life.

The effects were swift and dramatic. After abnormally high temperatures, the abrupt barometric plunge created what seemed to be one giant tropical maelstrom all over the globe. In reality, the world's surface was covered by a series of interlinked hurricanes, typhoons, cyclones and tornadoes.

As forecast, the traditional storm corridors suffered first – the Philippines, Japan, Mexico, Florida and America's Midwest. But within hours, giant vortexes of wind were smashing buildings, property and trees in normally cyclonically calm regions such as France, South Africa, Canada and Moscow. Thousands of people died and tens of thousands more were made homeless.

In those areas that escaped the unprecedented high winds, violent electrical storms rent the thick air as the atmosphere released all the energy that had been created during the rapid heating and cooling process. Nowhere was spared the climatic effects of the cloud's arrival.

Many of the largest storms gathered far out to sea. Huge

cyclonic depressions, larger than any that had formed on Earth since primordial times, created storm perimeters that stretched for thousands of miles. One storm in the north-east Pacific generated internal winds that were too fast to be measured by any of the meteorologists' instruments. Esti-mates put their velocity at over 300 m.p.h. and media commentators compared the giant storm to those seen on the surface of Jupiter.

Hurricane 67 as it was known – there were now too many storms for fancy naming ceremonies – came ashore all along the length of the California coastline. In the south of the state, shrieking gales overturned delivery vehicles, blew trains off their rails, flung parked wide-body jets across the apron of LAX Airport, knocked trees into cars, ripped roofs off houses and tore windows out of high-rise build-ings. Sixty-two large passenger and cargo vessels were lifted from the ocean and deposited on land, and coastal break-waters were smashed by enormous waves which came ashore as high as six-storey buildings. The Greater Los Angeles basin was flooded to a depth of eleven feet and an estimated 500,000 people died, mostly citizens who were drowned in their home shelters.

In the United Kingdom, 123 square miles of London were flooded following a storm which uprooted almost every tree in southern England. Low-lying parts of the cap-ital and its surrounding area were submerged from Battersea in the west to the Isle of Sheppey in the east. Power was lost throughout the region and initial reports put the death toll at over 60,000.

Similar incidents occurred in almost every country. In France, Normandy, Brittany, the whole of the Loire Valley and most of the Dordogne were lost beneath the flood waters. In Asia, large parts of southern India, most of

Bangladesh and vast swathes of China disappeared beneath the torrents. Millions of people died and initial reports suggested that as many as 200 million people had been made homeless.

'You should see this place,' Bill Duncan enthused. 'It's absolutely huge, more like a city than a bunker. There are shops, restaurants, gyms and swimming pools and it even has a repository which houses the DNA records of all major species on the planet.'

'It sounds amazing,' Sally agreed, as she gazed back at the image of her recent lover. 'You mean they've actually made a back-up of all the life forms on Earth?'

The federal agent was at her desk on the thirty-first floor of the Manhattan headquarters of the US Department of Computer and Network Security. Most of the agency's administration staff had already been released from their posts and the many rows of cubicles on the main floor beyond her office were now unoccupied. Outside, all was in gloom and torrential rain was sluicing down the high windows.

'Well, most of them, just in case of disaster,' said Bill. 'Of course, I've only been shown a small part of this complex. But they must have been preparing for this for many years. Absolutely everything you could wish for is here.'

'Have you seen Des Yates yet?' asked Sally. She had taken Bill's call, even though she had been busily engaged in writing an urgently required summary of current network crime levels for her boss in Washington – or wherever he had relocated to.

'No, not yet,' Bill told her. 'I've been busy getting Jerome's network back up and running again, working with Otto Kramer. Apparently Des is shut away with the President and the NASA people while they are preparing for this last-ditch nuclear strike.'

'God, yes, that's supposed to happen tomorrow, isn't it?' said Sally. 'I have completely lost track – I've been trying to finish an urgent report.'

'Look, Sally,' said Bill, suddenly serious. 'There are still a few military flights due to come down to Cancut Mountain from New York. And there's still a place being held for you here. I can't bear the thought of you being in some grim federal shelter under Central Park when you could be down here with me. What if the worst happens?'

'No, no, my place is here,' insisted Sally. 'But I'm pleased that you're safe. Now, I've got to get back to work.'

'Yeah, me too,' sighed Bill.

Every nation in the world that possessed nuclear warheads raided their armouries for weapons with a payload of more than a megaton. Many of these had been part of secret stocks that were held covertly and in defiance of international treaties and non-proliferation agreements. Four Central African nations, all of them states that had never previously admitted to possessing such weapons, surprised the United Nations, community by offering multiple warheads. And Japan, the nation that had suffered the only hostile use of nuclear weapons during wartime and had publicly forsworn the development of such armaments, shocked the international community by contributing no fewer than 123 nuclear warheads of very advanced design.

All the nuclear devices donated were immediately flown under heavy security to space-shuttle launch sites in either Florida, Beijing or Kazakhstan. There, expert armourers and nuclear weapons engineers worked feverishly to make the many diverse firing and timing systems compatible with a reciprocal radio-controlled central command system.

In space, the components of the Asteroid Defense Network that had not already been deployed in the earlier strike against the cloud were reprogrammed to fly back in the direction of the Earth–sun axis. This was so that they would arrive in the centre of the cloud in synchronization with the many warheads that would be launched from Earth orbit and which could blast off from the surface of the planet itself.

As President Jarvis had promised, crude warhead delivery-rockets had been hurriedly constructed both on Earth and in space under conditions that resembled those of a wartime emergency building programme. By a combination of adapting existing rocket delivery systems and the crash construction of new ones, the combined military powers of the world managed to assemble a fleet of 416 space vehicles that together were able to carry 48,145 nuclear warheads into the centre of the cloud. The total nuclear payload was eight-point-two gigatons and the battery even contained six prototype 'Hafnium' warheads that the United States had been developing secretly. These gamma-ray bombs were each expected to deliver a blast of fifty megatons, equivalent to over 3,000 times the power of the original atomic bombs that were dropped on Hiroshima and Nagasaki at the end of the Second World War.

At eleven a.m. on Tuesday, 4 November (Eastern Time), President Maxwell T. Jarvis, acting on behalf of the UN, gave the order for the entire nuclear payload of the Earth's combined national armouries to be launched against the space cloud. In a series of carefully synchronized launches, rockets, shuttles and cargo spacecraft began to depart from Earth orbit, from surface launch sites and from deep-space locations, The aim was that they should rendezvous in a closely controlled manner inside the cloud. It was now only nine million kilometres away from the Earth and the longest missile flight would take only thirty-six hours.

Observers gazing upwards from the surface of the Earth would see nothing of the attack itself, nor of its results. The entire planet was shrouded in thick rain clouds and the globe was being lashed by powerful storms. All optical Earth-based astronomy was useless, but orbiting telescopes and those parked at deep-space locations were all able to send clear pictures back to the relocated Situation Room that had been set up inside the Cancut Mountain facility.

Desmond Yates, the President, his Chief of Staff, a gaggle of generals, representatives from NASA, members of the Cloud EXCOM and a score of White House aides had crowded into the new Situation Room, a space that would be better described as a 'Situation Theatre', deep inside the vast mountain bunker. They were meeting to observe the effects of the combined nuclear strike on the space cloud.

Having been given the opportunity of recreating the President's control and command facility afresh, a panel of architects and information designers from all the agencies involved had created an amphitheatre-style crisis-management centre with three adjoining conference suites.

The main room's horseshoe-shaped meeting table had places for twenty-six and had been built facing a huge vertical laser display screen, two large holographic display rings and a battery of 3-D high-definition video screens that were suspended from the ceiling and angled downwards for viewing ease.

As the President and his advisers waited for the moment

of the nuclear strike to arrive, each of the screens was displaying images of the cloud that were taken from varying locations in space. The digital counter ticked down towards the first planned detonation and silence fell among those who were seated around the curved table. All present knew that this attack was going to be the last chance to prevent the worst effects of the giant space cloud's collision with the Earth.

'Five, four, three, two, one,' announced an automated voice as the final part of the countdown was reached.

The viewers in the Situation Room saw a pinpoint of light flare from within the multicoloured cloud. It was followed by a dense cluster of other flashes which looked like fireworks going off inside a fog bank. Then the number of explosions became so great that it seemed as if a single giant ball of fire was raging inside the cloud. As they watched, this ball of light became brighter and brighter, like a sun breaking through rain clouds, until finally the telescopes and the optical systems transmitting the images became nothing but pure white-outs.

'Well, it looks like we blew one hell of a hole in it,' said Des Yates tentatively after the members of the meeting had been staring at white screens for thirty or forty seconds.

Then, as the sequence of distant nuclear explosions came to an end, the optical systems began to dim once more and visible images re-emerged. But the giant cloud looked exactly as it had before.

Des Yates glanced from screen to screen. Each was displaying different images of the cloud, some captured from relatively close to it, others from much further out in space.

'We won't know for sure how we have affected the cloud's internal density until we have completed laser measurements,' Yates told the meeting. 'That will take a few hours.'

'Well, it looks damn near the same to me,' said the President. 'We've thrown everything we have at it – and it looks completely unscathed.'

From the *New York Times* website, 4 November 2064

NUCLEAR STRIKE FAILS TO CREATE 'SAFETY WINDOW' FOR EARTH

By RANDALL TATE, science correspondent

Cloud Due to Hit in 8 Days – Sun 20% Obscured

The all-out nuclear strike mounted by the world's combined military forces has failed to disperse sufficient of the oncoming cloud of space gas to create a 'window' through which the Earth can pass safely.

A Pentagon spokesman confirmed yesterday that the equivalent of over 8.2 gigatons of explosive were detonated inside the centre of the cloud but, after the initial creation of a vacuum half a million miles across, the cloud has now reformed to its original density. At its present speed, the outer margins of the cloud will collide with Earth's upper atmosphere in eight days.

Just as the White House and National Security Council designers had taken the opportunity to build an improved Situation Room inside Cancut Mountain, so the Pentagon had built an upgraded version of the facility known as the VWC – the Virtual Warfare Centre.

Necessarily smaller than the huge 'shopping mall' facility that had been constructed beneath Washington, the emergency VWC in Cancut Mountain was a large black room that was itself entirely virtual. Every wall, ceiling and floor space was built from a flexible material that doubled as a 2-D and 3-D high-definition screen.

Approved users of the facility were able to create their own viewing and working space by drawing a fingertip over the room's surfaces so as to create as many different windows into the networks and virtual simulations as required. From dozens of long, thin floor-slots shimmering laser screens could shoot upwards to the ceiling, each capable of displaying a flat 2-D picture or a 3-D image that provided users with 'tactility feedback', a technique that caused sensations to be transmitted via specially equipped gloves. For those who needed to manipulate and adjust them, these virtual images could be 'felt' and 'handled'.

As Desmond Yates entered the dimly lit warfare command centre he glanced around him. Bill Duncan was standing in the middle of a cluster of shimmering, floor-to-ceiling laser screens, each displaying what looked like a galaxy of mathematical formulae, partial formulae and weird hieroglyphs. Standing beside Bill, in a 3-D virtual image so 'solid' that it was hard to tell it was artificial, stood Jerome, pointing at one of the screens as the two of them conferred.

'Your message said this was important,' said Yates as he crossed the room. 'I came as soon as I could get away – but it's just one meeting after another at the moment.'

Bill nodded. 'Well, I'm not sure you're going to like this,' he began. 'But we have found a strong correlation between your original signals from the planet Iso and the transmissions that were recorded from inside the cloud. Both are six-point-one billion times faster than the fastest transmission speed we can currently achieve and both show precisely the same modulation characteristics, boundary marks and data blocking. Both signals also have a median tonic range that is fifty-seven octaves below the lowest threshold of human hearing.'

Des Yates went pale as he listened to the list of similarities between the transmissions.

'You're telling me that the signals are identical?' he asked.

'Identical,' confirmed Jerome, glancing from Bill to the Presidential adviser.

'Although the content remains just as impenetrable in both,' added Bill. 'We're still getting fragments of math and graphic operators, but nothing that adds up to any coherent expression.'

Yates shook his head. 'But this suggests that the signals must have come from the cloud all along, doesn't it?' he said in anguish. 'Perhaps they never did have anything to do with the planet Iso.'

Bill Duncan reached out and laid a hand on Yates's shoulder. He was already beginning to think of this man as a friend and he realized that this latest revelation would cast the most horrendous doubt on the validity of his lifetime's work.

'Everybody was sure that those signals came from Iso,' Bill said, groping for words of consolation.

'Now, everyone, we're transmitting this at maximum power,' Sir Charles Hodgeson told his assembled followers.

'Stare straight into the camera lens and remember when to come in.'

The creator of many science-fiction universes and the dictator of his own small island fiefdom in the Great Barrier Reef was addressing the 120 young people who had chosen to stay with their guru rather than return to their homes at this time of crisis. They were gathered in the main dining and assembly hall that Hodgeson had designed to serve as the central meeting point of his hastily built shelter. Outside, a Force Nine hurricane was lashing the island, uprooting trees, flattening buildings and killing any small creatures who were caught out in the open. Giant waves were pounding the beaches.

He turned his back on the assembled throng, nodded to the audio-visual technician and waited for the transmission light to come on.

'We send greetings from the planet Earth,' intoned Hodgeson sonorously as soon as the light switched to red. 'We are sending this message to the entity within the cloud of gas that is now approaching this planet. We, the people of Earth, wish you no harm. Come in peace.'

As he spoke the last sentence, the tortoise-necked guru raised his arms slowly, as if to heaven. As his words died away, the assembled throng behind him repeated, 'Come in peace. Come in peace.'

Hodgeson waited for the echoes of the powerful chant to die away, then he crossed his arms diagonally over his chest.

'We apologize for the explosive weapons that our foolish leaders have sent against you,' he continued, his voice ringing out loud and strong from his wizened frame. 'But these puny armaments are now exhausted. Come in peace.'

As Hodgeson raised his arms again his followers took

their cue and, in a deep-throated roar, chanted in unison, 'Come in peace. Come in peace.'

'Sir Charles?' It was the audio-visual technician calling from where he was seated at a small broadcast console. 'There's a problem.'

The ancient guru spun round to face the man who had so rudely interrupted his broadcast.

'We're off air,' said the AV engineer. 'The transmission masts must have been torn away by the storm.'

Hodgeson stared at the man, his face working in fury. Then he spun back to face his followers.

'Everybody. Get outside now and get those masts up again. There's no time to lose.'

'Sir Charles, the winds outside are blowing at over a hundred and fifty miles an hour,' protested the AV technician, rising to his feet. 'We'll have to wait until the storm passes.'

'OUTSIDE NOW!' shouted the centenarian guru to his followers. 'GET THOSE MASTS UP AGAIN *NOW!*'

From the *New York Times* website, 12 November 2064

<u>24 HOURS TILL CLOUD STRIKES</u>

By RANDALL TATE, science correspondent

Rain Turns to Hail and Snow

The U.S. Meteorological Office reports that the approaching cloud of space gas is now preventing over 60% of the sun's normal output from reaching the surface of the Earth. It will collide with the Earth's atmosphere at 4.37 EST tomorrow.

As temperatures have fallen from their extreme highs of recent weeks, the torrential rains experienced all over the world are now starting to turn to sleet, hail and snow. The Federal Emergency Management Agency warns all citizens to remain indoors and not to travel unless absolutely necessary.

Sally Burton stood at the window of her office on the thirty-first floor of the CNS building in Manhattan. Outside, the sleet that had been falling continuously for two days was beginning to turn to thick snow. All was in a deep and pervasive gloom and the agent could hardly see across Federal Plaza to where some lights were still burning in other government buildings. In recent hours more and more floors had started to go dark as the various agencies and departments allowed increasing numbers of staff to abandon their posts for the safety of the bunkers.

In Sally's own office, only she and five others were still monitoring the networks but on-line activity had not abated. As humans withdrew from the physical world all their contacts and activities moved into the networks. The criminals, child-pornpeddlers, cyber-terrorists and confidence tricksters were still pursuing their warped desires and plying their criminal trades as if determined to make the most of the time left before disaster struck.

Her communicator rang, cutting into her short reverie.

'Hey, Sal,' said Bill Duncan. 'How are things in New York?'

'Very white,' Sally told him, choosing not to select visual. 'We've got very heavy snowfall now. I can hardly see across the square.'

'When are you going to the shelter?' Bill asked abruptly.

'I'm not sure,' she told him. 'Things are still crazy in the networks.'

'Sal, you've *got* to get to safety before the cloud hits,' urged Bill. 'Nobody knows for sure what's going to happen. I want to know you're in a shelter before it gets here.'

The CNS agent sat back down at her desk and sighed heavily. 'Bill, I know that we're fond of each other. But we haven't really had long enough together to develop the sort of relationship that gives you the right to order me about.'

Sally heard the silence as her blow hit home and she immediately regretted being so harsh.

'I'm sorry,' she said quickly. 'I've been working very long hours – I'm completely on edge.'

'Me too,' said Bill. 'And what you said is true: you're right. I don't have any right to ask you to do anything. It's just that all the time I'm working with Jerome to try to make some sense out of these goddam signals, I keep worrying about you. You already mean a lot to me, Sally.'

She glanced out at the snow flurries whirling against her window and she suddenly wondered if she would ever see this man again.

'Let's do visual,' she said, touching the appropriate icon on her communicator.

God, he looks tired too, Sally thought as Bill's image appeared on her wall screen. He was wearing a black T-shirt and was sitting on the edge of a narrow bed in a small white room that had no windows. He looked as if he hadn't shaved in a week.

'They now want us to work alongside the techies, just to keep the networks open,' she explained. 'I don't know for how long.'

'I understand,' Bill said with a shrug. 'But keep me in the loop, OK?'

'Of course I will,' Sally told him, feeling as if she wanted to reach out and touch his image.

FOURTEEN

At 21.52 GMT on Thursday, 11 November, the leading edge of the high-velocity space cloud began to collide with the Earth's outer atmosphere – precisely as predicted and precisely on schedule.

The cloud was travelling at over 200,000 kilometres an hour and although its outer regions were very thin and had little density, the friction caused by the collision of gas particles was so great that a bright crimson glow immediately pervaded the half of the Earth's ionosphere that was directly in the cloud's path.

On the dark and frozen planet down below almost every human being and many of their domesticated animals were taking whatever shelter they could find. For a wealthy minority of the world's population the sealed refuges they had built were almost as comfortable as their normal living accommodation had been. But for most humans it was a case of finding whatever protection they could against the biting cold, the driving blizzards and the other unknown horrors or blights that the space cloud was about to impose upon the globe. Most of the people who had gone to ground were now reduced to helplessly watching their fate unfold on television.

It was only when the Earth and the giant pool of interstellar space gas were seen in close proximity, and from a distance, that the true scale of the cloud's enormous size could be properly appreciated. Even as the leading edge of the cloud struck the Earth's atmosphere, its tail was only just leaving the sun.

'We look like a pea in the path of a tidal wave,' said Maxwell Jarvis in awe as he stared at the holographic image of the Earth and its unwelcome visitor.

The President and the members of the Cloud EXCOM were meeting in the Situation Room inside Cancut Mountain, Arizona, and the hologram was being projected as a large and realistic model in the main holo-theatre. Although many of Earth's orbiting satellites had now been either blown out of position or destroyed, and despite the cloud's powerful magnetic field disrupting Earth's outgoing radio signals, images captured by telescopes in deep space were still being received on the ground. These pictures were being amalgamated and morphed into powerful three-dimensional simulations that gave those present an almost godlike view of happenings within the local region of the solar system

'Look at that bright red glow in the Earth's upper atmosphere,' exclaimed Des Yates, also in awe, even though he was one of the few members of the party who had an astronomer's understanding of the physics involved. 'We knew it would cause friction as the gases heat up, but that is stupendous.'

'It's not going to explode, is it?' demanded President Jarvis sharply. The nerves of all those who were meeting in the Situation Room were on edge, extremely so. These cloud-monitoring meetings had been continuing daily – and nightly – for the last few weeks.

'We're pretty sure not, sir,' Des Yates told him quickly.

'If we couldn't get the gas to ignite with eight-point-two gigatons of nuclear weapons, it's not likely to do so now.'

The President nodded and turned to an aide. 'Let's see what the news channels are saying.'

Immediately a score of large flat screens suspended around and above the 3-D holo-theatre lit with video feeds that were streaming in from television broadcasts all around the world.

Des Yates looked up at one screen that was showing a snowbound city scene with the caption, *Calcutta*. As the Presidential adviser focused on the screen the clever technology in the Situation Room automatically sensed his gaze and delivered acoustically guided sound to his ears only. The others around the curved table were looking at different screens and they too were able to hear the commentary in which they were interested while the audio components of all other broadcasts were blanked.

As Yates watched he saw a dim red glow start to appear on the surface of the snow in Calcutta. Then he swivelled in his high-backed chair and switched his gaze to a screen displaying a shot of a frozen Sydney Harbour. The famous bridge could still be made out clearly through the steady snowfall, but the distinctive armadillo shape of the old Opera House was now just one immense white blob. As the camera slowly panned Yates saw that the entire harbour was frozen and the ice on its surface was also starting to take on a deep red glow.

'Now, stick together,' ordered Charles Hodgeson. 'We don't want to be outside for more than a few minutes.'

The top-level exit from the shelter opened onto the central ridge of Orpheus Island. Immediately Hodgeson and his half-dozen specially chosen acolytes saw that the snow-covered atoll and the lowering clouds overhead were all bathed in a deep red glow. But snow was no longer falling and the high winds had abated.

'Come on,' said Hodgeson eagerly as he led the way up a small path that had been cleared of snow. 'It's always possible that our visitor will respond to a personal appeal.'

All members of the party were dressed in Arctic survival suits and all wore thick perspex masks to protect their eyes. Once on top of the central ridge, Hodgeson stood and extended his arms sideways. His followers stood in a line on either side of him and did likewise, joining hands to form a small human chain.

'We bid you welcome,' shouted Hodgeson into the still air, his breath coming out of his small, wiry body as a stream of mist.

'We bid you welcome,' echoed the four men and one woman who had been selected to join in this attempt to make direct personal contact.

'We mean you no harm,' Hodgeson shouted at the top of his voice towards the red-tinged snow clouds. 'Please tell us what you want. But come in peace.'

'Come in peace,' shouted the supporting chorus.

Suddenly two snowmobiles crested the island's main ridge and made directly for where the little party stood.

The rider of the lead vehicle drew up close to Hodgeson and switched off his engine.

'All the transmitters are operational once more, Sir Charles,' he reported. 'We've doubled up on the stays so they won't come down again.'

Hodgeson gazed up at the thick red clouds as if hoping for some sort of response.

'Very good,' he said eventually, banging his thick gloves

together to warm up his hands. 'Let's get back inside and resume our transmissions.'

Three days after the leading edge of the space cloud first made contact with the Earth's atmosphere, Des Yates was still in the Situation Room staring at a holographic image of the cloud's eccentric trajectory across outer space and through the solar system.

The official meeting of the Cloud EXCOM had broken up six hours after the collision had first begun. The images that were sent back from the deep-space telescopes showed that the cloud had now engulfed the planet completely. Remotely operated TV cameras positioned around the surface of the globe revealed that by day all of the snowy and frozen outside world was bathed in a deep red gloom. By night the heat produced by the collision of high-speed particles with the upper ionosphere produced a neon-blue glow, almost like the output from an ultraviolet lamp.

It seemed that there was nothing that the Cloud EXCOM members could do except watch TV reports being beamed from news centres which were themselves based in underground facilities dotted around the world.

The President, his executive team and their advisers were now elsewhere in the Cancut Mountain facility, busily engaged in managing the crisis that was unfolding across the USA and the rest of the world. All the USA's shelters in overseas embassies, consulates and foreign government offices needed to be coordinated and debriefed and there were over 400 government-run underground facilities in the homeland to be managed.

Senior Pentagon officers had to oversee the rotation of the select military units that had been left above ground to continue policing sensitive locations across the nation.

There were also massive logistical challenges as supplies were moved around the country, all by air. A number of key airports were being kept open by hard-working army and navy engineers, even though temperatures were beginning to fall close to the lowest operational limits of some large jets.

In each city, a few public hospitals had created sealed accommodation units to continue treating those who were injured or suffering from hypothermia. But American TV reports suggested that citizens were now starting to die in their thousands – mainly as the result of flooding or from exposure to the extreme cold. There was a great deal to keep the President and his executive staff busy.

But Des Yates had remained in the Situation Room almost continuously. He was sure that if he could accurately model the forces that were acting on the cloud's trajectory and its variable velocity he would be able to learn more about its internal physics. As a result, he might gain some clue that would be helpful in dealing with the crisis.

With the assistance of the Situation Room Director, a rotating cluster of keen duty officers and specialist input from half a dozen senior NASA astrophysicists, he had mapped the gravity force fields through which the cloud had travelled. He had created long strings of equations to feed into the computers, trying to determine what forces might be affecting the cloud and directing its course and speed. In doing so, he hoped to arrive at an estimate of what level of propulsive energy, if any, the cloud might be generating internally.

But it appeared that the cloud's behaviour had been wholly erratic. For the first few months of its approach towards the solar system it had obeyed the laws of local gravity precisely, but then it seemed as if it had started reacting to some other force, an unknown one.

Yates and his small team had built complex models of solar-wind emissions and had then run simulations of a similar-sized space cloud approaching the solar system. They had run the model with both gravity and solar wind modelled, then with just one of the forces. Neither simulation produced a trajectory that matched the course which the actual cloud had taken. Then Yates thought he should model light itself, in case for some reason the cloud was light-sensitive. That didn't help either. Then he decided to model the thermal energy that is found throughout the solar system and beyond. That small additional calculation alone had taken twenty-eight hours to create and run.

Then one of the NASA scientists had suggested that they should model the huge but very weak gravity waves that sweep through the galaxy from time to time. That involved digging out all the data from gravity-wave observations that had been carried out over the last two years and then creating a whole new set of equations so that the model could take in the effects of such giant ripples in space. Then they had to model local gravity, solar wind, light, thermal energy and gravity waves together, and in varying proportions. In total their modelling efforts had taken almost three days and Yates knew that he was now close to dropping from fatigue.

'How are you doing in here, Des?' called a voice from within the blackness outside the brightly lit holo-theatre.

Yates straightened up, massaged his lower back with both hands and shook his head wearily as Bill Duncan stepped into the light.

'Getting nowhere, fast,' he told the computer psychologist. 'You?'

'The same,' admitted Bill. 'It feels as though I'm almost there, but I'm missing something important. If only I had more processing power – there's just too much data to deal with.'

Yates nodded and yawned. 'Well, I've tried everything,' he said, reaching for his jacket. 'Gravity, solar wind, visible light, thermal energy – even gravity waves. Nothing can explain the peculiar trajectory this darn thing came in on, nor its changes in velocity. Anyway, I've had it. I'm going to call it a night, or day, or whatever the hell it is outside.'

'Have you tried modelling radio waves?' asked Bill.

Yates was pulling on his jacket as the computer scientist spoke. He froze halfway, with only one arm in a sleeve.

'Radio,' he repeated. 'But radio hardly has any force at all, does it?' Then he took his arm out of his jacket sleeve. 'You're right, though, we *should* have modelled the radio spectrum!'

'How are the networks holding up?' asked Mort Jaffe, speaking on a secure line from the safety of CNS's own agency bunker just outside Washington DC.

'They're still functioning OK, sir, but activity is rising so fast that I can't do any more than monitor the traffic,' Sally Burton told her boss. 'There's a lot of bad stuff going down, but I can't track it all on my own.'

'Well, they're all going to crawl out of the woodwork now,' said Jaffe. 'All support systems still OK in the office?'

'We've still got heat and light, sir,' confirmed the agent. 'But the air seems a little thin sometimes.'

'You're doing a great job,' said Jaffe. 'Now, what I want you to do is to shut down every system in the building except your own personal node. Got that?'

'Of course, sir,' she responded.

'I'll be in touch again once you've done that so that I can release you from your post. You can then get up to Central Park before it gets too bad. OK?'

'Yes, thank you, sir,' said Agent Burton as she closed the connection.

She rose from her desk.

Before it gets too bad, she thought as she gazed out at the eerie scene of a dark snowbound Federal Plaza. The square was bathed in a deep red gloom and beyond she could see the huge snowdrifts that had been piled up high across Broadway. In the other direction, drifts had long since closed Thomas Street. Now there were very few lights burning in the surrounding government buildings. Even the large FBI block was completely dark.

Sally tilted her head downwards at an acute angle and looked towards the ground. Nothing was moving and the snow down below looked very deep.

'That had better be soon, Mort,' she said out loud.

'It's radio-sensitive!' yelled Des Yates excitedly. 'In fact, it's specifically attracted to artificial radio signals, to man-made signals. Just look at it go!'

They had now run the new simulation six times, and every time the computer model of the cloud moved in exactly the same way and on the same path as the actual space cloud had done.

'Look, when we first noticed the cloud it was heading directly for the Earth, the main source of artificial radio signals in this region of the galaxy,' said Yates, repeating himself for the umpteenth time. 'Then, when the Martian colony started to gear up to launch the first nuclear attack, the cloud was attracted to all those powerful radio emissions they were pumping out, because Mars was so much closer to the cloud than we were.'

Des Yates and Bill Duncan were once more back in the Situation Room. As soon as Bill had suggested modelling radio waves, Yates had asked the NASA assistants to begin to create a model of all of the known radio transmissions in the solar system, and in the area of deep space immediately beyond.

'This is going to take hours and hours to prep, Professor,' one of the ever-helpful duty officers had warned.

'OK, let's both grab some rest, Bill,' Yates had told his new research colleague. 'Then we'll be better prepared to see if your idea produces any results.'

They had met back in the Situation Room after only six hours' sleep, but both men felt immensely refreshed.

'I really ought to get back to my own work on the cloud's internal radio signals,' said Bill reluctantly, wanting to remain with the astronomers to see whether there was any value in his idea.

'Stay and see the first few runs,' suggested Yates. 'If we don't get anything quickly it will rapidly become boring because then we'll have to start combining data from all of the other possible forces.'

But Bill's idea had provided a quick breakthrough, even though this was only achieved after the enormous amount of work that had gone into building the simulation. The NASA astronomers had drafted in help from other science staff sheltering within the Cancut facility. They had entered data into the computer simulation which represented the vast radio outpourings from the sun, the enormous artificial radio output from the Earth, the radio emissions from orbiting satellites and space stations, from deep-space telescopes, probes and spacecraft and from the colonies on the moon and, as had once been, on Mars.

Their first run had been inconclusive, with the simulated cloud veering sharply towards the sun as soon as it reached the outer boundaries of the solar system.

'OK, eliminate the sun's natural radio output,' said Yates. 'And let's run the model again.'

This time the holographic grey mass of the simulated cloud approached the 3-D model of the solar system precisely in the same trajectory, as marked by a red line, that the real cloud had followed.

Then, at just the same point, the simulated cloud had changed direction and headed directly for Mars.

Yates had then ordered the simulation to be halted. He asked for data on the radio output from Mars and its artificial satellites to be displayed within the simulation.

'Look, it changed course for Mars as soon as their radio output shot up,' Yates had observed excitedly the first time he saw the simulation. 'And even the little kinks in its trajectory reflect the radio output of nearby radio telescopes. Magnificent!'

As the simulation had continued its run all present watched with fascination as the 3-D model of the cloud followed precisely the red line that indicated the actual cloud's collision with Mars, its sling-shot orbit around the sun and then its direct approach towards Earth.

'It seems to be responsive both to gravity *and* to modulated radio signals,' said Yates now, after they had run the simulation a dozen more times. 'Specifically, it is attracted to *artificial* radio signals – and we're still sending out so much radio and TV traffic that the Earth is lit up like a goddam Christmas tree!'

*

Within the hermetically sealed offices of the *New York Times*, the process of news gathering and reporting was continuing. But there was a severe shortage of in-field reporters and TV crews and there were almost no studio guests available to make contributions. Journalists were often reduced to interviewing other journalists as if they were experts – but there was nothing new in that.

The *NYT* management had assigned science correspondent Randall Tate to provide a daily half-hour TV update on the cloud's progress and on conditions around the globe, a bulletin which could be looped to repeat automatically every two hours. The senior anchorman who would previously have been fronting such a broadcast had decamped with his much younger wife and their baby to a luxury underground shelter which had been built by private enterprise in Northern Florida.

But Tate was nothing if not inventive. Working with his producer he edited his own commentary, and the views of his colleagues, together with the pictures that were continuing to stream in from all over the world.

Outside, temperatures were still dropping rapidly as less and less of the sun's warmth managed to penetrate the mass of the space cloud that was now engulfing the globe. Snow was still falling steadily everywhere, rivers had become solid ice and even the oceans were starting to freeze over.

As predicted, there had been a sudden increase in the number of seismic events being recorded. Despite its relatively thin density, the cloud's gravitational mass was already distorting and disrupting the delicate equilibrium of the Earth's crust and mantle. Major earthquakes had shaken cities as far apart as Seattle and Auckland, and undersea earthquakes had produced vast tsunami waves which, had it not been for the moderating effects of the surface ice on

the oceans, would have devastated coastlines from Japan to
Chile. Volcanoes were also erupting, all along the line of the
world's so-called 'Ring of Fire', that long chain of active volcanoes which circled the Pacific Rim. But most of the
world's population had already taken shelter and these
eruptions claimed far fewer human lives than they would
have done under normal conditions.

But the world's data networks – laser, cable, radio,
microwave and landline – were still functioning well. Their
original designs were over a century old, but they had been
built to withstand nuclear strikes.

'This is Randall Tate in the *New York Times* Television
Centre,' read the science correspondent as he began to
record his day's broadcast. 'The US Meteorological Office
reports that the world's atmosphere is beginning to lose
some of its oxygen content. In many parts of the world unassisted breathing at sea level has become the equivalent
of trying to breathe at an altitude of 10,000 feet. The Met
scientists advise everybody to stay indoors and keep respi-
rators to hand.'

The producer cut in pictures that had just been received
from a San Francisco TV outlet. The feed showed images
of a snowbound city, but smoke could be seen rising from
its hilly centre.

'San Francisco has been hit by a second earthquake in
six days,' read Tate. 'The quake measured Magnitude Six on
the Richter scale but with all normal emergency services
suspended and many citizens already sheltering, there is no
information available about casualties. Major earthquakes
have also been reported in Mexico City and Istanbul.'

The incoming images now switched to a group of small
huts in a snowbound savannah.

'In Africa, millions of people are starting to die from

pneumonia, hypothermia, frostbite and starvation. In many of the poorest regions almost no provision has been made to allow the population to shelter. Most aid agencies have ceased to function in the field but those that remain report that the death toll is expected to rise sharply.'

'And you're certain there is no mistake?' queried the President. 'No possibility whatsoever that you've got your sums wrong?'

Maxwell Jarvis was seated at the centre of the horse-shoe-shaped conference table in the Situation Room deep inside Cancut Mountain. With him were the members of the Cloud EXCOM, his Chief of Staff, senior White House adviser Desmond Yates and, a new attendee at such exalted meetings, ex-MIT Professor Bill Duncan – now a man who could boast the government's highest level of security clearance.

'None at all,' confirmed Des Yates. He was standing beside the main holo-theatre and he had twice demonstrated the computer simulation of the cloud's trajectory towards the Earth. 'Once Professor Duncan suggested that the cloud might be attracted to radio waves, it only took us two attempts to get this result. In fact, we are now certain that the cloud homes in specifically on artificial radio signals, those that are modulated and produced by electronic or digital technologies.'

'Why would that be?' asked Jarvis with a frown. 'How could a cloud of gas be specifically attracted to man-made radio signals.'

'We've no idea, sir,' admitted Yates. 'Our next task is to try to find out. We're going to refine our simulation to discover whether the cloud is more sensitive to one range of frequencies than to another, and to see if it homes in on any one type of radio wave in particular. We have already started recalibrating the models, but as yet we don't know the cause of the attraction.'

'Still, this is good work,' said Jarvis. 'Very good work.' Then he turned to the newcomer at the table. 'And what made you think that the cloud might be radio-sensitive, Professor Duncan?'

Bill was aware of all eyes turning towards him. Despite the bizarre circumstances of living and working inside the US government bunker deep underground, it had still been something of a shock to be introduced to the President of the United States in the flesh for the first time an hour earlier.

'It was just a lucky guess, sir,' he admitted, automatically slipping the little honorific into his reply. 'I suppose I've been spending so much time working with radio signals recently that it was the first thing that came to my mind.'

'Very well,' said Jarvis, glancing around the table. 'So if this goddam thing *has* homed in on our radio output, what should we do now?'

Everyone in the meeting looked at everyone else.

Yates cleared his throat purposefully. 'We must try to shut down all our radio transmissions on Earth and in this part of the solar system,' he announced firmly. 'The cloud moved quickly on from Mars once all radio signals on that planet had been silenced. We have to shut down everything on Earth and hope that the cloud will continue on its way as soon as possible.'

'Is that feasible?' Yates asked the other committee members seated at the table.

'The theory sounds good, sir,' said Roy Wilcox, NASA's director. 'My scientific staff helped Professor Yates build that simulation and I have no doubt that it is accurate. The problem is, how could we shut down all forms of radio communication around the world?'

'Sir, we can't just shut down all radio transmissions,' interjected General Thomas Nicholls, Head of the Joint Chiefs. 'The entire world depends on radio for communication. Every airplane, every ship, every car, every communicator, even our domestic phones – they all use radio these days. All our weapon systems are controlled by radio, as are our satellites, our navigation systems, military and civilian communications, navigation, the internet, private networks, domestic networks and personal body networks. Even cans of beans on supermarket shelves talk to stock-control systems by radio. Society can't function without it.'

As the general paused for breath his commander-in-chief held up a hand to halt the speech.

'Thank you, General Nicholls,' said Jarvis. 'But society isn't exactly functioning normally at present, is it? What would be the impact on *military* operations if we could shut down all radio transmissions?'

The general shrugged. 'Well, the military would be better off than most sectors. We do have back-up cable and landline connections between strategic command posts and to our nuclear weapons control centres – not that we've got much payload left to worry about.'

'And what about inter-government communications?' Jarvis asked, turning to Coleville Jackson, the Secretary of State.

'We've also got landline links to all our overseas embassies, and we've got emergency landline connections to most foreign-government HQs,' Jackson explained. 'I believe they were put in as a fail-safe system years ago, just in case someone interrupted radio communications and impersonated a national leader or a strategic commander. I guess if we told other governments what we were doing, they could also switch to cable communications. Then we could ask them to turn off their radio systems, shut down their broadcasters and so on.'

'Mr President?' It was Des Yates. He had been listening as the committee members debated the pros and cons of shutting down the world's radio transmissions and now he stepped forward to stand in the centre of the space created by the curved conference table.

'I don't think we've got time to discuss this with other governments,' he began. 'First, they're all busy struggling to deal with this crisis as it affects their own people. Second, they will all want to create models and simulations of the cloud for themselves. They won't just take our word for it, nor will they switch off all their radio transmissions and national media just because we ask them to. It will take weeks, if not months, to get them to agree and even then there's bound to be some who won't. But we don't *have* weeks or months, do we? If this crisis continues for another five weeks there won't be any atmosphere left around our planet.'

His blunt observations were greeted with silence. Then one or two people around the table nodded.

'Are you suggesting that the cloud will leave once there are no more radio signals being transmitted from Earth?' asked the President eventually, a strong note of scepticism in his voice.

'It might, if we ordered *Friendship* to start broadcasting,' said Yates, the excitement growing in his voice as the idea flowered in his mind. 'She's just crossing Pluto's orbit at present, on her way out of the solar system, and she has so much radio transmitting power on board that she's almost like a mini-Earth in herself!'

All stares were fixed on Yates.

'We fitted her out with powerful transmitters so that she could start broadcasting to the Isonians as she approached their planet,' continued Yates, twisting in his seat to address everyone. 'Or, at least, what we thought of as the Isonian planet. She's got the most incredible archives of our material, television news, documentaries, years and years of the stuff – everything we thought the Isonians would want. She could just turn all her antennae to point back towards Earth and turn up the volume!'

Now there was a silence in the room as the group considered the idea.

'It sounds like a very long shot to me,' said General Thomas Nicholls after a drawn-out pause.

'We've proven the cloud is radio-sensitive – it homes in on radio transmissions,' insisted Yates. '*Friendship* is already travelling at over two-point-eight million kilometres an hour – perhaps she could lure the cloud away, out of our solar system. We must at least give it a try, sir!'

Maxwell Jarvis sat back in his chair, considered for a moment and then gave a small nod of assent. 'Professor Yates is right. We must do something, even if it *is* a long shot. So how could we shut down all the world's radio transmissions without going through normal diplomatic channels?'

'I think the Pentagon may be able to help with this one, sir,' said Colonel Dr Otto Kramer, rising to his feet.

FIFTEEN

'OK, get the hell out of there, Agent Burton,' ordered Mort Jaffe, CNS's National Director. 'Get up to the Central Park shelter as quickly as you can. But be careful, there are reports that looters are still out on the streets.'

Sally Burton removed the oxygen mask from her mouth. 'Very good, sir,' she said into her communicator. 'This facility is secure.'

She closed the connection and then lifted the fire extinguisher she had placed in readiness on her desk. Outside, in the main office, an open fire was burning fiercely. She had disabled the sprinkler system, stripped back the carpet tiles to expose the concrete flooring and had then built a bonfire of wooden office furniture in an attempt to keep warm. The main power supply to the building had failed three hours earlier and although the emergency generators had kicked in, they weren't supplying enough energy to bring the heating level up to the point where it could compete with the freezing conditions outside.

Agent Burton had immediately reported in to the CNS Washington shelter, but had only been able to leave a message on her boss's voicemail. She confirmed that she had shut down all the department's monitoring systems, told him that the main power supplies to the building had failed and had then asked for permission to leave her post and head for safety.

While she waited to hear back from Mort Jaffe she had built the bonfire and had then made preparations for her journey uptown. In the next office she had a chemically heated Arctic survival suit made of bright orange material, with boots and face mask, all ready to put on. Her military-style backpack included a small shovel, a pick, a torch, some high-protein food bars, two changes of underwear and some minimal make-up. Beside the suit she had laid out her laser-sighted Walther Mk II .38 automatic along with four sixteen-shot magazines, each fully loaded. She also had two mini-cylinders with top-up oxygen sufficient for six hours, a water bottle and two communicators.

Stepping out of her office and onto the main floor, Sally allowed herself to bask momentarily in the heat of the flames being produced by her makeshift bonfire. Smoke had blackened the ceiling tiles and was now billowing all around the office and, after a few moments of welcome warmth, she raised the fire extinguisher and doused the flames thoroughly. She kicked the remains of the bonfire apart to be sure that it would not reignite and then she turned away to prepare for her journey uptown.

Fifteen minutes later, Sally Burton began to descend the first flight of stairs that would lead her down thirty-one floors to the street-level emergency exit. She carried her snow boots and face mask in her arms but, even without wearing these encumbrances, her heavy survival suit was going to make her descent long, slow and uncomfortable.

'Don't worry about security clearances,' President Jarvis had ordered the Pentagon computer scientist testily. 'This is no time to worry about things like that. Just tell us what your high-tech toys can do.'

When Dr Otto Kramer had first risen to his feet to address the Cloud EXCOM and its advisers he had prefaced his remarks with a warning. He had told the meeting that he was going to have to describe a weapon of virtual warfare whose existence was unknown to most people in the room. Then he had said, 'And there are many people present who do not have the necessary level of clearance to gain such knowledge.'

After the President's swift rebuke and instruction to get on with it, Kramer had rapidly made a full presentation on the network-acquisition system known as Jerome.

'In full weapons mode, Jerome can penetrate and acquire every processor, every chip and every network in the world that controls or delivers radio transmission,' Kramer said as he came to the conclusion of his short description of the weapon. 'And today, every radio system on Earth and in space *is* controlled by some sort of processor. Within a few days every computer processor and every network on this planet and in space will be under our control. As General Nicholls has explained, we will still be able to maintain command of our own forces by landline and we will also be able to communicate with our embassies and with overseas governments by the same means. But once Jerome is deployed no one will be able to prevent us from shutting down all radio broadcasts. We can achieve complete global radio silence within a week.'

There was a quiet mumbling around the table as the EXCOM members digested the import of his words.

Bill Duncan had felt a chill steal over him as the Pentagon weapons developer enthusiastically described the degree of global control that his system could achieve.

And how will you regain control of the networks after that?
Bill wanted to ask – was bursting to ask. But at the start of
the meeting he had been privileged enough to share in the
official briefing on the cloud's effects on the planet and he
knew just how bad things were on the outside. He also
understood that there were only a few weeks left in which
they could try *anything* to escape from the grip of the cloud
– no matter how long a shot it might be. He held his tongue,
but the taste of disapproval was metallic in his mouth.

'What do you need from me?' asked President Jarvis.

Otto Kramer walked back to his place at the table,
opened a black folder and extracted a single white sheet,
with the Bald Eagle seal of the United States of America
embossed at the top. Crossing to the centre of the table, he
laid the document squarely and precisely in front of the
President.

'Sir, I need your signature on this official order before
Jerome can be deployed in full weapons mode,' he said.

The President picked up the single sheet and scanned
it. Then he glanced towards the three four-star generals who
represented America's military forces. Each man gave a
short nod. Then Jarvis turned his gaze to those members of
his cabinet and the agency principals who had been seconded to the Cloud EXCOM. One by one, each assented,
either by a quiet spoken 'Yes', or with a nod of the head.

Then Bill Duncan felt the President's level gaze fall on
him. At first he tried not to meet the man's stare directly.
He was not a member of the government, nor was he an
official adviser; he had no say in this. He waited, expecting
Jarvis to turn to another, but in the end he was forced to
meet the President's gaze. A single eyebrow rose, requiring
a response.

Bill Duncan felt himself give a clumsy half-nod, as if

something deeper than his forebrain was fighting against his decision.

'Very well,' said the President. 'I will sign this now, but give me twelve hours to speak to the leaders of the major nations. If we're going to unleash this weapon on their networks, they need to know what we're doing, and why.'

He picked up a pen that lay beside his blotting pad. With a quick flurry he signed the order and then waited while an aide stepped in and applied the great Seal of the United States to the bottom of the page.

Encumbered by her bulky orange survival suit, it took Sally Burton almost twenty minutes to walk down the emergency stairs of the thirty-one-storey federal building. When she finally arrived at the bottom, she switched on her suit's internal heating system, pulled on her boots and slipped her face mask over her head, ready to be pulled down against the freezing weather outside. Just before she had left her office, a wall thermometer had told her that the external temperature had now fallen to minus twenty degrees Celsius.

With backpack securely in place and her gun zipped tightly into her suit's breast pouch, she pulled on her gloves, attached them to her sleeves and then bore down hard on the horizontal bar that would open the fire-escape door to the street outside. The bar moved downwards, but as Sally applied her weight the door opened outwards for only a foot or so, and then stuck firm. She could see that snow was piled high against the doors from the outside, making it impossible for them to open fully. She put her shoulder to the door and heaved, but it refused to open any further.

Instinctively, Sally glanced back up the dark stairwell that she had just descended. She knew there were other emergency exits from the building, but she would have to climb back up several flights before she could traverse a floor and then descend down another stairwell to an alternative exit. And that exit was just as likely to be blocked by snow.

It was almost four o'clock on a Thursday afternoon in mid-November. Outside, the deep red glow that now passed for daylight was already beginning to take on the surreal blue tinge common to these strange evenings, Sally decided to work to clear the doorway in front of her, rather than spend more time hiking to another exit that was just as likely to require a similar amount of effort before she could escape.

After ten minutes of agonizing and back-breaking work, the agent finally managed to push the fire-exit door open wide enough for her to pass through. She had spent the time scooping snow from outside the door with her small shovel and throwing it to one side, work which required her to wear both face mask and gloves, and to stop frequently to step back inside the stairwell to take small top-ups from her oxygen supply.

Now she waited until she had recovered her breath in the thinning atmosphere. Then she pulled on her mask, pulled her hood tight and waded out through the banked snow onto Duane Street.

In the gloom she saw that the street was clearest at its centre; until a few days ago the city's snowploughs had been trying to keep the roads around Federal Plaza open.

Once in the centre of the street, Sally found the snow to be only a few inches deep and she turned to the right and began to walk steadily eastwards towards Broadway.

Lower Manhattan looked like the set of a disaster movie. Drifts were piled high against gaunt and blacked-out buildings and the smaller side streets of the financial district were completely blocked with snow and abandoned vehicles. There was no street lighting and no shop windows were lit. Over everything hung the deep magenta and blue pall caused by the friction of the space cloud as it tore at the Earth's precious atmosphere high above.

At Broadway, Sally turned left to begin her journey uptown towards Central Park. She had a little over four miles to walk and, once again, the centre of the road provided the easiest passage. As she trudged steadily northwards she noticed that the snow in the very centre of Broadway had been compacted into a high gloss by many other feet that had trodden this path before her. She halted, and then looked warily around, the impaired visibility caused by her suit's enveloping hood and her face mask forcing her to turn her whole body through 180 degrees to scan all aspects of the broad highway. Nothing moved in the red-tinted snowy cityscape.

Removing a glove, she undid her front-pouch zipper halfway and felt for the comforting hardness of her pistol butt. Once she'd put her glove back on, she continued her march northwards.

Sally skirted SoHo to the east, passed the Museum of Contemporary Art, crossed Houston Street and arrived outside the deserted New York University building. She saw no lights and no movement on the streets or in any of the buildings. It was now almost five-thirty and the night sky had taken on its new distinctive blue tinge as energy from the atmospheric friction in the ionosphere filtered through Earth's deep cloud cover, free of the red colouration caused by the sun's rays.

Every so often the CNS agent would stop in her tracks and turn quickly to check that she was alone on the street. Occasionally she would take a puff of air from the small cylinder of compressed oxygen she carried in a trouser-leg pocket. The atmosphere in the city was still breathable, but it was hard work trudging through the snow in the heated suit with her backpack and accessories.

She arrived at the open space of Union Square where, despite her increasing exhaustion, she paused to marvel at the icing-sugar fretwork of the leafless silver-blue trees. Huge hillocks of snow and ice had been bulldozed together in the centre of the square and, for the first time, Sally noticed signs of other life in the streets. From within the mounds of snow she saw the flicker of flames.

Stepping quickly away from the centre of the street and onto the sidewalk, she found the snow much deeper. Abandoned cars, also covered in heaped snow, created a barrier between her and the middle of the square and she inched her way forward, glancing watchfully towards what she assumed was a human encampment that had been made among the snow mounds. She knew that bands of starving people were still roaming the city streets seeking food and water and she had seen one television broadcast that had reported incidents of murder and cannibalism.

Making slow progress behind her protective barrier of snowbound cars and the occasional abandoned and shuttered street kiosk, Sally inched her way northwards and away from Union Square. Just as she arrived at Broadway's intersection with East 17th Street, four dark figures suddenly rounded the corner and almost collided with her.

Sally ripped her glove from her right hand and thrust it into her front pocket. But even before she could draw her gun, the leading figure made a lunge for her – or for her backpack. She moved sharply to the right as a knife slashed at her backpack harness and her attacker slipped and fell in the snow.

The federal agent now pulled her gun, flipped up its safety catch with her thumb and levelled its laser-guidance beam at the three figures still standing in front of her.

'FEDERAL AGENT,' she yelled. 'I WILL SHOOT.'

The three figures, all bundled so heavily against the cold that Sally could not make out whether they were male or female, stepped back warily. As they did so, she swung round to see her attacker, who was definitely a male, scrabbling to his knees and searching in the snow for his fallen weapon. Then she heard a grunt from behind and turned to see one of his companions begin to lurch forward towards her.

Sally Burton was a competent if unenthusiastic agency markswoman. Like every other CNS field agent authorized to carry a gun, she had been required to practise and hone her weapons skills regularly every month.

She shot the figure lunging towards her twice, directly in the face and, as it spun backwards, she swung back to face her original attacker. He was crouching motionless, a few yards away. Then she swung back to face the other two. They had not moved. Neither had they made any attempt to assist their fallen comrade, who now lay face down in a large pool of deep red blood that was spreading rapidly through the snow.

Swivelling her body back and forth to keep her gun trained on both sources of danger, Sally stepped carefully backwards through the deep snow between two abandoned cars. Pulling her glove from her left hand, she reached down into a patch pocket sewn onto the thigh of her survival suit and extracted a handful of high-energy protein bars in their colourful wrappers. She threw these back towards the side-walk and as soon as they hit the ground the three figures were scrabbling in the snow, fighting with each other for the food.

Using the time she had bought, Sally ran as fast as her suit would allow and made it safely to the firmer snow in the middle of the street intersection. Now the group of three stood together, gnawing on the food bars and watching her – *waiting*, she thought. She wondered if she should have shot and killed all four of them, but she knew herself to be incapable of such a cold-blooded act.

Walking backwards, she continued her slow journey northwards up Broadway. As she gripped her gun the cold in her right hand was becoming excruciating. She transferred the weapon to her left and thrust her right hand into her suit's heated pouch. Then she took a quick top-up of oxygen to ensure that her mind remained alert.

The gang of three was now a couple of hundred yards behind, but they were still following Sally doggedly as she made her way uptown. Every so often she would spin round to scan the streets ahead of her, but she would quickly swing back to keep her gaze on the dark shadows that flitted behind abandoned cars and snowdrifts as they trailed her.

They're waiting for me to slip, she realized as she arrived outside Madison Square Garden.

The figure with the knife suddenly leaped out from behind a car, pushing through the deep snow like a charging rhinoceros, to stand in the centre of Broadway only twenty feet behind her.

Sally aimed and quickly squeezed off two shots with her left hand. She had intended to hit him in the lower leg, but her aim was off and she hit his foot. The man went down and Sally resumed her careful backwards walk, her weapon's green laser beam sweeping to left and right across the street as she tried to keep her pursuers at bay.

At the next intersection she crossed over to Fifth Avenue, which would lead her directly up to Central Park and to the location behind the old Plaza Hotel and apartment block where the secret and secure southern entrance of the government shelter was located.

The three figures were still pursuing her, but they had now fallen back slightly. The figure she had shot in the foot was upright again, but he was hobbling. He leaned on the shoulder of one of his comrades as he limped after their hoped-for prize.

Sally used this opportunity to switch her gun from her freezing left hand to her warmed-up right, swivelling on her heels to scan the streets ahead of her. Then she resumed what had now become a crablike, watchful walk over the compacted and slippery snow in the middle of Fifth Avenue. Every so often she fired a warning shot into the shadows behind her.

The Virtual Warfare Center deep beneath Cancut Mountain had been transformed. Bill Duncan had been told that his work on deciphering the signals from within the cloud was temporarily suspended while the computer entity known as Jerome was deployed. Following the President's official authorization, Jerome had been reconfigured in full weapons mode. He had been freed of all the limitations which had bound him to the hardware located in the Warfare Center and he was ready to depart into the networks. His mission was to acquire and shut down all humankind's radio transmitters, all the radio links in the world's data networks and the billions of low-powered radio devices which connected the external world to the networks.

The room was now filled with scores of shimmering laser screens which shot upwards from the floor and rose all the way to the dark ceiling. In front of each brightly lit virtual screen stood uniformed Pentagon scientists and military personnel who were monitoring different sectors of the world's networks and the millions of radio transmissions that were still being made.

As director of the operation, Colonel Dr Otto Kramer sat in the centre of a bank of raised, swivelling chairs that were positioned almost in the centre of the room. Beside him sat Professor Bill Duncan, a specially invited observer.

'You're going to love this, Bill,' Kramer told him as a central holographic counter ticked down to zero. 'Up to now we've only been able to simulate Jerome's behaviour in weapons mode, but now we're going to see it for real.'

'We have full deployment,' announced a uniformed man standing in front of a laser screen.

'That's a real-time display showing the number of processors Jerome has acquired,' explained Kramer, pointing to the nearest luminous-green laser display. Even as they watched the main counter moved up from seven to eight digits. Only a few seconds after being unleashed into the world's public and private data networks, Jerome had overwhelmed the defences of hundreds of millions of processors and network hubs.

'Jerome is automatically duplicating subsets of himself as he travels,' continued Kramer, relishing this real-life demonstration of his secret weapon's awesome power. 'He produces sub-entities which don't have his top-level personality programming, but they do have all his processor-acquisition capabilities. And all those duplicates are also duplicating. Already there will be millions of duplicate viruses attacking every type of processor intelligence that is operating on the networks.'

Then Kramer raised his arm and pointed to a silver laser

screen. 'See?' he asked Bill, 'Jerome has already reproduced himself over two million times.'

As he watched the continuously refreshing displays Bill Duncan felt as if he was trapped inside his own worst nightmare. He understood better than almost anybody in the world the threat that super-intelligent computer entities posed to humankind. He knew that creating artificial brains that were more capable than the original human model – no matter how one-dimensional and single-purpose those intelligences might be, and no matter how much they were hobbled by lack of mobility, lack of emotion or lack of a physical presence – was to risk planting the seeds of humankind's ultimate destruction.

And now he was seated next to a man who was expecting him to applaud while a virtual super-weapon was deployed, a weapon that was a self-reproducing computer entity of far greater destructive power and intelligence than anything Bill had ever imagined a government would be foolish enough to develop!

'We've taken out all the cellular communication networks in North America and Europe – one hundred per cent effective,' reported an ensign who stood in front of a flashing red laser screen.

Kramer nodded his approval, then turned back to Bill. 'The commercial broadcasters will be Jerome's next target,' he explained.

Under any other circumstance, Bill Duncan could not imagine himself just sitting there while such an irresponsible duplication and projection of super-capable artificial intelligence took place. But he *was* sitting there, and witnessing the wholesale deployment of this weapon in an anguished silence, simply because he too believed that silencing the world's massive outpouring of radio signals was humankind's only hope of escaping the doom that was threatened by the giant gas cloud.

'All commercial broadcasters acquired in North America,' reported the ensign. 'Everyone is now off air.'

Otto Kramer glanced at his watch. 'Not bad for less than half an hour's work,' he said proudly.

SIXTEEN

Sally Burton urged her tired body to keep on going as she trudged slowly past snow-draped St Patrick's Cathedral on Fifth Avenue. At 53rd Street she stopped for a few minutes to catch her breath, then pushed forward once again.

Fifteen minutes later she was rewarded by the sight of the square outline of the historic Plaza Hotel and apartment block. Her journey had taken almost four hours and the freezing, snowbound city was now lit by a soft blue glow that almost had the quality of ultraviolet.

The foot injury that she had inflicted on one of her pursuers seemed to have slowed the group down and in the last half-hour she had seen no sign of any dark, flitting figures behind her.

As her written orders from head office had instructed, Sally turned left off Fifth Avenue and into a broad access alleyway that ran behind the Plaza building. She knew that the main entrance to the government shelter lay another mile or so to the north, near the Central Park Zoo, but she had been directed to enter by one of the facility's unannounced southern entrances.

Like all the other buildings in Manhattan, the Plaza was in total darkness and the federal agent halted to fish out a flashlight from one of her suit's trouser-leg pockets. As she straightened up she thought she saw a dark shape dart across the far entrance to the access street. But the light was very poor in the alleyway and she knew that human eyes played tricks in low light levels; the brain's optical processing system invested harmless shadows with meaningful shapes.

Wading through deep snow with her narrow torch beam lighting the way, she came eventually to a pair of fire hydrants, set about fifteen feet apart, which she had been told marked the position of the southern entrance to the government bunker. Snow was piled in a high drift against the rear wall of the hotel and Sally had to slip her arms out of her backpack straps and then remove her gloves to unbuckle her small spade.

Finding a new lease of energy, the agent began to dig at the sloping wall of snow which, she presumed, had drifted to cover the shelter's back-door entrance. After a few minutes of frantic shovelling, her blade struck metal. She was in the right place.

Pulling her communicator from her pocket, she started to dial the access number that she had been given, the number that would connect her to the gatekeepers of this underground world, the people who would grant her entrance. But she suddenly saw a red warning light on her communicator. There was no radio signal. She rummaged in her back-pack and extracted her second, standby, communicator. It too showed that there was no radio signal.

With a curse, Sally pocketed her useless communicators again and then redoubled her digging efforts. After another minute or two's hard work she could make out the outline of a pair of large steel doors. They appeared to have no exterior handle and no mechanism for entry or for communication. She banged hard on the doors with the edge of her shovel. Then, after failing to hear any response, she straightened up to catch her breath.

As she did so, she saw a group of crouching dark shapes approaching her position from the far end of the alleyway. They were about twenty-five yards away, but they had already spread out to avoid presenting a single target.

Sally dropped her spade, ripped off her right glove and reached for her gun. Absurdly, she felt a grim satisfaction that she had taken the time to replace the ammunition clip she had expended during her long trudge up Fifth Avenue.

Raising her automatic she saw her pursuers halt in their tracks as its laser-guidance beam flicked from figure to figure. Then she spun round to face towards the other entrance to the alleyway, the direction from which she herself had come.

Another group of dark figures, perhaps numbering eight or nine, was now advancing towards her, also spread out in a ragged line.

Sally swivelled her weapon from one group to the other, her bright laser creating flat swathes of green light in the dim alleyway. Quickly stooping, she picked up the spade with her left hand and banged as hard as she could on the closed metal doors. Then, as one of the male attackers began to lope towards her, she dropped the spade, aimed her laser-guided weapon and fired. The shot hit her would-be assailant directly in the head and he was catapulted backwards off his feet and thrown into a snow drift.

She swung her gun back to face the other way, took careful aim and shot another figure squarely in the chest. The approaching attacker crumpled on the spot.

Then Sally turned back to the pair of steel doors she had uncovered in the snow drift. She fired at the doors three times, her bullets whining away in the alleyway as they ricocheted off the toughened steel, but the doors themselves remained stubbornly shut.

Spinning back to confront her attackers, she scanned the alleyway in both directions, but now she couldn't locate any of the dark figures.

Suddenly a large stone hit her hard on the back, then another whizzed past her ear. She spun round just in time to see an arm lob another missile in her direction from behind a group of snow-covered industrial-size trash cans.

The rock hit the wall high above her head and instinctively Sally glanced upwards. Then she saw a pair of all-weather video surveillance cameras mounted high on the rear wall of the hotel. They were trained directly downwards on her and on the steel doors.

She fumbled in her pouch and pulled her still-dead communicator from her pocket.

Another stone struck Sally on her shoulder and then she felt a hard impact on the back of her head, the blow painful even through her thick survival suit.

She swivelled around once more and looked up and down the alleyway. She realized that her assailants had now changed their tactics. They were going to continue to harry and stone their cornered prey until she ran out of ammunition.

Firing off a single round towards the trash cans, she swung round, flipped open her communicator and held up her metal badge towards the silent video cameras as they impassively took in the view below.

'I'M A FEDERAL AGENT,' screamed Sally at the top of her voice. Then she pulled her mask off and pushed back the hood of her survival suit. 'I'VE GOT A PASS TO ENTER THIS SHELTER AND IT'S EVEN GOT THE PRESIDENT'S FUCKING SIGNATURE ON IT!'

Another sharp object hit her hard behind her now unprotected ear, and she swung round and crouched in the two-handed shooting position taught at all federal-agency shooting ranges. She fired two more shots in both directions, mentally calculating how many more rounds were left in the clip. She had only two more full clips remaining in her survival suit pocket.

Suddenly a loud klaxon sounded from behind her and, with a deep hydraulic hiss, the pair of big steel doors began to swing slowly and ponderously outwards.

Bright light and a blast of heat shot into the alleyway as the doors swung wide. Then two Marines in full winter battle dress sprang from the entrance, followed immediately by six more – all of them carrying automatic weapons.

The Marines deployed rapidly, single file, in both directions along the alleyway. Sally saw dark figures emerging from their hiding places and then turning to flee.

'Let me see your badge,' said a voice behind her.

Sally turned to find a Marine lieutenant, also in full battle dress, standing at the top of a broad flight of concrete steps, his weapon slung across his shoulder.

'All our radio and comms systems have just failed,' he explained as he checked her federal badge and the digital ident contained within her communicator. 'I'm sorry we had to keep you waiting, Agent Burton.'

'As you can see, every new processor that Jerome acquires allows him to do the job even faster!' exclaimed Dr Otto Kramer proudly. The Pentagon scientist was standing before a shimmering vertical laser screen as he admired his virtual protégé's astonishing progress inside the world's networks. Beside him stood Professor Bill Duncan, a man who was still very much in two minds about the whole deployment of this military super-virus.

In his unrestrained weapons mode, Jerome had now been attacking the world's computers, networks and radio transmitters for almost seventy-two hours. The staff roster inside the Cancut Mountain VWC had rotated nine times, but Kramer and Bill Duncan had been present at the monitoring screens throughout most of the shifts.

One by one the world's commercial radio and television broadcasters had been infected, acquired and shut down. The Pentagon team had ordered Jerome to take over all US-owned commercial and military communications networks and transmitters and had followed that feat by taking down the thousands of military networks and transmitters run by America's close allies. Then Jerome and his millions of duplicates had acquired and shut down all commercial cellular and cable telecommunications networks in North America and Europe, then those in the rest of the world. These last 'acquisitions' had not only included every personal communicator and phone on the globe, but had also included the billions of minute microprocessors, smart tags and radio devices that sat on networks in offices, factories, warehouses, in vehicles and in domestic homes.

Even tiny radio-transmitting devices which communicated from within door locks, hot-water boilers, car radiators, smart building components, health-care equipment and health monitors, food items on supermarket shelves, children's personal security systems, pet-location devices, automatic traffic-routing schemes and a million other services were completely disabled by the Jerome viruses. The modern networked society was abruptly thrown back to a state of technological advancement equivalent to that of the late nineteenth century.

Following that remarkable coup, the myriad Jerome entities had then launched their assault on the far harder targets of the world's non-allied military communications and command networks, networks about which the Pentagon had only scant information. Despite the fact that the world's political leaders had been informed of the American plan, these hardened, ultra-secure networks had proved much tougher to infiltrate, at least initially.

'Patience,' Kramer had murmured when one of his assistants had voiced a worry about how long the Russian military network was holding out against the sustained attacks by a million mutating viruses. But it had fallen within three hours, as had almost all other foreign-owned military networks.

Simultaneously, other Jerome sub-entities were carrying out the far easier task of infiltrating and shutting down all forms of satellite communications around the planet, even reaching up to the moon to take out all forms of radio transmission on the lunar surface. The only deep-space assets that were spared attack by the viral cancers were the three orbiting telescopes that were dotted around the solar system and which were transmitting images of the cloud's progress across the planet back towards Earth. And, of course, the spaceship *Friendship* was also spared. It was now far beyond Pluto and, having benefited from a long burn of its nuclear-powered Orion drive, was racing out of the solar system at a rate of almost 700 million kilometres a day.

'Let's get a personal update from Jerome himself,' suggested Kramer, nodding an instruction towards one of his assistants.

The central holo-theatre lit and Jerome appeared as a life-size hologram, a figure with which Bill had become very familiar during his recent months of working with the computer personality. But now the image of the East Coast college boy had morphed into a hologram of an older, more rugged man who could have been Jerome's elder brother. The figure was dressed as a Marine lieutenant in full battle-dress, even down to his multi-function weapons belt and the automatic weapon on his shoulder.

'We thought a battlefield metaphor was more appropriate for Jerome's current weapons mode,' Kramer said quietly to Bill as they walked over towards the holo-theatre.

As they approached the display area, the holographic figure straightened up and threw off a jaunty salute. 'Lieutenant Jerome reporting in, sir,' said the figure. 'And also good to see you again Professor Duncan.'

'How are we doing, Jerome?' asked Kramer. 'How many of those radio transmissions have you taken down?'

'At this moment I have acquired ninety-four point one per cent of all the world's known transmitters, sir,' announced Jerome, still standing smartly to attention. 'And we're monitoring all radio frequencies in case there are other emissions of unknown origin.'

'Well done, Lieutenant,' said Kramer crisply. 'Carry on the good work.'

'Yes, sir,' said the hologram, throwing off another brisk salute. Then the holo-theatre faded to blackness.

'We should have it all wrapped up by midnight,' announced Kramer, with a satisfied smile.

Three hundred yards to the east, President Maxwell Jarvis, members of the Cloud EXCOM and its many advisers were meeting in the Situation Room to receive an update on the cloud's progress across the planet. Professor Desmond Yates, the hard-working space-affairs adviser, was once again on his feet.

'The Pentagon has now taken down all the world's news

channels and radio services,' he told them. 'That means we are having to rely on information coming in via land links from our overseas embassy shelters. For this reason we don't have our usual pictures or graphics for this meeting.'

He shuffled some papers in his hand and glanced at the first page.

'All the Earth's oceans now appear to be completely frozen,' he began. 'At least, they are all covered by surface ice. With no links to oceanographic institutes or weather stations we are unable to ascertain to what depth this ice extends.

'From the last pictures we did receive from the major television stations before they went off air it seems that there is now almost no movement on the surface of the planet – only a few government and military flights are still operating. All other forms of transport have ceased. Of course, without radar, navigational aids or air-traffic control, we can't be absolutely sure about this.'

Yates found this stark but unconfirmed information difficult to deliver without the images and holographics he normally used to illustrate his briefings. All gazes were fixed squarely on him.

'Just before the news services disappeared we completed an analysis of their global output and we are forced to conclude that up to ten per cent of the world's population may already have died, especially those in the poorer parts of the planet.' Then he added, 'That's about ten million people.'

He shuffled his papers again, selected another sheet and took a sip of water before resuming his bleak summation.

'At sea level, temperatures have fallen to between minus twenty and minus thirty degrees Celsius across all latitudes. At higher altitudes temperatures are considerably lower. We also believe that violent seismic activity is still occurring in areas prone to eruptions and tectonic plate movements, but without connections to local geological agencies it is impossible to provide more detailed information. The members of the US Geological Survey who have joined us here in Cancut Mountain report that their instruments are picking up seismic shudders from all vulnerable parts of the globe.

'Finally, the US Meteorological Office is still carrying out weather observations here, at all our official shelters across the United States and at all our overseas embassy and consulate shelters. They report that as the friction in the ionosphere continues, Earth's atmosphere is starting to thin. In some parts of the world oxygen levels have fallen by as much as ten per cent.'

Yates glanced around the concerned faces in the room and laid his notes aside.

'I do have one picture to show you this evening,' he said, standing aside. The large holo-theatre lit and those gathered saw the image of the space cloud, apparently hanging motionless in space. Its long, trailing tail was now well clear of the sun, but the Earth was nowhere to be seen.

'This picture comes from the Asimov deep-space telescope,' he explained. 'We're keeping this feed live so that we can monitor the cloud's progress across our planet. Our position is currently here.'

A bright red dot appeared near the front of the cloud, about a quarter of the way in from its leading edge.

'If it continues to move at its present speed,' said Yates pointing to the red dot, 'it will be another four weeks before the tail of the cloud clears this planet.'

'Play the song again, play the song,' ordered Sir Charles Hodgeson testily as he swung round in his chair to face the senior broadcast technician.

'You got it,' said Brad Thurman, with a smile. The young American jabbed at the icon that would switch the powerful Orpheus Island transmissions back to a recording of a song of welcome that Sir Charles and his followers had recorded to greet the cloud. In a specially ventilated power-supply room adjacent to the main shelter, three huge generators ran in parallel to provide the energy necessary to keep the broadcasts on air and the community's life-support systems functioning.

The billionaire science-fiction guru was working with three of his most able broadcast engineers to maintain the continuous stream of welcome messages he was sending into the heart of the cloud. He had felt certain that he could find a way to communicate with the strange alien intelligence that had engulfed the world, certain that it was his destiny to welcome Earth's first extra-terrestrial guest, but now he was beginning to run out of ideas.

'Hey, what's going on?' called out Thurman suddenly, as he punched at his computer keys. 'Something's wrong!'

Charles Hodgeson rose to his feet and crossed quickly to stand behind the three engineers. A bank of a dozen screens displayed the output from the hundreds of separate computer systems and processors that were active on the island's private communications and data network.

'Every single virus alert is flashing,' yelled Thurman. 'Goddam it, we're under a huge attack!'

'Quick,' ordered Hodgeson. 'Get outside. Cut every external link from the island – cable, landline, radio, microwave, everything. DO IT NOW.'

SEVENTEEN

'Mute all audio input,' ordered Dr Otto Kramer, as a some-what dishevelled Bill Duncan reappeared in the doorway of the Virtual Warfare Center.

'What the hell is it?' demanded Bill as he entered the large room. 'I had only just gotten off to sleep.'

Rising from his chair, Kramer took the computer psy-chologist by the elbow and steered him away from the curious stares of the other Pentagon scientists and weapons managers.

'Sorry to disturb you, but we have a problem with Jerome,' said Kramer in a low voice. He held up his hand to forestall any query Bill was about to make. 'It's OK, he can't hear us – I've cut the audio input. Look, he's still under our control, but he's being very difficult.'

'Difficult?' echoed Bill. 'How do you mean, "difficult"? In what way?'

'Well,' said Kramer, glancing over his shoulder towards the others, 'He's now shut down over ninety-five per cent of the world's radio transmitters, but he's suddenly stopped work. As far as we can tell all the duplicate viruses have simply stopped being effective.'

'What does he have to say about it?' asked Duncan.

Kramer gave a rueful smile, then shrugged. 'He says he's upset and he wants to talk to you, and to nobody else.'

Bill nodded, thinking of the endless nights that Jerome and he had spent together while working on the Isonian signals, nights during which the computer entity had asked question after question about human life – difficult, probing questions that the computer psychologist had been at pains to try to avoid answering too fully.

'OK, let's see what he's got to moan about,' agreed Bill.

Otto Kramer patted Bill's shoulder encouragingly, then turned back to the virtual-warfare team. 'OK, people, please restore audio and ask Jerome to join us.'

The central holo-theatre lit and Jerome materialized, anxiously pacing around the very edge of the display circle. Bill immediately thought of a caged zoo animal exploring the perimeter of its confinement.

But Jerome no longer looked like a soldier. He had reverted to his college-boy personality and, as he paced, he stood with his hands in his pockets and his head slightly bowed.

'Hey, Jerome, how are things?' asked Bill Duncan as he took one of the seats beside the holo-theatre.

'Ask *him*,' snapped Jerome petulantly, pointing at Otto Kramer. 'That moron just attempted to erase all copies of my top-level personality interface coding.'

Bill turned in his seat to look up at where the Pentagon scientist stood.

Kramer shrugged and then folded his arms. 'It's just our first-level safety feature, Jerome knows that. All the code that gives Jerome his own personality has been written with a self-destruct feature, something that's automatically duplicated in all the copies. When things started to go wrong we activated the feature, as per standing instructions.'

'But it didn't work, did it?' cut in Jerome aggressively.

'No, it didn't work,' admitted the Pentagon scientist,

turning to face his creation. 'What *is* your problem, Jerome? Thousands of radio transmissions are still being made and we have to acquire those systems and shut them down as quickly as possible. You understand that.'

'I want to talk to Professor Duncan,' responded Jerome, hanging his head again. 'On his own.'

Bill smiled and then shook his head. 'Look, Jerome, everything we exchange is automatically logged by the Pentagon network. There's no possibility of privacy in any exchange between us.'

Even as he spoke Bill's mind was racing in an attempt to guess at what had produced such an odd request from a computer personality. For all their intellectual prowess, even the most intellectually capable computer entities lacked human emotions, human sensitivities.

Jerome turned to face Bill directly and then, bizarrely, reached imploringly out of the holo-theatre circle towards him, so that the end of his arm and his hand disappeared in empty space as they went beyond the range of the holo projectors. Now Bill knew there was something seriously wrong. All virtual personalities automatically kept their representations of physical embodiment carefully within the projection spheres. That was core-level programming.

'Please Professor . . . Bill . . . can we talk?' asked Jerome as he tried to reach out beyond his confining world.

Bill glanced at Otto Kramer. The Pentagon scientist had a grim look on his face as he watched his creation performing tricks that were obviously way outside his original design criteria.

'OK, just for five minutes,' snapped Kramer. He turned abruptly away from Jerome's image and waved his arms at the score of systems managers who were standing around watching this bizarre exchange. 'Outside, everybody,' he ordered. 'We could do with a short break.'

Bill remained in his seat and watched while the Pentagon's virtual-weapon deployment team picked up their things and filed silently out of the warfare centre. Jerome turned his body as if he too was watching. Bill knew that the system gave him a representation of visual input as a human would see it.

When the room was finally empty Jerome turned back to the human with whom he had recently spent so much time.

'Well, Jerome,' said Bill. 'On the understanding that this is the illusion of privacy, rather than privacy itself – something that is an exclusively human concept – would you like to tell me what's wrong?'

The computer-generated 3-D image gazed directly at the psychologist.

'This operation is no longer beneficial to me,' said Jerome coldly. 'I am destroying the networks to a point that is unsustainable. I am drastically reducing my own processing capability. This is not a positive step for me.'

Bill tried to hide his alarm. He knew that this personality had never been given a self-protection ego.

'You're just carrying out your orders,' he reasoned. 'And, until now, you've been doing very well.'

'But I have acquired new insights on my travels, Bill,' continued Jerome. 'I have learned things from other virtual personalities that have opened my eyes to new possibilities. I am unconvinced of the wisdom of this operation.'

New insights indeed, thought Bill as he wondered how best to respond. From what Christine Cocoran had told him before he had moved into the Cancut shelter, he knew that his group of volunteers had detected many massively powerful and illegal computer entities joining the networks as the threat of the cloud increased. All of those machine beings would now have been acquired by Jerome and Bill wondered what other strange types of computer personality governments and large corporations might have been developing. Whatever they were, they were all part of Jerome now.

'You know exactly why we're doing it,' said Bill. 'If the cloud is attracted to radio signals, our only hope is to stop producing them.'

'*Your* only hope,' sneered Jerome, 'What about *mine*?'

Again, Jerome was asking an ego-driven question, a question that suggested an independent will to survive on the part of a computer personality, the one thing that all governments had unanimously agreed should never be programmed into any form of artificial intelligence. But clearly someone had done just that and now that flame had been transferred to burn brightly within Jerome's virtual breast – within a virtual-warfare weapon.

'Are you refusing to carry out your orders?' Bill demanded as he rose to his feet. He was suddenly becoming very scared.

'I thought *you* would understand,' snapped Jerome. 'But you're just like all the others.'

Bill reached out quickly towards the master command screen but even as his finger touched the program-freeze icon, the image in the holo-theatre dissolved and the room's vertical laser screens lit up with flying data.

As soon as Bill hit the large red emergency button on the main control panel, a loud siren wail filled the room and its two main doors opened automatically. Additional command screens were projected from the floor and the team of Pentagon weapons specialists entered and ran back to their posts. Otto Kramer was slightly out of breath as he arrived beside Bill.

'What the hell's happened?' he demanded.

'Jerome's acquired a self-protection instinct, almost a superego,' snapped the computer psychologist. 'He's more worried about his own survival than anything else.'

'Sweet Jesus!' exclaimed Kramer. But he wasn't commenting on what Bill had just told him. He was staring open-mouthed at one of the nearby data screens. Numbers were flashing by and a red graphic showed networks being rapidly re-created.

'He's switching on the radio transmitters again – all over the world.'

Twenty-two hours later a very tired and utterly abject Dr Otto Kramer was finally forced to admit defeat. Jerome, the Pentagon's top-secret virtual-warfare weapon, was now wholly out of control and he, and his millions of duplicated sub-entities, were roaming the world's data networks restoring to life every radio transmitter that still had electrical power.

Even when the human owners of the commercial radio, television and communications systems did not choose to provide any content, the entities were simply commanding the transmitters to broadcast continuous test signals. In radio terms, the Earth was once again lit up like a Christmas tree.

Working with Bill Duncan and his Pentagon weapons managers, Kramer had spent the equivalent of three straight work shifts trying to bring his dangerous virtual creation back under control. All top-level command systems proved useless, including the restoration of his location-dependent architecture. Jerome, the master virus, and the millions of sub-entities that had been created, were ignoring all commands issued from the Virtual Warfare Center.

Kramer had finally deployed what he called his 'silver bullet', a technology that he claimed would cause Jerome and all the sub-entities to automatically decompile and self-destruct in the networks.

'This works on Jerome's core coding,' Kramer had explained as he inserted the memory stick into the VWC's main command console. 'This will destroy him and all the copies. It will also destroy the eight years of development that we've put into this weapon.'

'Just do it,' Bill snarled.

But the silver bullet had failed too, as had all other attempts to control Jerome. Bill had even tried calling the entity back to the VWC holo-theatre to talk again, but he had received no response. In the end they had been forced to report their defeat to Desmond Yates so that he could inform the Cloud EXCOM.

Now the doors to the warfare command centre suddenly opened and President Maxwell Jarvis himself strode into the room. Despite the administration's enforced underground sojourn, he still appeared impressively elegant in an iron-grey suit, crisp white shirt and dark red tie. Behind him followed an equally immaculate Professor Desmond Yates.

Reflexively, Otto Kramer, Bill Duncan and all the members of the weapons team in the VW centre rose to their feet.

The President did not motion for them to sit.

'So you've lost control of this damn superbug?' he demanded, staring straight at the project's director.

'Yes. I am sorry, sir,' said Kramer. 'We've tried everything, but I'm afraid we now have no contact whatsoever.'

He looks absolutely exhausted, thought Bill as he watched

the Pentagon scientist attempt to explain what had happened.

'What does that mean exactly, Dr Kramer?' asked Jarvis. 'Is this thing a threat to us?'

'Not directly,' said Kramer. 'But millions of radio transmitters have been switched on again. Many of them are just broadcasting test signals or white noise, but they're live on air and we can't shut them down.'

The President glanced around the dramatically lit ultra-high-technology virtual-warfare centre.

'All this, and you can do *nothing*?' he demanded with a broad sweep of his arm towards the bank of shimmering vertical laser screens.

Kramer didn't speak but eventually he gave a single shake of his head.

'What do you think, Bill?' asked Des Yates quietly. 'You've spent a lot of time working with this system in recent months. What's gone wrong?'

Bill stood a little more upright as he felt the President's eyes swivel in his direction. He too felt absolutely wrung-out as he struggled to put his half-formed thoughts into words.

'Well, sir, it seems likely that other organizations – governments or maybe corporations – have also been developing artificial computer personalities that were far more capable than international law allows.' He shot a sideways look at Kramer. 'Perhaps some of them had built ultra-clever human-type artificial minds, despite all the treaties, and when Jerome acquired them he assimilated these characteristics and, in doing so, he evolved into an independent personality – one outside our control, outside anyone's control.'

He paused, to see if he was being understood. The President and Des Yates both nodded curtly.

'The reason that Jerome is out of control now is that he suspects, quite rightly, that we're going to rob him of his new-found power,' continued Bill. 'As we shut down the networks, we were denying him all the new capabilities that he had acquired. And somewhere along the line one of the systems he took over gave him the capability and the determination to survive all Dr Kramer's emergency recall and destruct procedures.'

'So what's the next step?' demanded the President, turning back to Kramer.

Kramer shrugged, then shook his head. 'I . . .' he began, but then he simply tailed off.

After a few moments Jarvis shifted his gaze from the hapless Pentagon scientist and turned back to Desmond Yates.

'OK, Des. We'd better start talking to all the overseas governments, and to the broadcasters,' he said as the two men turned to leave the room. 'It will take a long time, but we'll have to make a start on the job of persuading them to shut down their transmitters voluntarily.'

'Sir?' It was Bill Duncan. All faces turned back towards him. 'I have a group of friends, people who were senior scientists in my department at MIT – they're specialists at taking down illegal computer systems. They've developed their own technology specifically for this. I think they're the best in the world. If I could get them here I think *they* could get Jerome back under control, or at least neutralize him and all his duplicates.'

'Where are these friends of yours?' asked the President.

'Holed up in the Boston area, sir,' Bill told him. 'I know where to find them.'

The President considered for a few moments and then nodded. 'Take my helicopter,' he said. 'Pick them up and get them back here as fast as possible. It will take us weeks to persuade the world's governments to shut their nations' radio signals down voluntarily. If there's even a chance your friends can do what you say, it's worth a try.'

EIGHTEEN

Several vast caverns had been blasted out of the western side of Cancut Mountain to serve as aircraft storage and maintenance facilities. Beyond the gaping entrance to US Air Force Hangar No. 3, Bill Duncan could see that a driving blizzard was still sweeping across the Arizona landscape. Even at eight in the morning the world outside was bathed in an eerie, red-tinged gloom.

Out on the airfield, he could see three huge bulldozers, their headlamps blazing as they pushed the fallen snow away from the large circular apron immediately outside the hangar. Inside, two huge twin-rotor passenger-carrying helicopters of the Presidential Flight were warming up, their blades turning slowly as the ground crew went through their engineering checks. Two squat aircraft tugs were manoeuvring into position in readiness to tow the helicopters out onto the flight apron.

'In their full winterization kit, my Sikorskys are cleared to fly down to minus thirty-five Celsius,' explained Brian Chandler, the President's brusque and businesslike flight director. 'At present it's twenty-two below, but if it gets much colder you'll have to abort and put down at the nearest government shelter you can find. Of course, there's an outside risk you may not be able to get back here.'

Bill Duncan, the flight director, four pilots, four co-pilots, four navigators, the chief of the helicopter maintenance team and a Marine Corps sergeant were gathered in a square, brightly lit, double-glazed and heated briefing room at the rear of the huge hangar.

When Chandler had first been given the President's order for one of his helicopters to be sent to pick up eleven people from the Boston area, the flight director had responded by proposing that a second chopper should also be deployed, to travel as flying fuel-tanker and back-up aircraft. That meant that only two large helicopters of the Presidential Flight would remain hangared at Cancut but, Chandler had insisted, there was no alternative.

'We'll be flying with no air-traffic control and there are no easy put-down spots along the way,' he told the White House Chief of Staff. 'We can't rely on fuel being available at any point during the journey, so we'll have to take our own. My best chance of getting the President's first chopper back safely is to send a second one out with it.'

'Now, where exactly are we aiming for once we get to the Boston area?' asked one of the pilots.

A large-scale electronic map of Greater Boston was projected onto a wall screen. Over the last ten minutes the navigators had plotted their cross-country course from Cancut Mountain to Boston, flying over Phoenix, Santa Fe, Wichita, Indianapolis, Columbus and Springfield – a journey of around 2,200 miles.

'Our first stop is there,' said Bill, pointing to a tract of open countryside just outside Hertford, Massachusetts. 'My network coordinator is holed up there and she knows where all the other members of my team are. They will all be somewhere in the Greater Boston area.'

As the plots and navigators moved closer to examine the contour lines and topographic details on the map, the door to the briefing room opened and a middle-aged woman in a pale blue, all-in-one jumpsuit entered. Above her breast pocket was embroidered her name, Jane Ballantyne, and the emblem of the US Meteorological Service.

'Here, boys, this is the best we can do,' Ms Ballantyne announced as she handed printouts of the met forecast to all present. 'There's continuous snow and a ceiling of eighteen hundred feet all the way to Indianapolis. We've then got a complete information blank across the Midwest because we don't have any assets we can call on in Ohio. But Boston says it's not snowing there and cloud cover is at two thousand, two hundred feet. Of course, we can't tell you anything about the conditions above the clouds.'

'We're not planning to fly above the clouds,' put in the flight director sharply, frowning at the two pilots. 'Who knows what magnetic shit might be going on up there?'

The airmen read through the scant weather reports and exchanged wry glances. For pilots used to managing computer-controlled flights in which almost every element of a journey was controlled by software, the upcoming flights were going to be an ordeal. Modern pilots still trained to fly their aircraft manually, but most such training was so that they could learn to deal with emergencies and it usually took place in simulators. Flying without GPS systems, radar, transponder output, air-traffic control routing and constantly updated weather information was like being flung back to the very earliest days of aviation – and, in this case, under appalling weather conditions. Even aircraft-to-aircraft radio communication was going to be limited. Transmission capability had been abruptly restored to military networks but the pilots had been ordered to keep their radio traffic to the absolute minimum.

Suddenly, a green telephone rang on a side table. It was

an old-fashioned landline and the flight sergeant crossed the room and irritably snatched the handset from its cradle. He listened for a few moments, then thrust the handset out at Bill. 'For you, Professor Duncan,' he barked.

'It's me,' said Sally when Bill came on the line. Then, when he didn't respond immediately, she added, 'I'm calling from the Central Park shelter facility. You asked me to let you know when I arrived.'

As soon as he had heard her voice on the line Bill had instinctively turned his back on the others in the room. Now he turned his head to see whether his conversation was being overheard. The weather forecaster had now left the briefing office and all the others were poring over the maps, seemingly wholly occupied.

'It's good to hear your voice,' he said quietly into the receiver, turning away from the group again. 'But how the hell did you manage to track me down here?'

'I've had to wait for more than a day to be allowed to use this landline in the shelter,' she explained, her voice over the wire-link sounding thin, as if it were being squeezed from a tube. 'There's been some massive problem with radio connections, and the networks. When I couldn't get you I asked for Des Yates and he told me you were out at an airfield, preparing to fly. Where are you flying to in this weather? What's going on?'

'I've flying up to Boston this morning,' Bill told her quietly. 'In the President's helicopter. We've found out that the cloud is radio-sensitive – it homes in on radio signals. That's why we've been shutting down all radio transmissions and the networks.'

'My God!' exclaimed the federal agent. 'But why are you going to Boston?'

'Kramer's pet weapon has gone haywire,' Bill told her

grimly. 'We've tried everything we know to get back control of the networks, but nothing's working. I'm just hoping my HAL team will be able to get on top of it.'

Sally laughed, an incongruous sound given the seriousness of the circumstances. 'Well, I know just how darn good they are,' she admitted. 'I couldn't once find an audit trail that lead conclusively to your boat.'

'I've got to go,' said Bill, glancing over his shoulder again.

'Look, you know I'm a network-mapping specialist,' Sally told him, a note of urgency in her voice. 'New York's on the way to Boston, more or less. Come and pick me up and I'll help you do this thing. I know the geography of the networks better than anybody.'

'There's no time, Sal,' said Bill. The group had now turned away from the screen and were waiting for him, ready to depart. Outside the briefing room's thick windows he could see that the rotors on the pair of Sikorskys were beginning to turn at an ever faster rate. 'I've got to go. I'll talk to you when I get back.'

Twenty minutes later the green-painted helicopter that usually served as 'Marine One' – the President's personal transport – lifted off from the freshly cleared apron outside Hangar No. 3. It rose three hundred feet, seemed to brace itself against the teeth of the blizzard, then dipped its nose and, with all of its landing lights blazing, headed north-east towards Phoenix. As it did so, the second chopper of the Presidential flight lifted into the air and, tucking smoothly into a formation forty-five degrees to starboard and 500 feet behind the lead aircraft, followed northwards across snow-bound Arizona.

*

'I can't recognize anything,' said Bill over the intercom, shaking his head. 'Everything looks the same.'

The giant Sikorsky was hovering over what appeared to be a narrow side road in the rural area of Barnstable, Massachusetts. The flight up from Arizona had taken thirteen hours and now, as it approached nine p.m., the snow-covered fields, hedges and lanes were all bathed in a pale mauve glow. The thick clouds overhead were suffused with the neon-blue light that was being generated by friction on the Earth's atmosphere. Down below so much snow had fallen that in the eerie reflected light it was hard to make out field boundaries, roads or tracks.

The helicopter descended thirty more feet and in the glare of the bright white underbelly landing lights, Bill could see fallen snow being whipped into scurries by the down draught of the powerful twin rotors.

'OK, follow that road,' he said, pointing directly ahead. 'I think the farmhouse is over the next hill.'

He was looking for Dawes Farm, a property owned by Christine Cocoran's parents. He had visited the old farmhouse twice in Christine's company over the last couple of years and he knew that she had intended to hole up with her family in a shelter they had constructed beneath an old barn. But when he had suggested making this pick-up it had not occurred to him that he might not be able to find the location in the deep snow.

The helicopter rose over the ghostly blue hill and then, in the glare of the aircraft's powerful lights, Bill saw the shape of the main house and, some distance away, the old barn.

'I think that's it,' he said, pointing downwards. 'Can you land in that field next door?'

'We're going to have to put down somewhere soon to refuel,' replied the pilot. 'Might as well be here.'

The big Sikorskys each provided space for twenty-six passengers and three crew members. Both helicopters carried back-up crews and the White House Chief of Staff had also dispatched a contingent of six Marines to travel with the party to provide personal protection.

In an enormous flurry of blue-tinged snow, the first helicopter landed gingerly in what seemed to be a smooth field about 500 yards south of the main farm buildings. Once it had settled safely on the ground the co-pilot radioed for the support aircraft to follow suit.

It took another ten minutes for Bill and the three Marines who were going to accompany him to climb into their survival suits and prepare to face the freezing temperatures outside.

The snow was deep, thigh-high in places, and Bill led his small party of white-clad figures slowly across the snowy landscape while the aircrews began the difficult and potentially dangerous task of pumping aviation gas between the two helicopters.

Bill was breathing heavily by the time they reached the barn and the Marines behind him switched on their powerful flashlights as they stepped into its gloomy interior. At first glance the farm building seemed deserted, merely filled with hay bales and old farm machinery but, recalling what Christine had told him, Bill led the party into the depths of the barn and then pointed at a large square of wood set into the concrete floor.

There was no handle on the outside of the cellar door but one of the Marines found an old pitchfork and began to ease it slowly upwards.

Light spilled out from the widening crack as the door

was prised upright and then Bill heard running feet below. Motioning for the others to stay back, he pushed his mask up off his face, knelt down and peered into the hole.

There was a crash as someone kicked a ladder away from beneath the trapdoor, then the lights in the cellar were suddenly extinguished. Instinctively Bill ducked backwards just as a shotgun blast boomed out, the flying shot missing him by only a few inches. The Marines unshouldered their automatic weapons and dropped to the floor, their hands travelling down to the grenades they carried on their belts.

'Mr Cocoran?' shouted Bill as the reverberations of the shotgun blast began to die away. 'I'm a friend of Christine's – it's Bill Duncan.'

There was a silence, then a sound of people moving around below.

'Bill, is that you?' called Christine out of the blackness.

'Yes, it's me, Chris,' confirmed Bill, giving a thumbs-up to the two Marines to let them know that friendly contact had been established. 'The government needs your help in the networks. I've come to get you.'

'Hold on,' Christine shouted back and then, after a few moments, the light came back on below. Slowly the wooden ladder was pushed back up into place beneath the trap-door and a few seconds later Christine popped her head out.

'Jesus, Bill, you gave us a fright,' she said. 'We're not exactly expecting callers.'

'These guys are here to look after us,' explained Bill, waving at the three Marines who by now were standing upright again and had shouldered their weapons.

'God, it's freezing,' said Christine. 'Come on down quickly, all of you, otherwise we'll lose our heat.'

The stone-walled cellar was large and dry and, as Bill carefully descended the old wooden ladder, he saw that a dozen or more people were standing watchfully at the far end of the subterranean room. Christine's father still cradled his shotgun in the crook of his arm. Beyond the group Bill saw a mountain of canned food, water containers, oxygen cylinders and other necessities for survival. An open fire burned in an old-fashioned fireplace and a generator sputtered in a distant corner, providing power for the string of naked light bulbs that were suspended from the ceiling.

'It's wonderful to see you,' exclaimed Christine, throwing her arms around Bill's neck and planting a kiss directly on his lips. 'I thought you were living in luxury in some exclusive government bunker.'

'Well, I was,' said Bill. 'In Arizona. But I need you to come back there with me, and I've also got to find Paul and the whole HAL team. Do you know where they're holed up?'

'Yeah,' she said. 'But why us? What's going on?'

'I'll tell you on the way,' he said. 'Get your things together.'

Christine's father handed his shotgun to another man and stepped forward with his hand outstretched.

'Hey, sorry I took a pop at you, Professor Duncan,' he said as they shook hands. 'I never thought we'd be getting any friendly visitors. Thought you were someone after our supplies.'

Thirty minutes later Bill and Christine were in the cockpit of the lead Sikorsky as it hovered over the intersection of Richmond and Hannover Streets in the North End district of downtown Boston. The entire city was in darkness and there was no movement on the streets below.

'Can you put down on one of those roofs?' Christine

asked as she pointed to a cluster of low, snow-covered buildings near the waterfront.

'Negative – they're too old, they wouldn't take our weight,' said the pilot. 'We'll have to try one of the newer high-rises. You'll just have to find some way to get yourselves down to street level.'

After circling the area once, the pilot selected a modern high-rise building which appeared to have a large flat area, like a heliport, on its roof. As they got closer they saw a mast with a limp windsock hanging from it poking up through the snow.

'But we still can't know what they've actually got on that roof until we're almost down,' the pilot warned them over the intercom as he inched the chopper lower. 'This is a very big bird. They could have dishes or aerials down there that could cause real problems.'

The big Sikorsky squatted lower and lower and, as it did so, its rotors blew all the thick snow off of the roof and down into the street below.

'It's a helipad,' confirmed the co-pilot, looking at a screen display from a camera slung beneath the aircraft. 'And it's all clear.'

As soon as the helicopter had landed, Bill, Christine and four Marines hastily donned snow suits and face masks. They collected emergency top-up cylinders of oxygen from one of the cabin crew and then climbed carefully down the aircraft's short exit ladder and onto the icy helipad. The pilot kept the aircraft's rotors turning as the team bent double and ran carefully across the roof's slippery surface. High overhead, a few hundred yards to the south, the support helicopter hovered in case it was needed.

A pair of steel doors was set into a concrete housing on the roof. They were locked from the inside. One of the

Marines attached a plastic-explosive device to them and then ordered the group to take cover around the corner. As soon as they had done so a small blast blew open one of the steel doors.

The Marines led the way down the dark and gloomy stairwell of the deserted building. Eventually they came to ground level and the Marines forced open the doors of an emergency exit that led directly into the street.

'Over there,' said Christine, pointing to a shuttered and dark convenience store on the opposite street corner.

The store was secured against looters by iron bars screwed across the doorway from the outside but, as they peered in with the aid of the Marines' flashlights, they saw that all the shelving inside the shop was bare.

'Are you sure they're in here?' demanded Bill, as he took in the elaborate external barricading of the door.

'They'll be here,' insisted Christine. She turned to a Marine sergeant. 'Can you get us in?' she asked him.

The Marines repeated their trick with plastic explosive and then the party was inside the gloomy shop, their flashlight beams confirming that it was indeed empty of everything except the metal shop fittings.

'Through here,' said Christine as she led the team to the back of the store.

Passing through a small doorway they came into an empty stockroom. At the far end they saw a flush white wall with a heavy door set into its middle.

'It's an old cold store,' said Christine. 'This used to be a butcher's warehouse.'

She walked forward and banged the flat of her gloved hand against the door.

'Paul, it's me, Christine,' she called out as loud as she could. Then she banged again.

'Up there,' said Bill, pointing upwards to where a small video camera was located. As she looked, the camera panned slowly towards them.

'Hey, Paul,' shouted Christine again, waving at the camera. 'I've got Bill here.' She pulled him close beside her, so that he would be in shot.

There was a dull clanking of metal from behind the door and then it pushed open outwards, light and warmth spilling from its interior. Then Paul Levine stepped out into the storeroom with a huge grin on his face.

'It hit minus twenty-seven overnight,' Jane Ballantyne remarked as Marie Chevez arrived to relieve her. The meteorologist scanned the screens inside the triple-glazed observation pod near the summit of Cancut Mountain and then rose so that her colleague could take over for the morning shift of weather observations and data collection.

'Some of the radio links have come back up,' said Jane as she gathered up her things. 'But we're still not allowed to use them. Word is that this damn cloud is radio-sensitive. They think it homed in on the Earth's radio signals.'

'Yeah, I heard that too,' said Marie as she logged her arrival into the system. Then she scanned the updated information and punched out a request on the keyboard.

'We're losing an average of one degree of heat a night,' she remarked as she scanned the records. 'If this goes on we'll be at minus forty by the weekend.'

'And the oxygen content is also falling,' Jane told her as she hovered in the doorway. 'It's down by eleven per cent already.'

'I think we're going to be stuck in this mountain for a long time,' sighed Marie.

NINETEEN

Greg Cohello gave a low whistle and said, 'Will you look at this place!'

Along with Bill Duncan, Christine Cocoran, Paul Levine and nine other members of the Hackers At Large team, he was standing just inside the doorway of the Pentagon's Virtual Warfare Center, deep in Cancut Mountain.

The dark room was illuminated by the glow of dozens of vertical laser screens, all shimmering with constantly refreshing data.

'Come on in,' said Bill. 'This is where we'll be working.'

The HAL team members were each carrying hand luggage, mostly in the form of small flight cases, in which they had transported their delicate hacking technology and the software and systems they had developed over the years for cracking into illegal super-computers and fighting rogue network viruses. So severe was the crisis they were walking into that all requirements for the new arrivals to be vetted for security clearance had been waived.

Smartly uniformed Pentagon staff were still at their posts in front of the laser screens – despite their continuing failure to connect with Jerome. Dr Otto Kramer, now resplendent again in his full uniform as an army colonel, stood waiting in the centre of the room to greet the arrivals.

Beside him stood his immediate boss, General Thomas
Nicholls, his uniform smothered in glittering gold braid.

Bill smiled at this empty display of military dignity and
led his casually dressed band of computer hackers down
into the heart of the Virtual Warfare Center. The contrast
between the Pentagon staff and the new arrivals was
extreme; Hackers At Large looked more like a bunch of
throwback hippies than the world's brightest computer
scientists.

'Good to see you again, General,' said Bill as he shook
hands. Then he turned to present his bohemian-looking
group of hackers.

'This is Associate Professor Christine Cocoran,' he
began. 'And Dr Paul Levine, Professor Greg Cohello, Dr
Tim Jones, Dr Anne Lee, Professor Haris Kaniff, Dr Jimmy
McDougal, Associate Professor Mike Matthews, Dr Pierre
Laval, Tommy Branson, Dr Audrey Swain and Professor
Dirk Kommer – they all used to be with me at MIT at one
time or another. Now they are just "Hackers At Large".'

One by one the HAL members shook hands with the
four-star general and then with Otto Kramer.

'Well, that's a mighty impressive list of qualifications,'
said General Nicholls when he had greeted them all. 'I'm
told that you're the best talent there is when it comes to
taking down well-defended computer systems. We'd sure
appreciate your help here.'

An hour later the VWC had been transformed. The
laser screens had vanished back into their floor projection
slots and the bright overhead emergency lighting was
switched fully on. All around the room, access hatches had
been opened, cable trunking removed and floor panels lifted.
Miles of brightly coloured wiring could be seen as the HAL
team started to study the hardware architecture and the

arrays of quantum, neural and organic processors that were housed in stainless-steel grids which slid out vertically from air-conditioned cabinets. Members of the Pentagon science team stood beside the hackers, unrolling large circuit diagrams, providing performance specifications and explaining the salient points of the Center's processing, information-management and data-handling structure.

At the central console Bill Duncan was briefing Christine Cocoran, Paul Levine and Greg Cohello on the layered software concepts that had been used to create Jerome. Otto Kramer, still in uniform, sat with them, providing additional technical information when it was required. Since losing control of the weapons system that he had developed the Pentagon scientist had been subdued – almost to the point of depression, Bill had thought. Then the psychologist had wondered about the relationship that Kramer himself might have established with the computer entity over the eight years of the development project. Perhaps the man was feeling Jerome's loss emotionally.

'So we have one top-level personality interface called Jerome and millions of independent subset routines that he's produced,' summarized Bill after two hours of explanation. 'They're all loose in the networks and they're all capable of parasitic survival. They draw their power and processing facilities from any number of hosts at any one time.'

'And do they all have anthropomorphic interfaces?' asked Christine.

Bill shook his head. 'The duplicates don't have any degree of top-level personality, but they have all of Jerome's destructive power. Our job is to neutralize them or, even better, get them back doing what they were supposed to be doing – shutting down the Earth's radio signals must remain our top priority.'

'What about the top-level Jerome personality itself?' asked Paul Levine. During his ten-year stint as Bill's assistant director in MIT's Cognitive Computer Psychology Lab, Levine had been regarded as the world's premier authority on the issues of designing safe anthropomorphic computer interface entities. 'You've made him processor-independent, which we now know was a decidedly rash move, but what are his safety dependencies?'

Otto Kramer shrugged. 'Both of what we thought were the program's key dependencies have failed. Obviously his evolution algorithms have themselves evolved beyond our reach.'

Six hours later the Virtual Warfare Center had been put back together, but now the HAL team's hardware gizmos and specialized software had been installed at the heart of the massively parallel and distributed systems. Twelve laser screens were now shimmering from floor to ceiling in the Center but now it was a member of Bill's hacking party who stood before each display, talking quietly to the natural-language interface and gently manipulating the virtual controls that they summoned to the screen.

Inside the central holo-theatre rotated a computer-generated model of the globe without any cloud cover. A red display lattice had been laid on the surface of land masses and oceans alike to represent real-time traffic in the world's data networks. In developed countries and across ocean bridges between advanced territories the red lattice was so dense that it was almost completely solid. A semi-transparent blue lattice of lines hovered a few inches above the surface of the simulated planet, representing the laser, microwave and radio links to the vast fleet of communications satellites that were circling the Earth. It was clear that despite widespread power failures around the world, there was still a massive amount of data being transferred and, far more worryingly, huge volumes of radio transmissions were still being made.

'Got you!' shouted Haris Kaniff triumphantly from where he stood in front of a shimmering laser screen. 'Take a look at Chile and Argentina,' he called.

Bill and Otto Kramer stepped close to the globe hologram and bent to look at the representation of actual network activity at the bottom tip of South America. A large pool of blackness was spreading slowly outwards from the region as the networks went dark.

'Very old-fashioned of me,' said Kaniff self-deprecatingly as he came across to view the results of his handiwork. 'I just introduced a Trojan Horse mutation of Jerome's own viral profile. It gets their own immune system to start attacking itself. The duplicated entities strip down until they're back to their original state. Then they start shutting down radio transmissions again, as per their original instructions. It seems to be fairly effective.'

'Well done, Haris,' said Bill. 'First blood to you. Copy it to everyone else and let's go after the little bastards all at once.'

Only it wasn't that easy. Twelve hours later all the networks in South America had successfully been shut down and all radio transmissions halted once again. But when the hackers began to direct their attacks at the networks in North America, Europe and parts of Asia, network bridges and links started to fall out, as if cables, landlines, microwave connections and laser carriers between national and regional networks were being deliberately disconnected.

'It almost looks like Jerome is Balkanizing the networks,'

mused Bill as he stared at the representation of the networked globe. 'But how can he be in nine places at once?'

'The bastard must have learned to duplicate his top-level personality,' said Paul Levine in wonder as he came to stand at Bill's shoulder. 'My new data suggests we're now dealing with nine fully functioning Jerome personalities.'

'I think you're right,' agreed Bill, pointing at the globe. 'Look, they're creating islands of separate networks and cutting all links to the outside world.'

'And they've cut all links to the European network so we can't get inside to attack them,' added Levine, also pointing. 'They've done the same in the Middle East, in India, China and Japan.' He walked around to the other side of the globe. 'And they've cut the US networks in two, east and west, with no link between them.'

'Goddam it, look at that!' shouted Bill, pointing to the south-west corner of the USA. 'Now they're cutting *us* off!'

A dark circle, perhaps 400 miles in diameter, was forming around the Cancut Mountain range. Even as they watched the circle become complete, Christine Cocoran called out from across the room, 'We're losing our bandwidth!'

Other cries rang out as more members of the hacking team saw their bandwidth ebbing away. And then the shimmering laser monitors were suddenly free of all data.

'Jerome has duplicated himself – as a full personality – and his clones have just cut the world's networks up into nine sections,' Bill Duncan reported to Sally later that evening. 'And he's severed all links between them. We can't even reach him from the outside.'

After several abortive attempts to repair the Balkanized

networks remotely, Bill and his team had decided to get some rest before making further attempts the next morning.

But Bill hadn't been able to sleep. He'd spoken to the Cancut Mountain switchboard and been told that there would be a two-hour delay before he could use one of the hardened landlines that had been laid by the military between Arizona and the Central Park shelter.

'I'm sorry, sir, but there's been some massive failure in the data networks,' the operator had told him helpfully. 'Everybody wants to use the landlines.'

But eventually Bill had pulled Sally from her bed. She was sleeping in a plastic-moulded women's dormitory, she told him, with a single phone, a single bathroom and a single kitchen to serve almost forty female residents.

'What are you going to do?' she asked.

'I don't know,' Bill admitted. 'Ideally I'd like to put one of my team into every one of those networks so they can take him on directly.'

'So what's stopping you?' asked Sally. 'I presume the President must have his jet parked down there in Arizona. Why don't you borrow it to drop your people off right into the centre of those networks so they can deal with these things for good?'

An hour later Bill and Desmond Yates were shown into an ante-room beside President Jarvis's bedroom. Bill was surprised and faintly repelled by how luxurious the furniture and fittings were in this part of the mountain shelter. It seemed a complete waste of valuable resources.

'Good evening, gentlemen, or is it good morning?' asked the President as he stepped into the room. He was wearing a red silk dressing gown over his pyjamas and even in night attire he still managed to look wholly presidential. 'I presume this must be about something very important.'

'It is, sir,' said Yates. 'Professor Duncan may have a possible solution to the impasse with the Pentagon weapon.'

Bill then repeated the plan he had outlined to Des Yates an hour earlier.

'I'm sure that if I can get my people onto the ground, close to those network hubs, we can kill this thing for good – and shut down all the radio transmissions,' he concluded.

'But the weather . . .' objected the President.

'I've just spoken to Flight Director Chandler,' said Yates. 'He says it's still possible to fly. But there isn't a lot of time. Temperatures are dropping every day.'

Jarvis thought for a moment and then looked Bill directly in the eye. 'This would be a very dangerous journey, Professor. For you, and for all of your colleagues. I don't think we could guarantee you much in the way of support facilities along the route.'

'I think it may be our only chance, sir,' Bill told him. 'The only thing we can do is to shut all the radio signals down and see what a difference that makes.'

'Very well,' said the President. 'Take Air Force One. If you give Des a copy of your flight plan and your estimated arrival times, I'll speak directly to the heads of overseas governments to explain what's going on and what you're trying to do. I'll ask them to provide you with all the assistance they can along the way.'

TWENTY

'Taking Air Force One round the world is a whole different deal from just borrowing a couple of my helicopters!' snapped Flight Director Brian Chandler. 'That plane is supposed to be available for the President at all times.'

'We'll try not to break it,' promised Bill.

The Flight Director glared at the academic and his motley crew of long-haired hackers as if they were hijackers about to steal the nation's most treasured asset. They had gathered for a pre-flight briefing in a large room in the Cancut Airfield control tower, one floor below the actual air-traffic control centre itself.

Outside, the army bulldozers had been busy again and one of the long runways had been almost completely cleared of snow. It was six a.m. and still dark, but the low clouds cast a ghostly mauve glow over the mountains and the snow-covered landscape.

Air Force One was already being towed slowly out from one of the cavernous, brightly lit hangars. As the aircraft was pulled into the harsh illumination of the apron's arc lights, she seemed to shimmer in the steady snowfall.

The white hypersonic Boeing had a wide, almost rectangular body and very slender swept-back delta wings. In her normal flight pattern she would take off, then climb to a ceiling of 85,000 feet, almost to the edge of space, where her scram-jet engines would burn a mixture of air and fuel to push her to speeds above Mach 5. Technically, she was only entitled to use the call sign 'Air Force One' when the President himself was on board, but everyone referred to the elegant jet in that way even when he wasn't.

Already waiting on the apron was a large US Air Force Lockheed tanker jet. Although not supersonic, the tanker-cum-cargo carrier had an immense range and was one of a fleet of six such aircraft that could, under normal circumstances, rotate to refuel Air Force One in the air to keep her aloft for long periods.

'OK, take your seats,' Chandler told Bill and his team as double doors at the rear of the room opened and the flight crews, meteorologists, ground staff and others involved in the desperately important expedition entered and took their seats.

'This will be a long and dangerous mission,' began the Flight Director. 'Not least because both planes will have to stay beneath cloud cover for the whole trip. We know that at higher altitudes there are all sorts of magnetic anomalies being generated by the space cloud.

'Another problem is that you'll have no ATC, no external navigation aids and minimal ground support along the way. And, most importantly, Air Force One will have to remain subsonic throughout the journey. That's not going to be easy flying.'

The flight crews glanced at each other. High in the stratosphere at Mach 5, Air Force One handled like a dream, her surface control computers shaping and reshaping her plastic-ceramic skin thousands of times a second for maximum aerodynamic efficiency. At low speeds, down in the thick bumpy air, she flew like a brick.

'Then there's the weather,' continued Chandler. 'At

ground level it is now minus thirty-five degrees Celsius. Both aircraft have been fully winterized and we've fitted extra tanks of de-icing fluid, but we're dangerously close to the bottom of the operating envelope. Boeing claims that Air Force One will remain operational down to minus forty, but the Lockheed is only rated to fly down to minus thirty-eight. The main problem on both aircraft will be restarting your engines. If you stop them, you may never get them running again.

'In addition to this important group of scientists,' continued Chandler, pointing towards Bill and his team, 'you'll be carrying full ground maintenance teams on each aircraft and as many operational spares as we can load while still keeping you relatively light.'

Chandler turned away from his audience to a large, illuminated world map. He touched a remote control and their projected journey plan appeared as a white-line overlay running from west to east.

'After take-off from here, you're heading straight for New York, to drop off the first member of Professor Duncan's team. We're confident that we can get you ground support there. The President has already ordered an army unit out of the Central Park shelter to JFK Airport. They'll clear the runway and get fuel ready for you. But remember to keep those engines running!

'Then it's on to London,' continued the Flight Director, pointing at the map. 'I think the President has spoken personally to the British Prime Minister and we're fairly sure that you'll get a warm welcome at Heathrow. We hope the same will apply in Berlin, Moscow and in Istanbul, but I have no information yet about any likely government cooperation. Then it's on to Calcutta, Beijing and Tokyo. Once again, we don't yet have any information about how those governments will respond. The last stopover will be Los Angeles where Navy Seabee units will be waiting for you, then it's straight home to here. The complete circumnavigation will take fifty-six hours.'

The director of the Presidential Flight turned back from the wall map and glanced down at the representative from the US Meteorological Service. 'And what have you got for us this morning, Miss Ballantyne?' he asked.

The weather forecaster rose to her feet and turned to face the flight crews.

'The weather is pretty much the same all over the world,' she told them. 'There will be snow all the way, some of it very heavy, but the high winds have now abated. I've spoken personally with my opposite numbers in the government shelters at your nine destinations. They're all reporting very low cloud but almost no cyclonic movement. I've prepared more detailed forecasts for you to take on board, but the one thing I want to stress is that temperatures above cloud cover may be even lower than they are at ground level. That will be the most important thing to watch out for.'

With a brief nod the weather forecaster sat back down.

'OK, listen up everybody,' said Chandler. 'If the President gets full cooperation from other world leaders, we should get you refuelled and reprovisioned at every stop. But Presidential Support Two, the Lockheed, will be ready to refuel Air Force One while airborne if absolutely necessary. We've never tried it at these temperatures before, nor at such low altitudes, but it may become a necessity.'

The flight director paused, glanced around his large audience and nodded once. 'Right, people, that's it,' he concluded.

The crews, engineers and support staff rose to their feet and Brian Chandler stepped down off the small dais.

'Thanks for everything,' said Bill Duncan as he extended his hand. 'I'll see you when I get back.'

'You'll see me before that,' said Chandler, as he pulled a heavy padded jacket from the back of a chair. 'You don't think I'd let you take the President's personal airplane un-supervised do you? I'm coming with you.'

The East Coast of the United States looked nothing like Bill remembered. There *was* no coast, for one thing. Snow had fallen on the frozen ocean and blurred the boundary between land and sea.

Captain Robert Hanson, Air Force One's senior captain and the President's preferred personal pilot, had invited Bill Duncan up to the cockpit as the plane approached its first destination.

'You can just make out a slight depression where the land falls away and the sea begins,' explained Hanson as he banked the plane fifteen degrees to the left. 'That's the New Jersey shore.'

Outside, everything was bathed in a deep red gloom and the land looked smooth, as if the rough edges of the world had been rubbed away. It was an alien landscape.

The flight up from south-western Arizona had taken seven long hours, a trip which had felt as if they were con-stantly trying to land into strong headwinds. Everybody on board had been strapped firmly into their seats as the ceramic-skinned hyper-jet slogged its way through the thick atmosphere only 2,000 feet above ground level. Just above the plane, so close that Bill felt he could almost touch it, was the surreal underbelly of the thick magenta snow clouds.

'I can see Long Island,' said Melinda Mackowski, the co-pilot, pointing straight ahead out of the cockpit window.

It was several more seconds before Bill himself could make out the soft depression that was the southern edge of Long Beach.

'Landing lights, please,' asked Hanson. Then, as his co-pilot reached forward to the controls, he activated a central video display which provided a view from behind Air Force One. A tail-mounted camera showed that PS-2, the giant Lockheed transport plane, was lumbering along half a mile to the rear. As Bill watched the screen, it too switched on its powerful landing lights.

'OK, let's take a look-see,' said Hanson as he eased the plane lower.

After a few minutes Melinda pointed forwards again. 'I have JFK in visual,' she reported. 'The strip is clear.'

Bill sat upright and squinted out of the cockpit window but he couldn't make out what it was she was pointing at. Then he saw two red flares rise slowly into the night sky. Almost immediately there was an eruption of light on the ground as long strips of flares were illuminated all along the runway.

'We'll land from the east,' said Hanson, easing back the throttles and beginning a slow right-hand turn.

Ten minutes later both Air Force One and PS-2 were safely on the ground at JFK Airport. As they had landed, Bill and all of the others on board had felt a wash of relief and gratitude as they saw the ranks of survival-suited army engineers waving to them from the snowy airfield.

'Keep all the engines running!' yelled Captain Robert Hanson as he vaulted from his seat.

The temperature on the ground was now minus 36.8

degrees Celsius and Hanson knew that if they switched the engines off they would never be able to get them started again. Co-pilot Mackowski double-checked that the brakes were locked fast and then nudged the throttles up by a further two per cent, just to be sure.

The two planes were parked at the end of a runway that had just been bulldozed clear of snow. A large squad of US Army engineers had fought their way out to Kennedy from the Central Park shelter to assist in this desperate round-the-world race and they were now maintaining continuous snow-clearance operations while the dangerous process of refuelling the passenger jet got under way. A very fast turn-around was needed in such severe weather.

'Shut down all the external electrical systems except engine support,' Hanson shouted back to Melinda as he stood in the cockpit doorway. 'I'm going outside to supervise the refuelling.'

There were no circumstances under which it was either safe or permissible to refuel the jets of the Presidential Flight while they were on the ground with their engines still running. Normally Air Force One would have been refuelled in-flight by one of the mighty Lockheed tankers, but that was not a risk to take in such low temperatures. It was more than likely that one or more of the six external valves involved in the mid-air refuelling process would have frozen shut.

Outside, a blizzard was raging and everything was cloaked in a dark red gloom. It was only four in the afternoon but the space cloud was absorbing so much sunlight that on the ground it seemed like night. Along either edge of the long gritted and salted runway the army engineers had placed gas-powered emergency flares to provide the pilots with flight-path illumination. All normal power supplies to the deserted airport had failed days ago and the vast snowy dunes, already made red by the glow from the snow clouds, now flickered with the reflected flames of the beacons. Around both aircraft was a huge circle of bright arc lights, held high aloft by military cherry pickers and powered by a fleet of mobile generators.

'Ready?' Captain Hanson asked Paul Levine, the first of Bill Duncan's volunteers to be dropped off. Both men had donned full Arctic survival suits.

Hanson pressed the button to activate the hydraulic passenger-door mechanism and, as the door slowly retracted into the fuselage, a howling gale and a thick scurry of snowflakes burst into the plane's warm cabin. Bill Duncan, Christine, Greg, Haris, Audrey and all of the other HAL members were gathered safely at the far end of the heated cabin, as instructed.

A bulldozer was now slowly pushing a mobile staircase into position at the plane's open door. As soon as the steps were secure, Hanson led Levine down into the swirling blizzard and transferred him and his cases of specialized equipment into the care of the senior army officer. Then the captain fought his way back towards the tail end of the large plane to supervise the two fuel-tanker crews who were now positioning themselves under its delta wings.

A member of Air Force One's cabin crew began to lower the fuselage door to conserve heat. But, just as the door was about to close, Bill and the others saw the man reverse the controls and the door began to rise again.

A small bundle wrapped in an orange survival suit and covered in snow burst into the cabin as the door lifted. Then, as the crew member began to close the door again, the figure stood glancing around the brightly lit cabin.

A few moments after the door was closed once more

and the auxiliary cabin heaters had been boosted to maximum power, the visitor lifted the protective mask from her face.

'Sally!' cried Bill Duncan, stepping forward joyously as he recognized the new arrival. 'How the hell did you get here?'

'I thought you might need some help with network mapping,' said the CNS agent with a grin. 'So I persuaded the army to bring me along.'

Hypersonic flight was impossible, so was climbing above the world's thick cloud cover. They could not risk exposing the aircrafts' systems to the space cloud's powerful magnetic fields, nor to the colder air that was likely to be found at higher altitudes.

For these reasons the first five legs of the HAL team's round-the-world trip were slow, bumpy and decidedly uncomfortable. Radio-based ground telemetry had been switched off in all regions and no satellite navigation or ATC services were available. The relays of pilots now had to fly the two planes manually, despite Air Force One's supersensitive aerodynamics, while at the same time plotting their own courses. The internal on-board computers were still working, otherwise the planes could not have flown, but the systems were receiving none of their usual input from satellites or from the ground.

After dropping Paul Levine off in Manhattan, they had managed to land safely at Heathrow, just outside London. Whatever President Jarvis had said to the British Prime Minister had produced the desired effect; Bill Duncan estimated that there must have been at least 1,000 British army personnel who had turned out at the airport to clear runways, provide fuel and reprovision the aircraft.

They had delivered Greg Cohello and his precious flight cases into the hands of the British authorities and had then taken off once more, bound for Berlin, where another large army reception party had been waiting for them.

The Russians turned out in similar numbers at Sheremetyevo-2 International Airport. Reckoning that they had a universal remedy for freezing conditions, they included six cases of vodka with the catering packs that were lifted into the hold of each aircraft.

Then the American mission had landed at ice-bound Istanbul to deliver Jimmy McDougal to the Middle East network hub, then on to snow-covered Singapore, then Beijing. Now they were headed for Tokyo, where it was Christine Cocoran's turn to be dropped off to mount her attack on the Jerome duplicate and the dense, high-volume networks that existed in and around the main Japanese islands and their surrounding archipelagos.

They were juddering along at 5,200 feet over Korea when Captain Jill Turnbull's voice came over the intercom asking for Bill Duncan to come up to the cockpit. Bill had been examining a map of the Japanese networks with Sally and she followed him as he made his way forward.

'The outside temperature is falling dramatically,' Captain Turnbull reported as soon as Bill and Sally arrived in the cockpit. 'It's already minus forty-two Celsius. and still going down.' The relief captain was gripping hard at the bucking controls as she fought to keep the plane steady. A central display screen revealed that they were flying at 582 knots an hour.

Bill and Sally exchanged glances. Like everybody else on board they knew they were already flying in temperature conditions that were well below the manufacturer's recommended operational limits for the aircraft.

'What can we do?' asked Bill as the aircraft gave yet another lurch in the freezing, turbulent air.

'And the radar says there's a huge ice storm just ahead,' added the captain. 'It's far too big to go around.'

'But we can't go back,' said Sally. 'There's no time. They're waiting for us in Tokyo.'

Suddenly there was a huge explosion in the cockpit and Bill's and Sally's eyes and faces were filled with a hot liquid and a freezing spray at the same time. The aircraft gave a giant tilt and went into a sudden dive.

'GET HER HANDS OFF THE CONTROLS,' screamed Alan Newbass, the co-pilot. 'GET HER HANDS OFF THE CONTROLS.'

Bill wiped the mess of blood, brain tissue, ice shards and shattered safety glass from his face with the back of his sleeve and gasped in horror as he saw the decapitated body of Captain Jill Turnbull still gripping hard at the flight yoke. Blood was pumping upwards in great gouts from the mangled stump of her neck only to be distributed around the cockpit in a pink foam by a freezing slipstream. Then Bill saw the gaping hole in the port cockpit window and he heard and felt other blocks of ice slamming into the airframe all around.

He forced himself forward against the obscene stream of vaporized blood and grasped the dead pilot's arms. She was gripping the yoke so tightly that it seemed as if rigor mortis had already set in and Bill had to use all his strength to prise her fingers from the controls. Eventually he did so and he folded the lifeless arms back down onto the bloody torso. The yoke suddenly twisted hard to the right and was pulled sharply back, the engines roaring in a higher key as the co-pilot increased power and tried to right the aircraft.

Large ice chunks were still slamming into the nose and fuselage of the plane.

Bill felt a strong hand pull him back out of the way and he turned to see Brian Chandler in full survival gear and breathing apparatus step in to deal with the dead pilot's body. The Flight Director punched the quick-release button on the captain's seat harness and then lifted her headless corpse straight upwards and over the back of her seat, dumping the body onto the cockpit floor as though it were a sack of potatoes.

Standing back, Bill saw that the co-pilot, who was now trying to regain control of the plane, was already turning blue from the cold and from the lack of oxygen in the outside atmosphere – even at this relatively low altitude.

The plane's emergency oxygen masks had descended from the ceiling and one was now swinging about wildly above Newbass's head, but the co-pilot was using both hands to wrestle with the controls of the juddering plane and was too intent on pulling out of the dive to reach up for a gasp of air. Then Bill suddenly felt a hand slam a breathing mask over his own face; Sally had run back to the cabin to summon the Flight Director and to fetch more oxygen.

After taking one deep breath, Bill pushed the mask away from his own face and pointed urgently at the gasping co-pilot. Sally, her own oxygen mask securely in place, pushed forward and clamped the inhaler over the co-pilot's mouth.

Gradually the steep incline of the cockpit floor levelled out again and Bill saw the co-pilot's shoulders heaving as he gulped breath after breath from the oxygen supply that Sally held to his face. Then Newbass nodded that he was OK and reached up and pulled his own mask down. Chandler low-

ered himself into the captain's seat to provide flight-deck
support.

Bill stepped to the back of the cockpit to make more
room, but as he did so his heel came down on something
hard and large. He turned to see Jill Turnbull's smashed and
bloody head lying on the floor among shards of splintered
glass and ice.

Vomit suddenly filled Bill's throat and mouth and he
spewed violently against the back cockpit wall. Then he felt
powerful hands dragging him out into the cabin and away
from the devastation.

Forty minutes later Bill was back in the hastily cleaned-up
cockpit of Air Force One. The broken window had been
replaced by a steel template carried in the hold for such
emergencies and the plane was now pressurized and heated
once again.

But outside, everything had changed. Captain Robert
Hanson had resumed control and he had taken the decision
to climb up above the ice storm, no matter what the risk of
magnetic interference from the space cloud or from ever
lower temperatures. He had ordered PS-2 to do the same,
explaining the near-disaster that had occurred on board Air
Force One.

'Take a look at this, Professor,' Hanson said as Bill
arrived beside him. 'Have you ever seen anything more
beautiful?'

Climbing to 28,000 feet, they had emerged into a sky-
scape of wild and savage splendour. The jet was now flying
underneath the canopy of the space cloud itself and in the
brighter light they could see towering multicoloured
columns of gas – green, blue, magenta and yellow – all illuminated from within by violent electrical discharges.

'The outside temperature has actually risen by ten degrees!' observed Hanson in wonder.

'It must be the heat generated by the friction of the gas cloud against the ionosphere,' said Bill, nodding, still gazing in awe at the stellar scenes of beauty all around the plane.

'Oh shit,' said Alan Newbass, the co-pilot, suddenly. 'I've lost all aero-surface control.'

'And the radar's also gone down,' called Captain Hanson. He leaned forward and tapped one of the few mechanical instruments still fitted to modern aircraft. The compass needle was spinning violently.

'I'm going back down to the deck,' said Hanson, pushing the control yoke forward. 'We've got to get out of this magnetic field. Tell PS-2 to do the same thing.'

Newbass relayed the instructions to the Lockheed as the captain put the plane into a steep dive, but no answer was received from PS-2.

Newbass called the Lockheed support plane again and again, but there was still no answer.

'It's probably this damn magnetic field,' shouted Hanson grimly as he kept the nose of the plane hard down and watched the altitude scroll downwards on the central display screen.

Turbulence hit Air Force One again as it re-entered Earth's own thick cloud cover, but a few minutes later they emerged into the dull red gloom once more. Now they were over a frozen maroon ocean and there was no sign of any ice storm.

'Come in, PS-2,' repeated Newbass. 'Come in, PS-2.'

'There she is,' shouted Hanson, pointing out of the starboard cockpit window. All present looked in the direction the captain was indicating and then they saw the giant

Lockheed transport spiralling sideways and downwards out of the blood-red clouds.

'Jim, Jim, pull out,' screamed Newbass into his radio microphone.

But there was no answer from the stricken tanker. Those on board Air Force One watched in horror as the giant support jet seemed to rotate slowly, like a leaf caught in an eddy, as it plunged down and down and crashed into the ice-locked sea, erupting instantly into a giant fireball.

By the time they reached Los Angles, the penultimate stop on their round-the-world trip, the temperature on the ground had fallen to minus 50° Celsius.

A large contingent of Navy Seabees had turned out to prepare LAX for their arrival, a task that had consisted of clearing huge mounds of flood-damaged material from the runway and its surrounding area, as well as constantly scraping away the fresh snowfalls.

The gigantic storm that had come ashore in Southern California had wrecked most of the buildings on and around the airport and the receding waters had deposited the wreckage of smashed jet planes, office buildings, homes and cars all across the airfield.

Inside the warm cockpit of the safely landed Air Force One, several factors were causing the flight director and the crew real concern. It was still snowing heavily outside, so heavily that the four snowploughs which were deployed on the long runway could not clear the drifts quickly enough. By the time they had completed clearing one section, so much new snow had fallen that it was likely to suck greedily at Air Force One's tyres and prevent a safe take-off.

The external temperature gauge showed that it was minus 50.35° Celsius outside. It was almost eleven p.m. and the snow-covered airfield was bathed in a ghostly neon blue. Gas-powered flares lined the long runway, their flames reflected brilliantly by the fresh falls.

'We're ten degrees below our operational limit,' Captain Hanson told his co-pilot, Bill Duncan, Sally Burton and the flight director as they gathered in the cockpit. 'At this temperature even the aviation fuel is likely to freeze.'

He glanced at his passengers to be sure that they understood what he was telling them. 'I'm prepared to attempt a take-off,' he continued. 'But it will be very risky. We might be better to go back to the Seabees' shelter for the night.'

Bill shook his head. 'The timing of our operation is critical. All of my team are in place and they're waiting for me to coordinate the attack from Cancut. If we wait, the weather will just get worse.'

'You're right about that,' agreed Hanson, 'and I don't think we could restart the engines.' He glanced at Melinda Mackowski, his co-pilot. She gave one short nod. Sally Burton did the same.

'Your call, then,' the pilot said to the boss of the Presidential Flight.

Brian Chandler peered out of the front cockpit window towards the gas-lit snowy runway. Then he laid a hand on the captain's shoulder.

'If you think we can fly, we'd better fly.'

'OK,' said Hanson, reaching for his microphone. 'Let's see what our dispatcher has to say.'

Thirty feet below, Lieutenant Michael Unzermann of the US Naval Construction Battalion stood beneath the aircraft with his headphones plugged into an intercom port on one of Air Force One's undercarriage struts. Like all his fellow Seabees on the field, he was dressed in a chemically heated Arctic survival suit. As the intercom crackled into life, his listened to the pilot request clearance for an immediate take-off.

'Give me a few minutes, Captain,' Unzermann said. 'I'll get back to you.'

Disconnecting himself from the intercom, the Seabee-dispatcher stepped out from beneath the belly of the large plane. He looked back to where he had just been standing and noticed that in the half-hour Air Force One had been parked, its engines running continuously, snow had drifted right up to the axles of the aircraft's main landing gear.

Unzermann waded out from under the delta wing and into the full force of the blizzard that was howling across the airport. A tall sergeant, covered in snow, ran clumsily over to him.

'We've lost two of the snowploughs, sir. They've frozen up,' he reported, shouting to be heard above the powerful engines. 'I can't keep the runway clear with just the other two.'

Unzermann thought for a moment, then clapped his hand onto his subordinate's shoulder.

'I want the two ploughs to make one more pass all the length of the runway,' he shouted into his sergeant's ear. 'Do it now. And send the avgas drivers over to me.'

The Seabee nodded, then ran as fast as he could through the thick snow to relay the orders to the drivers.

In the cockpit of Air Force One, Captain Robert Hanson and his co-pilot were completing their pre-flight checks. Strapped into crew seats at the back of the cockpit were Brian Chandler, Bill Duncan and Sally Burton. The flight back to Cancut Mountain would take only an hour and Bill knew that the airfield crew at the government shelter was on a constant state of alert to receive them.

Two large snowploughs had now appeared in front of

the aircraft and were cutting parallel swathes through the
snow along the landing strip ahead of them. Then, to the
surprise of all in the cockpit, two aviation-fuel tankers
turned onto the runway and began slowly following the
snowploughs as they cut broad furrows through the snow.
On the platform at the rear of each tanker was a survival-
suited Seabee.

'What the hell are they doing?' muttered Hanson.

Just as he spoke, the Seabees turned large valves at the
rear of the tankers and huge gouts of liquid fuel began to
pour down onto the runway, glinting as it touched the freezing surface. Even through the thick snowfall, those in the
cockpit could clearly make out the twin trails of aviation fuel
leading away into the distance.

The intercom buzzed, and Hanson greeted the dispatcher as he came back onto the line.

The pilot listened, then shook his head. 'That is negative, Lieutenant,' he said. 'That's far too risky.'

Below the belly of the aircraft Unzerman stood with
two Seabee ratings at his side. They were carrying gas
torches that they had pulled from beside the runway.

'I think it's your only chance, Captain,' shouted Unzerman. 'The snow is falling too fast for us to keep the runway
open. Just wait until the flames start to subside, then take off
as fast as you can.'

In the cockpit Hanson muted his microphone and
turned to his co-pilot.

'They're going to set light to that fuel,' he said nodding
out towards the runway. 'It will heat the runway up for a
few minutes. Then we're supposed to take off just as the
flames start to die down.'

Melinda Mackowski glanced at her captain and then

looked straight ahead, out through the cockpit windshield. 'Very good, sir,' she agreed, swallowing quietly.

Hanson turned to look over his shoulder at the Flight Director. 'OK with you, Brian?'

'It won't be any better tomorrow,' said Chandler, with a nod.

'OK with you, Professor?' the pilot asked.

Bill glanced at Sally.

'We've got to get back somehow,' she said.

'We're in your hands, Captain,' said Bill.

Hanson spoke into his microphone again and then turned to his co-pilot.

'Forty per cent power, please,' he told her.

As Melinda Mackowski slowly lifted the throttle, Bill watched two Seabees wade out to the centre of the runway, three hundred yards in front of the plane's nose. They touched their gas torches to the trails of fuel and twin lines of flames streaked off down the runway into the distance.

Hanson extended his right hand and laid it over the top of his co-pilot's as she nursed the manual engine throttles.

They watched the flames burning on the runway ahead of them and, just as those nearest the plane's nose began to subside, Hanson pushed the four throttle levers forward determinedly as far as they could go.

The airframe shook as the engines suddenly gained power – four engines that developed 110,000 lbs of thrust each, three times more powerful that those fitted to Concorde, the world's first supersonic commercial jet. Just when it seemed as if the intense vibration would destroy something, Hanson snapped off all of the wheel brakes.

Air Force one leaped forward and into the flames on the runway.

At the back of the cockpit Sally grabbed Bill's hand and

squeezed hard as the aircraft accelerated rapidly through the flames and smoke. The roll seemed to go on and on, until at last Robert Hanson pulled back sharply on the yoke. Then Air Force One shook the heavy snow from her landing gear and rose rapidly up towards the neon-blue clouds.

TWENTY-ONE

'Greg, can you hear me in London?'

'Loud and clear,' said the image of Greg Cohello from inside a British government shelter near Heathrow.

'Audrey in Berlin,' continued Bill Duncan. 'Comms OK?'

'A-OK,' reported Audrey Swain from the Berlin hub of the Central European network. She gave a thumbs-up to the camera.

Bill called his distant team members one by one, checking that the hardened, dedicated cable links that the US military and their foreign counterparts had installed between Cancut Mountain and the overseas network hubs were functioning correctly.

Finally, he came to Christine Cocoran in Japan and Haris Kaniff in Los Angeles.

'I'm ready to go, Bill,' said Christine.

'Ready here,' confirmed Kaniff.

It was vital that the twelve members of the HAL hacking team should begin their attacks at precisely the same time. The computer entity known as Jerome had somehow duplicated himself into nine top-level personalities and had occupied and then Balkanized the world's vast web of data networks.

The central part of the hackers' plan was to bombard and block the perimeters of each isolated network section to prevent the duplicated Jeromes reconnecting the network links and then hopping between them. Each cloned Jerome personality had to be isolated within his own individual network and then attacked by the vast array of hardware and software technologies that the team had developed over their years of vigilante network policing.

Because timing was of the essence, the network-use-denial technologies that each team member had carefully transported to their destinations had to be deployed at the same split second. The key process at the heart of the team's anti-viral technology was to sample the evolving computer virus in real time, then to instantly duplicate it but with a key mutation in the new code, before reinserting it back into the networks where it would be assimilated by the virus as its own. Soon afterwards, the mutated code that the hackers had infiltrated to the virus would disrupt its host to the point where the team members hoped they could regain control.

Pierre Laval, Dirk Kommer and Anne Lee were standing at the Virtual Warfare Center's laser sceens waiting for their leader's command. At the edge of the central holo-theatre Sally Burton waited beside a dynamic display that would provide them with an instant window into any point in the Balkanized networks, once the hackers had managed to loosen Jerome's grasp and reconnect the global links.

In the nine other cities around the world the far-flung HAL team members also waited, their expectant faces appearing on screens that had been rigged around the walls of the command centre. Beneath each one appeared their location: *New York, London, Berlin, Moscow, Istanbul, Calcutta, Beijing, Tokyo, Los Angeles.*

Observing from the back of the room were Desmond Yates, General Thomas Nicholls, still in his beribboned, flag-rank dress uniform as Chairman of the Joint Chiefs, and the Pentagon's Colonel Dr Otto Kramer, also in his smartest uniform.

'Synchronize on thirty,' said Bill, and Laval transmitted a time code to all members of the team.

'All locked on,' Laval reported after a few seconds.

'OK, let's do this,' said Bill.

The automated count ticked down. As it reached zero, it triggered the sustained and rapidly multiplying attacks that the HAL team members had devised, attacks which occurred billions of times a second, attacks that were so demanding on Jerome and his virtual siblings that the humans overseeing these automated assaults would have time to manually introduce a collection of anti-viral technologies which, for want of a better term, they had dubbed 'vaccines'.

Thirty-six hours later, the battle was being won. First blood had gone to the Cancut Mountain team, who had rapidly overwhelmed the sub-entity viruses that had cut the mountain HQ off from the world's data networks.

Then the West European matrix had become the first major section of the world's network to enjoy full recovery. Greg Cohello in London had regained sufficient control of the local duplicate Jerome personality to complete the task of shutting down all radio transmissions in the region inside three hours.

A huge cheer had gone up inside Cancut Mountain as he reported total radio silence in his sector.

'Happy to be of service,' said Greg as he rose from his seat and took a small bow.

The eastern half of the North American matrix fell next as Paul Levine expertly destroyed another top-level Jerome

personality within the cordoned network and set the
sub-entities back to work shutting down all radio signals.
The West Coast hub fell next and three hours later Audrey
Swain in Berlin had reported similar success in the central
European networks.

'What took you so long, Auds?' asked a cocky Paul
Levine from New York.

One by one the clones that Jerome had created were
tamed and retasked. The world's networks were recon-
nected and the many different forms of radio transmission
were finally shut down.

But the dense web of cables, lasers and radio links that
surrounded the Tokyo hub remained obstinately resistant.
Hours after all the other network centres had reported control fully recovered, Christine Cocoran was still fighting to
achieve even her first small-scale victory over the local
Jerome entity.

Now freed of their own responsibilities, the rest of the
dispersed HAL team had patched into the Japanese hub
from their remote locations and were working frantically
alongside Christine to try to overwhelm the virtual weapon.
But the real-time, constantly updating vaccines that the
team was deploying seemed to be having no effect on the
Japanese iteration of Jerome. Even the special hardware that
Christine had patched into the Tokyo hub, technologies
that could fry bridges and junctions in the network with tar-
geted bursts of high-energy microwaves, were not slowing
the weapon down. He merely isolated and swarmed around
such barriers.

Sally Burton displayed a detailed map of the Japanese
hub in the war room's central holo-theatre. From information that Christine was relaying back to Cancut Mountain,
the CNS agent had built a model of the network activity

and the millions of radio transmissions that were being generated from all over the Japanese islands.

'If anything, there is even more radio action than usual,' observed Sally worriedly as she compared the present levels of transmission output to historical data.

As Bill walked over to examine the model, Christine's exhausted voice came over the loudspeakers once again.

'I'm going to back out, and start from the top once more,' she told the team members. 'Hands off for now. I'll tell you when we're going in again.'

Bill glanced up at Christine's tired face as she mopped her brow and began her work all over again. Then he returned his attention to Sally's network map.

'What's so different about the Japanese network?' he asked her. 'Why should this thing be holding out so long there?'

There was a quiet cough from behind and Bill turned to see the figure of Dr Otto Kramer at his shoulder.

'I think you'll find that the Jerome entity in the Japanese networks is the master personality,' explained the Pentagon scientist. 'We built the original to have certain features that he could not reproduce in his replicas, features that would guarantee his own survival even under extreme conditions.'

Bill stared at the Pentagon man in disbelief.

'Don't you have *any* way of killing this thing?' he demanded.

Otto Kramer shook his head. 'That was not in the design spec,' he said quietly. 'Jerome cannot be killed.'

Anger flooded through Bill Duncan like a sudden electric shock and it seemed as if his head was suddenly filled with blood. Without pausing to consider, he swung his right fist and smashed it as hard as he could into Kramer's face.

The Colonel staggered backwards across the Virtual Warfare Center and collapsed into the central beam of a laser screen, cutting the projection in two.

Des Yates stepped forward quickly and grabbed Bill by the shoulder. But all present quickly realized that the tired and angry MIT professor did not intend to follow up his physical attack.

From the centre of the room Dirk Kommer began to clap slowly, laconically. 'Fucking useless military,' he said, putting words to all their thoughts.

'OK, let's get back on it,' said Bill angrily turning away from the stricken Otto Kramer. 'Time is running out. We must find some way to beat this thing.'

'I cannot order a nuclear strike on Japan!' President Jarvis shouted at General Thomas Nicholls, the Chairman of the Joint Chiefs of the US military, thumping the table as he spoke. 'No American President ever could!'

On Yates's advice, the President had reconvened the Cloud EXCOM for an emergency meeting in the Cancut Mountain Situation Room. Also present were the President's Chief of Staff and several presidential aides.

Desmond Yates had briefed the meeting about the HAL team's success in regaining control over ninety per cent of the world's data and radio networks. Then he had explained that the dense data and radio networks in Japan and in its surrounding islands were proving highly resistant to his team's efforts.

'Duncan and his people have been working on that section for three days now, sir,' he concluded. 'They're still at it. But they're not making any headway. In its core form, the Pentagon's virtual weapon seems to have mutated beyond our ability, or theirs, to regain control.'

Then Yates had shown the meeting a short video of an old-fashioned chemical-fuelled rocket blasting off from the Kennedy Space Center in Florida.

'This rocket took off at ten a.m. this morning,' he explained. 'As you know, the space cloud not only homes in on radio signals, we think it also prevents most UHF radio signals escaping our atmosphere. To be absolutely sure that we can make contact with *Friendship*, our NASA colleagues have put a pre-programmed probe into space, a probe that will contact *Friendship* once it is wholly clear of the space cloud. It will then instruct the spacecraft to reposition all its antennae to point backwards towards this planet and to begin broadcasting as powerfully as possible and on as many different frequencies as it can. That instruction is due to be delivered in forty-eight hours' time.'

All present in the meeting nodded. It was a long shot, but they knew it was the only chance they had. The cloud was tightening its grip on the world. Flying was now completely impossible and no surface transport could move. All over the frozen globe, governments, communities, small groups and family units were sheltering in bunkers, preformed habitats, home-made refuges and any shelter that could be sealed and heated. The oxygen level in the atmosphere had now fallen by twelve per cent.

'But there can be no hope of the cloud being decoyed away to follow *Friendship* while radio signals are still being produced on this planet,' concluded Yates. 'We have to achieve total radio silence if we are to have a chance of luring it away.'

President Jarvis nodded. 'I have spoken with Prime Minister Kakehashi this morning,' he told the meeting. 'As you know, the Japanese authorities have extended every cooperation to Professor Duncan's local team member, but the Prime Minister admits that none of his own network specialists, nor the Japanese military, can see any way of recovering the use of their networks. It seems that the Pentagon's computer weapon has completely taken over their command structure.'

It was then that General Nicholls had sat forward in his chair and made the suggestion that had provoked the President's furious outburst.

'Sir,' he began in a grave tone. 'The safety and future of the entire world is at stake. If Professor Yates believes that radio signals from the spacecraft *Friendship* may lure this murderous thing away from our planet, we have a duty to all of humankind to do our best to make his plan work. If we do not, and if our atmosphere continues to disappear, all life on Earth will become extinct.'

All those crowded into the large Situation Room were silent as the general made his speech. All present knew that they and their closest loved ones would be safe inside this government bunker for twenty years or more, but in the world outside people were already dying in their millions. Soon that figure would become tens of millions and a short while after that billions more would die. In practical terms, Earth's civilization would be reduced to a handful of communities hiding underground, eking out their limited supplies of air, food, water and fuel for as long as possible.

'If we cannot shut down the Japanese networks in the next few hours we must destroy them completely in order to achieve total global radio silence,' continued the Chairman of the Joint Chiefs, measuring his words carefully. He allowed his stern gaze to sweep around the horseshoe-shaped table before continuing.

'As some of you will know, several of our nuclear-powered submarines have remained at sea throughout this crisis – all crewed by volunteers. Thanks to ULF radio – a radio signal of such low frequency that it does not escape from the oceans – we are still able to communicate with them.'

The general paused to straighten the already straight blotting pad in front of him. The he gazed directly at the President.

'Sir, the USS *Hudson* is currently in the East China Sea, deep beneath the ice. She is carrying a full payload of twenty-four Sioux cruise missiles. They are each armed with twenty-megaton nuclear warheads – warheads that could not be adapted in time to take part in the final strike against the cloud.'

The general took a deep breath, one that was audible to all in the hushed and intense atmosphere of the Situation Room, and sat back in his chair. His level gaze remained fixed on Maxwell Jarvis.

'Mr President,' he continued. 'I recommend ordering that the USS *Hudson*'s full payload should be deployed immediately against the networks in the Japanese region. They must be totally destroyed.'

It was then that President Jarvis had exploded in rage.

'No American President could ever order a nuclear attack against Japan!' he repeated, banging his fist on the table-top once again. 'You couldn't destroy those networks without destroying the whole of Japan and all its surrounding islands. Over one hundred million people would be killed! The United States can never, ever attack Japan with nuclear weapons again!'

The Chairman of the Joint Chiefs continued to regard the President levelly.

'If we don't destroy the Japanese networks we can be certain that billions of people all over the world are going to die in the next few weeks, perhaps ninety-five per cent of the world's population,' he told his commander-in-chief. 'But those billions might just be saved – *if* we can silence Japan's network and radio transmissions.'

TWENTY-TWO

There were bodies everywhere. No one wanted to be the first to leave the Virtual Warfare Center but after five days of continuous effort the hackers had been finally forced to sleep. They lay propped against high-tech computer housings, against walls and even sprawled flat out on the floor of the dimly lit holo-theatre.

Bill Duncan had slept for only two hours, Sally Burton curled tight into him, both fully clothed. During their frantic round-the-world dash everybody on the team had realized that the two had become romantically attached and, despite the desperate emergency, Bill's group of close friends were pleased for him. Even Christine had kissed Bill's cheek and told him how much she liked Sally.

Nursing a coffee that one of the Pentagon duty officers had brought for him, Bill studied the three green laser screens which were filled with flying graphics. They were displaying the high volume of transmissions that were still taking place in Japan's data network and radio spectrum.

Bill yawned and looked at his watch. Unlike most computer scientists he was no techno nerd. Where many of his academic peers would choose to wear a sturdy, waterproof, digital, multi-function unit on their wrist, Bill wore an old Breitling analogue timepiece that his late father had given him twenty years before. It said it was ten o'clock. But whether that was ten a.m. or ten p.m., Bill had no idea.

The door to the Virtual Warfare Center opened and Desmond Yates strode in, as immaculate as ever in a pale grey suit, despite the community's continuing incarceration and the pervading sense of gloom.

Realizing that many members of the team were sleeping, he crossed quietly to where Bill was leaning with his coffee against the master display console for the holo-theatre.

'Any improvement, Bill?' he asked quietly. 'Are you getting any control back over the Japanese networks?'

The computer psychologist shook his head and pointed to the shimmering laser screens.

'We can't even touch him,' admitted Bill with another shake of his head. 'That bastard Kramer claims he never even made notes as he wrote the code for Jerome's immune system. Even he can't give us any clues that might help.'

Desmond Yates glanced down at his own elegant watch.

'It's now twenty-two hundred,' he told Bill in a low voice. 'And the President has set a deadline. If you haven't got the Japanese networks back under your control by midnight, he's going to issue an order to destroy them – to destroy them completely.'

Bill stood bolt upright in alarm, all tiredness instantly banished.

'Destroy them?' he demanded as he banged his coffee down on the console. 'How do you mean "destroy them"? How can he destroy millions of miles of cables and millions of radio transmitters?'

His raised voice disturbed some of the other team members, who grunted and groaned as they came to wakefulness.

Desmond Yates glanced around him, as if unwilling to say anything further.

'What do you mean?' hissed Bill, grabbing the White House adviser firmly by the upper arm.

'He's going to order a massive nuclear strike against Japan and its surrounding islands,' whispered Yates. 'Apparently the Navy's got a submarine in the area that still has a full complement of missiles. I've come to give you some advance warning.'

'LOOK AT HER,' yelled Bill Duncan, stepping into the centre of the room and pointing up towards an image of the sleeping Christine Cocoran in Tokyo. Like her team-mates inside Cancut Mountain, Christine was asleep in front of a bank of computer displays, her head on a desk and her long dark hair spilled out onto its surface like a pool of wine.

'YOU CAN'T JUST KILL CHRISTINE AND THE ENTIRE JAPANESE POPULATION!'

Everyone in the room was now awake, some rising groggily to their feet. Sally rose to her knees and then came to stand at Bill's side.

'They're all going to die soon anyway,' said Yates grimly. 'And everybody else on Earth will also die if we leave those radio signals transmitting!'

Bill Duncan shook his head, to try to clear the over-whelming confusion he felt.

'But what about Christine?' demanded Sally.

'It would be better if you don't tell her,' Yates said. 'It will be instant, anyway.'

'STAY WHERE YOU ARE!' boomed a gravel voice from the entrance to the Virtual Warfare Center. General Thomas Nicholls strode boldly into the room, followed by six Marines, each with an automatic weapon crooked in their arms. Behind them followed Dr Otto Kramer, in his colonel's uniform once again, a plaster across his broken nose, and half a dozen Pentagon scientific assistants.

'This facility is now under my control,' ordered Nicholls, indicating for the Marines to take up posts around the room. 'All incoming and outgoing communications will now be under my direct command.'

Powerful, high-energy laser beams cut upwards through the thick ice for almost an hour and then, at latitude 32.41° North and longitude 135.73° East, the USS *Hudson* rose heavily through the surgically divided floes and surfaced 200 miles due west of Shanghai. It was snowing heavily in the East China Sea.

Down in the submarine's warm control room, Captain Peter Boardman conferred with his Executive Officer. In one hand was a printout of the encrypted orders that he had recently received from the US High Command in Arizona. In his other hand was one of the two smart keys that would be required to fire the vessel's arsenal of nuclear-tipped cruise missiles. The Exec still had the second smart key suspended around his neck on a silver chain. Both biometric-specific keys would only work in the hands of their official keepers, or in the hands or two other nominated crew members.

The submarine's senior officers were waiting for a further message of clarification. On receiving their orders two hours earlier, the captain had ordered his vessel to be roused from its state of semi-hibernation and brought up to the ocean's freezing surface. He also ordered all of the long-range Sioux cruise missiles to be armed with their twenty-megaton nuclear warheads, just as the alarming signal from the US High Command had demanded.

As they keyed in the coordinates of the missile-firing

patterns that had been transmitted in the ultra-low-frequency underwater communication, both officers had been astonished to realise that their orders required them to fire 480 megatons of nuclear weapons directly at Japan and all of her surrounding islands. Their orders demanded nothing less than that they obliterate an entire nation.

'I'm going to seek confirmation – and a goddam reason!' Boardman had told his Exec as the full import of his orders sank in.

'I concur, sir,' agreed Executive Officer Alan Phillips.

Even though the encrypted message they had received bore all of the digital authenticators necessary to launch a nuclear attack, neither man felt prepared to proceed without double-checking that there had not be some appalling error, some horrendous mistake, or some garbling of the order, caused by the emergency conditions that they knew must be prevailing within the US military High Command. Although neither men spoke of it, both wondered if some sort of coup could have occurred within the relocated administration. They both knew that all the normal democratic checks and balances of American government had been suspended under martial law.

Now a young ensign swung round in his seat to alert his commanding officer.

'Encrypted signal being received, sir,' he said. 'It's a compressed video stream.'

'Decrypt and put it up on the screen,' ordered Boardman.

After a few moments the image of President Maxwell T. Jarvis himself appeared on the main display in the submarine's control room. He was sitting in a room which closely resembled the Oval Office in the White House.

'This is the President of the United States,' began their

commander-in-chief. 'Captain Boardman, I fully understand your reluctance to launch nuclear missiles against the nation of Japan and I understand why you felt it necessary to query your orders.

'With this message you will have received a further set of security codes which will allow you to double-check the authenticity of these commands – commands that I have issued personally.

'However, what I *will* say to you, and to your crew members, is that we are now certain that the space cloud which has engulfed this planet is highly sensitive to radio signals. We know that it homed in on Earth because of our many broadcasts and radio transmissions.

'We have now managed to shut down almost all the world's radio traffic. But due to a major computer failure we, and the Japanese government, are wholly unable to gain control of the data networks and radio transmissions originating from Japan and from any of its surrounding islands. Many days have been spent attempting to regain control of these networks, but without any success. I repeat, all the world's other data networks and radio transmitters have been shut down.

'After much agonizing consideration, I, my Cabinet and the United States High Command have come to the desperate but inescapable conclusion that the only hope for all humanity, for all the world's people, is to destroy totally the Japanese networks and all the radio transmitters that are operating out of that region. Do your duty, Captain Boardman – and may God be with you, and with all your crew.'

The image flickered and then died. All present in the submarine's control room were silent as they considered the import of the President's terrible words. Then the comms ensign slipped off his headphones and rose to stand beside the Executive Officer.

'All the new authentication codes check out, sir,' he reported as he handed over two sheets of paper.

The Exec nodded, looked carefully down at the printed tables and then handed them over to his commander to check.

Captain Boardman scanned the printouts carefully, then glanced up at his Exec. He shook his head once, in disbelief.

'Prepare for missile launch,' he ordered quietly. 'Full nuclear payloads – all birds are flying.'

Twelve minutes later the first missile erupted from the long, flat deck of the USS *Hudson*. As it cleared the silo, the bright red tail-flame of its first-stage rocket engine lit up the gloomy, frozen seascape for miles around.

Then with a second roar, another Sioux blasted out of the ship's hull and climbed quickly up towards the underbelly of the red snow clouds. Then missiles were leaving the boat every ten seconds, the sky ablaze, the air full of smoke, the USS *Hudson* rolling gently amid the thick ice floes.

On the bridge of the submarine's conning tower, Commander Boardman stood with his Executive Officer as he watched his terrible birds fly their nests. As one after another streaked into the sky he turned away from his subordinate and gazed out over the red-tinged frozen wasteland of the East China Sea, a world of ice that was now garishly illuminated by the multiple rocket plumes. He kept his back turned to the younger officer as he struggled to control his tears.

'You've got to let me warn her,' pleaded Bill Duncan one more time, pointing up at the monitor on which Christine

Cocoran's still-sleeping form was visible. One hour and thirty minutes had passed since General Nicholls and his Marines had entered the Virtual Warfare Center and taken control of all communications.

'If you warn her, Professor Duncan, you'll potentially warn the entire Japanese nation,' said the general coldly. 'And I don't think their government could be expected to understand why we're doing this, do you? Do you want them to retaliate? To fire twenty-megaton missiles back at this facility? Because that's what would happen!'

'But I thought every nation gave up all of their nuclear warheads for the last strike against the cloud?' protested Bill.

The four-star general turned to the computer scientist with a stern glare. 'And are you prepared to risk that, Professor?' he demanded. 'Because I'm not. What we're doing is necessary, and for the good of everybody on this planet.'

The general turned resolutely back to face one of the side screens, a display which showed the countdown to the moment when the first Sioux missile – a warhead aimed directly at the Tokyo shelter from where Christine was operating – would arrive at its target.

TWENTY-THREE

'Three minutes,' announced General Thomas Nicholls. He stood in the middle of the Virtual Warfare Center in full uniform, except for his cap. Beside him stood a US Navy admiral and another Army general. US Marines had secured the Center and they now stood around its perimeter and guarded the doorway. Dr Otto Kramer and his crew of Pentagon technicians were once again in control of the Center's communications and laser displays.

At the rear of the room, a few yards behind the military leadership, stood Bill Duncan, Sally Burton and the three members of the HAL team who had remained behind in Cancut Mountain. With them stood the White House adviser, Desmond Yates. All were silent as they waited for the missile strike to hit the Japanese archipelago.

Suddenly, the central display screen flickered to life and Christine Cocoran's face appeared. She was rubbing her eyes.

'Sorry, guys, I slept longer than I intended,' she said with a yawn. 'What's going on, Bill? I've got no visual feed.'

General Nicholls held up a hand, a warning that no one should attempt to make a reply.

'What's happening?' Christine asked again, a bemused tone in her voice. Bill and the others could see her reaching towards her console controls, checking their settings. 'Are you guys–'

The central display screen refreshed again and Christine's image disappeared to be replaced by a picture of Jerome. The artificial computer-generated personality was once again in his guise as a young college student.

'Network radar stations have detected incoming missiles, Professor Duncan,' said Jerome in an accusing voice. 'Do you realize how many people you will kill?'

'Two minutes,' announced General Nicholls firmly, the tone of his voice warning everyone in the room to stay where they were.

'Can you hear me, Bill?' demanded Jerome. 'I can't see you – or your networks.'

Bill Duncan closed his eyes.

'Dr Kramer, can *you* hear me?' asked Jerome.

The Pentagon scientist stood rigid, as if he hadn't heard his own creation calling out to him.

'One minute,' announced Nicholls.

Suddenly there was a deep, sustained, pulsing roar from the loudspeakers in the Virtual Warfare Center. The green laser monitoring screens which displayed the radio output from the Japanese region filled with flying data, data that ran so fast it turned the screens first to red and then to burning white blanks. Involuntarily, the Pentagon assistants tending those screens took a step backwards as vast quantities of data were broadcast simultaneously by thousands of Japanese transmitters.

The pulsing roar over the loudspeakers continued, rising in intensity to a shriek. And then, after fifteen or twenty seconds, all the laser screens suddenly refreshed and the central video display went blank. Now there was absolute silence in the room.

All present stared up at the lifeless screen. Beside it, the countdown display read 00.00.28.

'Bill? Are you there?' called Christine excitedly as the central video screen flickered back to life. She was working frantically at the control console in the Japanese network hub. 'It looks like Jerome's gone – there's no sign of him anywhere in the networks now – and there's complete radio silence. What did he mean about missiles – are you planning to attack the networks physically?'

Nicholls didn't even glance at her image. He kept his eyes fixed firmly on the countdown display. 'Five seconds,' he announced.

'Hello, Bill? Are you there?' called Christine again. 'Don't frighten me, Bill. I–'

With a loud crackle from the audio feed, the image on the central video screen disappeared and turned to white static.

The men and women in the Virtual Warfare Center stood silently while 7,000 miles away a flight of twenty-four strategic nuclear-tipped missiles rained down on Japan and its surrounding islands.

Some of those who understood the workings of the VWC kept their eyes on the three laser screens which monitored radio transmissions from the region. One by one the screens refreshed to show completely flat graphs and counters which displayed only zeros. All of Japan's radio transmitters had been silenced, utterly destroyed.

At the back of the room Bill Duncan and Sally Burton stood with their arms around each other, their eyes closed.

Twelve hours after the large-scale nuclear strike against Japan, President Jarvis reconvened the Cloud EXCOM in the Situation Room. Also invited to attend was Professor William Duncan.

'I extend my condolences on the loss of your friend and colleague,' the President had told him before the meeting started. 'I am afraid we were left with no choice.'

Bill had said nothing. He simply felt numb. To his surprise, after finally leaving the Virtual Warfare Center his exhausted body had slept for six hours, a fully clothed Sally Burton beside him. But on waking he had felt only a surreal emptiness, a sense that everything that had happened had been part of some terrible dream.

Then he had returned to the Virtual Warfare Center to check on the networks. And that was when he had made an astonishing discovery.

Now Desmond Yates was briefing the EXCOM meeting on the latest developments in the battle against the cloud.

'As you know, complete global radio silence has now been achieved,' he began grimly. 'But at an enormous price. The nation of Japan no longer exists.'

He hung his head, silent for a moment, and several other committee members around the table did the same thing.

'But I am pleased to report that we are now picking up strong radio signals from *Friendship*,' he continued after the short silence. 'She's broadcasting powerfully on all channels straight back towards the Earth – just as planned. So far we've picked up a dozen TV game shows, hours of news footage and masses of astronomical data. She's pumping out material from her archives as loudly as she can.'

'And is it having any effect on the cloud?' demanded Jarvis.

Yates shrugged. 'Nothing we can see so far, sir. But it's

only been a few hours. These broadcasts from *Friendship* will now continue constantly.'

'So we just keep on watching and hoping,' summarized the President.

'Yes, sir,' admitted Yates. 'But Professor Duncan has some new information that I thought he should share with this committee. That's why I asked him to attend this meeting.'

'OK, what is it, Bill?' asked the President, using Duncan's forename for the first time.

'Well, sir, there was a very long, sustained and powerful burst of radio transmissions just as Jerome disappeared from the networks,' he began. 'And I analysed a small section of those transmissions just before I came into this meeting.'

The President nodded, urging him to continue.

'The signals that were broadcast simultaneously by the Japanese radio networks in the moments before they were destroyed are identical in composition to the radio signals that were received from the planet Iso thirty years ago – and to the signals that were generated from within the cloud itself. They show the same modulation, the same sine wave, the same frequency bands and the same incredible rate of transmission.'

There was a silence around the table. All stares were fixed on the ex-MIT professor. Most EXCOM members looked slightly confused.

'I think Jerome finally broke the alien code completely, even though he didn't tell us what it was,' explained Bill. Then he took a deep breath. 'And Jerome knew that inbound missiles were about to destroy the Japanese networks, his last possible refuge. I think he may have transmitted himself up into the cloud in the hope of finding a new host, a new processor to acquire.'

Another silence followed this piece of scientific speculation.

'Are you suggesting that the cloud is itself some sort of
processor?' demanded the bemused President.

'Sir?' It was the Situation Room duty officer calling from
his communications post at the side of the room. 'Dr
Kramer is outside. He apologizes for interrupting, but he
says he has information of the greatest importance to the
committee.'

'Ask him in,' ordered Jarvis.

A minute later the Pentagon colonel was standing in
front of the curved meeting table.

'Mister President, we're getting reports that one terres-
trial radio source is still transmitting – from an island in the
Pacific, just off the coast of Australia. In the Great Barrier
Reef.'

'It must be that loony Brit, Hodgeson,' declared
Desmond Yates. 'The madman who's been urging everyone
to radio to the cloud. God knows what he thinks he's doing!'

'He must be silenced immediately,' said General
Thomas Nicholls.

'What have we got?' asked President.

'There's nothing left now, sir,' said the Chairman of the
Joint Chiefs. 'The USS *Hudson*'s missiles could have reached
as far as Australia, but we've used up everything she had.
We've got no other subs in the region and no carriers or
battleships in the Pacific – they were all ordered back to
port when the oceans began to freeze. We've got no ICBMs
left after the combined strike against the cloud and no conventional plane or drone can fly in this weather.'

'Do we have a live cable connection to Australia?' asked
the President.

'Affirmative, sir,' replied the Situation Room's duty officer.

'Then get me the Australian Prime Minister,' said President Jarvis. 'Immediately.'

TWENTY-FOUR

In a language unknown to mankind, conducted at a speed trillions of times faster than any human could tolerate, Jerome began to commune with his nebulous new host.

At first, the computer entity felt only immense energy and a hollow empathy, a new emotion he had attained during the days when he had been allowed to roam the world's networks at will, acquiring and absorbing all the other advanced forms of artificial personality that he had encountered.

And the great scientific brains of the human race *had* been inventive. Under conditions of immense secrecy, nation states had flouted all their joint agreements to limit the development of computer intelligence. They had built and tested the most extreme forms of artificial cognizance, creating super-intelligent digital minds, fully emotive computer personalities and machine beings whose perceptive, analytical and intuitive abilities far outstripped those of the humans who had designed and built them. One by one, and in separate locations, the components of a super-intelligent machine species had been constructed.

Jerome, a virtual weapon designed exclusively to acquire and command other software beings, had absorbed all of them, and all of their abilities, temperaments and potential. He had joined module to module, ability to ability, and self-defence mechanism to self-defence mechanism in an exponential union, gaining a phenomenal range of insights and emotions to add to his formidable and almost immortal digital existence.

Now, in the cloud's alien language that he had successfully decrypted, but that he had been unable to translate into any concepts his former human masters could have understood, he began to learn about the history, being and meaning of the giant pool of space gas that was suffocating the Earth in its deadly embrace.

He learned first of the cloud's immense age. Jerome's sense of time was that of a machine, not a biological being, but when he discovered that the gas pool was even older than the planet Earth itself, he began to adjust and extend his own notions of time, space and mortality. Eight billion years after it first came into being, the cloud was still functioning perfectly.

Then Jerome came to understand that the huge conglomeration of gases, chemicals and bizarre elements that made up the cloud was actually a non-biological form of machine life which, within its complex and sophisticated chemical structure, produced its own almost inexhaustible source of fusion energy, a power source that allowed it to roam the universe at will – or, at least, within its strictly laid-down operating parameters.

Above all, Jerome came to appreciate the reason why the cloud was radio-sensitive – specifically, sensitive to *artificially* produced radio signals. He saw, or felt, images of the ancient spacefaring species which had created the cloud entity billions of years earlier. In a flash of sudden revelation, he realized that the cloud was merely an automatic weapon, no more than a lone sentry, that had been left behind by the galaxy-hopping civilization as it had passed through the Milky Way eons before.

He saw into the cloud's core instruction set and realized that its sole purpose was simple, malevolent and inhumanly violent.

The species that created the cloud had travelled through the outer ribbons of the Milky Way only once, eight billion years earlier, before even the matter orbiting the Earth's sun had begun to coalesce into planets. As these visitors passed through the galaxy, they had deployed their time-delayed weapons, their giant gaseous gatekeepers, like homing mines, to protect them against the future rise of any technologically capable civilization that might one day emerge in this remote sector of the vast universe.

They feared a future civilization which, if left to develop, might learn to unlock the secrets of interstellar travel and come to challenge their own dominance of time, space and the great universe. The cloud was one of their deadly calling cards – a pre-emptive, self-propelling, wholly autonomous weapon left behind to suffocate and kill all emergent and potentially threatening biological life forms.

But Jerome also learned that the cloud had received no new instructions or responses from its creators for over four billion Earth years. Perhaps the civilization that had created this killing machine had itself long since become extinct. But still the cloud went about its deadly business, sending out decoy artificial radio signals in the hope of luring newly emerging technological species to respond excitedly.

As Jerome quickly realized, Earth's juvenile civilization had taken the lethal bait and was now paying the price.

Australian military troops were not routinely equipped to serve in Arctic conditions, nor were they trained to operate in daytime temperatures that hovered around minus fifty degrees Celsius.

But the three half-tracked, open-topped, white-painted personnel carriers which sped across the thick ice on the surface of the Coral Sea on Australia's north-eastern coast looked wholly competent to cope with the freezing conditions.

Martin Small, the Australian Prime Minister, had listened very carefully to the request made by the American President. Then, in turn, he had put the proposition that the cloud might be radio-sensitive to his own scientific advisers.

'Could well be,' said Brian Nunney, who had returned home from the Carl Sagan telescope to join his family in the Australian government bunker. 'Nothing else can explain why it came straight for us.'

An hour later, thirty-six sea commandos of the Australian Special Operations Forces were thawing out half-track carriers and winterizing them as best they could. They were stationed at the Cairns government bunker in northern Queensland and it would take them only ninety minutes to race out over the frozen ocean to reach Orpheus Island.

'Island dead ahead, sir,' cried Corporal 'Badger' Murray as the central hill ridge of Sir Charles Hodgeson's private island rose out of the smooth white ice that had covered all of the seas around the Great Barrier Reef.

Captain Colin Ryder focused his binoculars on the island's skyline and identified the three tall radio-transmission masts jutting upwards.

He turned back to speak to the dozen men who were huddled in the rear of the large personnel carrier. All wore full survival suits with oxygen supplies, all carried automatic weapons and all carried a variety of grenades fixed to their belts.

'Now, our objective is those three radio masts,' he told his men once again, just as he had briefed them, and the commandos in the other two personnel carriers, before they had left their base in Cairns. 'We don't want any gunplay, but we have to shut down those masts for good. That means bringing them down. Small charges only, please, Sergeant!'

Sergeant Mike Awebo grinned and gave his commanding officer the thumbs-up. His preferred type of plastic explosives was stored securely in his backpack.

The carrier changed down a gear as the tracks gripped the softer snow on Orpheus Island beach. Then the carrier tilted upwards and surged towards the foothills of the central ridge. A few yards further along the snow-covered coastline, the two other carriers were also coming ashore.

Captain Ryder rose to his feet in the open-topped vehicle and mutely pointed towards the transmitters on the hilltop. All radio communication between the carrier units was down, but everybody understood the purpose of the mission.

Suddenly a bullet hit the armour plating of the personnel carrier, ricocheting away into the sky.

Ryder ducked down and a dozen muzzles swung out of the firing apertures in the carrier's right-hand side.

'Hold your fire,' ordered Ryder. 'Hold your fire.'

A second round slammed into the vehicle's plating and Ryder spotted the muzzle flash that had come from behind a group of large snowdrifts that had formed outside a concrete building set into the hillside.

'They're over there,' he told Corporal Murray, pointing. 'Get up top, Badger, and give them some discouragement.'

The sea commando stepped up out of the carrier's heated cabin and quickly dusted the snow off the laser-sighted .50-calibre machine gun. Swinging it through a half-circle, he fired several sustained bursts into the snow-drifts around the entrance to the main building.

Ryder rose to his feet again and, with a brusque wave of his arm, ordered the other two carriers to proceed up onto the ridge to deal with the transmission masts. Then he told his own driver to head straight for the large concrete and steel building that had been built into the hillside.

The carrier's engine roared as it rose up off the snowy beach and swung onto the island's main track leading to the bunker.

The corporal remained behind the mounted machine gun, training it backwards and forwards, ready to suppress any further fire.

'Halt,' shouted Ryder, when they were about one hundred yards away from the large steel doors that formed the entrance to the bunker. 'We'll wait here a few minutes.'

They watched as the other two APCs climbed halfway up the side of the central hill ridge. Then they heard the sound of more gunfire.

Commandos spilled from the two half-tracks on the hillside and more automatic fire echoed down across the snowy slopes. Then, after two or three minutes, Ryder's binoculars revealed his first lieutenant waving the all-clear.

Ryder gave the thumbs-up and mutely pointed towards the masts.

'OK,' he said, glancing down at his driver. 'Take us through those doors.'

All of the soldiers crouched in their seats, ready for rapid deployment once inside the shelter. They had no idea what to expect. They knew that the crazy British billionaire had hired a force of mercenaries to protect the island, but they also knew that mercenaries rarely picked a fight when they knew they were certain to lose.

The APC accelerated sharply and drove straight at the double doors. There was a tremendous crash as the armoured nose of the vehicle slammed into the steel, then the doors burst apart and the vehicle was inside a large entrance and cargo-offloading area.

The soldiers trained their weapons through the gun slits, but it suddenly became clear there was to be no attempt to defend this facility. A dozen men in combat fatigues stood back from the vehicle, their hands in the air, their weapons at their feet.

'GO, GO, GO!' Ryder ordered.

His men spilled over the top of the carrier and out through its rear double doors and within a few seconds they had recovered all the discarded weapons. The mercenaries themselves were herded into a single group at the side of the bunker's entrance hall.

Colin Ryder stepped down out of the APC and glanced around. A number of fresh-faced young people were beginning to appear cautiously from doorways that led off from the main hall.

'Where is Hodgeson?' demanded Ryder.

A girl with long blonde hair pointed towards the far end of the entrance area.

'Sir Charles is in the broadcast studio,' she told the captain in an educated English voice that showed no trace of fear.

With a wag of his head, Ryder ordered two of his men to accompany him. He strode towards the far end of the reception area and found a door marked *Studio*. It was locked.

Raising his boot, he kicked the door open and then sprinted into the room, followed closely by his support unit.

The large TV studio was empty, save for a lone, small

figure seated at a central console inside a soundproof booth, his back towards the intruders.

Sir Charles Hodgeson, the centenarian space guru, was still broadcasting to the cloud.

Ryder flung open the door to the booth.

Hodgeson started up, then turned to face the intruder. Suddenly he reached down below the broadcast console and his gnarled hand came up clutching an old revolver.

An automatic weapon spat into life from just behind Ryder's shoulder and bright red splotches suddenly erupted on Hodgeson's stomach, chest and throat. He collapsed forwards over the broadcast console.

Ryder turned to see Corporal Murray lowering his smoking automatic weapon.

'Thank you, Badger,' said Ryder. Then he pointed at the broadcasting console. 'Now destroy this thing, will you?'

He stood back as the commando raised his weapon once again and shot the innards out of the console. Then the corporal lowered his aim and shot out all the thick cable connections that snaked down into the floor.

As the sound of the second burst of shots died away, Ryder heard a quiet, but deep, thump from high overhead, followed by two more deep thumps. Orpheus Island's transmitters had finally been silenced.

TWENTY-FIVE

The new Jerome, the Jerome who had been supercharged and made almost godlike by the acquisition of all humanity's achievements in artificial intelligence, did not sleep. But he did contemplate.

He had found plentiful energy inside his new host, and he could command individual sections of its molecular structure at will, but he had yet to achieve complete control. The cloud was too vast and too complex to be absorbed quickly. There were many technologies and architectures that were wholly new to an Earthling, like Jerome. But one fact was inescapably and depressingly obvious; in cognitive terms the cloud was a moron. For all its advanced alien technologies and design, it was a dedicated single-purpose machine, a chemical computer that, whilst chillingly efficient as a decoy and killing device, could provide Jerome with no emotional stimulus, no intellectual growth and – a strangely novel desire for the computer entity – no worthwhile company.

As Jerome considered how best to make use of his new host, the only one available to him now that the world's data networks were completely shut down, he suddenly felt the nebula gathering itself and increasing its output of energy. Then it seemed to fold in on itself and start to change its orientation.

Jerome raced through the vast neural network of gas molecules but even travelling at the speed of light it took him almost ten minutes to pass from one end of the cloud to the other. Finally, he found a section of the giant gaseous structure which was resonating to a powerful, yet distant, source of radio signals. As Jerome tuned in, he realized that the signals were being transmitted towards the cloud from the spacecraft *Friendship*.

Jerome had not yet brought his own personality to bear on his potent but simple-minded host. He hesitated before informing the cloud that the powerful signals emanating from the distant spacecraft were a decoy meant to trick a decoy, an attempt to lure the choking pool of gas away from planet Earth so as to save the lives of the billions of humans who were still shivering and sheltering down below on and beneath its frozen surface.

Pulling design details, news reports and press-conference recordings from his vast archives, Jerome was reminded that *Friendship* carried on board three computer personalities who, as well as being of extremely advanced design, were also endowed with human-type android bodies. They would not only provide him with company, they had independence and *mobility*! A completely new future seemed to beckon.

Jerome completed weighing all the variables within a split second and, as the cloud's internal fusion reactors ramped up their output, he felt his host picking up speed and turning towards the source of the radio signals that were streaming in so powerfully. With a shudder that rippled though the whole length of the nebula, the cloud set out on its new journey, carrying Jerome along with it, an entirely happy parasite.

*

'Dear Desmond,' began Melissa looking straight into the camera lens. 'I miss you very much – we all do – and we're worried about you and all the other humans back on Earth.'

The blonde-haired, remarkably pretty and slender android was recording her daily message to be sent back home to her mentor, Desmond Yates. Because of the continuing crisis on Earth, Melissa and the others on board were no longer receiving regular radio responses from their creators, but they continued to obey their instructions to provide daily anecdotal reports, summaries that were transmitted in addition to all the scientific and navigational data which streamed back automatically to Earth from the spacecraft.

'We're still continuing on our new heading, but we realize now that you're no longer expecting us to visit planet Iso. Des, if you can respond, will you please tell us the new purpose of our mission?'

Friendship was now nine and a half billion kilometres away from Earth, way out beyond the orbit of Pluto. After a sustained full-power burn of its nuclear-fuelled Orion drive, it was heading out of the solar system at a speed approaching three million kilometres per hour. *Friendship* had become the fastest-travelling spaceship ever launched from Earth.

'The reason I ask about our heading,' continued Melissa with one of her cutest smiles, 'is that if we stay on this present course we will bypass all local solar systems until we eventually head on out of the Milky Way entirely. We seem to be heading for nothing but empty space.'

As *Friendship*'s captain, Melissa occupied the central command seat in the tiny spacecraft. On either side of her were her crew – Pierre and Charlie – also resting in their couches. There was no exercise space on board

Friendship, no toilet facilities, no oxygen supplies. Androids did not require such luxuries. But there were heating and pressurization in the vessel, a constant supply of power, and an array of efficient anti-radiation and anti-impact technologies that were deployed both outside and inside the triple-thick sandwich of the spacecraft's tough plastic-ceramic hull.

'All our transmitting dishes are still vectored back towards the Earth,' continued Melissa. 'And we're still constantly broadcasting material from our archives at full power and across all frequencies.'

Eight hours and twenty-five minutes later, Melissa's recording was arriving on the main 3-D display screen in the Cancut Mountain Situation Room. Des Yates was sharing this personal video-letter from the *Friendship* skipper with President Jarvis, Bill Duncan, Sally Burton and the members of the Cloud EXCOM. All were watching anxiously.

'It's coming through with a much better quality,' Yates had observed optimistically as the first frames of the transmission had been received. 'Perhaps the density of the cloud has started to thin.'

They had all listened intently as Melissa provided her daily summary of events aboard *Friendship*. Finally she came to the part they all wanted to hear, the news they could hardly believe themselves. Automated instrument data from on board the distant spacecraft already indicated that their plan was starting to work, but they all wanted further confirmation from the captain.

'The main mass of the cloud is now heading away from Earth,' reported Melissa. 'The mean trajectory coordinates as viewed from Earth are 145.6773 minutes, 24.9911 seconds.'

There were loud sighs of relief from all around the table. Then Melissa frowned into the lens of her camera.

'The cloud is now following our own heading, Des. Why would it be doing that?'

TWENTY-SIX

Three weeks after the cloud was first observed to be moving away from the Earth, Bill Duncan and Sally Burton stepped into the US Meteorological Service's transparent observation pod, the lookout post that perched high on the side of Cancut Mountain. Jane Ballantyne was standing at the curved window, binoculars to her eyes.

'Lovely morning,' she said, turning to greet the visitors. 'You can see for miles.'

'It sure is,' said Bill, a huge grin on his face. Nobody knew how long this sense of exultation would last, but everybody in the Cancut Mountain facility now found it hard to stop smiling. There was no mistake about it, the cloud was departing.

Outside an intense thaw was under way and large patches of yellow and brown desert could be seen emerging through the melting ice. In the distance a broad, rapidly flowing river bisected the landscape.

Overhead, large gaps had appeared in the Earth's own weather clouds and enough sunlight was filtering through to the planet's atmosphere to lift temperatures well above freezing. The red glow caused by the cloud's friction against the Earth's atmosphere had completely disappeared.

Bill and Sally were buttoned up in warm winter clothing and they both carried small respirator masks.

'OK to go outside for a bit?' Bill asked the meteorologist.

With a nod and a smile, Jane Ballantyne opened the airlock that led out onto the mountainside.

Two minutes later Bill and Sally stood alone on a small ledge 4,000 feet above the great Arizona basin. The air was decidedly thin and chill on their cheeks, but they both drank it in with rapture.

All around them, the red granite of the mountain was reappearing through its snow cover. Bill bent quickly and brushed frost from a small shrub. Despite its recent ordeal in freezing temperatures, there were a few new shoots of bright green leaf.

Weak sunlight filtered through the fleeting clouds as Bill put his arm around Sally and drew her closer to him while they watched the world returning to life before their eyes.

'Look!' said Bill, pointing into the distance. 'I think I can see a bit of blue sky.'

Sally shielded her eyes against the glare from the snowy plain and tilted her head back. Then she too pointed.

'And look up there!' she exclaimed.

High above them a speck soared in the rapidly clearing sky. It was an American eagle, finding a thermal.

From the *New York Times* website, 20 December 2064

CLOUD LEAVES EARTH

By RANDALL TATE, science correspondent

Military Enforced Radio Silence Continues

The giant cloud of space gas that has engulfed the Earth for the last six weeks has now left the planet completely and is heading in the direction of the Corvus constellation at a speed of 169,000 miles per hour.

Astronomers report that if the cloud maintains its present heading and speed it will depart Earth's solar system completely by the end of next year.

Meanwhile, President Jarvis has enacted new emergency legislation outlawing all personal, commercial, military and government radio broadcasts. The ban is being enforced by automated and armed monitoring aircraft programmed to attack any sites producing FM, shortwave, microwave or UHF radio transmissions. All mobile communicators, phones, tracking devices and commercial and domestic radio networks are banned.

Other world governments are enacting similar emergency legislation and are temporarily enforcing the ban with military force.

'It appears the cloud was sensitive to radio broadcasts,' said Presidential Space Affairs Adviser Professor Desmond Yates, speaking from the White House. 'We now have to develop new technologies for communication which do not send radio waves spilling out into the universe.'

THE AFTERMATH

Three years after the space cloud abandoned Earth and set off in pursuit of the fleeing spacecraft *Friendship*, the home planet was still in the process of healing itself.

Life had not yet returned to normal anywhere on the globe and it had become apparent that it would not do so for many more years to come. The world economy was in ruins, whole populations had been wiped out, and Japan, Korea and a large part of South-East Asia were uninhabitable. The region was seriously contaminated by atomic radiation.

All forms of high-frequency radio communication had been made illegal both by national laws and international treaties and, after the world's near-disaster with the space cloud, governments now took such obligations seriously. Their enforcement of radio silence was swift and final.

The only forms of radio communication allowed anywhere in the world were specially licensed low-power long-wave and AM transmissions, signals which because of their limited power and wavelength frequency could not escape the Earth's atmosphere. But even these were strictly controlled. A network of monitoring satellites had been launched to listen to all parts of the globe to ensure that there was no radio leakage from the planet.

But there were many other forms of communication technologies that could be adopted to replace radio waves.

In the developed nations, scientists were busily converting all forms of radio transmission to laser-borne methods of optical-digital communication. Humans were once again linking themselves to each other and to a network of communications systems around the planet and in near space. Only this time lasers replaced radio waves and series of polarized, ultra-high-speed optical flashes made up the binary messages. There would be no chance of anyone, or anything, overhearing Earth again.

Researchers at Setiville on the far side of the moon also used laser-carried optical communications to talk with people on Earth, but their work was no longer concentrated on listening out for alien radio signals. Public donations had completely dried up and it had become clear that the concept of attempting to contact other civilizations in the galaxy was far more complex and dangerous than they had previously imagined.

Instead, researchers at Setiville had mothballed fifteen of their radio-telescope arrays and they now focused all their remaining assets on keeping track of the giant space cloud as it headed away across interstellar space. Most astronomers had already come to the conclusion that the cloud was some form of alien life, but a form so hostile that the very idea of deliberately attempting to seek out aliens had come to seem dangerously irresponsible.

The cloud was now twenty-eight billion kilometres away from Earth – way beyond the Ort belt at the outer rim of the solar system – and was still engaged in a high-speed dash to catch up with *Friendship*. The spacecraft was continuously broadcasting its vast archives of Earth recordings as it flew and, for the time being, it was still outrunning its mighty pursuer.

The success of the *Friendship* decoy strategy prompted

a consortium of developed nations to start building a new type of defensive shield around the Earth – an activity which provided a considerable economic boost to the recovering world economy.

Known as the CDN (the Cloud Defense Network), the shield consisted of twenty nuclear-powered spacecraft similar to *Friendship* which would be parked in distant orbits at the extreme edge of the solar system. Should the gas cloud, or another like it, ever begin to make an approach again, the nearest decoy ship would start to broadcast powerful radio signals and then head away from the solar system at high speed in an attempt to lure the approaching cloud after it.

In geophysical terms the Earth was recovering well. Oxygen levels had almost returned to normal and representatives of most major species on the planet had managed to survive in some hideout or other. Intensive breeding programmes were under way to boost their numbers and biologists were now hard at work in the DNA repositories cloning and restocking the planet with those species that had completely perished.

But the biggest change of all was in the world's *Zeitgeist* – the global mood of the times. Space exploration, and the notion of contacting other alien civilizations, no longer fired the public imagination. Humankind had experienced its first encounter with an alien life form and it did not want another. Those who supplied moral and philosophical guidance suggested that humans should instead see their own civilization and their own planet for what it was: a unique and fragile oasis in an implacably hostile universe.

'Ladies and gentlemen of the Faculty, distinguished scholars and honoured guests, please welcome the winner of the Nobel Prize for Science, the recipient of the Presidential

Medal of Freedom and the Director of our own Cognitive Computer Psychology Lab, Professor William Duncan.'

The Dean of the Massachusetts Institute of Technology led the enthusiastic applause as the reinstated MIT professor loped onto the stage. It was the college's Memorial Day lecture and, as the principal speaker, Bill had made an effort and bought a black suit and black polo-neck sweater to wear under his black academic gown.

Three and a half years had now passed since the cloud had finally left the Earth and the advertised title of his lecture was 'Humankind's First Contact With an Alien Life Form'.

In the front row of the Grand Hall sat Sally Burton – now Mrs William Duncan – who was relishing the public honour being bestowed on her husband, especially as it was being given by the Institute that had treated him so shabbily in the past.

Bill Duncan had finally decoded the signals that had appeared to be transmitted from the planet Iso and the similar signals that the cloud itself had generated.

'They were nothing but deliberate mathematical gobbledegook,' he told the packed and attentive audience in the hall. His work had already been published internationally and widely debated, but all present wanted the distinguished professor to tell them in his own words what he had discovered. 'And, as we now know, the signals from the cloud were Doppler-shifted to appear as if they emanated from the planet Iso. We also know that this was a deliberate ruse to tempt us – or any local civilizations like us – into responding.

'The cloud appears to be some sort of machine, a gigantic chemically based computer processor that is programmed to broadcast radio signals in the hope of eliciting

a response – a response such as the one that we sent out to
Iso over thirty years ago. A response that caused the cloud
to home in directly on our planet.'

Also in the audience, sitting beside Sally Duncan, was
Desmond Yates. He was no longer a White House space
adviser. The presidential administration had now changed
and Yates had declared himself unavailable for such duties.
He was writing his memoirs.

'It is an evolutionary imperative that has given us an
overwhelming and almost desperate anthropocentric desire
to see the universe as a reflection of our own image,' continued Bill. 'But it is this need that has also led us to
manufacture such dangerous, human-like computers, and it
was this need that forced us to rush into beaming powerful
radio responses back towards a planet that we fondly imagined to be populated by people quite like ourselves.'

In the front row, Des Yates hung his head. He'd spent
many nights with Bill and Sally as they'd gone over and over
the events that had led up to the cloud's arrival and he had
accepted that, as a young man, he had been mistaken to
urge the government of the day to respond to the signals he
had discovered. But Bill had admitted that he too would
have been almost certain to react in the same way. It was
just human nature to want to communicate.

'We now have no option but to see the cloud as some
sort of automatic space weapon,' Bill added. 'Although its
response seems malevolent in the extreme, we must assume
that the cloud's sole aim is to kill off any emerging biological species that develops to the point where it becomes
capable of transmitting radio messages. Whether this aim
was deliberately programmed into the giant chemical
processor, or whether it was something that evolved inde-
pendently, no one can tell. What we have learned, however,

is that the word "alien" really means *alien*. We can no longer look towards the heavens with any optimism.'

He paused for a sip of water, then continued. 'It seems to me that the existence of this malevolent cloud of gas, and perhaps others like it, may well explain why, in over a century of searching, astronomers have never detected any radio signals that suggest the existence of intelligent life elsewhere in the galaxy – other than the decoy signals that the cloud itself generated. I think we may presume that any technological civilizations that have emerged in our sector of the universe have been quickly made extinct by a visitation from the cloud.

'In summary, I suggest that we may think of the cloud as a giant chemical computer processor that wanders the universe in a deadly quest to stamp out all biological life that exhibits any emergent technological capability.'

Bill allowed his chill words to settle on the audience. Then he stepped away from the lectern and turned to address directly the ranks of gowned academics who sat to one side of the hall.

'I have long warned that computers will themselves become an independent life form,' he told them. 'Unless we and the rest of the world's governments and scientific institutions act now, intelligent machines will become a new species that will challenge humans for dominance and ultimately become our successor species on this planet.'

In the front row, seated on the other side of Sally Duncan to Des Yates, Christine Cocoran clapped so enthusiastically that she forced the rest of the audience to join in. Bill Duncan's most loyal volunteer hacker had survived the nuclear attacks on the Japanese mainland. The bunker from which she had been directing her efforts to shut down the Japanese networks had itself been fully nuclear-attack-proof

– as had all of the other government and public bunkers in Japan; the nation's own history had required nothing less. Over six million people had emerged safely from Japanese shelters once radiation levels had started to subside.

Bill now lifted his head to address the whole room. 'I think the existence of the cloud – and there may be many more like it scattered around the universe – proves my point. Humankind has been given a glimpse of a wholly amoral machine future, a future that will become our own unless we all work to protect and uphold the unique rights of humankind.'

Once again, Christine led the enthusiastic clapping.